Number One Millbank

Also by Terry Lovell:

A Camera in Colditz
An Invasion of Privacy

Number One Millbank

The Financial Downfall of the Church of England

Terry Lovell

HarperCollins*Publishers*

HarperCollins*Publishers*
77–85 Fulham Palace Road, London W6 8JB

First published in 1997 by
HarperCollins*Publishers*

Copyright © 1997 Terry Lovell

1 3 5 7 9 10 8 6 4 2

Terry Lovell has asserted the moral right
to be identified as the author of this work

A catalogue record for this book is
available from the British Library

0 00 627 8663

Printed and bound in Great Britain by
Caledonian International Book Manufacturing Ltd, Glasgow

This book is dedicated to Sheila, Dorothy and John,
who know the heat of battle … and to Alexandra, Toby,
Janice, Sam, Sophie, Jessica and Elizabeth.

Never, ever give up … especially when
it is 'against all hope'.

Contents

CHAPTER ONE

A Storm Breaks

The press statement issued by John Prodger, chairman of the Oxford Diocesan Board of Finance, on 12 July 1992 was a political gesture intended to exploit fully the headline scandal that had just exploded around the Church Commissioners, a powerful body responsible for the investment management of the Church of England's assets portfolio, valued three years earlier at almost £3 billion.

The statement had not been Prodger's idea; it wasn't his style. He was a convivial old Etonian, a retired personnel director of an international corporation who had been chairman of the diocesan board of finance for less than two years. Now and again he had heard disquieting gossip on the diocesan boards' grapevine about property investment difficulties, but he reckoned others, longer in the political tooth, were in a more influential position than he to ask the right questions of the right people if necessary.

But, like almost everyone else in the Church of England, from Lambeth Palace to the most far-flung parish church, he had been stunned by a two-page article in the *Financial Times* the previous day which, under the headline, 'Unholy Saga of Church's Missing Millions', revealed that, through high-risk property speculation which had incurred massive borrowings, the Church Commissioners' investment policy had led to a loss of £500m in the value of their property portfolio, a figure that would finally be nearer to £624m.[1] That the Commissioners, long considered in the property world to be paragons of commercial prudence, and whose investment income was responsible for a major part of clergy stipends and

1

paid virtually all of the Church's pensions bill, could be capable of such recklessness defied belief.

But while the likes of Prodger remained incredulous at the news, others were seizing the opportunity to manipulate the *Financial Times'* exclusive disclosure to their advantage, and the Commissioners' public embarrassment. For some time there had been a simmering hostility between the Diocese of Oxford and the Church Commissioners – culminating in a High Court battle – over the ethics of their investments in general and those in South Africa in particular, which allegedly encouraged the exploitation of black workers employed by multi-nationals at sub-standard salaries and working conditions.

At the heart of the affair was the First Church Estates Commissioner, the redoubtable Sir Douglas Lovelock, who chaired a committee of much-respected figures in the City and property world responsible for the Commissioners' investment strategies. Although the implications of the story had no bearing on the ethical investments issue, in a Church of England that at times can be as Machiavellian as Westminster, the circumstances presented the chance to add to the intense discomfort that Lovelock and his colleagues were enduring – and Prodger, as chairman of the diocesan board of finance, was considered to be the man for the job.

On the day of the story's publication, he was approached by a senior diocesan official who suggested he issue a statement to the national press urging an inquiry into the Church Commissioners' activities. A diocese ought to react quickly, he was told. Why not Oxford? Prodger was invited, as he described it, to 'stick his neck out'. Being a good team man, he agreed to do so.

On his behalf, a statement was issued. In the following day's newspapers, it formed the basis of a story claiming that the Archbishop of Canterbury, Dr George Carey, was 'under pressure' over the massive slump in property investments. The statement issued by the Diocese of Oxford, combined with the advice of others within the Church, caused the Archbishop to move swiftly. That same day, he announced a review of the Church Commissioners' financial strategies, conceding that 'serious points' had been made about investment judgements. The tactic of the Commissioners' opponents within the Diocese of Oxford had achieved its purpose.

Dr Carey made the announcement in York, where the Church of England's law-making executive, the General Synod, were about to begin their business. The *Financial Times* had published its story to coincide with the session for maximum impact. As an investigative article, by features writer John Plender, it was hardly a deep-throat *tour de force*. It was largely based on careful scrutiny of the Church Commissioners' annual reports and accounts, reinforced by inside information and the informed interpretations of property and financial experts. Nevertheless, it was conclusive in revealing a staggering level of property value losses, which exposed gross mismanagement of the Church of England's assets.

Predictably, the story led to a succession of speculative media reports of the Church in crisis; of threats of closure to historic churches now too costly to maintain; of a considerable shortfall in the Commissioners' contributions to clergy stipends and pensions, which would have to be met by churchgoers; of parishes merging to reduce costs; and of a significant reduction in the number of clergy. They were fears that would wrack the Church of England for some time to come.

Three months later, on October 8, the Archbishop announced the formation of what would be known as the Lambeth Group, a seven-man independent body – although some would challenge the claim – headed by the Bishop of Chelmsford, the Rt Revd John Waine, himself a Church Commissioner, and aided by three other Church Commissioners, plus a senior member of the Church of England's Central Board of Finance, and two City businessmen. The Archbishop also announced the appointment of leading financial consultants, Coopers & Lybrand, to play a leading role in the investigation. Their presence increased criticisms of the inquiry's impartiality. Long-standing advisers to the Commissioners, they were at the core of the discredited accounting strategies endorsed by Sir Douglas and his colleagues to help conceal the financial consequences of their investment follies.

Sir Douglas, now besieged on all sides, assumed a sanguine attitude, declaring that he welcomed the investigation, adding that all organizations should undergo periodic examination. 'The present moment,' he announced boldly, 'is just the right moment to do so.' For Sir Douglas, and others involved, there could never be such a moment. The investigation would reveal reckless property investments, unethical conduct, massive borrowings of hundreds of millions of pounds, and a level of administrative incompetence that would cause a Parliamentary inquiry to accuse the Commissioners of acting with 'unbelievable naivete'.

When, on April 20, 1991, Dr George Carey, the one-time electricity board office boy and son of an east London hospital porter, emerged from Canterbury Cathedral as the 103rd Archbishop of Canterbury, he believed that the ordination of women priests would present his most daunting challenge.

From the chair of St Augustine, the first Archbishop of Canterbury, Dr Carey had urged the Church to 'set above our divisions the urgency of witnessing to our nation that there is a God who cares and loves all people. We shall only be able to do this if we stand together.' His words were interpreted as an appeal for unity within a Church which in recent years had become deeply divided as muscular churchmen of the traditional quarter locked theological horns with the more liberal and feminist factions.

But the issue of women's ordination would be a minor matter compared to the financial scandal which, even on the day of Dr Carey's enthronement, was ready to break. Its eruption, and all that followed, would lead to the most radical changes to the Church in England since the Reformation.

It would also enter the name of Dr Carey, as Chairman of the Church Commissioners, into the history books as the first Archbishop of Canterbury to appear before a parliamentary select committee inquiry to face public questioning. Such was his predicament that he was moved to declare that, unless the Church acted on certain proposed reforms, 'then perhaps my career is on the line.'

The administrative offices of the Commissioners are based at No. 1 Millbank, a seven-storey Grade II listed Edwardian Baroque building designed by W. D. Caroe in 1908, and whose elegant marble and oak panelling interior is in somnolent harmony with the weighty business of the Church of England's fiscal affairs. It is situated in the shadows of Westminster Abbey and Parliament, where, ironically, stands the statue of Oliver Cromwell, the Puritan revolutionary who, even with his Roundhead Army, observed a parliamentary critic, was less successful than the Church Commissioners in bringing the Church of England to its knees.

At the time of the Commissioners' calamity, their work was carried out by a staff of 280, who occupied almost half the building; about one-third was rented out to commercial companies, and the rest to church bodies such as the Church Pensions Board, which administered the clergy pension fund, and the Church Urban Fund, set up to help inner city relief programmes.

The first floor accommodated the office of Sir Douglas, the First Church Estates Commissioner, a position comparable to that of company chairman in a corporate structure. In keeping with historical tradition, the appointment is formally recommended by the Prime Minister and approved by the Queen at a salary of £62,000. Although he sat on a number of committees, including a General Purposes Committee which made recommendations on how the Commissioners' investments income should be distributed, the First Church Estates Commissioner's central power base was the chairmanship of the Assets Committee, responsible for generating just over 25 per cent of the Church of England's annual running costs of about £600m.

By his side, as the Second Church Estates Commissioner at the time of the Commissioners' disgrace, was the Rt Hon. Michael Alison, the grandiloquent Tory MP for Selby, North Yorks, a former minister of health with 30 years' parliamentary experience, who was credited by a Christian newspaper as 'the man who brought Christianity quietly to Downing Street.'[2] Alison's role, which began in 1987, was to answer questions on behalf of the Commissioners in Parliament. There was a Third Church Estates Commissioner, Mrs Margaret Laird, a former head of religious studies at a private school in Bedford, and a woman of solid social virtues and faith, whose appointment was largely titular.

The Commissioners' power lay exclusively in the hands of Lovelock and the Assets Committee, whose authority, to the chagrin of the more liberal and cynical within the General Synod, was unique within the Church of England. While the Church Commissioners had statutory guardianship of the Church of England's assets, the First Church Estates Commissioner and the Assets Committee had total control over their management and investment, an authority vested in them, ironically, to increase the Commissioners' income generating efficiency.

The First Church Estates Commissioner was also an *ex officio* member of the Board of Governors, an august assembly of senior churchmen under the chairmanship of the Archbishop of Canterbury, which was technically responsible for the management of the Commissioners' duties, and which, in a multi-layered bureaucracy that inspired wide-ranging and costly inefficiency, was served by no less than five committees.

While the Assets Committee was subject to any 'general rules' issued by the Board, in reality it meant little. The First Church Estates Commissioner was established as a person of almost supreme authority whom few within the Church of England, including the Archbishop of Canterbury, could openly challenge without creating a constitutional crisis. It was a position of power that sat well on the shoulders of Lovelock, a former senior Civil Servant of formidable intellect and ego.

The Church Commissioners numbered 95, most of whom came together once a year to rubber-stamp annual reports and accounts before they were submitted to the General Synod. But there was scant interest in an event which was little more than a congregation of distinguished senior churchmen dutifully playing their appointed part in an administrative ritual of little importance or attraction, other than the splendid hospitality that was inherent on such occasions, and the oleaginous politicking pursued by those keen to advance their old-boy networking.

Following the Archbishop of Canterbury, as their *ex officio* chairman, were the Archbishop of York, 41 diocesan bishops, the three Church Estates Commissioners, five Deans or Provosts, ten Clerks in Holy Orders, ten laymen appointed by the General Synod, four laymen nominated by the Queen, four people nominated by the Archbishop of Canterbury, two aldermen representing the City of London, and a representative of the universities of Oxford and Cambridge. The rest of the Commissioners were automatic *ex officio* Government appointees – the Prime Minister, the Home Secretary, the Chancellor of the Exchequer, the Lord President of the Privy Council, the Speaker of the House of Commons, the Lord Chief Justice, the Master of the Rolls, the Attorney-General, the Solicitor General, and the Lord Mayors of the Cities of London and York.

They reflected the historical link between Parliament and the Church Commissioners, whose origins, in part, go back to an Act of Parliament introduced in 1836 to rationalize the income of a Church whose wealth lay largely in the hands of a number of privileged and politically powerful bishops.[3] Out of that Act came the Ecclesiastical Commissioners – the two Archbishops, three bishops, three church laymen and five 'Principal Officers of State' – whose purpose, among others, was to investigate and correct financial inequalities, abuse and corruption.

The Ecclesiastical Commissioners set about readjusting the levels of income of the Archbishops and bishops, which came chiefly from land and estates left to the Church dating back to the Middle Ages, to the benefit of poorer sees. It caused bitter protests from those bishops who lived well off the fruits of the Church's inherited resources. They had argued loudly against the formation of the Commissioners, claiming that Parliament had no right to interfere in the affairs of the Established Church. It was a plaintive cry that would be heard again in Parliament 160 years later in the aftermath of the Church Commissioners' more recent fiasco.

But the bishops' outrage reached a new pitch at the introduction four years later of an Act of Parliament which went much further in removing the financial sinecures they had long enjoyed. The Ecclesiastical Commissioners Act of 1840, known as the Cathedrals Act, brought about sweeping changes which empowered the Commissioners to claim the revenue from the estates of cathedrals and the endowments of certain offices, which the Commissioners declared redundant, for distribution to poor parishes. The money was to make 'additional provision for the cure of souls in parishes where such assistance is most required in such Manner as shall ... be deemed most conducive to the efficiency of the Established Church'. A year later, the Commissioners were able to distribute to parishes the considerable sum of £4,000 in capital grants.

But even in those early years, the Commissioners were soon in trouble. Their financial management proved so inefficient that by 1844 they were soon unable to make any further grants to the poor parishes. They had completely miscalculated how much income would be available, a strategic deficiency that their successors in No. 1 Millbank would inherit. To increase their accountability, all diocesan bishops, three deans, six more laymen and five judges were added to their number. It was a costly error.

Their composition became so unwieldy that management policy was inconsistent and difficult to frame. More and more of the day-to-day business fell on the shoulders of a man called Charles Knight Murray, who, since the formation of the Ecclesiastical Commissioners, had been in charge of administration and finance. Unbeknown to the Commissioners, he became a director of the London Chatham and Dover Railway and began speculating in railway shares.

It was a venture that contributed to a personal financial crisis, which he attempted to resolve by intercepting money drafts totalling £7,000, worth today about £243,000. It also led to his public disgrace in October 1849, when, amidst growing suspicions, he confessed his misdeeds. The Commissioners decided not to prosecute, and Murray emigrated to Australia where he became a high-ranking official in the New South Wales Government and a senior member of the New South Wales Bar before his death in 1865.

As a result of Murray's infamous activities, a parliamentary select committee inquiry was held, which led to parliamentary legislation in 1850 reconstituting the Ecclesiastical Commission, one of whose principal effects was the emergence of a new body to be known as the Estates Committee – the forerunner of the oligarchical Assets Committee 113 years later – whose purpose was to protect the interests of lessees to whom land and property was rented. To the Estates Committee was appointed a clerical and lay member from the Commissioners' board and three additional laymen, who would be known as Church Estates Commissioners. Another principal effect of the Ecclesiastical Commissioners Act of 1850 empowered the Commissioners to take over and manage estates to ensure more equitable distribution of the Church's income.

In these early years, the Commissioners were widely unpopular, mistrusted by bishops and an embarrassment to government ministers. Their opponents believed them to be iniquitous and absurd, while economists thought them wasteful and unbusinesslike. There was considerable support for their abolition. In 1856, at the second of three parliamentary inquiries into their activities, the third Marquess of Salisbury, Conservative MP for Stamford, the future Lord Salisbury and Prime Minister, asked of Spencer Walpole, a Church Estates Commissioner from 1856–58, and a former Secretary for the Home Department, whether he 'contemplated the Ecclesiastical Commission being a permanent body'. Replied Walpole: 'It is now, and I do not see how it can be otherwise.' It has since been observed that the existence of the Commissioners turned on the following exchange. 'You do not see any way of getting out of it?' asked Salisbury. 'I do not,' came the reply.

During the next decade – in 1860 and 1868 – Acts of Parliament increased even further the powers of the Ecclesiastical Commissioners, allowing them to take over the estates of bishops, deans and Chapters, corporate bodies who managed the estates to raise income for salaries and the maintenance of buildings. This 'acquisition', by far the biggest vested in the Commissioners and which provided them with the bulk of their assets, made them one of the biggest owners of land and property in the country.

However, most of the Commissioners' income came through their agricultural interests – they owned 250,000 acres of agricultural land – and they began to broaden their investments only in 1910, including a £3m investment in War Stock during the First World War, with a further £2.5m in a War Loan. It wasn't until that year, due to the slow development of their resources, that the Commissioners were able to introduce a general scheme to augment clergy income. Over the next 20 years, their income levels varied with the economic fortunes of post-war years, but, by 1948, the Commissioners were issuing annual grants totalling nearly £2m out of an income of £5.2m, which also paid for the maintenance and upkeep of cathedrals and churches.

During that year, on March 31, the Ecclesiastical Commissioners ceased to exist. They were merged with Queen Anne's Bounty, a charitable corporation established by Royal Charter in 1704 to restore to the Church of England special taxes claimed by the Pope in the 13th century before they were appropriated by Henry VIII. These taxes, known as 'first fruits and tenths', required the clergy to pay the whole of the first year's income from their estates and one-tenth per year thereafter. The restored funds produced the considerable income in those days of £16,000 per year, which was used as capital grants to provide financial assistance to the poorer clergy.

In 1924, by which time nearly £9 million had been paid in capital endowments to poorer benefices, Queen Anne's Bounty became responsible for the maintenance of all parsonage houses, and, later, the authority for approving the purchase and sale of parsonage houses. By 1948, it was paying an annual average sum of £225 to over 100,000 incumbents, or more than £2.25 million per year.

Between 1900 and 1935, there were four attempts to bring the functions of the two bodies together, much of whose work, from parsonages and benefice income to issuing quarterly stipend cheques to the same clergymen, was a costly duplication. This was the principal logic behind the proposal to merge, but efforts to bring the two bodies together were thwarted, at least initially, by mutual suspicion. An influential force pressing for a merger was the Church Assembly, the predecessor of the General Synod, which had been created through the Church Assembly (Powers) Act of 1919 to empower the Church of England to legislate on its own affairs, and which now wanted to establish a more formal and constitutional relationship with the two bodies. There was also a political motive – there was some resentment that the Church had no say on appointments to the Board of Commissioners, which put it outside the Assembly's control or influence. Finally, the constitution of Queen Anne's Bounty laid down that every Queen's Counsel automatically became a governor, which had caused it to become impossibly unwieldy. By 1947, the number of governors had grown to more than 700.

In 1935, the boards of the Ecclesiastical Commissioners and Queen Anne's Bounty agreed to merger proposals contained in a report commissioned by the Archbishop of Canterbury following a resolution by the Church Assembly. But, in a world where nothing moved at a great pace, the process was interrupted by the outbreak of the Second World War. It was not until 1943, when the Church Assembly set up a joint committee, that the proposal was revived. The committee proposed that the amalgamation of the Ecclesiastical Commissioners and the Queen Anne's Bounty should make way for the Church Commissioners, originally named the Church Bounty Commissioners.

Through the Church Commissioners Measure – the Church of England's equivalent to an Act of Parliament – passed by the Church Assembly in 1947, and approved by Parliament, which nevertheless retained the right to reject the Church Assembly's legislation, the Church Commissioners finally came into existence, with 'all functions, rights and privileges' of the two bodies. On 1 April 1948, with assets of £210m, of which £70m came from the coffers of Queen Anne's Bounty, the Church Commissioners were created to 'promote the more efficient and economical administration of the resources of the Church of England'.

1. Lambeth Group report, July 1993, Para. 422.
2. *London Link*, Summer 1996.
3. *The Ecclesiastical Commissioners*, J. W. Cook CBE, official solicitor to the Church Commissioners, 1977–1985.

CHAPTER TWO

Foundations Laid

Within six months of the merger, the Church Commissioners' governing body, the Board of Governors, gave its support to a radical new investment strategy to increase income, which led the way to fundamental and far-reaching changes in the traditional portfolios. It led to the dumping of safe but low yield gilt-edged shares and fixed interest securities for more profitable ordinary shares – and, more spectacular, a gradual process of moving out of fixed rent, low profit residential property, much of which was on 99- or 999-year leases, into office and commercial property which could be let at far more lucrative rents.

There were two key players behind this initiative: Sir James Brown, the Commissioners' first Secretary – a post equivalent to chief executive – who was later promoted to the office of Third Church Estates Commissioner in 1954, and an astute and energetic chartered accountant named Mortimer Warren, who joined the Commissioners as financial secretary after 21 years with the Queen Anne's Bounty. The recommendations he produced in a report soon after his arrival at No. 1 Millbank led to this new strategy.

It was actively supported by Sir James, who played a principal role in the formulation and implementation of the constitution of the Church Commissioners, empowering them to broaden the scope of their Stock Exchange dealings. Sir James' role ensured that the Commissioners were not restricted, as both the Ecclesiastical Commissioners and the Queen Anne's Bounty had been, by constitutional clauses which permitted Stock Exchange investments in gilt-edged shares and fixed interest securities only.

Warren's report was warmly received by the then Archbishop of Canterbury, Dr Leonard Fisher, the first Chairman of the Church Commissioners. He had publicly expressed his enthusiasm for an increase in the clergy stipend, which, in 1948 was, on average, only £475 per year,[1] not much more than the average manual worker's wage of £348.[2] In the economic gloom of post-war Britain, and with the emergence of the phenomenon of inflation, many clergy, particularly in the inner cities, were existing on the bread-line.

But the move into riskier investments had its opponents. The more traditional Church Commissioners, suspicious of any departure from long-established practices, recoiled at the worldliness of it all. However, concerns were soon assuaged by the performance of the new investment policies, which by the early fifties were producing much-welcomed improvements in income. Ten years later, Warren was knighted for his contribution to making the lot of the clergy a temporally more happy one.

The Commissioners' more aggressive investment policy gathered pace with the appointment in 1954 of Sir Malcolm Trustram Eve, later Lord Silsoe, as First Church Estates Commissioner. A 60-year-old lawyer and army officer who had fought with distinction in the First World War, Gallipoli, Egypt and Palestine, Eve was also appointed that year to the post of First Commissioner to the Crown Estate Commission, the body responsible for managing government land property, which he would hold for the next six years; and the following year he sat on the Prime Minister's Committee on Administration of Crown Lands.

He was a man of distinction, socially and professionally, with the added virtue of excellent contacts in the property world. He also understood the political and cultural structure of No. 1 Millbank – he had been Third Estates Church Commissioner for two years, a position to which the former Secretary, Sir James Brown, was now promoted. Eve, who knew how to manipulate the system, was much respected, but also feared for his despotic style. A retired member of the Millbank staff, recalling his days under Trustram Eve, said: 'There was only one way of doing a thing, and that was his way. He would very rarely brook any opinion contrary to his own. He would most certainly have turned in his grave at the naivete and foolishness of the Commissioners' commercial judgements of recent years.'

On 5 January 1954, shortly before Trustram Eve's appointment, Mortimer Warren, his reputation established as a man of shrewd financial perception, became Secretary to the Commissioners. The appointments brought together an even keener and weightier combination of authority, expertise, energy and vision, which gave impetus to the pursuit of ever bolder property investments. Twelve months after his arrival, Trustram Eve authorized the disposal of low-yield property on a grand scale: the auctioning of freehold shops, business premises, pubs and long-lease residential properties across 65 acres of the central London borough of Paddington. Until the mid-1940s, the Church Commissioners had owned some 500 acres of the borough, part of the Church of England's historic assets dating as far back as the Middle Ages.

Apart from the substantial capital it would raise for reinvestment, the disposal was welcomed by the Commissioners for other reasons. The area was rife with prostitution, and the Church of England had been periodically embarrassed by sensational newspaper stories gleefully linking another brothel scandal to the landlords. Disquiet had also been expressed within the Church itself that its work was being funded by 'tainted' money.

The auction announced by the Commissioners was the first of its kind, and one of the biggest. Until then, the sale of residential property to owner-occupiers, and local authorities for slum clearance and redevelopment, or to private investors, had been substantial but piecemeal. News of the auction attracted much interest, particularly among a new breed – the speculative property developer – who in a post-war, bomb-blitzed London ready for redevelopment emerged to make their fortunes. Among them was Max Rayne, the 37-year-old son of a Polish immigrant, who left the RAF as a corporal, with a lot of ambition and a small gratuity. He invested both in property, and it was the beginning of a remarkable rags-to-riches story.

Returning to work at his father's rag trade business, Carlton Coats, which had been interrupted by the war, Rayne took a mortgage on offices in Wigmore Street, a prime property area of central London, for his father's business. He sub-let the rest of the property and soon realized it promised a more profitable future than the rag trade. It encouraged him to set up British Commercial Property in 1947, with ownership split between himself, his father, and a solicitor skilled in commercial conveyancing.

The ambitious Rayne soon established a reputation as a particularly shrewd operator. Twelve months after British Commercial Property was formed, the company bought a property for redevelopment in nearby Mount Street. It was funded by Norwich Union on the recommendation of Sir Edward Gillett, a chartered surveyor and senior partner in Daniel Smith, Oakley & Garrard, estate agents and chartered surveyors, of St James's Street, Whitehall, a long-established and much-respected company which had the trust of London's traditional landowners. Sir Edward had not known Rayne long but he had become sufficiently impressed by his business acumen and style that he had no hesitation in recommending that Norwich Union fund the project.

It marked the beginning of a mutually profitable association between Rayne and the aristocratic and well-connected Sir Edward, who enjoyed the professional esteem of many in the property world. Among Sir Edward's acquaintances was Trustram Eve, the newly-arrived First Church Estates Commissioner. It was Sir Edward's company of chartered surveyors – in conjunction with Hunt & Steward, of Parliament Street, Whitehall – whom the Church Commissioners engaged to handle the auctioning of the Paddington Estate on January 14, 1956.

However, when news of the auction reached Rayne, an audacious idea came to him and he set off for Sir Edward's office to put a proposal. It was remarkably simple but would help lay the foundation of his future success. It was that the Church Commissioners should go into partnership with him, Max Rayne, to redevelop a part of the estate known as Eastbourne Terrace, situated on a prime site opposite Paddington Station. Why should the Commissioners sell the freehold, he argued, when they could retain ownership and enjoy the top market rental income it would generate?

Sir Edward, who might have been taken aback by such a suggestion coming from a company of relatively little substance, nevertheless went to No. 1 Millbank to represent Rayne's case, vouchsafing for Rayne's business judgement and skill, as he had with Norwich Union. The proposal appealed to both Silsoe and Warren. It led to Rayne and the Church Commissioners forming a company known as West Regional Properties in which both parties had an equal share.

It was a triumph for Rayne, an unknown quantity to the Church Commissioners, and yet on whose confident analysis of the market they were ready to finance the entire redevelopment costs of £1.75

million, while Rayne himself put up just £1,000. But his judgement proved sound. By 1966, the joint venture had a value of £5.8m. The Church Commissioners' share was £2.9m, a considerable improvement on the estimated £400,000 it was expected to attract if it had gone to auction.

The relationship that developed between Rayne and Silsoe was such that, as a director of New River Co. Ltd, founded in 1619 and the oldest company quoted on the Stock Exchange, Silsoe used his influence to get Rayne appointed to its board for the purpose of producing and providing development expertise. The success of Eastbourne Terrace also led to a strengthening of the relationship between Rayne and Sir Edward Gillett to a point which led to Gillett being appointed chairman of several companies with which Rayne was associated with the Church Commissioners and the Portman Estate.

In 1967, the Church Commissioners bought Rayne's share in West Regional Properties for £2.9m, and in 1985, thirty years after the two parties came together on the Eastbourne Terrace partnership, the three-block row of office buildings was sold by the Church Commissioners for £12 million.

Four decades later, 77-year-old Lord Rayne – made a life peer in 1976, 11 years after marrying the eldest daughter of the 8th Marquis of Londonderry – maintains that his proposal to the Church Commissioners was motivated by altruism, an alien quality in the cut-throat world of property development. Chairman of London Merchant Securities, a leading property development company in which he acquired a controlling interest shortly before the success of the Eastbourne Terrace development, the dapper, silver-haired figure of charm, courtesy and undiminished acuity said:

> I was very confident that they should be tackling the redevelopment themselves, and in the end I think they must have been persuaded by my argument. My comment to Sir Edward, which he passed on to them, was that I felt they were missing an opportunity of doing something themselves. With my colleagues, I was able to demonstrate the possibilities and they were persuaded. I thought it was an opportunity that it would be wrong for them to lose.

As a result of the success of Eastbourne Terrace, the Church Commissioners abandoned any further thoughts of simply selling off property without first fully investigating the potential for speculative property development. Thanks to Rayne, they quickly came to realize the huge profits to be made in co-partnership ventures. So came into being the Church Estates Development and Improvement Company (CEDIC) in 1956, formed purely to hold shares in property development ventures.

The first major partnerships between Rayne and CEDIC took place that year through a company called West London & Suburban Property Investments Ltd. However, this time there was a fundamental difference in the structure of the partnership. In this instance, Rayne found the land, 5.5 acres of office buildings in the Tottenham Court Road area of London, and with profits 40–60 per cent in his favour. The only similarity with Eastbourne Terrace was that, once again, the Church Commissioners would provide all the finance, a total of £4m. The land itself, which formed most of the Cartwright Estate and was being auctioned to pay off death duties, was bought by Rayne for £320,000 before the auction opened. A further £475,000 was spent on acquiring small adjoining plots of land, and a little more than £3m on constructing new buildings.

Just eight years later, in 1966, the value of the Cartwright Estate had almost quadrupled to £11m, in addition to which the Church Commissioners were receiving a very handsome income. This partnership continued until 1987, when Rayne bought out the Church Commissioners' interests for £40m. They claimed that the estate required a considerable injection of money to ensure its future, funds which 'could be better deployed elsewhere'.

By the end of the fifties, the Church Commissioners were becoming ever more involved in commercial property, continuing to dispose of fixed-rent property as well as agricultural land. In London alone, they had sold 300 acres of property and land to local authorities. Even so, such was the Church's vast accumulation of property and land, that by 1962 the Commissioners still owned 30,000 houses, including six housing estates of 1700 houses, and 211,464 acres of agricultural land. By 1966, CEDIC's investments in co-partnership developments were principally in office buildings – the most ambitious of which was the £9m Paternoster development near St Paul's – at a total cost of £38.1m. Other projects totalling £20.4m had already been completed.

But the Commissioners' boldest venture took place in 1970 when CEDIC joined forces with three leading property developers – Max Rayne's London Merchant Securities, Wates and Great Portland Estates – to redevelop 90 acres of its Hyde Park Estate. It consisted almost exclusively of housing built more than 120 years earlier which, as with much of the Paddington Estate, had been more or less abandoned to the ravages of time and overcrowded, low-income tenants.

Ambitious plans were drawn up for the redevelopment of the entire area. From a political perspective, it was considered to be a brave project; landlords in those days had a reputation for ruthlessly exploiting tenants. But neither the size of the project nor the thought of public criticism could deter the Commissioners' enthusiasm. Indeed, they pursued the initiative one bold stage further. In their first venture as a sole operator, they built 238 apartments in the Sussex Gardens area at a cost of £4m.

Business relationships the Church Commissioners formed in those days continued for the next two decades. In the early eighties, under the co-partnership name of Myddleton Square Properties, the Commissioners and London Merchant Securities developed The Angel Centre, an impressive office block in Islington, North.London, at a cost of about £24 million, of which the Commissioners provided two-thirds. LMS, through the New River Co. Ltd, owned the site and had obtained planning permission, but wanted an institutional funder to spread the investment risk.

However, according to a senior member of the Millbank staff at the time, Lord Rayne was not happy with the Commissioners' terms. Although it was his idea and site, the deal was structured 52–48 per cent in the Commissioners' favour, with both parties sharing equally the development costs, and the Commissioners also insisted on the freehold. '[Lord Rayne] thought we were being unduly grasping,' said the former staff member. But Rayne had the last word, when, in 1991, as a consequence of their financial follies, the Commissioners were forced to sell their interests in The Angel Centre to LMS for £24m, a figure said to be well below its market value.

Despite the Commissioners' successes in the commercial world, they had no shortage of critics in the equally volatile pastures of the Church Assembly. There had long festered within its assorted political ranks an undercurrent of resentment of the unique powers and authority of the small group of men who were the force behind the

Commissioners' success. They had absolute control over the Commissioners' assets, from crucial investment decisions to the distribution of the Commissioners' income, as well as responsibility for staff and agents, the control of administration expenses, and the right to act on behalf of the Commissioners 'in matters of urgency'.

At the head of this powerful group, then known as the Estates and Finance Committee, was Lord Silsoe, the First Church Estates Commissioner, whose autocratic style perfectly fitted the sweeping powers of his office.

The committee was so constituted that unless two of the Church Estates Commissioners agreed, the committee's consensus view could be vetoed, and, in certain matters, two of the three could even act on the committee's behalf without consultation. In effect, the three Church Estates Commissioners had exclusive power over assets valued at the time at nearly £303m.

Such was the extent of their control that the three Commissioners met weekly to discuss their investments and to make any necessary decisions which would be approved as a formality at fortnightly meetings of the Estates and Finance Committee. When swift stock market decisions had to be made, they would be taken by Lord Silsoe, or even the Secretary and senior members of staff, who worked closely with the Commissioners, and who had available the advice of a panel of experts recommended by the Governor of the Bank of England and the Chancellor of the Exchequer. The committee's powers were designated at a time when there was considered a need for quick and efficient decision-making. Sir James Brown and Sir Mortimer Warren believed it was imperative that the income-generating agenda of the Church Commissioners was not encumbered by the heavy infrastructure of the Ecclesiastical Commissioners and the Queen Anne's Bounty.

But the Finance and Estates Committee had become a victim of its own success, which, some argued, was due to its dealings in worldly business to the exclusion of more Christian but less profitable investments, such as low-cost housing. While the Church of England quietly and formally applauded the increased income, there were some who saw profit as a secondary consideration, a tension that would continue to plague the Church and culminate in periodic outbursts of fractious disunity. But the greater force at work – and one that would also surface with equal acrimony in later years – had more to do with power than policy. The Finance and Estates Committee was considered by many, including a number of Church Commissioners themselves, to be too powerful for the good of the Church. Silsoe's authority needed to be challenged and his committee to be made more accountable.

Such was the persistent criticism and influential lobbying at senior levels within the Church that it led to the Archbishop of Canterbury, Dr Michael Ramsay, appointing a committee to consider 'whether improvements can be made in the administration of the Church Commissioners'. In a letter in late 1962 to Lord Monckton of Brenchley, whom he appointed to chair the committee, Dr Ramsay praised the way the Commissioners had 'looked after and developed' the Church's property and money, but added that he had 'come to the conclusion that this very success as well as the passage of fourteen years may have made changes desirable'.[3]

The committee consisted of deputy chairman Sir Edwin Herbert, Sir Maurice Dean, Sir Arthur fforde and Sir Alfred Owen. Their brief was to examine the work of the Church Commissioners as a whole. But, inevitably, due to its central authority and powers, their attention was largely focused on the Estates and Finance Committee. The committee's findings, published in September 1963 in what came to be known as the Monckton Report,[4] confirmed disquiet among the laity, clergy and Church Commissioners, who believed they had insufficient say in the way income was distributed. The clergy, in particular, also felt the Estates and Finance Committee did not understand or consider parochial feelings in its decision-making. Their feelings were due, in part, to 'the immensely powerful and possibly rather isolated position of the three Church Estates Commissioners', said the Monckton Report.

The exclusive powers of the three Commissioners and the Estates and Finance Committee were also blamed for a deteriorating relationship between the Church Commissioners and the Church Assembly. The report added:

> It was suggested to us that a part of the explanation could be found in the Commissioners' constitution under which such considerable power and policy control is in fact exercised, not so much by the Commissioners at their annual general meeting or even by the Board of Governors, as by the small Estates and Finance Committee and by the three Church Estates Commissioners, in particular.

The report stated that there was

> ... a general feeling that too much control has been put
> in the hands of the Estates and Finance Committee and
> the three Church Estates Commissioners: that the repre-
> sentatives of the Church Assembly, in spite of the fact
> that they are in a majority on the Board [of Governors],
> do not exert as much influence as might be hoped and
> that, in spite of the care taken to collect information,
> decisions about distribution [of funds] are sometimes
> taken upon inadequate information and with insufficient
> knowledge of public opinion in the Church and of the
> complete needs of the Church and the calls upon it.

The Monckton Report, which was subsequently approved by the
Church Assembly, made 11 recommendations, ranging from
the functions and composition of the Church Commissioners and
the Board of Governors, which would remain intact, to the importance of improving the Commissioners' relations with the Church
Assembly and the dioceses, as well as the Church of England's public image. But its more significant recommendation came in the
breaking up of the Church Estates Commissioners' power base, the
Estates and Finance Committee, in whom, the report said, 'too
much responsibility has been concentrated'.

As a result, the committee ceased to exist, with its functions
divided between two others: the Assets Committee and the General
Purposes Committee. The Assets Committee would manage the
Commissioners' investment portfolios, and report annually to
the Board of Governors on the level of income available for distribution, while the General Purposes Committee, the Board of
Governors' 'principal committee', would be responsible for the allocation of income, and its members of 'position and experience'
could 'bring to bear ... the thoughts and feelings of the Church'. It
would also control administration expenses; be responsible for
staffing matters and the appointment of solicitors and agents; act as
the general executive committee of the Board of Governors; and
act on behalf of the Board of Governors in matters of urgency
'other than those relating to the management of assets'.

The Monckton Report also led to the end of the Church Estates Commissioners' direct control over investments. Only Lord Silsoe, as the First Church Estates Commissioner, was appointed, as chairman, to the new Assets Committee, supported by a bishop and three 'specially qualified' lay Commissioners appointed by the Archbishop of Canterbury. And while all three were appointed to the General Purposes Committee, again with Lord Silsoe as chairman, the Second Church Estates Commissioner, Sir John Arbuthnot, became a non-voting *ex officio* member, and their number was balanced by two diocesan bishops, three clerical Commissioners and three lay Commissioners.

The Third Commissioner, Sir Hubert Ashton, was also appointed chairman of two other committees to emerge from the report – the Pastoral Committee to advise the Board on pastoral matters and the Houses Committee to advise on the houses of diocesan bishops and clergy – while the Second Church Estates Commissioner, who represented the Commissioners in Parliament, was excluded from all committees, apart from his *ex officio* membership of the General Purposes Committee.

The report claimed that, as an MP and member of the Church Assembly, he couldn't 'for long hope to carry the kind of burden imposed by his present undifferentiated responsibilities'. It would probably have been nearer the unkind truth to say that, his political connections apart, he was considered to be of little practical value to the Commissioners' business and that his seat could be better occupied by someone of more qualified expertise.

Following the report's recommendations, the joint powers of the three Church Estates Commissioners were redefined and the functions of the Finance and Estates Committee repealed under a measure passed by the General Synod and approved by Parliament as an amendment to the Church Commissioners Measure of 1947.

The investigation into the administration of the Church Commissioners was widely welcomed, as were the recommendations of the Monckton Report. Their implementation was seen as a major step in ensuring greater accountability of the Commissioners' assets management. Many were also pleased by the recommendation that the Commissioners should give 'full consideration' to suggestions in the report for improving relations with the Church Assembly and the dioceses.

But, in the ensuing years, the Church Commissioners, and the Assets Committee in particular, would prove to be no more popular with the Church at large. For the next three decades, the Commissioners would continue to be accused of being too distant and remote from the cares and concerns of parishes, while the Assets Committee would remain condemned as an impenetrable clique, with too much power and of too little accountability for the Church's good.

In 1969, 21 years after Sir James Brown and Sir Mortimer Warren had set the Church Commissioners on a revolutionary route to greater wealth, Lord Silsoe, the third figure at the heart of their success, retired as First Church Estates Commissioner. By then, the income of the Church Commissioners had increased from £5.6m from assets of £118.6m in 1949 to £23.27m from assets of £412.404m. But while the level of clergy stipends had more than doubled, inflation meant that the clergy were barely any better off than when the Church Commissioners came into existence. Nevertheless, but for the Commissioners' dramatic change of investment policy, the impecunious state of many clergy would have been even more severe.

The payment of stipends was only one demand on the Commissioners' income, which was divided into two parts − to meet the requirements of the statutory obligations inherited by the Church Commissioners from the Ecclesiastical Commissioners and the Queen Anne's Bounty; and that which was available for discretionary distribution. The first call on the Commissioners' income in those days was the payment of clergy stipends, followed by contributions to curates' stipends, pensions for retired clergy, contributions to repayments of parsonage mortgages, the stipends of archdeacons and bishops, and contributions towards the stipends of deans, canons residentiary and cathedral servants. Surplus income, if certain year on year, might go to permanently augment parish stipends, or to the pensions of clergy and their widows, or as one-off grants, for example, to fund capital works on parsonage houses, or Church buildings in new housing areas.

However, the world judged the wealth of the Church of England on the basis of its assets and income, not on the harsh reality of the bills it had to pay. It was believed to be awash with money, even by many within the Church itself, an image encouraged by the success of the Commissioners' investments in property and shares.

By the time the Monckton Report was published, the Commissioners had already become well established as a major player in the property development world. They were not only keenly sought as partners in major property ventures, but their financial might was such that they were able to loan millions of pounds to property development companies, even to the likes of Lord Rayne and Basil and Howard Samuel, of Great Portland Estates.

By now, the Commissioners were no longer seen by the City as unenterprising keepers of the Church of England's wealth, content to rely on the modest fruits of safe and traditional investments. Willing to play the property and shares markets to the full, they became regarded as astute entrepreneurs funding some of the most ambitious property development in recent times.

1. GS333 *Differentials*, Central Stipends Authority report to the General Synod, May 1977, p. 84.
2. *British Labour Statistics: An Historical Abstract.*
3. Published in chapter one of the Monckton Report.
4. 'The Administration of the Church Commissioners for England', report of the Committee appointed by the Archbishop of Canterbury, 1963.

CHAPTER THREE

Increasing Demands

The decision by the Church Commissioners to become more adventurous in their investments was considered within No. 1 Millbank to be unavoidable. With increasing demands on their income, fuelled by inflation, it was believed the Commissioners had little option but to move into more lucrative markets. However, the success that followed the expansion of their property and shares portfolios, while applauded in the City, was not so widely acclaimed within the Church of England itself.

It laid the ground for increasing conflict between two factions: those who argued the Commissioners had no function but to use the Church's historic assets to realize the maximum profit to fund clergy stipends and pensions, and those who believed, with equal fervour, that the Commissioners' stewardship should follow more closely the teachings of Jesus Christ, with greater concern and compassion for the plight of the deprived and disadvantaged. Over the next three decades the schism would harden over the issue of ethical investments – that is, money invested in companies such as breweries and arms manufacturers, and those operating in South Africa in particular. This would result in an acrimonious legal confrontation in the High Court.

But even before then, the Commissioners were making the news, and many enemies, by the way in which, having disposed of much of their dilapidated property in the more unattractive areas of London, they began increasing rental income from residential property in the more fashionable areas of the capital to the cost of low-income families. Equally controversial was their decision to impose staggering rent increases – in some cases as high as 100 per cent – on their commercial tenants. Local Labour MP Arthur Latham urged churchgoers and clergy 'to bombard the Commissioners with protests. I know the Church needs money, but it should have a sense of responsibility towards its tenants.'[1]

In times when private tenants had little legal protection and were often at the mercy of unscrupulous landlords, the activities of the Church Commissioners, as one of the biggest and wealthiest land and property owners in the country, were keenly covered by newspapers, which usually reinforced the public perception of a rapacious Church of England exploiting the poor and defenceless.

Concern within the Church caused the Monckton Committee to diplomatically underline the problem in its report. Acknowledging the City's respect and interest in the Commissioners' successful development of the Church's assets, the man in the street, said the report, got 'misleading ideas' from what he heard or read. He didn't distinguish 'between the Convocations, the Church Assembly, the Church Commissioners and the priesthood ... The news that he hears and reads about any of these is news about "the Church" – and, if there is anything in it of which he disapproves, it is the Church as a whole that is apt to get the blame.' The report recommended that the Commissioners bear in mind the importance of giving an accurate presentation of the public image of the Church of England.

The Commissioners insisted that, as landlords, their conduct in dealing with their tenants was beyond reproach. In earlier years this might have been true. The Commissioners had played a pioneering and progressive role in providing low-rent housing for working-class families in Walworth and Lambeth. They worked closely with the likes of social worker Octavia Hill, who devoted her life to improving the lives of the socially deprived, and after whom the Commissioners named their housing estates in the two areas.

But with the change of policy in property investment to produce greater income, the lives of thousands of their tenants would suffer, with the reputation of the Commissioners as caring and responsible landlords much diminished. Even at the time of the Monckton Report implementations, the Commissioners were planning the redevelopment of their Hyde Park Estate, a 90-acre triangle of terraced houses ranging from Edgware Road to Bayswater Road and Sussex Gardens and occupied by working-class families, which would prove widely unpopular and cause great hardship. To the Commissioners, the commercial equation was simple: exclusive, high-class property represented massive rent increases.

However, the impact on the lives of their tenants could be devastating, as the Hyde Park Estate redevelopment programme, which the Commissioners embarked upon with London Merchant Securities, Wates and Great Portland Estates, starkly illustrated. Hundreds of homes on the 90-acre site were demolished to make way for 763 luxury apartments and 112 houses at a cost of £12m. More homes were also demolished in the Commissioners' separate £4m Sussex Gardens redevelopment to build a further 238 luxury apartments, over which they enjoyed total control and profits.[2]

The Revd Kenneth Bartlett, who arrived at St James' Church in Sussex Gardens in 1963 to work with the homeless and needy, was appalled by what he saw. His church bordered the redevelopment area, and he witnessed at first hand the ruthlessness of the Church Commissioners. He said:

> They ran down the estate by buying terraced houses all over west London, into which they decanted families as the opportunities arose to move them on. Then they demolished and redeveloped the entire area. They had declared that they were going to turn it into the most exclusive residential area in London, which they proceeded to do. But it was very disruptive and completely destroyed the community. It was so tragic to see what it was doing to ordinary families.
>
> As a young curate, I was attempting to minister to people in the area, people who needed help and support. I was trying to preach the message of God's love and the Church's concern for His people, while ... the Church's appointed representatives were busy clearing the parish of these people in harsh and uncaring style. The area has never recovered as a residential area. It is more an area where companies buy apartments for executives. The Commissioners had no regard whatsoever for the way in which their decisions broke up families. They were simply an obstacle to greater profits, and one which had to be removed as soon as possible.

Bartlett was so staggered by those early experiences that he founded the Paddington Churches Housing Association, a voluntary group which campaigned for low-cost housing for the unemployed and homeless, and later became assistant chief executive of the Government-funded Housing Corporation, founded in 1974 to help fund non-profit making housing associations which provided accommodation, particularly for the elderly, at 'fair rent' levels.

As a senior official of the Housing Corporation, he drew little applause from No. 1 Millbank when he publicly announced that Peter Rachman, a notorious rogue landlord of his day, had attracted a great deal of public opprobrium for making life difficult for a few hundred people, while the Church Commissioners had made life impossible for a few thousand people. Looking back on those days, he added: 'Scriptural teachings and the Church Commissioners passed each other on parallel lines.'

Spurred by the success of the redevelopment of the Hyde Park Estate, the Commissioners turned their attention to the nearby Maida Vale Estate, a sprawling 160-acre area of terraced houses, also occupied by low-income families. But here the Commissioners decided on a different strategy. They decided to 'gentrify' the area by modernizing properties and increasing the rent, which the vast majority of their tenants simply couldn't afford.

Forced to move on, the Commissioners were then able to welcome a professional class of tenant who could afford the rent increases. Maida Vale gradually became a prime residential area, but, again at the cost of great hardship to poor families. Such was the concern caused by the Commissioners' activities as landlords that the Nuffield Foundation funded an investigation by an independent housing research team.[3]

It led to a report published in May 1981 which revealed the depth of the Commissioners' 'gentrification' policy over the previous 10 years. It confirmed that cheaper rented property on the Maida Vale Estate had been rapidly eroded, 'with the poor ... being pushed out by the rich'. The report claimed that in one particular fashionable street, the only unimproved properties were those occupied by less well-off families who had resisted all efforts to move them out. The fight to stay in their homes had been long and exhausting, 'with considerable effects on their lives'.

There was evidence, too, that the Commissioners had moved other families into accommodation in less salubrious parts of the estate at lower rents to encourage them to move out. The Commissioners were accused of pursuing a housing improvement policy without apparent regard to the consequences to the housing market and in direct conflict with Westminster City Council's housing strategy. 'There should be concern throughout the Church of England about whether the price of the Commissioners' responsibility for paying the clergy and maintaining Church property must be the destruction of the housing chances of the poorest section of London's population.' According to the Revd Bartlett, the Commissioners even bribed tenants to move out. 'A number of people I knew were paid off to leave, so [the Commissioners] could revamp the property and let it at a higher rent. The Commissioners were quite determined about that sort of thing.'[4]

The Commissioners responded to the Nuffield Foundation report, in a statement issued by the First Church Estates Commissioner, Sir Ronald Harris, who had succeeded Lord Silsoe in 1969, by denying the charge that the Commissioners were 'engineering gentrification' at the cost of poorer families. Harris claimed that certain properties scheduled for improvement had to be vacated and families moved to other accommodation where rents were 'unlikely' to be more expensive.

Following publication of the report, the Commissioners, who between 1975 and 1981 received £500,000 in improvement grants and had enjoyed substantial tax benefits, announced in late 1981 that 2,000 properties on the Maida Vale Estate would be placed on the market. The properties, between 80 and 100 years old, were in such a state of disrepair that the cost of repairs would total 'millions of pounds'. A senior consultant, who was involved in the decision to put the property on the open market, said, 'I wanted [the Commissioners] to get out of it because my experience in housing is that you are onto a political loser and all you get is "aggro".'

The Commissioners said that the properties would be offered to tenants at discount prices. But this gave little comfort to many working-class tenants who, even then, were unable to buy their own homes, as the Commissioners' own annual report and accounts for 1983 confirmed. Sales, it said, were proving 'particularly successful on the estate, where prices realized ... rose by around 15 per cent during the year'. It added that a number of tenants' associations – formed to act on behalf of low-income families who could not afford to buy their own homes, even at the 20 per cent discount offered by the

Commissioners on vacant possession – had failed to 'put together bulk purchases of whole sections of the estate'. It was followed by 'a surge of sales of individual units'.

The move was widely unpopular amongst tenants who, with good reason, believed their homes were threatened. In July 1985, three hundred from the Maida Vale Estate lobbied the General Synod in protest at a decision by the Commissioners to sell five houses after the occupying families had been unable to buy them. It was done, admitted the Commissioners, to 'concentrate the minds of tenants' associations and the residents about what should be done about the houses, and we put them on the open market to see what would happen. We have now sold them ... and we think it is ... very satisfactory.'[5] In 1986, when the sale of properties on the estate passed the £100m mark, the Commissioners reported tersely that 'further progress had been made in selling residential properties which tenants were either unable, or unwilling, to purchase'. The fate of those tenants was not mentioned, but clearly the Commissioners had succeeded in moving them on.

Seventeen months after the publication of the Nuffield Report, its claims about the way in which the Commissioners had upgraded property to attract higher rents at the expense of low-income tenants was confirmed by no less an authority than the Social Policy Committee of the Church of England's Board of Social Responsibility. The committee's report, *Housing and Homelessness*, proved even more scathing of the Commissioners than the Nuffield Report.[6]

It suggested that the Commissioners should not only face critical questioning about the sale of residential property on the Maida Vale Estate, but also about their policy governing the sale of church land and property. A substantial part of the report focused on a different area of their business activities – the sale of redundant churches. The committee discovered that it was the practice of the Commissioners to sell to the highest bidder, even to the exclusion of church-based housing associations working to provide low-cost housing for the homeless.

The report, which supported a claim by housing associations that the Commissioners should give priority to 'socially valuable projects', said the Commissioners frequently accepted the highest bid for a redundant church, rather than wait until a housing association had been able to raise the necessary finance to make a realistic offer.

The Commissioners were also unwilling, the report suggested, to wait for a district valuer's assessment in case it undermined a site's full market potential.

The chairman of the Social Policy Committee, the Suffragan Bishop of St Germans, The Rt Revd Brother Michael SSF, said the issues covered by the report presented 'critical questions about ... how the Church of England sees its responsibilities about the use of its properties'. He added that he wrote the report with an 'underlying belief that the provision of an adequate supply of housing is fundamental to the well-being of society and that there must be a Christian concern to ensure that access to housing is given equitably to all'.

Following a debate in the General Synod on the plight of the homeless, the report was distributed to dioceses, where, amidst the Church's prosperous shires, it disappeared without trace. Fifty years earlier, when the Church of England was very much more the Tory Party at prayer, the Bishop of Southwark, shocked by the social privations of the poor, had said that the housing conditions of three-and-a-half million people in England and Wales were 'a practical denial of the belief in the Fatherhood of God'. As a result of his speech, a five-point action plan, endorsed by the Archbishops of Canterbury and York, was produced. It, too, went largely unheeded.

One of the more illuminating examples of the Commissioners' aggressive commercial attitude was the sale of a redundant church in Bishops Bridge Road, Paddington, in 1985. Holy Trinity Church, more than 100 years old and declared redundant six years earlier, had gradually succumbed to the brutalities of the weather, vandalism, and, above all, public disinterest. But there were hopes that its sale and demolition would make way for 80 sheltered flats for the elderly and a community centre for the benefit of some of the 1,600 homeless families in the area.

Behind the proposed development was a housing association which had put in a bid of £900,000. But it was turned down by the Commissioners in favour of an offer of £1.5m from Rosehaugh plc, one of the largest property developers in the country. Their bid was accepted, claimed the Commissioners, on the recommendation of the local diocese, 'so as to enable more provision to be made for the areas in greatest need'.[7] Given the desperate local needs, it was a comment which must have brought a sardonic smile to the housing association officials.

By way of compensation, the Commissioners announced in their annual report and accounts that 'a substantial grant' from the sale proceeds should be awarded to youth work in Paddington 'in recognition' of a young people's club which had been held in the church's crypt, one of the few places in the neighbourhood where youngsters could meet in safety. It was subsequently decided, however, that the grant – £200,000 – would go towards the cost of building the community centre for the homeless. But neither local youth nor the homeless saw a penny of the grant. It went, instead, on improving a property owned by the Diocese of London in Newton Road, Bayswater, which was then rented out to a medical practice at a lucrative rent. According to Mr Roger Clayton Pearce, Secretary to the Diocese of London's Pastoral Committee, it was 'for the benefit of the local community. I am not sure what the property is worth today. It is a long-term investment.' It was, he confirmed, owned by the London Diocese, 'although that is not to say that the Church Commissioners might not have put some money in as well, but I am fairly certain in saying it is our investment as opposed to theirs'.

Out of the debris of Holy Trinity Church rose a block of luxury flats, which were put on the market at up to £400,000 each. Not long after their completion, the Church Commissioners purchased £1.109m-worth of shares in Rosehaugh and by December, 1989, had increased that shareholding by a further £500,000. By June 1991, Rosehaugh became a victim of recession and went into receivership, but not before the Church Commissioners had sold their shares at a handsome profit.

During the 1980s, the Commissioners sold four redundant churches in Paddington. One was used to provide sheltered accommodation for the elderly, while three went to property developers for luxury housing, contrary to the wishes of the congregations.[8] The sale of Holy Trinity Church for luxury housing was a decision that deeply saddened its vicar, the Revd Adam Duff. He campaigned hard for the site to be sold to the housing association to benefit the poor in the district. 'It ... did the Church little credit. It was an area of great social deprivation. The decision by the Commissioners, and indeed the diocese, caused a good deal of local anger and understandably held the Church up to charges of hypocrisy, being, as it was, so uncaring about the weak and the vulnerable, those whom Jesus commands us to help.'

Between 1969 and 1995, the Church Commissioners raised £25.8m, of which £21.5m was passed on to dioceses, through the sale of 1,453 redundant churches. Of these, 63 were sold to housing associations. They were churches which could not be sold off for more profitable commercial projects. But, even then, the Commissioners frequently preferred to deal with housing associations which were not registered with the Government-backed Housing Corporation, and which, not bound by its rules and regulations protecting the interests of tenants, were driven more by commercial enterprise than social concern. As a profits-driven business, such associations invariably had access to larger funds, which greatly enhanced their chances of doing business with the Commissioners. Said the Revd Bartlett:

> It was a widely recognized danger to sell to an unregistered housing association. No other reputable body, as far as I know, ever sold to an unregistered association. The legal obligations on them were far fewer, and they could get rid of tenants much easier. Unless a housing association was registered, it had no value at all. Of course, the Commissioners were happy to sell to them because an unregistered association could offer more money. It was not restricted by certain legal obligations, which made it easier for them to raise the kind of capital that would meet the Commissioners' expectations.

In December, 1985, by which time Holy Trinity Church had been demolished, a commission, which had been set up two years earlier by the Archbishop of Canterbury, Dr Robert Runcie, to 'examine the strengths, insights, problems and needs of the Church's life and mission' in deprived inner-city areas, published its report. Led by Sir Richard O'Brien, Chairman of the Bank of England, commission members had gone into the inner cities to see for themselves the reality behind the headlines and official statistics on unemployment and homelessness. The experience, said the report, *Faith in the City*, had left them 'deeply disturbed'.[9]

The residential property holdings of the Church Commissioners, landlords to 4,300 tenants, from wealthy professionals in Hyde Park to low-income families in Walworth and Lambeth, were so great in some parts of London that they significantly influenced rent and property prices, said the report. Referring to the implications of Commissioners' statutory obligations to maximize income to fund clergy stipends and pensions, they also faced 'particular pressures' to sell low rental property to commercial developers. But it was a policy that 'may well encourage the local community to conclude that the Church does not seem to care about housing and the needs of local people'.

The report, which also confirmed the Commissioners' process of 'gentrification' to force low-income families out of the Maida Vale Estate, adding that it 'may occur elsewhere, too', believed that any future involvement by the Commissioners in housing should be through non-profit making housing associations, rather than as part of an income-generating policy. The report highlighted the difficulties housing associations had faced in dealing with diocesan authorities, who represented the Commissioners' policies at local level. The sale of a redundant church, they complained, would take place without them being aware that it had even been on the market. 'Housing associations, seeking to work in co-operation with diocesan authorities and develop a long-term strategy, have felt that their request for partnership was unwelcome.'

Local community groups had also been frustrated by what they saw as 'an impenetrable procedure' in trying to contribute to discussions on possible community uses for redundant churches. The report, which recommended earlier and more open consultation with housing associations and community groups when redundant churches were to be sold, added:

> We have been told that some people have gained the impression from their dealings with the Church in property matters that it finds it too much trouble to take non-financial matters into account. The conversion of a church building into luxury flats … conveys an image to the local community of a rich and perhaps uncaring institution.

The commission members were 'glad' to be reassured by the Commissioners that during the previous 15 years – from 1970 onwards – 70 per cent of redundant churches had been used for purposes 'benefiting the local community'. But, once again, it was an ambiguous phrase that encompassed a wide range of community activities from arts and crafts to storage and light industry. In truth, very few went, as the Archbishop's Commission might have hoped, to help the socially disadvantaged. Between 1969 and 1990, 1,300 churches had been made redundant, but only nine had been converted to provide low-cost social housing. Although under the Church of England's Pastoral Measure of 1969, the Commissioners were not obliged to sell a redundant church to the highest bidder, as *Faith in the City* pointed out, profit was still the principal consideration.

However, such was the negative public perception of the Commissioners as landlords, the report itself – and the Church of England – was bitterly attacked for comments which dared to be critical of the Thatcher government's inner-city housing record. Mr Terry Dicks, Tory MP for Hayes and Harlington, challenged the integrity of *Faith in the City*, when the Commissioners 'were one of the worst landlords London has ever seen'.[10]

The Commissioners, stung to public reply, said the allegations should be substantiated or withdrawn. A spokesman for the Commissioners said: 'Any landlord with 5,000 residential units may make mistakes but at least our heart is in the right place. I can think of many landlords who are worse than us.'[11]

But the Commissioners' dealings with their tenants sat incongruously alongside pronouncements by senior churchmen through the eighties who castigated the evils of market-driven materialism. A notable example was provided in a business magazine interview given by Dr Robert Runcie in October 1989, during which, in similar tone to the *Faith in the City* report, he was critical of a market-driven economy and a Thatcher government which, he believed, had failed the deprived and disadvantaged.[12] He claimed that they were in 'days when the simple dictates of profit and self-interest are recognized as the dynamics of industrial success – but to regard them as the sole dynamics of society or an organization is fatal'. They were, of course, the very dynamics that dictated the Commissioners' management of the Church's assets. And they would indeed prove fatal.

The interview took place shortly before a conference held by Dr Runcie at Church House, the administrative headquarters of the General Synod, to examine the possibilities of redundant church property being used for low-cost housing. The conference, which promised much, ended feebly. It was hoped that the Commissioners would give greater consideration to low-cost housing when disposing of redundant churches, but the Archbishop said he could not solve the central conflict the Commissioners faced in deciding between maximum profit and social needs.[13] It was considered by the Commissioners' critics to be a pusillanimous statement which gave tacit approval to uncaring property investment strategies, and it illustrated perfectly the tension within the Church of England between the Commissioners' legal obligations and Christ's teachings.

At this time, the First Church Estates Commissioner was the ill-fated Sir Douglas Lovelock, a man who, in fulfilment of his duties as he saw them, paid almost obsequious homage to the bottom line. Certainly there was no room on his agenda for such negative considerations as low-cost housing for the poor and needy. He was not prepared to invest the Church's capital in socially valuable projects even when a reasonable profit was possible. His attitude was exemplified at a meeting in early 1989 with the Joseph Rowntree Foundation, a £7m-a-year registered charity whose housing trust supports a wide range of social housing.

The foundation's director, Richard Best, a member of the Church of England's Social Policy Committee and former Director of the National Federation of Housing Associations, had gone with his financial director to No. 1 Millbank to try to persuade Sir Douglas to consider investing in social housing as a profitable commercial proposition. He was convinced the foundation had 'a winner' in index-linked loans to housing associations, which offered 'a tremendous market' for investors looking for safe, long-term investments. Best, whose foundation went on to invest £10m in social housing through housing associations, was willing to invest alongside the Commissioners to encourage their involvement.

'There were at that time excellent investment opportunities for putting money into housing associations on an entirely commercial basis, where one could get some rather good returns, but at the same time would be supporting the end product of social housing,' he said. As large investors of 'the right sort', he had hoped the Commissioners would show the way to others. But he was to be sorely disappointed. 'Sir Douglas felt they had seen residential property in years gone by, and they didn't want to see it again … But Lovelock was not at all interested. I think he thought it was a very eccentric suggestion. I felt frustrated because I didn't really feel that the message we had brought had been heard.' Lovelock told Best that the Commissioners had better investment opportunities in commercial properties, which caused Best and his finance director to respond by claiming that they were proving 'an unsafe market'.

By the end of 1989, with high interest rates beginning to bite, the Commissioners were experiencing a serious downturn in the rental and capital values of their commercial investments. On the other hand, the prudent investment of housing association loans proposed by Best led, by March 1996, to a £10bn market, attracting both pension funds and insurance companies. But, at the time of Best's visit to Sir Douglas's office, the First Church Estates Commissioner was immovable. Unless, it seems, it suited the Commissioners' political sympathies – as the case of the Cruise missile site in Molesworth, Cambridgeshire, suggested.[14]

To extend the site, the Ministry of Defence negotiated the purchase of an adjoining 1.6 acres of land owned by the diocese of Peterborough. The ministry offered £1,400 for the land, while the Christian Campaign for Nuclear Disarmament, keen to block the planned extension, was able to raise £2,100. Yet it was the ministry's bid that the Commissioners accepted. The Revd Robert Anstey, vicar of Gretton and Rockingham, agreed, on behalf of the Christian CND, to put his name to a High Court injunction to halt the sale of the land to the Ministry of Defence on the grounds that, as the Commissioners themselves had so frequently claimed, they were legally obliged to seek maximum profits. In March 1985, the High Court injunction was granted, and the land remained in the ownership of the diocese. Said the Revd Anstey, now retired: 'I gather the Commissioners accepted the bid from the ministry because they did not care for the politics of the CND.'

Apart from demonstrating a remarkable flexibility of policy when it suited, the decision also illustrated the autocratic indifference the Commissioners were capable of displaying towards the General Synod, which had passed a motion condemning first use of nuclear weapons. As Cruise missiles were part of NATO's first use strategy, the sale of land to aid that strategy was seen as being contrary to the spirit of the Synod's wishes. Similarly, the Commissioners overrode a motion by the Synod opposing the sale of redundant churches to non-Christian faiths. In February 1983, St Luke's Church, Southampton, was sold to Singh Sabha Gurdwara, a Sikh sect, for £80,000. It was an issue over which there was bitter division within the Church of England, and the Commissioners' dismissal of the Synod's views gained them few friends.

But one of their more curious deals was planned in 1982, when the Commissioners began negotiations to sell properties in London worth £30m to an offshore company called Hillingdon Investments, registered in the Isle of Man on 7 August 1981 with capital of 2,000 £1 ordinary shares.[15] However, the directors of the company suddenly resigned and were replaced by two business-women from Sark in the Channel Islands. Five months later, they also resigned, to be replaced by a woman administrator and an Indian barrister.

At the same time, the Commissioners had also agreed to accept a bid from Hillingdon Investments of £166,000 for seven properties in central London, rather than a collective bid of £325,000 by the tenants. Once again, for reasons which were never made public, they were prepared to accept less than the highest bid. At the time, Mr David Long, a senior executive officer to the Commissioners, was quoted in a newspaper as saying that the Commissioners were 'satisfied' with the company, although he later said, 'I didn't work in the estates and commercial property department. I simply passed on the information they gave me for the media.'

On 15 December 1982, the matter was raised in the House of Commons, when Mr William Hamilton, Labour MP for Fife Central, requested from Sir William van Straubenzee, Tory MP for Wokingham, then Second Church Estates Commissioner, details of 'the circumstances in which the Church Commissioners sold several of its London properties to a company known as Hillingdon Investments registered in the Isle of Man'. Sir William confirmed that Church Commissioners' representatives had held discussions with the company concerning 'the possible sale' of a number of commercial properties. But the Commissioners had been informed by the company that it no longer wished to proceed.[16] A few months later, the company went into receivership.

Negotiations on behalf of the Commissioners were carried out by Cluttons, an international company of chartered surveyors and property consultants with headquarters in Berkeley Square, London. A partner in the company at the time, Mr Peter Stratton, said: 'I very vaguely recall the name of Hillingdon, but I really can't remember any of the detail.' Cluttons declined to divulge any information relating to their past dealings with the Commissioners. 'It is the principle of confidentiality that exists with clients,' said Mr Martin Sankey, a senior partner. According to Millbank, there was no record of the negotiations with Hillingdon Investments.

This aborted deal coincided with the retirement of Sir Ronald Harris as First Church Estates Commissioner after 18 years' service. His reign, beginning in 1969 after five years as Secretary, had vigorously reinforced the ambitious commercial property investments policy set by his predecessor, the more aloof and didactic Lord Silsoe.

Harris, the son of the general secretary of the South America Missionary Society, spent his early years in Colchester, Essex, and went on to Harrow and Trinity College, Oxford, achieving a first in modern history. A distinguished Civil Service career, which began in the India Office, took him during the Second World War to the post of secretary to Cabinet Secretary, and subsequently civilian staff officer to Lord Louis Mountbatten, then Supreme Allied Commander in South East Asia. In 1947, he became principal private secretary to Lord Pethick-Lawrence, the Secretary of State for India, before moving to the Treasury as head of the Imperial and Foreign Division, and, in 1952, returning to a senior position within the Cabinet Office. After four years as Third Secretary at the Treasury in charge of its overseas expenditure and aid programme, Harris, then 51, was appointed Secretary to the Church Commissioners in 1964.

With this impeccable Civil Service pedigree, he had been eminently suited to the regime of No. 1 Millbank, whose structure was closely modelled on the bureaucratic disciplines of Whitehall. His appointment five years later to the post of First Church Estates Commissioner was an inevitable progression. With his ever-present bow-tie immaculately in place, he settled into its chair – and that of Chairman of the Church's Central Board of Finance in 1978 – with urbane ease.

Harris, who died in January 1995 at the age of 81, was widely respected within Millbank for the way in which he understood the needs of the Church and the spirit of Synod. Unlike Silsoe, who was singularly apathetic towards Synodical business, Harris would attend debates which offered little professional interest. A member of the Board of Governors who knew him well said: 'He wasn't a person for whom finance was the be-all and end-all. He was concerned with the good of the Church, the good of the clergy, and doing what was right in meeting the needs of the time, but with caution, and to see that it was all done within the synodical context.'

As for the tenanted property controversies in which the Commissioners became embroiled during the seventies, particularly the Maida Vale Estate, his former colleague believed that the evangelical Harris would have been unaware of the hardships they caused. 'While he was aware of the duty the Commissioners had to get the best possible profit from their investments, he was far from unmindful of its possible effects on the well-being of others. Whatever might have happened at the street level, so to speak, I am quite sure it would not have been with Sir Ronald's approval.'

His time as Secretary had given him a complete understanding of the Commissioners' property and shares portfolios, which he continued to ambitiously expand. Particularly successful was his endorsement of an initiative to establish a presence in the US commercial property market. A former Second Crown Estate Commissioner whose frequent visits to farms had gained him considerable agricultural expertise, he also improved the quality of the Commissioners' agricultural holdings to see the price of farming land soar in the early seventies.

Harris' astute leadership saw the Commissioners' income grow rapidly, until, by his departure, it stood at £70m from capital assets of £1,442m, compared to £23m out of £412m on his appointment in 1969. He had successfully maintained the Commissioners' investments strategy to a degree which increased the average clergy stipend to £5,800, a substantial improvement on the late sixties when more than half the clergy were paid less than £1000 a year although the crippling cost of inflation meant that most clergy were only marginally better off.[17]

Inflation had also seriously eroded the value of contributions from the Church of England's 13,663 parishes. In July 1971, the Central Board of Finance, the financial executive of the General Synod, announced budget cuts of 15 per cent, while four years later, the Bishop of Chelmsford, the Rt Revd John Trillo, believed that inflation was proving so devastating to the Church's finances that it threatened the existence of churches of non-historic value. He added that if the rate of inflation at that time continued the Church 'was in danger of becoming the community's poor relation.'[18]

In the same year, 1975, the Commissioners warned that their income – it was £34m the previous year, less than half of total expenditure – couldn't hope to keep pace with inflation. The gap could only be filled by the giving of church members, and it was necessary to raise a further £11.3m to maintain the clergy's living standards, principally through increases to stipend and pensions of retired clergy and clergy widows. More than a third of rectors and curates were on stipends of less than £40 a week, which were planned to be increased to an annual minimum of £2,400 at a cost of about £3m.

Between 1968 and 1978, the effects of inflation had been so great that donated income was reduced in value by nearly one third. It led to an appeal by the Church Commissioners and the Central Board of Finance to church members to give £1 for every £1,000 of annual income. Over the next four years, donations increased from £52.3m to £95.6m, a cash increase of 83 per cent, but even then, with inflation over that period at about 62.5 per cent, the increase in real terms was reduced to 12 per cent.[19] The consequences of these inflationary pressures had further constrained the Commissioners to pursue a maximum profit policy, argued their allies.

Nevertheless, the Church of England had a deft touch in producing ammunition for their critics. While the Commissioners were calling on parishioners to show greater generosity, and the future of curates as well as churches was threatened due to financial shortfalls, a Lambeth Conference was proposed to which bishops worldwide would be invited at a reported cost of hundreds of thousands of pounds. Another public relations gaffe was a costly proposal by the General Synod that all debates of Synod should be published in book format. Such grandiose plans never failed to draw the fire of those who needed little excuse to attack the establishment.

Both proposals were strongly criticized in an open letter to his diocese by one of the establishment's most vociferous opponents of his day, the Bishop of Southwark, Dr Mervyn Stockwood. Of the proposal to publish synodical debates, he wrote: 'At a time when we are compelled to reduce our incumbencies and curacies because we cannot afford to pay priests, we are expected to pay for the doubtful privilege of reading speeches, many of which would have been all the better had they never been uttered.' Like the proposed Lambeth Conference, it would be 'the man in the pew who pays for all this'. He called on churchgoers to oppose alleged overspending by the Church of England, 'a top heavy and expensive organization'.[20]

At this time, in 1975, one of Stockwood's fellow bishops was also making the news with the Church Commissioners.[21] Questions were asked at the Synod about the expenditure of £201,000 – worth today about £1.3m – on new homes for the Bishop of London. Following the closure of Fulham Palace as the Bishop of London's official residence on the retirement of Dr Robert Stopford, his successor, Dr Gerald Ellison moved to a prestigious three-storey terraced house in Cowley Street, Westminster, around the corner from offices of the Commissioners in Millbank, on which £101,000 was spent by the Commissioners to purchase the lease and refurbish to suit the new bishop's comfort. However, the bishop was of the opinion that his new residence was 'just not' suitable.

The Commissioners agreed to purchase the lease of a similar but larger house in nearby Barton Street. The combined costs of the lease and conversion – which gave the entire top floor over to the bishop's accommodation, with the rest of the house to his offices and his chaplain's flat – came to £100,000. It was considered a colossal expenditure by Commissioners who were responsible for another, more iniquitous, property conversion and refurbishment policy a few miles away in Hyde Park, Maida Vale and elsewhere.

Many people in the parishes viewed the Church Commissioners with a high degree of suspicion as self-serving political appointees deaf to the heartbeat of the grassroots body. The Commissioners' executive staff at Millbank were seen as careerists living off the fat of the Church. Such disapproval was expressed in a pamphlet headed 'No. 1 Millstone', distributed by a radical group of clergy and laymen calling themselves 'Parish and People'. They urged the sale of Millbank, with offices to accommodate the Commissioners' administration relocated in 'a development area to show the Church cares for areas of high unemployment'. They were also critical of the high salaries and Civil Service style of staff selection. 'Clergy may not apply', said the pamphlet.

It was into this world of eclectic and cloistered ecclesiasm, united by one God and disunited by almost everything else, that the imposing figure of Sir Douglas Lovelock arrived on 1 February 1983 to occupy the office of the First Church Estates Commissioner on the first floor of No. 1 Millbank. One of his favourite quotations was a line from Robert Browning: 'A man's reach should exceed his grasp, or what's a heaven for?' Lovelock, for a short while at least, would be in paradise.

1. *London Evening News*, 31 January 1978.
2. Oliver Marriott, *The Property Boom*.
3. *The Guardian*, 5 May 1981.
4. Recorded interview with author, 5 November 1996.
5. *Daily Telegraph*, 3 December 1985.
6. *Housing and Homelessness*, Social Policy Committee of the Board for Social Responsibility of the Church of England, CIO Publishing, October 1982.
7. Annual Report and Accounts, Church Commissioners, 1985.
8. Institute of Housing, March 1990.
9. 'Faith in the City, a Call for Action by Church and Nation', the Report of the Archbishop of Canterbury's Commission on Urban Priority Areas, December 1985.
10. *Daily Telegraph*, 3 December 1985.
11. Ibid.
12 *Director*, 1 October 1989.
13. *The Independent*, 27 December 1989.
14. *The Guardian*, 9 March 1985.
15. *Daily Mirror*, 1 December 1982.
16. *Hansard*, 15 December 1982.
17. Church Commissioners' Report and Accounts.
18. *London Evening News*, 3 March 1975.
19. John Smallwood, *Slothful Stewards? Giving in the Church of England*.
20. *London Evening News*, 10 November 1975.
21. *London Evening Standard*, 13 November 1975.

CHAPTER FOUR

Going Shopping

The appointment of Sir Douglas Arthur Lovelock offered the opportunity of a splendid end to the career of a distinguished civil servant. It was one that began at the age of 17 in the Home Office, and which took the former grammar schoolboy from Streatham, south London, through ascending seats of executive power in the Ministry of Supply, the Ministry of Defence and the Department of Trade and Industry, until reaching its zenith in 1976, when he was appointed chairman of Her Majesty's Customs & Excise, and where he remained for six years. It was a career that Lovelock reviews with pride. ('If I may be forgiven a moment of conceit, I was the first person to be promoted all the way from clerical officer to Permanent Secretary.')

His interest in the position of First Church Estates Commissioner was more than professional. He was active in his local parish church a member of the parochial parish council and various committees – and, at the age of 58, claimed a desire to use his administrative skills for the benefit of the Church of England. First word of the position came through Sir Robert Armstrong, then head of the Civil Service, who had been asked if he knew of anyone suitable to fill Harris's shoes. It appeared to have been a difficult task. It seems that Lovelock, who took up office some two months after his predecessor's retirement, was by no means the first name that came to mind. 'They trawled around the Civil Service for quite a bit before settling on Douglas, who was, I think, about fourth choice,' said a former colleague.

In any event, Lovelock was flattered to be invited, and acknowledged his interest with enthusiasm. Armstrong, said Lovelock, made it clear that he wasn't trying to get rid of one of his senior mandarins, 'but I had always been involved in the Church of England in a fairly low capacity ... I thought I could make a real contribution to the work of the Church Commissioners and the Church at large.'

Unlike Sir Ronald Harris or Lord Silsoe, Lovelock had no experience either of the Stock Exchange or the property world, which, claimed the former colleague, led to considerable covert opposition to his appointment. The Commissioners' ambitious and aggressive investments required the stamp of a hard-headed businessman, it was believed, rather than the more political and administrative skills of a civil servant. It allegedly failed for lack of a suitable opponent.

Lovelock wasted little time in letting others feel the weight of his authority. Again unlike Harris, he made it clear that he was not prepared to pay court to the work of the General Synod. Although chairman of the Church's Central Board of Finance, responsible for the Synod's budget – an appointment he inherited from Harris, who saw it as an opportunity to improve relations with the Synod – Lovelock, said a member of the Board of Governors,

> took a more laid-back and detached role ... and consequently was less effective in holding the thing together. Ronald Harris would sit through debates on totally non-financial subjects to express his support, but Douglas Lovelock very quickly made it clear that he would appear when he was needed as a Commissioner, he would appear when he was needed as chairman of the Central Board of Finance, otherwise he'd got better things to do.

Lovelock's arrival at No. 1 Millbank coincided with early signs of recovery in a western economy that had been severely blighted by high inflation. For the first time for several years the Commissioners' income from both the shares and property portfolios began to show significant increases. As a closed fund unable to attract new money, their policy of selling off residential housing for property sectors promising greater income continued unabated. They were also disposing of much of their less glamorous regional office property, concentrating on prestigious, high-grade offices in central London.

In pursuit of better growth potential and to diversify their property investments, the Commissioners moved into the US property market through a wholly-owned subsidiary company called Deansbank Investments Inc, which was launched with an allocation of £28m from £77m raised during the year from the sales of static property investments. Twelve months later, the Commissioners' stake in US commercial property had increased to £38m, and a further £14m was earmarked for joint development ventures. They now owned substantial office complexes in Austin, Texas, and Tampa, Florida, and an impressive research and development centre in San Jose, California.

Nearer home, as the economy became more buoyant and recognizing the beginnings of a new shopping trend, they were sufficiently encouraged by income growth to move into US-style shopping malls.[1] Although compared to some later projects, it was a modest event – a 130,000 sq ft development at a cost of £27m – what came to be known as Tower Ramparts in Ipswich, Suffolk, marked the introduction in 1984 of a major turn of strategy that offered them the promise of great riches; but which, as they became ensnared by unbridled ambition and speculation, proved a major factor in their financial downfall.

Two men who would play a full part in that downfall were coming to prominence within the Millbank hierarchy. One was Jim Shelley, who, on 1 August 1985, was appointed Secretary to the Commissioners, giving him widespread control of Millbank. He was responsible to the Commissioners, as invested by their constitution, 'for the conduct of all business in their name and on their behalf'. In matters of urgency which required a decision, he had the authority, when neither the chairman nor the deputy chairman was available, to do so without reference to the Assets Committee until its next meeting. It was flawed licence for a person described by many as an eternal optimist incapable of saying no.

The slim, impeccably-mannered Shelley, 53, had been employed in the offices of the Church Commissioners for almost 31 years. He joined the pastoral department as a lower-grade executive officer on September 20, 1954, was personal assistant to Lord Silsoe for several years, and went on to work in the parliamentary and general department, and the investments and housing departments before being appointed assistant secretary to the estates, residential and agricultural department in 1972. He then became Under-Secretary of the estates department, Secretary to the parliamentary and general department, and, finally, Secretary to the Commissioners.

Although they had both come through the ranks of a civil service culture, Lovelock and Shelley had little else in common. If Lovelock was arrogantly intransigent, Eton-educated Shelley was considered malleable and complaisant to a degree of desiring to be all things to all men. He was, said a senior Commissioner, a man 'with whom you had to take the smooth with the smooth. James was that sort – very elegant, very well-connected and very stylish.' His lack of business experience, compounded by what was considered to be an obligingly benign personality, provoked strong opposition to his appointment.

It came from the same group who had opposed Lovelock's appointment, and for much the same reasons. As Shelley himself admitted privately, he, like Lovelock, knew very little about the property game. In the words of a bishop: 'We did need a shit, you see, and he wasn't the right sort of shit. He would have made a marvellous ambassador. But we weren't in that sort of world. He was a very pleasant person but not necessarily best suited to imposing his authority. Instead of a top civil servant, we wanted a top businessman. I claim nothing from it, but if we had got our way, we would not have been in this state.'

The anti-Shelley faction lobbied for another Millbank executive – Patrick Locke, a graduate of Wadham College, Oxford, a lover of 18th and 19th century literature, and a member of the Athenaeum. He joined the Commissioners in 1957, was appointed Stipends Secretary and Estates Secretary, and at this time was Under-Secretary General. Fifty-one-year-old Locke was considered the better choice because, said the senior churchman, he was 'a bit of a street fighter, one for close combat'. Another described him as 'the sort of person you know will take you to the cleaners if you play poker with him'.[2] But Shelley's opponents lost the day. 'The remnants of the old establishment were still in power,' said one. On the same day that Shelley was appointed Secretary, Locke was appointed his deputy.

The other central player in this ill-matched trinity was 38-year-old Michael Hutchings, who, four months earlier, had been promoted to the £51,000 post of Commercial Property Manager, the most senior executive position in a department responsible for property management and administration, and where he had worked, latterly as Principal and senior executive, for 14 years. Hutchings brought his own unique qualities to the management and administration of the Commissioners' property portfolio. A charming and overweight lover of good food and wine, who cherished first-name terms with head waiters, reputedly of independent means, he enjoyed life to the full, which meant during business trips to America on the QE2 – fear of flying prohibited air travel – he would be accompanied by a selection of expensive wine.

Hutchings, the only son of wealthy upper middle-class parents, was born in Hampstead, north London, attended Haberdashers Aske's School and went on to St Andrew's University, near Edinburgh, where he studied astronomy, physics and chemistry with indistinction. Through a tutor whose parents had connections at No. 1 Millbank, he began work at the age of 23 in the pastoral department assisting in benefice duties. Six months later, he was transferred to the estates department responsible for property management and administration.

He was, as he puts it, a 'very green bag carrier' and 'mouthpiece' for John Millard Barnes, the Development Officer, a title changed, on Hutchings' appointment 12 years later, to Commercial Property Manager. He regarded Millard Barnes as his patron and mentor and continued to view him many years later with misty-eyed affection. 'He taught me everything I knew about property. He was very good. He was entrepreneurial in character. He wasn't what I would call a standard institutional surveyor. I did miss him.'

Hutchings' career at No. 1 Millbank was confined exclusively to one department – property. But it gave him a comprehensive grounding in the Commissioners' property development and investment activities. While he possessed no professional qualifications, it was said that such shortcomings were more than compensated than by a sharp brain, shrewd judgement and a keen opportunistic eye for a lucrative property venture. It was reportedly his instinct for a good profit that earned him promotion to commercial property manager. A senior Commissioner commented: 'I heard his name mentioned as someone who had a golden nose when it came to real entrepreneurial flair.'

But, for all his natural talents, others saw Hutchings' dilettante inclinations as a handicap in the ruthless world of property developments. A former managing director of one of the biggest property development companies in the country, who knew Hutchings well, said: 'He was a delightful personality who was born 100 years too late: a Victorian country gentleman of substantial private means enjoying a Victorian country gentleman's lifestyle. Great company, an engaging man, but in a different world.'

These three key figures, with all their limitations and differing degrees of experience, came together to safeguard a property portfolio valued in the mid-eighties at £967.2m, representing almost half of the Commissioners' total assets of £1,944m, at a time when the Assets Committees were embarking on some of the biggest speculative property developments in Europe.[3] Of course, they were not alone, having behind them the collective wisdom and expertise of Lovelock's all-powerful Assets Committee, who enjoyed, in the name of the Church Commissioners, supreme control over their assets. They were men whose knowledge and experience were crucial in advising on investment policies, which would then be implemented by the Commissioners' executive property staff and agents. They were, in effect, non-executive directors, nominated by the Archbishop of Canterbury, and received no payment, although their involvement with one of the biggest investors and property developers in the country would do their professional networking little harm.

A prominent force within that power base was its deputy chairman, Brian Howard, who was appointed a member of the Assets Committee and Board of Governors in 1977. He was deputy chairman of Marks & Spencer until his retirement in March 1987, when he became non-executive deputy chairman of Hull-based Northern Foods, the £940m foods conglomerate, until his retirement in 1996. Howard, described as 'a very institutional man' and a stout defender of the status quo, got on well with Lovelock.

The committee's other property expert was Christopher Briant CVO MBE, who had been a senior partner in chartered surveyors Daniel Smith, Oakley & Garrard, whose principal, Sir Edward Gillett, had been responsible for introducing Max Rayne to the Commissioners in the pioneering mid-fifties of Lord Silsoe's reign. But Briant's experience was chiefly in residential property. Large-scale retail projects were not his particular skill, and he very much played second fiddle to Howard's lead. He became a member of the committee in 1981 and retired in 1989, when his place was taken by David Male, then President of the Royal Institution of Chartered Surveyors, and consultant to

Gardiner & Theobald, an international project and cost management company.

The committee's Stock Exchange experts were Joel Burnett-Stuart, chairman of merchant bankers Robert Fleming, and a member of the Stock Exchange Advisory Panel, who was appointed in April 1984; and David Hopkinson, who was chief executive of M & G Investment Group, then one of the largest units trust businesses in the country. He knew his way round the political corridors of Millbank and the General Synod, to which he was elected in 1970. He was appointed a Church Commissioner in 1972, and had sat on the Commissioners' General Purposes Committee and Board of Governors.

Giving the committee the benefit of his extensive agricultural expertise was Sir John Starkey, a former Sheriff of Nottingham, who ran a successful fruit-growing business called Starkey's Fruits in Southwell, Nottinghamshire. He became a member of the Assets Committee in 1984, and spent much of the time arguing, unsuccessfully, with Lovelock for greater reinvestment in their agricultural assets, which totalled 170,000 acres, including 474 farms of over 50 acres, rather than Lovelock's favoured policy of selling off land at every opportunity for reinvestment in more pro-fitable sectors.

Bringing up an ample rear was the Bishop of Peterborough, the Rt Revd Bill Westwood, a self-described 'Thatcherite bishop', a rumbustuous and outspoken personality, who said he once told the Rt Revd Michael Turnbull, the Bishop of Durham, that he was 'too Christian for his own good'.[4] His presence on the Assets Committee was intended to offer ethical guidance. Instead, he was more inclined to ask questions about property and equities which were generally unwelcomed by those committee members who claimed to know best. Starkey and Westwood might be described as the Asset Committee's loose cannons, and not considered close to Lovelock.

The Assets Committee met ten times a year, for about two hours, in an oak-panelled room in Millbank – it had been fortnightly until 1980 when it was agreed that meeting so frequently was too burdensome – to fine-tune investment strategies which were decided every 12 months, generally about May. On property matters, Hutchings had, in effect, supreme executive control, while Shelley played a more active role in Stock Exchange investments. His responsibilities and duties touched every part of the Millbank management and administration. He had little time, even if he had

had the experience, for the myriad meetings necessary in exploring and negotiating new property development proposals. He was happy to give Hutchings free rein.

They were responsibilities that Hutchings welcomed. He enjoyed his work enormously; the sense of importance that came with its power and prestige as one of the most influential people in the UK property scene, the boardroom intrigue and politics, the cut-and-thrust of closing a deal, the wining and dining with well-known figures in the property world; it offered a high-profile platform that suited his cavalier personality perfectly. So much did he revel in the professional and social esteem that he claimed that he personally subsidized his five-star lifestyle. One of the Commissioners' property advisers commented: 'He was in his element. He saw himself as one of the biggest property entrepreneurs in the universe.'

By his side, subordinate to his office, was a four-strong team of retained agents – representing Hillier Parker, Donaldsons, Cluttons and Chestertons – each specialists in their own property fields, who, in return for their expertise, received handsome consultancy fees and commissions on completed deals. Their companies had worked with the Church Commissioners over many years. Their analyses and recommendations on a proposed development were invariably accepted without question.

While he made his own contact with developers, Hutchings also briefed the agents who would return with propositions to fit the property investment policy decided by the Assets Committee. If Hutchings' 'golden nose' appreciated the fragrance, he would 'work up' a proposal with the agent and submit a detailed report to the Assets Committee on site, costs, feasibility and potential income levels. They were rarely knocked back. By that stage, only the contracts were left to be signed.

One of the Commissioners' more successful and highly-regarded agents was Chestertons, a leading firm of consultants, whose association with Millbank went back to the early fifties when the company managed the Commissioners' residential Hyde Park Estate and, later, the Maida Vale Estate after Hunt and Steward, a company involved with the Commissioners over many years, and who had been joint agents in the Eastbourne Terrace development with Max Rayne, fell out of favour.

The Commissioners' dealings with Chestertons took place through William Wells, a smooth, gregarious workaholic and a third generation property man. He joined Chestertons in 1959 after being lured away from Max Rayne's London Merchant Securities, preferring a career as a property consultant to a property developer and investor. In 1983 he was appointed chairman of the company, which, four years later, became Chesterton International. The appointment consolidated a relationship in which Lovelock and his Assets Committee vested their absolute trust and confidence, while his company enjoyed the bounty of their patronage.

When the Assets Committee, keen to take early advantage of the spending boom that was gathering pace in the mid-eighties, decided to invest more heavily in retail shops, it was Wells who first mooted the proposal that they should look to US-style shopping malls and retail parks. Brian Howard, as deputy chairman of one of the biggest department stores in the country, was the principal mover behind this new policy, a judgement endorsed by Lovelock. Such was the Assets Committee's conviction that major retail ventures would provide massive profits that it announced plans to schedule 50 per cent of its commercial portfolio in the retail sector; in fact, it finally came closer to 60 per cent.

With the construction of Tower Ramparts, the shopping project in Ipswich, under way, the Assets Committee's next step into the retail sector was bold indeed. The proposition was taken to Hutchings by Wells who had heard that Sir John Hall, the founder of Newcastle-based Cameron Hall Developments and saviour of Newcastle United Football Club, was looking for an institutional investor to back an ambitious retail venture in the north-east. In fact, the plan was breathtaking – 1.5 million square feet of retail and leisure facilities on a 100-acre site near the city of Gateshead, which would also provide more than 6,000 jobs in a high unemployment area. The project, the Gateshead MetroCentre, would be the first, and biggest, in Europe.[5]

Hall had already bought the site and had begun some construction, financed by a personal overdraft facility of about £30m. Several heavyweight funders were apparently keen to talk to Hall, but the Commissioners won the day because they were prepared to let the self-made millionaire, the son of a coal miner, play a principal role in its development, a condition crucial to the deal.

The first phase, which cost £130m, with £70m short-term funding from Royal Scot Leasing, was opened with 210 retail units in October, 1986. Brian Howard proved he was prepared to put his company where his mouth was – Marks & Spencer was among the first major tenants. The second phase, which included a further 90 retail units and a leisure complex, plus a ten-screen cinema, was completed by the end of 1987 at an additional cost of £55m, with £39m funded initially by Royal Scot Leasing.

But it was not long before the relationship between Hall and Millbank turned sour. According to Hutchings, a clause in their deal gave the Commissioners the option to buy out his residual share 'something like' five years after completion. But so strained were relations between the two sides that his withdrawal was negotiated and agreed two years before completion. Said Hutchings, 'John Hall was a very difficult person to work with. [The Commissioners] would like to have taken him out before they ever started. He still believed it was solely his project.

'We would hold these great meetings deciding what we would do, then he would get back to Newcastle and carry on regardless. He carried on acting as if he owned the place lock, stock and barrel.' William Wells, confirming the cause of the split, was called in to negotiate Hall out of the deal. Wells says it took many a long night to persuade Hall to accept the Commissioners' point of view. Hall finally agreed to sell his interest in the MetroCentre for £40 million, reports Wells. Hall declined to comment, other than to say, 'I thought we got on well together.'

Whatever the political wrangling, the Gateshead MetroCentre, within a 30-minute catchment area of 1.5 million people, appeared to be a triumphant success. It fired the Assets Committee's enthusiasm for similar projects, and almost before work on the MetroCentre had begun, another major shops project had been agreed – a joint venture with Sears Holdings, one of the UK's leading retail groups, for a 260,000 sq ft glass-covered shopping complex in Glasgow's city centre, which would be known as St Enoch's Centre, and include four major retailers, 50 shopping units, a food court and an ice rink at estimated cost of £57m to be shared by the partners. As with the MetroCentre, William Wells had recommended the deal to Hutchings and the Assets Committee.

By now, in late 1986, the Commissioners had, according to their own figures, invested £250m in shopping developments in the north. Looking for geographical balance to their portfolio, the Assets Committee approved two joint ventures in the south – Beechwood Place, in Cheltenham, a 124,000 sq ft covered shopping development at an estimated cost of £24m; and The Marlowes, in Hemel Hempstead, Herts., a far grander development of a 350,000 sq ft shopping centre at an estimated cost of £41m. The Commissioners' partners were Abacus, a subsidiary development company of Sir Robert McAlpine, and City Merchant Developers, whose chairman, Martin Landau, would soon become a key figure in the most ambitious of all the Commissioners' funding investments – a massive residential and industrial project in Ashford, Kent, and which would lose the Commissioners many tens of millions of pounds. (See Chapter 6.)

Landau, then aged 50, was a shrewd, dandified figure, who played to the full the stereotyped image of a hard-talking, cigar-smoking property entrepreneur, with homes in Montpelier Square, South Kensington, and the South of France. Educated 'in London', he reinforced his reputation for keen financial skills and an eye for a good development in the early eighties when he built up a property division for Guinness Peat and went on to set up City Merchant Developers. In March 1988 he merged forces with Martin Myers, chairman of Imry Property Holdings to form Imry Merchant Developers, of which he became deputy chairman with a £6.2m shareholding.

Landau knew both Hutchings and Wells well. He also knew the Commissioners' operational style. He had worked with them on many joint ventures, beginning 12 years earlier after a meeting with Hutchings. It came about when Landau approached the Commissioners for investment capital to redevelop an office block, Birchin Court, in Birchin Lane in the City of London. Hutchings, then under Millard Barnes, recalls that he wasn't keen on the proposal, claiming the appearance of the property, 'three buildings just massed into one, was so appalling'.

To encourage the Commissioners' interest, Landau asked Hutchings: 'What do you want – another quarter per cent on the yield?', referring to the interest rate that the Commissioners invariably charged for their banking services. That, replied Hutchings gleefully, would help. The project went ahead, with Wells as the Commissioners' agent. At the level of money the Commissioners were lending, a half or three-quarter per cent on top was, as Hutchings put it, 'well worth having'. '[The partners] used to get quite shirty. They used to say, "Aren't we partners, Michael?" And I'd say, "Yes, but we have administrative costs." They used to look at me!'

These, under Lovelock, were the Commissioners' palmy days, on the surface, at least. The timely sale of unattractive commercial property in central London – for which Wells would claim the credit as 'being one of the best things they ever did' – had provided the Assets Committee with the necessary liquidity to take full advantage of the eighties spending boom. Between 1985 and 1989, their retail shop investments increased massively, from £156.6 million to £460.3 million, an increase from 16.2 per cent to 48 per cent, and producing an income of £20.9m. But their true expenditure on retail projects was hidden in their annual reports and accounts, thereby concealing a recklessly high level of investment in one property sector.

The real figures, which were deliberately played down to avoid attracting critical attention, came to light following a report by accountants Coopers & Lybrand, who were engaged to investigate the Commissioners' investment activities as part of the Lambeth Group, the inquiry set up by the Archbishop of Canterbury, Dr George Carey, in the wake of the *Financial Times* disclosures (see Chapter 11). The report revealed an extraordinary degree of over-expenditure, which, due to poor planning, maladministration and incompetence, more than doubled the original estimated costs. The sum originally approved by the Assets Committee totalled £236m, but the final figure came to a staggering £517m.[6]

Between June 1986 and November 1989, the costs of 19 office and industrial projects, with two exceptions, also widely exceeded costs originally approved by the Assets Committee. The approved total was £321m but finally came out at £462m. The original costs of all projects authorized by the Assets Committee between July 1985 and November 1989, including the ambitious retail sector, totalled £557m. The final figure was £979m, a damning statement of expenditure alarmingly out of control. Some of it was due to amendments to specifications, construction problems, higher than forecast cost of borrowing and the failure or buying out of partners.[7] Some of the cost over-runs ended up on the Commissioners' table because of agreements which imprudently failed to ensure that the development companies were held responsible. Cost over-runs and buying out joint venture partners through default or design was a primary factor in adding over £200m to the Commissioners' development activities.

Landau, whose company, City Merchant Developers, and, later, as deputy chairman of Imry, was involved in some of the biggest joint venture development projects, denied that the projects either his company or Imry were involved in incurred cost over-runs: 'They were not cost over-runs in the true sense of the word, in that we said something was going to cost X and it ended up as double X.' Referring to The Marlowes as an example, Landau said that about halfway through the development they had the opportunity to purchase additional land. 'That's just one small item I'm giving you … but that wasn't originally planned.' Nor was the expenditure, which was authorized by Hutchings, and later approved by the Assets Committee. All the same, further land acquisition, variation orders and site problems were among the factors which added £89m to the final cost.

Hutchings blamed other reasons, from the rising cost of materials to poor design and inadequate surveys. As a prime example of over-budget expenditure, he cited the St Enoch's Centre in Glasgow, whose estimated cost of £41m, the Coopers & Lybrand investigation discovered, escalated to £68m by the time it opened its doors in May 1989. The progressive design of the two shopping-level building included the construction and installation of 30,000 sq m of sloping roof glass, which caused considerable technical problems. The Assets Committee had been assured by one of their advisers, in the words of Hutchings, that there was 'no state-of-the-art stuff with the roof'. They were advised that it was 'all good standard stuff'. The reality proved otherwise.

Said Hutchings: 'I think no one had really anticipated the complexity of producing a roof of that sort of magnitude. One of the main problems with that project was that the design was trying to keep pace with the contractors' requirements.' The technical problems were such, recalled Hutchings, that they led to a claim by the steel works contractor for £13m. 'They claimed that the drawings were inadequate and that they had to design things on the hoof, as it were.' The contractors, he said, finally settled 'for something like seven-and-a-half million. Throughout that job there were things that hadn't been thought through.'

One such oversight was the installation of an ice rink on the second level, which, in the summer, caused its own problems under the greenhouse effect of the glass roof. It resulted in the construction of a protective canopy at further considerable cost. But even that failed to resolve the problem and in mid-1985 the ice-rink was finally closed down to provide additional retail space. 'All along,' said Hutchings, 'there was a lack of planning foresight.'

The biggest budget over-run was the Gateshead MetroCentre – from £130m to £272m – the Commissioners' biggest single investment, although few outside Millbank would have known at the time. The Commissioners consistently listed its value in their annual report at 'over £20m', a ploy to conceal a dangerously overweight investment. The £40m buy-out of Sir John Hall and £55m second development phase took the Commissioners' total costs of ownership to £225m, a fact that the Commissioners wanted to conceal. But it was still £47m short of the final cost of £272m. Hutchings was unable to explain the shortfall.

'Even allowing for the payment to Sir John Hall, and all sorts of additions, such as the coach parks, new roads at the rear, and other rental-producing activities, I'm not at all sure how it could get to that sort of final figure. It was such a large scheme that we used to meet fortnightly and Jim Shelley was always around, so each stage was approved as we went along.' Wells claimed there 'really weren't' any cost over-runs. 'The additional expenditure went in buying out Sir John Hall,' he said.

The final costs of the MetroCentre and Ashford Great Park drew the following comment from a parliamentary inquiry set up in 1993 to investigate the management of the Church of England's clergy pensions. In a report published in March 1995, the all-party Social Security Committee commented: 'It is difficult not to conclude that the most senior staff and the senior Commissioner presented information which was so wide of the mark that the Church, Parliament and the public could only be misled as to the true cost of making these investments.'

In addition to attempting to hide the MetroCentre's true development costs in their annual reports, the Commissioners were less than accurate in trumpeting its trading performance. Hailed in their annual reports as an outstanding success, the Investment Property Database (IPD), the premier database for monitoring commercial property investments, told a different story: income had failed to even match inflation. Based on returns submitted by the Commissioners' agents from information supplied by Millbank, the IPD index covering a five-year period from 1986 to 1991 reported that the Gateshead MetroCentre yielded 5.5 per cent per annum on average, compared with an average annual inflation rate of 6.4 per cent.[8] Jim Shelley's claims in the Commissioners' annual report for 1988 – '[The MetroCentre] is now an established success and should bring the Commissioners considerable financial success in the years ahead' – were both misleading and unduly optimistic.

Beechwood Place, the Commissioners' fourth largest shopping centre of 124,000 sq ft, with 41 units and a car park, and situated in the centre of Cheltenham, presented its own problems, not least development costs which snowballed from an approved figure of £24m to £47m. As with the MetroCentre, Hutchings was unsure how such massive additional costs had been incurred. 'There were one or two of what you might call cosmetic refinements, but nothing that would have been that significant,' he said. 'Of course, there was the interest on the money the Commissioners borrowed, which at the end of the day increased substantially the cost of all these projects.'

The project, in partnership with London-based property developers Arrowcroft, was funded by the Commissioners and approved in early 1986 for completion in 1989. It opened, in fact, on 15 March 1991, over 18 months behind schedule – and £23m over budget. And the problems for the Commissioners were only just beginning. With the consumer spending boom a euphoric memory and recession biting deeper, the centre from the start was a letting agent's nightmare. It was anchored by one major store – Debenhams – and a restaurant. The massive development costs dictated unattractively high rents, which impacted heavily on the letting level. Its appeal to potential tenants was also diminished by inadequate car parking, the absence of a bus station linkage and poor signage. Even the inducement of reverse premium payments – with the the tenants' cost of fittings being paid by the letting agent – failed to significantly boost rental income. The centre, said a local observer, had become 'an embarrassment'.

1. Church Commissioners' Report and Accounts, 1983–1984.
2. *Daily Telegraph*, 8 October 1992.
3. Church Commissioners' Report and Accounts, 1983–1984.
4. Recorded interview with author, 28 March 1994.
5. Church Commissioners' Report and Accounts, 1985.
6. Coopers & Lybrand Report to the Archbishop of Canterbury; Lambeth Group Report, July 1993.
7 Lambeth Group Report, 19 July 1993, Appendix 4.
8. Ibid., Comparative Performance, p. 42.

CHAPTER FIVE

The Stakes are Raised

The Commissioners, alarmed at the drop in rental income in all sectors of their commercial property portfolio – although their concern was well disguised in their annual reports – and the increasingly poor prospect of successfully leasing their joint developments, decided on a course of action that would cost them many hundreds of thousands of pounds. It went in 'buying out' developers' interests where they were involved in so-called 'profit erosion' deals, which were a common practice between investment institutions such as the Commissioners and development companies.

These worked on the basis that the developers' profit was originally agreed as a percentage of the project's rental income after an initial return to the Commissioners. This percentage was paid as a capital sum upon successful completion of leasing, usually 12 to 18 months after construction had finished. The problem for the developer arose if the space had not been let during that time. The longer he took, the less profit he got; hence, 'profit erosion'.

On the other hand, in the light of a worsening recession, and with its adverse impact on rental potential, the problem for the Commissioners was that they needed to lease as quickly as possible, even at reduced rents, which could always be later increased in rent reviews. Reducing the rents, though, would not have been in the interests of the developers, as it would have reduced their profit share – and, under the terms of their agreements, it could not be done without their permission. The Commissioners were advised by Chesterton to pursue the only option: buy out their partners' letting interests. At least this way, it was argued, their investments would generate some desperately needed income. The cost of annulling a 'profit erosion' deal with Arrowcroft was allegedly as high as £500,000.[1] The Commissioners came to similar agreements for undisclosed sums with several other of their short-term partners, including Cussins Property Developments Ltd and Grosvenor Square Properties, who developed, respectively, Erskine House in Edinburgh and King Charles House in Oxford, both of which came in well over budget. According to the Coopers & Lybrand report, development costs of King Charles House were approved at £12m and finished at £16m, while Erskine House, approved at £9m, finally cost the Commissioners £27m – a massive 200 per cent increase.

The person behind the Commissioners' decision was Patrick Locke, who by now had succeeded Jim Shelley as Secretary. He was supported in his decision by William Wells. In some cases, said Wells, Locke had no choice – the partners were going bust and Locke didn't want to be caught with a partner in liquidation or in the hands of the receiver. 'I think we did recommend in one or two cases that they buy out their partners, and for extremely good reasons. If you've got a partner who has got the right of veto on everything [level of rents] and you, in the meantime, have put up all the money and you're getting no return on that building, then it's pretty damn important that you get a return as quickly as possible.' Wells, whose company, Chesterton International, took over as letting agents, added: 'That was one of the fragilities of the "profit erosion" deal. It was by no means peculiar to the Church Commissioners. Every single major investment institution learnt that lesson.'

But Hutchings was astonished by Locke's decision, particularly in the case of Arrowcroft. 'We had a very good deal with them, because, effectively, they were on line for absolutely nothing. They were responsible for some of the cost over-runs, and they never went into profit until the centre was fully let on 25-year leases, which they found very difficult to do. There wasn't a penny in it for them, and yet they got paid [off]. Every deal I did in that format was "profit erosion" ... because I couldn't see why we should take the letting risk. I suppose on average we got about two years' cover. I thought it was absolute madness to [buy the letting rights] because it was providing us with some sort of safeguard at a time when I could see the market was going a bit wobbly.'

The fact that the Commissioners were willing to buy out the developers' letting rights indicated their desperate need for income. But whatever Locke's reasons, he maintained a typically stony silence on the matter, declining to be interviewed. Although the Commissioners had bought out Arrowcroft's letting rights to give them control over rent levels, their efforts proved no more successful. Beechwood Place continued to prove difficult to let, and by 1993 more than 25 per cent of the shop units still remained vacant. Arrowcroft also declined to comment.

Hutchings maintained that a major factor in the cost over-runs was inadequate planning. He cited The Marlowes, the 350,000 sq ft shopping centre at Hemel Hempstead, as a classic example of how projects ran far from smoothly. There were, said Hutchings, serious problems with the land conditions. The bore holes to test land conditions had been sunk in the wrong place, he claimed. Chesterton, in the person of William Wells, was the agent. 'I really do think that when an agent produces a report, he ought to have looked into that. I don't see it's for the client to run round looking at land conditions.'

Costs were also substantially increased by a decision to buy additional land in the 'middle' of the site, which, alleged Hutchings, was 'totally under-designed in terms of architectural work. But once you are committed to one of these things it is terribly difficult to pull the plug and say we're not doing it. It turned into ... a damage-limitation exercise.' With that additional cost, which ran into several millions, rising interest rates, and the land problems, The Marlowes was 'a farce. All sorts of nasties were discovered. When we read the report from our agents, we were entitled to believe it had been researched and that we knew precisely what the costs were. But the more I sat at the meetings, the more I knew the costs were nothing like what they had said.'

However, Wells claimed that his company was expressly instructed by the Commissioners to have only a 'light touch' monitoring role. 'They looked upon the arrangement with Imry as the same type of arrangement they had had with Max Rayne and people in the past [when the developer provided the necessary development expertise]. Therefore we weren't required, or even asked – we were expressly told not to – to do anything other than have a light touch monitoring role, which would have been fine if they had been dealing with people who really didn't know what they were doing.'

But Martin Landau claimed that Wells represented the Commissioners throughout the development and attended meetings as the Commissioners' project adviser. 'It is unthinkable that an institution would put up tens of millions of pounds without a professional external adviser ... institutions traditionally, almost without exception, pay agents a monitoring fee to look after their interests.'

Hutchings was equally puzzled by Wells' claim. Confirming that Imry were paid to provide project management, he added that nevertheless Chestertons' role was 'not exactly a case of a "light touch". Their responsibilities were to make sure the Commissioners' interests were properly protected. And as The Marlowes progressed, it became apparent that Imry's project management ... was far from satisfactory. So what might have started as a fairly modest role [for Chesterton] developed into a full property management service at the end of the day.' Added Hutchings, 'I haven't the foggiest idea who instructed Chesterton to have a light touch monitoring role. I most certainly didn't, and I can't imagine who else would have done.'

The rising development costs caused considerable friction within the partnership, but it was the Commissioners who were at greatest risk. For they not only agreed to fund 50 per cent of the £84m development costs, they also borrowed money to loan on to their partners at an extra half per cent, which was part of their usual 'banking' operation. The deal was so structured that once various cost limits had been reached, each partner had to provide his proportion of the excess costs in cash. This they were able to do, but towards the end of 1990, Imry and Abacus had to meet their 25:25 share of the Commissioners' original investment. Unfortunately for the Commissioners, there were doubts, said Hutchings, that their partners could meet their shares.

William Wells was instructed to negotiate a solution. Imry Merchant Developers fulfilled their obligations by ceding their interest in Gracechurch Centre, a retail complex in Sutton Coldfield, near Birmingham, which they had acquired with the Commissioners the previous year for £60m. In a concerted drive to pay off massive borrowings, incidentally, the Commissioners later sold Gracechurch for a reported £58m. Wells also negotiated the buy-out of Abacus's interest, which gave the Commissioners sole ownership of The Marlowes. But, once again, they ended out of pocket, and with a huge development that failed to yield much-needed income.

David McAlpine, a director of McAlpines who, said Hutchings, was personally involved in the project, refused to discuss their deals with the Commissioners. The cost over-runs were a question 'you want to address to the people involved in the development side. I honestly think you are best talking to Mr Hutchings. He was there for the Church.'

The cost of The Marlowes, originally approved by the Assets Committee at £41m – half of the total estimated costs – ended up at £130m on completion in late 1990, representing an over-spend of more than 200 per cent. Commenting on the loans to McAlpine and Imry, Hutchings said: 'I'm not saying the deal we did at the end of the day was terribly clever, but they [the Commissioners] could have turned round to McAlpine and Imry and said, "Let's have our 'turn'."[2] But if you were thinking in those days of making loans to McAlpine and Imry ... I still don't have any doubts about loaning money to McAlpine and Imry ... you wouldn't think twice about it.'

The Commissioners' big mistake, according to Wells, was in loaning their partners' share of development costs, which, he claimed, was done by Hutchings to cream a half per cent profit on the loan. He claimed that he persistently advised the Commissioners against the practice of loaning money to their partners. 'I warned the Secretary, Jim Shelley, on a number of occasions from 1988 onwards, that I thought they were over-committing themselves to property, that I didn't like the way they were lending money to their partners ... and that he really had to do something about it.'

He said he finally put his concerns in a letter to Shelley in 1988, but claimed nothing was done. Exasperated by Shelley's attitude – 'we were between a rock and a hard place' – he decided to take his complaints to Patrick Locke, Shelley's deputy, in early 1989. 'He was the only person left me. I told him and, as a result of that, a few months later he took the whole matter to wherever he took it in order to blow the whistle.' He didn't know to whom Locke went. 'It wasn't my concern.'

He admitted that in going to Locke he was 'considerably surpassing' his obligations, 'but I did [so] because we had been involved in the Church for a long time and we felt very loyal to them and very concerned.' His complaint to Shelley, he added, was 'rather presumptuous, because they were the people who made the strategy, [but] one of the more dangerous things was actually going to the deputy Secretary behind the back of the Secretary.' Whatever Locke, alerted to Wells' fears, did is a matter for speculation. Locke declined to discuss the matter other than to say: 'I am not prepared to comment or speculate on matters of opinion.' Hutchings claimed he knew nothing of Wells' letter until Coopers & Lybrand began their investigation, nor, he said, had Wells expressed his fears to him, or at any meetings between the Commissioners and their partners. The letter also failed to reach the desk of Sir Douglas Lovelock. Said Lovelock: 'I never saw it. I was told about it afterwards and I was extremely cross that the letter hadn't been shown to me.' What would he have done if he had been shown the letter? 'It's not what I would have done. It is what the Assets Committee would have done. I would have insisted that the letter was shown to the Assets Committee.'

Wells' letter, according to the Coopers & Lybrand report, stated that the Commissioners' portfolio was 'in danger of becoming overweight in property, that future developments should be very selective and should only be undertaken on a pre-let basis'. However, according to Martin Landau and Martin Myers, Wells failed to follow the recommendations of his own letter. For some months later, in January 1989, Wells, according to Landau, was recommending that the Commissioners should proceed with the development of Ashford Great Park, a project in which they were centrally involved. Said Myers: 'They closed this deal with us … on land which was not only not pre-let, but on which there wasn't any planning permission.' It was something, said Landau and Myers, that 'mystified' them. 'Something doesn't seem to be quite right, does it?' added Myers.

Landau added that Wells also recommended a joint venture between the Commissioners and Imry which involved the £42m development of an office block, Colmore Row, in Birmingham, which went ahead without any pre-lettings. That was approved by the Assets Committee with Wells' support, in February 1989. Said Myers: 'The point I would like to make is that I'm a gamekeeper turned poacher, because I was 18 years with a professional firm as a chartered surveyor, and I know that if you recommend to your client in such uncertain [sic] terms not to do something and they do it, your position is untenable, is it not?'

Although he refused to be interviewed, Shelley, when he appeared with Lovelock before a Social Security Committee inquiry on 14 December 1994, claimed that the Assets Committee 'were being strongly advised' not to pre-let office property, 'because if you waited another year you would get another £2 a foot interest.' [3]

Wells was also a key figure during 1988, at the time of his protests to the Commissioners, in a 320,000 sq ft business park development in Banbury, Oxfordshire. It was a partnership with a newly-formed company called Oxford & Cambridge Estates and approved by the Assets Committee in February 1989 at a cost of £35m. The proposal was taken to Wells by Andrew Oakes, a former partner in chartered surveyors Richard Ellis, and who began his career with Chesterton in 1972. The 25-acre site was bought without planning consent for £3m through Chesterton who were acting for the landowners, William Holdings. Wells then negotiated its purchase, with planning permission, on behalf of the Commissioners at £5.5m. In commenting on his support of these projects, Wells claimed he had, in fact, written two letters – one in 1988, in which he claimed the Commissioners' property portfolio was dangerously overweight, and another in the summer of 1989, when he strongly advised against developments that were not pre-let. The Coopers & Lybrand investigation team had access to all the documentation, he said, although his office later admitted that copies of the letters could not be found.[4]

The events that followed the signing of the Banbury Business Park development give an interesting insight into the Commissioners' business culture. Oakes claimed to have had a better offer for the site, more than £6m, but he was hopeful of establishing a lucrative relationship with the Commissioners. By way of compensation, Wells agreed that Oakes would be paid £500,000 out of future profits. The deal was based on a 60–40 per cent split in profits in the Commissioners' favour. As was their usual practice, Wells also agreed, on behalf of the Commissioners, with DTZ, who were representing Oxford & Cambridge, that the Commissioners would pay 50 per cent of the development costs and loan Oakes his share.

Wells pulled the deal together, with Hutchings doing little more than celebrate the agreement at a very expensive lunch in Reading at Oakes' expense. 'Michael didn't really have a major input,' said Oakes. 'There were certain things they wanted us to do, which they felt would improve the lettability of the product. Michael had particular ideas about certain things. He was particularly keen on a particular specification for reception areas and toilet areas.'

Sadly for Oakes, it all ended in tears, when Oxford & Cambridge Estates, also involved in a major development scheme in Brentford, Middlesex, was severely hit by cashflow problems through the collapse of a syndicated loan bid. By mid-1990, when banks and investment institutions were rolling down the shutters, his company was forced into liquidation. Hutchings terminated the partnership, and, under the terms of the agreement, the Commissioners took full ownership of the development. Oakes was at least £500,000 poorer.

It led to a meeting at Millbank with a solicitor friend of Oakes, who also knew Shelley. The solicitor, believing that Oakes had been badly treated, beseeched Shelley to arrange some sort of payment to ease Oakes' losses. Shelley agreed to speak to Hutchings, who refused, claiming that Oakes hadn't 'performed'. It was unfair comment. It was the market, rather than Oakes, that hadn't performed. Nevertheless, Hutchings was adamant and rejected Shelley's plea to 'find a way'. Oakes was nevertheless subsequently appointed to promote and manage the business park.

The Banbury Business Park development also illustrated the influence that Wells exercised in representing the Commissioners' property portfolio. He was the driving force in its content, and successfully, to such a degree that it would have been 'unusual' for Hutchings, according to a chartered surveyor who knew them well, to have rejected a project recommended by Wells. Of the two, he was considerably more experienced and astute.

It was Wells who had recommended The Marlowes project. According to Landau, he was so keen for the Church to become involved that he agreed, on behalf of the Commissioners, to pay a 'signing-on' fee of £7m. Landau claimed that his company, City Merchant Developers, had three different institutions seriously interested in providing the capital – a Japanese group, the Church and another UK institution. 'I asked one of our colleagues to produce a report for us, so that we could compare the respective benefits of going with either one of these three companies.

'Because the Church … Wells … was keen to fund this, I went to them and said, "We would be delighted to do it with you, but you have to understand that we have other people who would like to do it with us. If you want to do it with us, you will have to make an attractive offer." He asked me what I meant by that and I said, "Well, you'll have to pay a signing-on fee," and he asked me how much that would be and I mentioned a figure, and he responded: "We will pay you a figure of £7m over and above all the development costs as a signing-on fee, which is yours, so that we can have the right to fund that development." They would have earned a big fee for recommending it. They begged us to the tune of £7m to let them fund it for us.'

Hutchings claimed to know nothing of such an agreement negotiated by Wells on behalf of the Commissioners. 'I would certainly have known about it … I don't think we would have swallowed that for a moment. If someone had … said, "Oh, by the way, there is £7m just for the privilege," you just couldn't justify it.' He could offer no explanation of how the payment went through at Millbank, other than it being added to the value of the site 'but I would have thought £7m difference would have been rather noticeable. I can only think that it must have been an initial payment for the land. I can't think how else it would have been done, and … it would have come under a heading something like "costs to date".' Wells admitted that he agreed to a £7m 'signing on' fee, which he said was a 'horrible word, the sort of snappy word which he [Landau] would use'. Rather, the payment was for a 'partnership share' in the development, and was made on condition that any cost over-runs would be met by their partners, Imry and McAlpine. Unfortunately, the Commissioners failed to invoke the clause when substantial additional costs were incurred and ended up paying an additional £60m. Said Wells, 'It beggars belief, but that was the way they were.'[5]

The payment of a 'signing-on' fee was described as 'amazing' by Mr John Parry, a former managing director of Hammerson UK Properties, one of the top five property companies in the country, a past President of the British Property Federation, and member of the Property Advisory Group to the Department of Environment. He added: 'To charge a fee for being allowing into a deal is quite astonishing. It is not something I would have ever agreed to, nor, in my opinion, would any other similar company in that situation. Whatever we paid at Hammerson, we paid for what we deemed to be "value". We didn't mind somebody taking a profit out of us, provided it was costed in to what we regarded as our commercial return. But to be expected to put in a bid for the right to negotiate is beyond belief.'

The accounting system deployed by the Commissioners, as revealed by Hutchings, was naive in the extreme. He explained, 'A certificate used to come in from Chesterton or another agent, saying this or that item of expenditure is approved and then the Commissioners paid the bill. Sometimes the bills were paid direct and sometimes it was done through a partner. Sometimes we would give them a global cheque, because it was much easier, and then let them distribute to all the people.'

Extraordinarily, payments were made without prior reference to Hutchings, who, as commercial property manager, was technically responsible for expenditure and cost control. The general procedure, he explained, was for payment requests to be sent to 'a girl' in the commercial property department. 'So what would normally happen was that Chesterton would write to her and say these payments are now due and she would authorize the cheque requisition, and that would then be counter-signed, probably by Shaun Farrell [Hutchings' deputy], or, if he wasn't there, I'd sign it.'

He admitted that he would not necessarily know what payments were going out or to whom. '[The girl] ran the finance side of the commercial property department, so she was the kingpin.' It was not a practice, he claimed, for any payments to agents to be referred to him. 'Perhaps it was a slack way of doing it ... but what used to happen was that Chesterton were confirming that the expenditure had been properly incurred, and, as the Commissioners' agent, that was considered good enough, because we wouldn't know ... say it was an architect's fee account, whether that was properly incurred or not. We were really relying on [the agents] to tell us what it was.'

The Coopers & Lybrand report heavily criticized the commercial property department's system of record-keeping, which failed 'to ensure that vital documentation was available'. Such items as fee rates and payment arrangements 'were not indexed and easily accessible'. The same criticism was made of the filing of documents recording the Assets Committee's approval of project budgets and major variations. In some cases, key documents, such as final versions of schemes approved, could not be located. Hutchings was disdainfully dismissive of this allegation, claiming: 'Well, they were all there up until my departure.' Besides, as he and his 'golden nose' were away from Millbank much of the time sniffing out high income-generating property deals, he believed that such matters came within the ambit of his deputy, who, he said, was in charge of administration and the day-to-day management of the property portfolio.

The Assets Committee's practice of providing loans to cover their partners' development costs was also criticized in the report for negating the principle of sharing development risk. It was a criticism picked up by the House of Commons' Social Security Committee, which, in its report of March 1995, commented: 'The best interpretation we can put on these activities is that they display unbelievable naivete.' It attracted wide media coverage, but it was unfair comment, if not indeed itself a naive one. It was a long-established practice for investment institutions such as the Commissioners to provide all the development costs while the developer provided the site and the expertise. That was the basis of the joint venture principle.

Nevertheless, the report revealed the shambolic management of the portfolio, with no cost control procedures to prevent major cost over-runs or formal post-development reviews, and there was such variation between the accounting methods of the Commissioners and their joint venture partners that their respective projections of profit levels invariably differed. Responsibility was concentrated in a small number of people so that it was difficult for proposals to be fully assessed against relevant data, 'or for the scale of concurrent developments to be adequately supervised'.

Due to the size of the commercial property department, added the Coopers & Lybrand report, the Commissioners relied heavily on outside advisers; agents were appointed managers of investment properties and were also responsible for carrying out external valuations of those properties. They also relied 'heavily' on agents to co-ordinate projects, monitor costs and submit regular progress reports. Moreover, risk analysis at the appraisal stage of the bigger joint venture projects appeared inadequate, with no consideration given to 'potential exit routes and concentration of risk'.

Hutchings' highly personalized style was well illustrated by his introduction of an 'incentivized' fees system, which blithely ignored the scale of fees recommended by the Royal Institution of Chartered Surveyors. Instead, he would insist on paying half the normal rate until a project was completed. 'It didn't go down too well with the professionals, but, essentially, I said, we can pay their fees if a project was a success. And if the thing was a great success, they got a bonus, which would actually give them more than what they would have got on a statutory basis. If the thing went a bundle, we'd make a lot of money, and it wouldn't actually hurt us to pay bonus fees.'

It was Wells' belief, and a central point behind his letter to Shelley and his subsequent meeting with Locke, that Hutchings was 'out of control'. He was referring chiefly to Hutchings' inclination to authorize major variations to projects, the least of which were what he considered to be last-minute improvements to facilities to enhance rental potential. Indulging his creative style in this way added considerably to cost over-runs, claimed Wells.

He said: 'It was ... embellishments to shopping centres by the dozen. Changing things because it was thought it would look nicer, which [was] the actual bane of our lives. And, of course, when you've got a building contract going, it costs a great deal more money with all the delays.' He claimed there were 'massive rows the whole time' with Hutchings. 'He was very astute, extremely bright, but he wasn't disciplined. He loathed to be disciplined. Nobody would discipline him back at Millbank.'

Wells' complaint of Hutchings' management style was confirmed by Sir Douglas Lovelock, who believed Hutchings 'had a few odd little ways about him'.[6] He said that Hutchings had suffered 'nasty, snide criticisms', which might have 'deeply upset' him, before adding: 'The only criticism I would ever make of Michael Hutchings is that it was very difficult to find out exactly what he was doing.' It was, at the same time, an unconscious criticism of Lovelock's own leadership. As chairman of the Assets Committee ultimately responsible for the Commissioners' property portfolio, he had recourse, through Shelley as well as the authority of his committee, to discover precisely what Hutchings was doing at any particular time. His failure to do so was an indictment of the Assets Committee's competence.

Hutchings agreed he had a tendency to impose cosmetic changes on certain developments, but these, he maintained, were in the interests of making a building more 'tenant-attractive' and thereby increasing rental income. 'It was either the bog-standard finish or something more attractive.' They were variations which Hutchings would authorize without hesitation. He was inclined to make a decision on the spot and expect its implementation five minutes later. Hutchings cited lack of patience as one of his more negative qualities. 'I'm very impatient. If I know I can do something in an hour, I am not going to wait for someone else to do it, and probably do it wrong.'

This unorthodox attitude was at the root of many of Hutchings' problems. Effectively in control of one of the biggest property portfolios in the country, he came to believe that his judgement and authority were virtually unassailable. His style was encouraged by the relaxed informality of the Assets Committee and executive structure within Millbank and enabled Hutchings to take upon himself major cost-increasing decisions without consultative reference to Shelley or the Assets Committee.

'It was terribly informal,' he confessed. 'I always felt that if I could actually show a return on what I was doing, and it was in the remit of the original investment decision, I didn't feel worried at all ... What we used to have is ... a monthly round-up, which was decisions I had taken over the month, which was then reported to the [Assets] committee, and then, if they wanted to discuss any of them, we could talk about it.

'If there was time to take [a decision] in advance [to the committee], fine. But, if there wasn't, then it was reported retrospectively, and if they were unhappy with it, that would cause a real problem. But, nevertheless, we did discuss it and they could have said, "Well, we don't think that's very bright", but that didn't happen.' Even if it had, he agreed, it would have been too late to rescind the decision, 'but, on the other hand, if some committee member had said, "This is outrageous" … you were dealing with partners who knew it would be up to us to unravel it. Ostensibly, it would be too late, but I never think anything is too late. If you've got somebody who's unhappy, it's beholden on you to go back and see if you can sort it out.'

Hutchings claimed that, despite his best efforts, the members of the Assets Committee weren't really interested in project progress, and showed little interest in his monthly financial reports. 'All the information was there, but it was glossed over. I can only comment from the amount of discussions that those reports generated, which was absolutely nil. I sometimes did think, when one had quite significant cost increases on particular projects, it was surprising that nothing was ever said. I used to gear myself up with the answers but there were never any questions.'

Lovelock believed that Hutchings' decisions and the delay in reporting cost increases to the Assets Committee were 'extremely unfortunate'. But he and his colleagues decided to go along with them, 'because we didn't want to lose what we had put in, or threaten our return'. There was also, he admitted, another factor: the Gateshead MetroCentre syndrome. Reports of its trading success encouraged the view that the property executive could do no wrong. It swayed not only their thinking on escalating project costs, but also in the expansion of the property portfolio, especially into shopping centres.

Agreeing with the comment of another member of the Assets Committee, who said they came to believe that Hutchings and his agents could 'walk on water', Lovelock said: 'In the early days, they were highly successful. Later on, they became less so. We were probably lulled into a false sense of security. Probably our thinking went a bit like this: we are not property experts. We have to listen to people who are. These people, our own property experts, our agents, and those on the Assets Committee who are property experts, all think that these things will be successful. We have no particular reason to think otherwise. The other things they have brought us have been very good, therefore we will agree. I think that was our thinking, and it was too complacent. I accept that.'

He said that responsibility for the decisions had to be borne by all members of the Assets Committee. 'Me, certainly, because I was the chairman. I could have found out. I didn't, and if I just say that I was busy on other things, that's a bit cowardly, [although] I was very busy on other things … being Chairman of the Assets Committee was a very small part of my responsibilities. But … there are things that we, and I, could have known if we had ferreted far enough.'

But while Hutchings' unconventional style generated wide criticism, the Assets Committee were no less undisciplined in observing their own property investment guidelines. They were, said the Coopers & Lybrand report, frequently amended to approve development projects 'for which there was great enthusiasm'. They succumbed to pressure to make quick decisions to take advantage of short-term opportunities, but failed take 'full account' of their cumulative effect on the portfolio. There was also criticism of a lack of any feasibility or 'acceptability' criteria at the project evaluation stage, neither were there any guidelines from the committee on the maximum proportion of the portfolio which could be invested in any one project. This led to the Commissioners' vulnerable exposure to major shopping centres not only costly in capital expenditure, but which impacted severely on rental incomes when the property recession severely hit consumer spending.

The pressures on the Assets Committee were caused, recalled David Hopkinson, the committee's Stock Exchange expert, by the property boom. 'There was no doubt that in 1985–6–7, it was quite difficult to find property development. The competition was such that they were difficult to find and I think that led into [the] difficulties.' Everybody had forgotten, he added, 'the hothouse of that world'. 'The thing wasn't run like the board of a company. It was run like a government department with some non executive directors really there for consultancy purposes.'

However, it was in this 'hothouse' world that shrewd agents, able to take ambitious property developments to the Commissioners, flourished. But the confidence that the Assets Committee apparently placed in its external advisers was not shared by all. There was criticism of the 'cosy' relationship between the Assets Committee and its agents. One member was 'worried' by the comments he claimed Lovelock would make to one of the agents about his smart suits and whether he had been to the races. 'These sort of remarks have no place … in hard decisions.'

One of the more outspoken critics was the Bishop of Peterborough, the Rt Revd Bill Westwood, a Church Commissioner for 13 years and a member of the Board of Governors, until his resignation in 1992 after six years on the committee. He quit, he said, because of the 'cosiness' which, he claimed, influenced the Assets Committee's decisions. 'When there was any sort of row [over a property decision] we always used to come down on the side of the agent ... and the only person who gave them a rough time was me.'

One of the Asset Committee's basic problems, he believed, was the infrequency of meetings – totalling about seventeen and a half hours a year – which prevented efficient control of the portfolio. 'We did not actually exercise control over the investments. How could we? We were seen as being in charge of them, but, looking back, that was a great mistake on our part to make that assumption. Stock market investments were pretty good. It was at the level of any other parallel group in the country. Our problem was on the property and there was only a couple of members at any given time who were *au fait* with the property world at that level. You were forced to trust your leadership in such Commissioners and staff.'

By 1990, the Commissioners' shopping centre bubble had burst. Over the next two years, the value of their retail assets dropped by £174m, from £615m to£441m, with retail income for the same period slumping to £30m from £35m. Retail developments werre proving impossibly difficult to lease and the cost of spiralling high interest rates, combined with development costs higher than expected, had a crippling effect on the Commissioners' income.

Burdened with a massive property portfolio of £1.7bn – 57 per cent of their total gross assets of almost £3bn – of which 36 per cent was in the retail sector, the Assets Committee embarked in 1990 on a major sales programme in a bid to ease short-term borrowings which, largely to finance their retail shops sector, had reached a staggering £518m. During the next few years, office property and smaller shopping centres were sold off in a fire sale of the century: in 1991, Trinity Quay, a 75,000 sq ft office development in Bristol, which cost £21m – £8m more than originally approved – was sold to National Westminster soon after completion for £18.5m; The Angel Centre in Islington, North London, went to London Merchant Securities for £24m – the same figure that the Commissioners put up in development costs 10 years earlier; and Birchin Court, undertaken with Landau's City Merchant Developers at a cost of £61m – a mere £7m over budget – was reportedly sold for £47m.

By 1993, the Commissioners raised, through the sale of 18 properties and two small shopping centres in Birkenhead and Sutton Coldfield, a total of £372m, helping to reduce borrowings to £224m. But their commercial property portfolio – at £872m, with £394m in the retail sector – was still grossly overweight with no sign of generating the income necessary to help meet the Commissioners' annual expenditure of £240m.

In 1995, the Commissioners' assets restructuring continued with the sale of two of their less-than-successful major shopping centres – The Marlowes and Beechwood Place – at considerable capital loss. In February, Beechwood Place was bought by a pension fund, Universities Superannuation Scheme, for £15.32m, less than four years after completion at a cost of £47m. A month later, The Marlowes was sold in an investment sale to Bourne End Properties, at even greater loss. With massive cost over-runs of £89m on completion in late 1990, it went for £45m.

In the same year, the Commissioners sold the jewel in their shopping centre crown – the Gateshead MetroCentre, their most ambitious retail venture, and upon which they staked a claim to shrewd and visionary funding. In October it was sold for £324m, with the Commissioners retaining the freehold and a 10 per cent share of income, to Capital Shopping Centres, the fourth largest property company in the UK. The disposal of the three shopping centres totalled more than £400m, which, in October of the following year, would be increased by a further £180m through the sale of their partnership in the St Enoch's Centre in Glasgow.

When news of the Commissioners' mismanagement of their assets first broke, there was justifiable anger within the Church at media claims that their folly had caused a loss as high as £800m. This wasn't so, it was rightly argued. The 'losses' were property valuation write-downs caused by the recession, the sort of misfortune which millions of mortgage-holders experienced. Once the recession ended, it was argued, and the market began to pick up, the Commissioners' properties would soon return to their former values. Losses could only be assessed if the downturn forced properties to be sold, which would then crystallize a loss or profit. Through the sale of their retail sector and about a third of their office sector at below market prices, combined with the considerable loss of expeccted rental income, it has been possible to do that. Actual capital losses to the Commissioners can be unofficially estimated to total more than £400m.

During these stormy years the Assets Committee's investments in America, which began in 1983 through Deansbank Investments Inc, a wholly-owned subsidiary based in New York, were faring no better. Between 1986 and 1989, the value of their property investments in the US increased from £56m to a peak of almost £120m, but hopes of getting a better yield than in the UK failed to materialize. By 1990, the growth in income and capital was proving so disappointing that the US property portfolio began to be scaled down. Office and industrial developments proving hard to lease were the target. By 1995, the portfolio was slimmed down to £59m, with further sales earmarked. Most of the revenue went to pay off US loans, which, as in the UK, the Commissioners had blithely run up.

As in the UK, the investments in America suffered from an imprudent level of borrowings to fund an over-ambitious strategy which, at a time of deep recession, failed to meet expectations. The move into the States was keenly favoured by Jim Shelley, who asked William Wells to prepare a report on the investment potential. It was a favourable report, which gave, said Wells, the pros and cons. 'What we said was, as one would expect, that in order to do it, you had to go there in a big way … but the potential returns were more attractive than they were getting in the UK.'

At Shelley's recommendation, the Assets Committee agreed to invest in US real estate, primarily offices and industrial, and gave their approval to set up Deansbank, of which Shelley was appointed chairman. Wells' company, Chesterton, was given management responsibility of the portfolio, and on the back of the agreement his company set up office in New York. He said: 'They made the decision and asked us if we would implement the decision for them, and therefore it was incumbent upon us to have a presence in the States.' Three years later, Chesterton International, as it had become known, decided to launch an international chain of offices, and, at the same time, considerably expand its operations in the States.

Shelley, with Wells, flew to the States three times a year to attend board meetings of Deansbank. Brian Howard was also an enthusiastic supporter of moving into the US, said Lovelock ('I was neutral'), and on trips to the States on behalf of Marks & Spencer would update himself on the Commissioners' investments. Wells believed the Assets Committee's decision was vindicated 'by doing a darn sight better than anybody else', although by 1987, a sharp fall in the value of the dollar and a worsening property downturn had the Assets Committee treading water and praying forlornly for better times.

Hutchings believed much of the failure of the US investments was due to high operating costs and poor growth. 'The high initial yields were quite exciting but the sheer cost of running that operation was enormous,' he said. 'It was like going back to the old days, when we were buying things at high yield and then there was absolutely no growth.' Hutchings' comments were confirmed by an institutional investor who said: 'Even a superficial examination of US commercial property investments would have revealed that the prospect of any substantial returns was unlikely in the extreme. The US market did not operate in that way.'

Wells' expertise was much respected by the Assets Committee's members. In matters of commercial property he was their principal agent. At one stage, according to Hutchings, Chesterton was handling 80 per cent of the commercial property portfolio. 'I didn't think it was very healthy at all, but, on the other hand, they produced the business. Lovelock used to think he was wonderful.' In 1990, the Commissioners paid Chesterton a total of £7.5m for agent and property management services. Lovelock said that he remembered the fee very well. 'It sounds very large,' he said. 'It *is* very large. But what people don't seem to understand is that, in addition to being involved in these development projects, Chesterton managed an enormous part of our residential estate.' William Wells was, he added, a man of total integrity, 'who thought he was, and sometimes was, bringing to the Church very good opportunities for development, some of which turned out better than others.'

According to the Coopers & Lybrand report, the Assets Committee minuted its concern that the Commissioners were becoming unduly dependent on Chesterton. But, commented Hutchings, it went no further. 'Their attitude was, "Let's hope some other agents come up with some good propositions".' The report recommended that the appointment of agents should be reviewed on a regular basis and subject to competitive tendering. Lovelock said that by then the Commissioners were already scaling down their involvement with Chesterton. 'Too many eggs in one basket,' said Lovelock. It caused 'over-strain of the senior partner [Wells]. He didn't neglect our affairs. We simply thought he was over-taxed.'

Wells disagreed, but two years after the news broke of the Commissioners' property debacle, Chesterton International, he said, continued to manage a significant proportion of the commercial property portfolio and relationships were 'very good'. He added: 'Coopers & Lybrand ... fully exonerated our role in this.

We believe we gave [the Commissioners] an outstanding service, and I think they would agree.' The quality of their commercial property folio was, he said, outstanding. 'They've got some superb office buildings in all the major centres of the UK. They have not made much money out of them because they got the timing wrong.' It was an error of judgement, which he added, he pointed out at the time.

Wells became a reported £1m richer in mid-1995 following the stock market flotation of Chesterton International, which numbered Marks & Spencer, National Westminster and Walt Disney among its clients.[7] The company, with 25 offices in Britain and 19 in Europe, the US, Asia and Australia, was valued at more than £50m. Following the sale of its substantial residential estate agency to the Prudential for 'a very nice price'[8] in 1986, it expanded rapidly with an aggressive acquisition policy driven by Wells. Merchant banker Robert Fleming, which guided the company towards limited company status two years earlier in readiness for going public, acted as adviser in the flotation. The chairman of Robert Fleming was Joel Burnett-Stuart, a member of the Assets Committee. In 1991, the Commissioners had £2.4m-worth of shares in Robert Fleming Holdings, rising to £9.28m in 1995.

In 1997, Wells, chairman of the NHS executive of the South Thames region of the National Health Service and who had been involved in a voluntary capacity with the NHS for many years, received a knighthood in the New Year's Honours List for services to healthcare.

1. Recorded interview with Michael Hutchings, 26 May 1994.
2. A 'turn' meant the interest on the money loaned by the Commissioners.
3. Social Security Committee, Second Report, *The Church Commissioners and Church of England Pensions*, 29 March 1995.
4. Recorded interview, 20 March 1997.
5. Ibid.
6. Social Security Committee, Second Report, *The Church Commissioners and Church of England Pensions*, 29 March 1995, Para. 253.
7. *London Evening Standard*, 3 May 1994.
8. *Financial Times*, 3 May 1994.

CHAPTER SIX

Ashford Great Park

Sir Douglas Lovelock had little understanding of the proposed development projects that came before the Assets Committee. To him, they were simply investments requiring speculative funding and his interest rarely strayed beyond the potential returns. As a traditional Civil Service generalist, with little understanding of the property market, he was perfectly content to be guided by his committee colleagues and the Commissioners' commercial property executive in Millbank. The disastrous exception to the rule – a singularly disastrous exception – was Ashford Great Park, the most ambitious scheme in which the Commissioners became involved, and one which illustrated an extraordinary degree of reckless incompetence among those responsible for taking the key decisions.

The beginnings of its history is found in the entrepreneurial initiative of two Scotsmen, Gerald Harte and Samuel Ellison, co-directors of Ellison and Harte Developments Ltd, a small Edinburgh-based property development company set up in January 1980 which specialized in identifying major development opportunities to sell on at a fat profit to bigger operators.

In the mid-eighties, Harte, formerly development manager and director of Ladbrokes for 14 years, and Ellison, an estate agent and surveyor of many years' experience, recognized the enormous property speculation potential of one of the boldest engineering proposals of the century – the Channel Tunnel. Their instincts suggested it could lead to the biggest deal of their professional careers.

Plans for a Channel Tunnel between Folkestone and Calais had been on the drawing board for some years, but had foundered for a variety of financial and political reasons. Now, in the booming eighties, the tunnel was considered for the first time as a serious co-venture. Talks finally led, on 12 February 1986, to a meeting between Prime Minister Margaret Thatcher and President Mitterrand in the Chapter House of Canterbury Cathedral where the two heads of state signed a partnership treaty between Britain and France agreeing their roles and responsibilities in the construction of the 32-mile tunnel. Work began on 1 December 1987 and was completed six years and nine days later, on 10 December 1993, at a cost of £10.75bn. A central part of the project was an international passenger rail terminal based in Ashford, a town about 13 miles from Folkestone. The terminal, a British Rail project, would also include a domestic rail station for Network South East, at a total of £80m and scheduled for completion by January 1996.

It was this particular development which caught the interest of Ellison and Harte. They had recognized the strategic importance of Ashford as an international terminal – and the enormous potential it created for large-scale commercial, industrial and residential development. The two men decided to follow their professional instincts and, as Harte put it, 'take a flyer'.[1]

In early 1986, their company moved to buy the options on key areas of land within a triangular sector of 2,000 acres between the villages of Mersham and Sevington, about four miles south-east of Ashford, a rural part of the town which since the late 1940s had been identified as a growth area. Ellison and Harte agreed an aggregate price of about £7,000 per acre, a premium price for largely agricultural land, and which, even though prices were heating up as the property boom continued, reflected a very high expectation of development value.

Ellison and Harte were convinced they were on to the biggest deal of their lives. They saw it as a golden opportunity for either a straight trading situation or a small equity stake in what might prove the biggest development of its kind in Europe. The next stage was to find an entrepreneur with the financial clout to exercise a land options bill of £14m. The man they went to see was a Yorkshire-based property developer called Jim Cookson, who at one time had been on the board of directors of the controversial

Centre Point, and with whom Ellison had done business some years earlier in connection with that project.

Cookson, a gregarious, sharp-suited operator, was managing director of Northern England Development Associates Ltd, a building and constructional engineering company, which he had set up in 1975 and was formerly known as Cosocon Construction Enterprises (UK and Middle East) Ltd. Its impressive address was Boroughbridge Hall, Boroughbridge, near Ripon, Yorks. At the meetings that followed between the three men, a deal was structured whereby Ellison and Harte agreed to sell their interests in the land options to Cookson for an initial payment of £655,000, followed by a further payment of up to £3.5m after deduction of expenses in the event of disposal of the land or shares to a non-connected party, or, alternatively, within six months of planning permission being granted which resulted in a land value of £44m or more.

However, once the deal was struck, Cookson was unable to find the money to pay the balance of the land options, but, he reassured Ellison and Harte, he knew some men who did. Said Harte: 'We had no idea of Cookson's financial standing, but he had sufficient to see through his obligation to us, and that was our immediate concern.' Even if Cookson had been in a position to put up the money, he wouldn't have risked his own. He raised the first tranche to pay Ellison and Harte their £655,000 through an investments company called Claret Developments Ltd based in Nun Monkton, near York, in return for an equity partnership. Its principal, David Aykroyd, first met Cookson some 12 months before Nedaclaret was formed. They became neighbours when the Cooksons moved into Bilton Hall in the village of Bilton-in-Ainsty, near York. Their business relationship was first established through another deal in which Aykroyd agreed to invest a substantial sum of money, and which made Aykroyd a nice profit. The two set up Nedaclaret on 28 April 1988, a holding company created solely for investing in Ashford Great Park.

Cookson's first call in his efforts to find a super-league investor was British Land, one of the biggest property development companies in Europe. But negotiations with chief executive John Ritblat began to concern property consultants Eric Atkinson and Colin Peacock, whose company Nimbus International Properties had been engaged, along with investment bankers Goldman

Sachs, by Cookson to help bring together the best deal. Cookson was under some pressure, because he was running out of time on the land options. If he failed to come up with several million pounds to exercise the options by certain dates, he would lose the land, plus the £655,000 paid to Ellison and Harte. According to Atkinson and confirmed by Harte, British Land repeatedly exploited the pressure by insisting on altering the terms of the agreement at the last minute.

Said Atkinson: 'There was a certain amount of stringing along [by British Land] in negotiations, knowing that there was a cut-off date. As the date grew nearer, the negotiating strength of British Land grew all the time. We advised Jim that he was being squeezed out.' Goldman Sachs, brought in to check out the financial calibre of possible investors, had others standing in the wings. But, according to Atkinson, he had a conversation 'out of the blue' with Kean Hird, an investments specialist and a director of Imry Merchant Developers.

Atkinson also claimed to know Imry's 47-year-old chief executive and managing director, Martin Myers, when they worked together some years earlier in the New York office of chartered surveyors Jones Lang Wootton. Myers was delighted by the approach from the Cookson camp, made all the sweeter by the opportunity to put one over British Land.

Said Atkinson: 'Imry were saying that they would do the same sort of deal. We tootled round that very night to see Imry and worked night and day to put the deal together.' Myers clinched the deal with Cookson and provided the money – at that stage about £5m – to meet the necessary option deadlines. Ritblat, in the words of Gerald Harte, 'was distressed' to learn that their deal was dead and that Myers had snatched it from under his nose.

One of Myers' first moves, to give him hands-on control, was to join the board of a company called Bigscan Ltd which, with a nominal share capital of £1,000, had been set up by Cookson on 30 March 1987 'to purchase and sell land', and whose registered office was subsequently given as Imry's. Manish Jayantilal Chande, Imry's financial director, was also appointed company secretary. With Myers on the scene, matters began to move apace.

A few months later, Bigscan Ltd was proposing a most ambitious two-phase development which would in effect create a mini-town at an estimated cost of £400m and with an estimated development potential of £1bn. On 25 November 1987 the company submitted a planning application to Ashford Borough Council for the first phase covering an area of about 600 acres, which in a subsequent planning application would be increased to 760 acres to include a 150-acre residential development for 1500 houses, a 124-acre business park of warehouse, distribution and business offices, a 105-acre leisure area, a 137-acre shopping and community centre, a 64-acre complex of five hotels and conference centres, 52 acres of highways, and 67 acres of lakes. Plans for a second development phase of 1400 acres included a light railway system linking the area to Ashford town centre and to a Customs haulage clearance depot for the Channel Tunnel.

The council requested further information, which Bigscan declined to give. Two months later, the application was refused by the council on the grounds of 'non-determination'. The council's planning chiefs feared the scheme was not only too ambitious but also failed to satisfy their concerns of how the company would deal with the amount of traffic and sewage the scheme would generate. Bigscan Ltd lodged an appeal and a public inquiry was set for 10 January 1989.

Weeks earlier, the news of the proposed development had broken in the local press. As a public relations exercise, Cookson held a public meeting in a local hotel in an attempt to pacify an army of hostile locals. His smooth-talking efforts to convince them that the proposed development would be very much for the benefit of the local community left his audience unmoved.

Local borough councillor Joseph Dean, a retired circuit judge, who chaired the East Ashford Rural Trust, a lobby group set up to oppose the development of the area, said, 'We knew land had been bought up all over the place, but we had no idea what was really going on ... Cookson's plans seemed to have a protean quality ... The way he put it over to us was that he could afford to give us all sorts of facilities and produce a marvellous development because he had bought a lot of land very cheaply. He was a pleasant, extrovert character; an amiable rogue.'

From the start of his company's involvement, Myers had been looking for a major investment institution able to provide huge development capital, and with the stomach to stand the risk. It was a project that required a super heavyweight. Enter the Church Commissioners, with their recently gained reputation for being willing to take on highly speculative property investments.

Taking a lead role was Imry's deputy chairman, Martin Landau, who knew the Commissioners and their property executive better than Myers. To him, the Commissioners were the obvious choice as funders, although he claimed there had been two or three 'national contractors' willing to put up the required development money. Imry could have even funded the project itself, claimed Myers. 'We had a £175 million facility, of which we had drawn about £80 million. We had ample funds to close the [land option] deals, so when we brought in the Church, we invited them in, not from weakness, but from strength. If they had passed it by, we would have taken it on board ourselves or we'd have found another partner.'

According to Hutchings, he played no part in the early discussions that followed between Landau, William Wells, with whom he initially discussed the project, and the Commissioners, although, he claimed, he made it known that he wasn't keen on the proposed project, telling Landau that, in his opinion, the project wasn't quiet 'Church-type stuff,' particularly as the question of planning permission appeared to be in so much doubt. 'I told him that I thought he was really going to have to work to push it through,' he said. Hutchings then set off for an extended holiday in France.

However, on his return to No. 1 Millbank seven weeks later, he found that the proposed deal had gone before the Assets Committee, which had given approval to funding the initial development costs, despite the council's refusal to grant planning permission. Hutchings claims he was astonished by the committee's decision. It was the first time, he said, that the Commissioners had run such a risk.

But a key factor in persuading the Assets Committee that Ashford Great Park was a project of immense potential was the enthusiasm of Sir Douglas Lovelock himself. As former chairman of Customs & Excise, he insisted he understood the potential of such business, and that the Channel Tunnel, with its inland customs clearance hall and international rail station, would attract a tremendous amount of commercial business and yield a most profitable income.

He said: 'I was always enthusiastic ... knowing what I did about the way in which customs and related matters would be handled in future, that is, not at the port of entry but inland. I always believed that once the tunnel was up and running, great prosperity would come to Ashford, partly because that is where a good deal of the customs clearance would be done, but also because of the fact that there was to be a great international station there, and, just as it has happened at Gatwick and Heathrow ... business would be drawn to it, and that the land that we owned would become very valuable.'

Such optimism, reinforced by the positive recommendations of the Commissioners' commercial property advisers, including Jim Shelley, won the day, although not the unqualified support and confidence of all the Assets Committee members. One, who declined to be named, claims he expressed disquiet over entering into a funding partnership with Imry and the totally unknown Cookson '[but] I was reassured by the property people that they knew what they were doing'.

Hutchings, who claims he was pressed on all sides to back the scheme, began to reconsider the chances of its success. Gradually he was able to overcome his early misgivings. He came to believe that perhaps it could work after all. 'At first, I thought, "I don't know what the answer to this is." I felt as if I was fire-fighting backwards. There were all these people saying, "It's only round the corner. You can get it [planning permission]".

'Then I took the view that it was shit or bust, and we actually had to make this thing work. I believed if we really worked at it, we'd probably do something. I had been over to Calais and I'd seen what they were doing [on the Channel Tunnel development], and I thought, "Crikey, if we can get this going, it will work." '

By 'working at it', Hutchings meant launching a powerful selling campaign to win over Ashford Borough Council. 'Really hard marketing, hard grafting. Kent County Council were totally in favour, but Ashford Council ... didn't want to know. Whether it was because they didn't like Cookson, who they thought was a wide boy, or whether they didn't like Imry, I don't know. But I thought if we sold ourselves as the Church, respectable developers, we might get somewhere.'

News of the Commissioners' involvement in the £400m first stage of the proposed Ashford Great Park development was made public in a news release issued on 2 December 1988. They declined to reveal the size of their investment, although it was estimated to be at least £30m.[2] The money was intended to finance the planning stages through to basic infrastructure, including roads and sewers.

However, in their annual report for that year, prepared, as usual, by Jim Shelley, their investment in Ashford Great Park was vastly underplayed at 'between £1 million and £3 million'. The Commissioners also played down the significance of the project itself, referring in only 38 words in the annual report to 'a long term development of a substantial site near Ashford in Kent. This is strategically situated close to the major routes to the Channel Tunnel and should prove an excellent investment.' The cost was underplayed as a calculated ploy to prevent any awkward questions on the wisdom of so much money being invested in such a highly speculative project.

The partnership agreement gave the Commissioners a 10 per cent shareholding for their estimated £30m investment, which, according to Hutchings, included loans to Imry and Nedaclaret to cover their share of the costs. The agreement was signed on 5 January 1989 between Imry, Nedaclaret and Paysystem Ltd – which became Cedarvale Ltd four months later – a subsidiary company wholly owned by the Church Commissioners and through which their money would be channelled. On its board as sole directors sat Secretary Shelley, Hutchings, and John Shirley, a Millbank employee. Cedarvale's company secretary was Paul Bussy, a senior member of the omnipresent Coopers & Lybrand.

On the same day, the Church Commissioners made a loan of £26m – most of which was borrowed from the Japanese bank, Sumitomo – to Ashford Great Park (Phase 1) Ltd, a company which had been set up by its chairman, Jim Cookson, on 25 April 1988 following its acquisition of Bigscan Ltd for £100, with Imry, Nedaclaret and Cedarvale as the shareholders. The £26m went to reimburse Imry Property Holdings for a similar sum loaned to Ashford Great Park (Phase 1) Ltd on 22 July 1988 to finance 'existing property commitments'.

In the light of the local council's refusal of planning permission, a serious obstacle that threatened to drag on for many months, it represented an extremely high risk for the Commissioners. Commented Gerald Harte: 'As there was no planning permission, it just didn't make any sense.' It was all the more senseless in that, once again, the Commissioners were taking on the funding of what was supposed to be a joint venture in which each partner would bear their share of costs.

On 22 July 1988, Imry Property Holdings plc also acquired 50 per cent of the share capital of Ashford Great Park (Phase 1) Ltd from Nedaclaret to give Cookson a handsome profit for his initiative. And on that day, Myers, along with Kean Hird, of Imry Merchant Developers, joined the board of Ashford Great Park (Phase 1) Ltd, along with property consultants Colin Peacock and Eric Parkinson, of Nimbus International Properties. Parkinson, who had brought Cookson and Imry together, later joined the board of European Land, Cookson's parent company. But shortly after the Commissioners joined the club of Ashford Great Park (Phase 1) Ltd, and once William Wells had advised the Assets Committee on the project's viability and potential returns,[3] a radical restructuring took place. According to Hutchings, the Commissioners insisted on the setting up of an unincorporated partnership, a special purpose vehicle which is not legally obliged to publish its accounts, but which was, claims Hutchings, the most tax-efficient structure for the Commissioners in the light of their charity status. It became known as The Ashford Great Park Partnership and appointed to chair its meetings was Peter Sutcliffe, a partner in Wells' company Chesterton International. Into its coffers went all the assets of Ashford Great Park (Phase 1) Ltd, which, in effect, became a shell company.

For his part, Myers claimed he was 'totally fuddled' by it all. He said: 'We were a public company, the Church is a charity, so there are different tax regimes, which have to be moulded. Then there were often third partners. There were often builders, or individuals … and what typically we used to do … was once we'd done the structure of the deal, the accountants and the lawyers all burned the midnight oil for extortionate fees to work out the structure that suited all parties. I think they had certain constraints [but] so long as their method of structuring didn't impinge our shareholders' rights, we were supportive of how they wanted to do it.'

Landau believed the setting up of the Ashford Great Park Partnership was, as Hutchings maintains, a device to protect the Commissioners' tax-free charity status, which prohibits taking part in property trading activities. Peter Sutcliffe declined to comment on the affairs of the Commissioners. He said: 'Before we go any further, I need to have clearance from the Church Commissioners that they are willing to participate in this venture, and I am not at all clear that is so. I would not wish to make any comment about someone else's business without their approval.'

On 10 January 1989, a public inquiry to hear the appeal lodged by what had been Bigscan Ltd, but now Ashford Great Park (Phase 1) Ltd, was opened. Local opposition was strenuously expressed through the East Ashford Rural Trust, representing residents, parish councils and 'other organizations concerned with the 21 parishes of the East Ashford rural area'.

Its representatives argued that the two-phase development would ultimately cover four square miles and would cause 'loss of important countryside, absorption of rural settlements and excessive and inordinate growth'. For Ashford Great Park (Phase 1) Ltd, it was claimed that the area would remain an undamaged or even improved rural area: 'the development concept envisages that only 25 to 30 per cent of the site areas would be developed with buildings, leaving 70 to 75 per cent of the land as landscape or waters'.

Local churchgoers were particularly angered by what was seen as the Church Commissioners' pursuit of profit at the expense of historic rural countryside and the undermining of local quality of life. Major John Varrier, a churchwarden of St Mary's, a Norman church in the village of East Brabourne, near the proposed site, said: 'We felt that our own church was almost stabbing us in the back and that the Church Commissioners were prepared to ride roughshod over our environment and people's local interests in order to make a lot of money.' Ecologist Dr Hilary Moorby also claimed that a survey carried out on behalf of Ashford Great Park (Phase 1) Ltd had 'vastly underestimated' the amount of flora and fauna of ecological interest that would be either destroyed or seriously degraded.

The protesters appealed to the Archbishop of Canterbury, Dr Robert Runcie, urging him to persuade the Commissioners to withdraw from the project. It was a forlorn hope. Although the Archbishop of Canterbury is chairman of the Church Commissioners, it is a titular title, with little executive power. Runcie would not have dared to have gone into battle on behalf of the protesters over such an issue, even if he had had the inclination.

In fact, a month after the public inquiry, Runcie, in response to the local residents' appeal for help, announced in a press statement that the project was the price society had to pay for economic growth. 'As a lover of Kent,' added the statement, 'I share the anxiety about the impact of the Channel Tunnel and can well understand fears about development in a hitherto unspoilt area. However, we have to face the fact that, in many parts of the country, that is the price we have to pay for economic expansion.'

By now, Hutchings' enthusiasm for Ashford Great Park had become so keen – or myopic – that on 6 October 1989, 10 months after entering the partnership, he decided to increase the Commissioners' shareholding through Cedarvale from 10 per cent to one third – with both Imry and Nedaclaret diluting their shares to their handsome profit. The cost of that third share, authorized exclusively by Hutchings, with Shelley's backing, increased Cedarvale's interest to £21.4m. This transaction was subject to a prior charge of £38.6m by Ashford Great Park (Phase 1) Ltd, which meant that Cedarvale would pick up the bill if Ashford Great Park (Phase 1) Ltd failed to meet its obligations. A further commitment was that Cedarvale was liable to contribute 45 per cent of the post-formation capital.

Because of the prior charge in favour of Ashford Great Park (Phase 1) Ltd, and the basis of distributing partnership profits and capital, the amount that could be distributed to Cedarvale was restricted to £8.57m. Their investment was accordingly written down to this value. This was the only provision made by Cedarvale. Extraordinarily, Cookson was writing down his investment while the Church Commissioners were writing theirs up.

But Hutchings' decision was all the more astonishing for its lack of forethought. No matter what confident reassurances he might have received from those around him, he could have no reason to be certain that the council's refusal would be overturned by the appeal to the Environment Secretary, Chris Patten. With little effort, given the Church Commissioners' network of well-placed contacts, Hutchings could have discovered that Patten's decision was imminent. If he had waited just six weeks, until 22 November, he would have learnt that the appeal would be turned down.

Hutchings at first denied that he had been responsible for increasing the Commissioners' shareholding. He put the blame squarely at the door of Sir Douglas Lovelock. Said Hutchings: 'He did it off his own bat ... and he reported to the Assets Committee after he had done it. There was nothing they could do about it ... I felt like a man with my hands tied behind my back ... It was a case of get what you can for a third.'

But when questioned again about the decision to increase the Commissioners' shareholding, he did a remarkable U-turn. 'That [decision] was mine,' he admitted. 'I did do that, because ... I felt I was on an unstoppable train, and if I was going to influence ... I think I felt from memory that if I was going to be a ten-percenter, I could get ten per cent with no control, with no chance of getting my money back, or I could be a third-percenter and actually lead the show. That might have been a mistake. I took the view that we were going to lose everything if we didn't get to grips with it.'[4] It was a decision typical of Hutchings' maverick style, and its logic, from any business perspective, was quite irrational.

Increasing the Commissioners' interests to an equal third substantially increased Cedarvale's risk exposure without any increase in control or influence. Myers and Cookson, with their joint shareholding, still remained in the driving seat. But Hutchings' comments also give a telling insight into the decision-making autonomy that Hutchings took upon himself, without immediate reference to his boss, Jim Shelley, or the Assets Committee.

Patten refused the appeal on the grounds of 'prematurity ... given that the proper vehicle for deciding the location is primarily a matter for the development plan process and given also that a review of the Ashford Local Plan is already in train'. Essentially, Patten believed that the proposed development was too big to be decided by the planning appeal process and justified its consideration as part of a local development plan under review at that time by Ashford Borough Council.

Now the Commissioners were exposed to a much higher risk, thanks to Hutchings' private enterprise, subsequently endorsed by Shelley. The two men were at a board meeting at the St Enoch's shopping centre in Glasgow when the news came through.

Hutchings' recollection of the casual dialogue between him and Shelley verges on the comical. Said Hutchings: 'The phone rings. It was some guy from Chesterton and he said: "I thought I'd let you know. He [Patten] has just turned it down." So Jim said, "Oh, what do you think we ought to do about that, Michael?" So I said, "Well, that's modestly serious, isn't it?" '

Attempting to explain the rationale of his decisions, Hutchings emphasized that they had the confidence of certain colleagues.

I had been told that [planning permission] was an absolute certainty. Besides, do you want to write your 10 per cent share off and sell to your partners, or do you believe that you can actually bring this one through? It was a hell of a risk, but what do you do? Do you write it off in one fell swoop?

The whole scene was set, and I think it would have been terribly difficult not to have the third, because I felt that we would actually be in some sort of control of what was going on. I felt there was a certain inevitability to it all. Although I hadn't been party to the first decision, I felt, well, this is right.[5]

Neither Sir Douglas nor Shelley were much troubled over the Commissioners' financial predicament caused by Patten's refusal, he claimed. Sir Douglas was 'not unduly concerned' and Shelley, who saw it as 'just a minor hiccup', was 'quite relaxed'.

Patten's decision led to Ashford Great Park (Phase 1) Ltd submitting two further planning applications in 1990 – they submitted five planning applications altogether – which were later withdrawn. It symbolized a year of zero activity, despite a misleading claim by Cookson in European Land's annual report and accounts for 1990, that the 'project will fund a large section of Ashford's southern by-pass' to link into the M20 motorway for access to the proposed development. Such funding had not been agreed, nor did it take place.

With equal audacity, he claimed in his 1991 annual report that European Land, as a partner in the Ashford Great Park Partnership, had entered into an agreement with Eurotunnel Development Ltd, owners of land which gave motorway access to the development, that 'enables the construction of major infrastructure work, opening up not only the first phase development but also access to the remaining 1,400 acres [of the proposed second phase development]'. Although Mr Nigel Ladkin, the company's commercial manager, refused to comment, no such agreement had been reached. It was merely Cookson hyping up the market.

But whatever was happening behind the scenes – and both Myers and Landau maintain it was 'a hotbed of activity' – there was certainly little happening on the ground due to Ashford Borough Council's opposition. Nevertheless, the Church Commissioners were continuing to pump in millions of pounds into the project, much of which went on generous consultancy fees.

Business, at least for Jim Cookson and David Aykroyd, his fellow director of Nedaclaret, was good. In 1988, shortly before the Church Commissioners became involved, they manipulated a highly lucrative shares-swap by issuing 49,999 £1 ordinary shares to Cookson's company, Northern England Development Associates Ltd, and the same number to Aykroyd's company, Claret Developments Ltd, in return for their companies' shares in Ashford Great Park (Phase 1) Ltd. They further issued respectively to the two companies 81,000 £1 ordinary shares and 19,000 £1 ordinary shares in return for their shares in Ashford Great Park (Phase 2) Ltd, the company formed by Cookson to develop the second stage of the proposed development.

But once, in effect, having sold their own shares to themselves, which they had valued at £200,000, Cookson and Aykroyd then put on their Nedaclaret hats to revalue those shares at a staggering £7.26m. The result of this shares-swap meant that Nedaclaret was able to pay handsome dividends to its ultimate holding company, European Land (previously known as Northern England Development Associates Ltd and then NEDA Ltd) which came into existence on 4 June 1990. European Land owned 65.5 per cent of Nedaclaret, and once fellow director Aykroyd received his 34.5 per cent payout, an interim dividend of £3.68m was paid to European Land, whose sole shareholders were none other than Jim Cookson and his wife, Susan True Cookson.

The extraordinary increase in the value of their shares was due to a dramatic revaluation of the land owned by Ashford Great Park (Phase 1) Ltd, which was enhanced from £7.61m in 1988 to appear in the books of the partnership at £21.56m in 1989. The revaluation was probably implemented shortly before the Church Commissioners became involved, and was a remarkably optimistic increase, given the council's refusal to grant planning permission. But it no doubt helped to convince the Church Commissioners that they were onto a very lucrative investment. After all, outstanding against that evaluation was the loan from the Commissioners of £19m, which, as with all other assets and monies, disappeared into the all-concealing Ashford Great Park Partnership account.

The Cooksons also paid themselves a dividend of £1.71m through European Land, whose profits increased from a mere £3,855 in 1989 to £6.15m in 1990 through its share of profits in the companies, Ashford Great Park (Phase 1) Ltd and Ashford Great Park (Phase 2) Ltd, in which European Land had a 32.75 per cent shareholding. The value of its shares in Nedaclaret were increased from £50,283 in 1989 to £5.15m in 1990, a figure based on Cookson's assessment.

But there were even more lucrative pay-offs to come for Cookson. As chairman of European Land, he doubled his salary – from £283,574 to £552,964, spent £147,807 on 'motor cars', believed to be his chauffeur-driven Turbo Bentley, and paid fees totalling £436,902 to J. Cookson & Partners, his project management practice. With a touch of irony, perhaps, Cookson, in his directors' report to 31 March 1990, attributed a substantial increase in pre-tax operational profits of £5.8m to European Land's 'experienced management and successful funding'.

1990 continued to prove a bonanza year for Cookson when, in January, Nedaclaret received a dividend after tax of £3.68m following the sale of the 1400 acres earmarked for the second phase of the Ashford Great Park development. It earned the Cooksons, as the sole shareholders in European Land, which owned 65.5 per cent of Nedaclaret, their share of a dividend that was possibly the only realizable profit in the land which he received, with, presumably, Imry receiving a similar pay-out.

European Land's accounts to March 1991 reveal that the Cooksons paid themselves a relatively modest dividend of £131,000, but Cookson increased his chairman's salary to £631,233, and paid himself a further £441,483 for services rendered by J. Cookson & Partners, his project management practice. He also paid consultancy fees of £190,636 to Nimbus International Properties, whose directors, Colin Peacock and Eric Parkinson, were also directors of Ashford Great Park (Phase 1) Ltd. According to Parkinson, the payment was principally to cover their consultancy work in bringing Cookson and Martin Myers together some two years earlier – and was finally met from profits made by Cookson out of the Commissioners.

But the most questionable payments received by Cookson took place during a 15-month period between July 1988 and December 1989 when he received a total of £1.35m for services described as 'marketing' and 'setting up'. The payments were made by Ashford Great Park (Phase 1) to European Land and began on 1 July, followed by regular payments of £75,822 thereafter on the first of each month through to December 1989.[6] Martin Landau confirmed the payments were made to Cookson.

'It was all agreed between us and the partners. It sounds a lot of money, but you've got to remember that it was agreed, and you've got to remember the size of the scheme.' Michael Hutchings also recalls the fees. He said: '[Cookson] was supposed to be project-managing the thing. I can't remember the fee, but I was pretty staggered when I saw it, and he wasn't actually providing the service.'

But the fees, revealed in a confidential summary of expenditure produced by Coopers & Lybrand in 1994, cannot be traced in the accounts of Ashford Great Park (Phase 1) Ltd because they were capitalized into the value of the land. The company secretary of Nedaclaret and European Land at that time was Mrs Jennifer Rennison, an experienced businesswoman and an associate of Cookson's for several years, who later became a partner in a property development company in York. When asked about the payments, she replied, 'I am going to have to refer back and talk to somebody regarding these issues, because we are starting to get into areas which aren't available to public record. I don't feel I am in a position to be able to make a statement on that.'

Later, though, she confirmed the money was paid to European Land. 'There was a payment of about £75,000 per month made to European Land (for project management) during this time.' These payments, however, could not be traced in European Land's accounts. But while Cookson was receiving £75,000 a month for his 'project management' services, a payment of £20,000 per month for the same services was also being made to Imry – and during the same period.

As with the payments to European Land, the payments to Imry were for 'setting up' and 'marketing', except for one payment of £125,000 under a heading of 'raising finance'. The payments began on 27 July 1988 and continued on an irregular monthly basis through to 30 December 1989. Including the £125,000, the total paid to Imry Merchant Developers was £408,600. According to Mrs Rennison, the dual payments were made during 'a period of transition, until Imry took over the project management'. As with the payments to Cookson through European Land, there is no trace of these payments in the accounts of Ashford Great Park (Phase 1) Ltd, again assuming they were rolled up into the land valuation.

In the board room of Imry in Grafton Street, in the West End of London, Martin Myers, with Landau by his side, said: 'There is no secret about the fact that Imry took fees, that Nedaclaret, as far as I can remember, took fees. We got substantial fees over a considerable period of time, so did Chestertons, and so did others ... we had the architect who took enormous fees ... there was the traffic engineer ... there were numerous consultants. There were many other concerns who were earning very much more than £75,000 a month ... I actually volunteered that the whole fee regime should be severely slashed because the fee structure was set up when we were quite optimistic about the scheme in the early days. Then the recession came and ... we had considerable discussions about everyone reducing their fees.'

That reduction, however, did not take place. He was unable to reveal details of fees paid because 'it would be inappropriate for me to give you the amounts paid. I would be divulging something which is none of my business.' They were payments, in any event, that the Commissioners, through Cedarvale, were ready to meet. As Martin Landau was quick to point out: 'The Church would have been the one who would have signed the cheques.' Considering the Church Commissioners' investment, those fees were averaging about £4m per year for three years.

By mid-1991, almost four years after the first planning application was submitted to Ashford Borough Council, the £1bn Ashford Great Park was no nearer to getting off the ground. A further two planning applications, which were slightly modified in response to the council's opposition to the size of the proposed development, were submitted by Ashford Great Park (Phase 1) Ltd, and refused. Despite the modifications, the council claimed that 'the scale of housing and economic development identified by Ashford Great Park (Phase 1) Ltd were too great'. They were turned down along with proposals submitted by other companies for various large scale developments around the town, said a senior planning officer.

The development the council preferred, which was considerably less ambitious and virtually adjoined the proposed Ashford Great Park site, was one being proposed by the council itself. Said the senior planning officer: 'What we were proposing was about 1,000 houses on 100 acres of housing land and 40 acres of employment land – land available for offices and factories – and what Ashford Great Park was proposing was approximately 150 acres of housing and about 140 acres of employment land.'

On 3 December 1991, a public inquiry was held into Ashford Borough Council's Local Plan. It was an opportunity that the Commissioners and their partners eagerly seized to lodge an objection against the council's development proposals, arguing that theirs were superior. The issue dominated the inquiry, which continued through to February 1992. Hedging their bets, the following month, Ashford Great Park (Phase 1) Ltd appealed against the council's refusal of an earlier planning application, an appeal subsequently upheld on the grounds that a decision would be 'premature' pending the outcome of the Local Plan inquiry.

It was eight months before the inquiry inspector's report was issued. But even then, as the public inquiry was being held, the Ashford Great Park project was fast heading into trouble. The Church Commissioners, who had guaranteed to fund Cedarvale, were now facing intense recessionary pressures caused by their massive property borrowings. They were rapidly running out of time, money and credibility.

According to newspaper reports and city speculation, Imry Merchant Developers, now part of the Imry Group, had its own financial worries. The property market was going into a tailspin. The Imry Group had been suffering for some months, and by September 1989 was taken over for £314m by an unquoted investment consortium called Marketchief led by Canadian businessman Stefan Wingate. Supported by a £200m loan from Barclays Bank, the consortium comprised Eagle Star, Prudential Bache and Development & Realization.

A few months later, in early 1990, Landau sold his shares and quit the company. It was precipitated, said some observers, by the arrival of Wingate, and an anticipated clash of strong-willed personalities. Others put it down to shrewdly getting out before the property downturn began to bite. He moved to Monaco as a tax exile from where he went on scouting expeditions in eastern Europe looking for development opportunities in partnership with pension fund Postel. Landau's departure left Michael Hutchings' portly frame quivering with anger.

Said Hutchings: 'I did actually have a good go at him, because we had no inclination at all that he was leaving Imry. As far as the Church was concerned, he was a key player. I said to him that it was outrageous. The first thing we read about it was in the press. He said he regretted it. He gave me all the background. Essentially, his father had just died and he had to become a tax exile, and all the rest of it. I said that we were partners, that he really owed us something.' In apparently settling the score, Hutchings was remarkably generous – in return for a very handsome fee, Landau was persuaded to act as a property consultant in other co-venture projects.

This arrangement drew criticism from Coopers & Lybrand in their inquiry. In referring to the commercial property department's reliance on outside agents and consultants, it said 'one project manager' was retained to oversee completion of certain developments in the UK 'despite being permanently resident abroad'. Landau, acknowledging that he was that project manager, was contemptuously dismissive of Coopers' comments: 'Shall I tell you something? There is such a thing called a telephone. Yes, for purely personal reasons, I went to live abroad, but that didn't stop me from thinking, advising, helping.' Perhaps not, but it did, all the same, prevent him from cost-effectively monitoring the Commissioners' developments in the UK, for which he was paid handsome fees.

The restraints of his tax status led to a series of business meetings in the south of France between Landau, Hutchings and Wells, which newspaper reports said went on for as long as a week. But Landau branded the reports as 'pure mischief', as were claims by Millbank insiders that the three men were 'far too cosy for far too long'. He said: 'They were brief meetings held for the purpose of discussing certain projects. There was no more to it than that.'

Wells complained that four or five times a year, 'I used to have to ruin my weekends by flying down for a day in order to make sure they conducted business in some sort of orderly fashion. How long they had been there, I wouldn't know … this was very much the Hutchings style and it was very much played to by Landau.'

The meetings, he confirmed, were to discuss a number of projects, 'and one or two other things. It was incumbent on me to ensure that stupid decisions weren't reached.' He had to pay his own expenses. 'They wouldn't pay mine; it was all part of the normal course of duty – but they, of course, paid Hutchings.'

Hutchings maintained that it was the most efficient way of deploying Landau's expertise. 'If I was in France, or Italy, if I was coming to and fro, we'd try and find a day when I would bowl up and we'd have a day and we'd do our business and then I'd go. William would fly in and that was that, although I wouldn't say he did it unhappily. But there was certainly no week-long jolly. The media reports of week-long junkets created totally the wrong impression.'

It was, nevertheless, an extravagant style of business meeting which caused critical comment. Lovelock claimed to be unaware of the meetings, adding later that they were 'not wise. But I don't interpret it in any sinister way. I continue to believe that all those concerned were people of integrity. It is not the way I would conduct business ... but the world of property is conducted in a rather different way, and Hutchings, although a loyal servant of the Commissioners, and an honourable one, was very drawn to the world of property.'

Shelley, who worked closely with Hutchings on the Ashford Great Park project, was unable to remember whether his colleague's trips were with the approval and knowledge of the Assets Committee. 'I believe they did go to the south of France on several occasions,' he said. But he had 'no idea' if they were for business meetings.

Back in the less hospitable economic climate of the UK, the Imry Group's fortunes were not improving. In June 1991 German investment banker Wolfgang Stolzenberg 'with international business interests' acquired control of the consortium to become chairman of the Imry Group. Barclays Bank, keen to see its money returned, agreed to refinanced Imry's borrowings with a £196m medium-term loan and guarantee. At the same time, a new company called Commercial Property Corporation – 'a vehicle for new investment, trading and development opportunities' – was formed as a joint venture between Imry and Vines Management Ltd, a company controlled by Myers to manage the assets of Imry.

Stolzenberg set up Chester Holdings (UK) Ltd, but the rescue packages and the drastic restructuring did little to reverse the Imry group's fortunes. In late 1992, Barclays Bank pulled the plug on Chester Holdings (UK) Ltd in an equity-for-debt deal when Stolzenberg and associates were unable to service the £196m loan. After acquiring 100 per cent control, Barclays announced on 17 December of that year some major surgery 'to remove uncertainty and enable Imry to operate in the property sector from a stable base'.

Imry Holdings Ltd and its subsidiaries were transferred from its parent company, Chester Holdings (UK) Ltd, to Imry Group Ltd, a new company owned by Barclays. Commercial Property Corporation became a wholly-owned subsidiary of Imry Holdings Ltd, of which Martin Myers was appointed chief executive. Wolfgang Stolzenberg and his associates resigned as directors of all Imry Group companies. Next to this high-powered wheeler-dealing, the Church Commissioners and their loans were small beer.

Myers adamantly refutes any claims that Imry at that time was in financial trouble. Of media reports about its difficulties, he gave the following explanation: '[The media] didn't understand the relationship between Marketchief and Imry. Imry was acquired by Marketchief for £314 million. This was a takeover. They chose to finance their acquisition in a certain way ... Imry was their only asset and Imry had to then pay dividends so they ([Marketchief] could service their debt [to Barclays Bank].

'I think the confusion happened because Marketchief actually changed its name to Imry Merchant Developers, right? Now Imry Merchant Developers – it's only a name – and when Marketchief hit trouble, because they changed their name to Imry Merchant Developers, while Imry was called Imry Holdings, which was the old Imry, whilst Imry survived the whole debacle, Marketchief disappeared and Barclays had to take their write-off at the Marketchief level, not at the Imry level. So Marketchief changed its name to Imry Merchant Developers and then changed its name to something else [Chester Holdings UK]. The old Imry Developers is now Imry Holdings, which survived and is still here, and I'm chief executive of it. I think the press and others were confused about that, but the fact is if Imry was in such financial trouble, why is still here and flourishing?' Despite Myers' tortuous explanations, Imry was in financial trouble and had to be rescued by Barclays.

1.   Recorded interview with Gerald Harte, 16 January 1995.
2.   *Daily Telegraph*, 3 December 1988.
3.   Social Security Committee, Second Report, *The Church Commissioners and Church of England Pensions*, 29 March 1995, Q. 315.
4.   Recorded interview with Michael Hutchings, 26 May 1994.

5. Ibid.
6. Source: Stewart Hamilton, Finance Director of Ellison and Harte Developments Ltd, and Lecturer at International Institute for Management Development, Lausanne (interview 14 February 1995), and Gerald Harte, co-partner of Ellison and Harte (interview 6 February 1995).

CHAPTER SEVEN

A Development Too Far

Nedaclaret was now dead in the water, and with it the Ashford Great Park project. Its parent company, European Land, went into receivership in August 1992. Between 31 March 1990 and 31 March 1992 its annual turnover fell from a peak £15.35m – much of it generated by the Ashford Great Park deal – to £1.98m, with pre-tax profits over the same period falling from £2.2m to a loss of £1.55m. Loans to the two companies, which the Church Commissioners had to write off, totalled £41.2m.

When European Land folded, among the casualties were consultants Eric Parkinson and Colin Peacock, who had helped to bring Cookson and Myers together. Said Parkinson: 'We were owed a lot of money. That episode around the time the receivers were called in was very difficult for Colin and me. It was an unhappy ending. European Land left a lot to be desired. The trouble with European Land was that there were so many inter-connecting companies. The whole basis of its corporate structure was unorthodox.'

Parkinson ended up working with the receivers to untangle Cookson's web of business dealings. He said that their efforts to sort out the company's affairs failed because 'for a small company it was highly complicated. It was designed for Jim's immediate family to prosper. As a non-executive director, I had attended board meetings and requested information from time to time but that information was always tardy. As for what went on at Nedaclaret, I wouldn't have a clue. The arrangements between Jim Cookson and David Aykroyd were between them.'

Cookson's partner in Nedaclaret, David Aykroyd, claims ignorance of much of the company's dealings, which, he insisted, were driven by Cookson. 'I was never really involved. I was involved inasmuch that I put money in to get Mr Cookson involved, and from then on I would receive a telephone call [from Cookson] saying we were doing things this way. I concurred from the outset with all his wishes on that. I can't say anything about the Commissioners' losses. I never got near the driving seat at all. Claret was only one-third of Nedaclaret, with Mr Cookson owning the other two-thirds.' Aykroyd, whose company, Claret, had been wound up, quit property investments to run a filling station in Nun Monkton.

'Mr Cookson wasn't the sort of person you could be involved in with if there was something on. He remained in the driving seat. I just sat on [the board], with nil investment as it were, waiting for a never-never situation that never came good. I just got back my original investment of £655,000' – the money paid by Cookson as an up-front payment in his deal with Ellison and Harte – 'when Imry bought half interest in the Ashford Great Park company.'

The Cedarvale gravy train was wheezing into the sidings by December 1991. Accountants Coopers & Lybrand, in auditing the finances of the Commissioners' subsidiary company for that year, reported that the partners were

> discussing future funding of the partnership. Until the discussions are complete, there is uncertainty as to the ability of the partnership to continue as a going concern. In addition to this uncertainty, the financial statements of the partnership have not been audited and we have been unable to satisfy ourselves as whether the investment in the partnership is fairly stated.

The financial affairs of the Ashford Great Park Partnership remain unaudited. To this day, the recipients, and the services they provided, of the many tens of millions of pounds invested by the Church Commissioners in the Partnership remain a mystery.

With the winding up of Cedarvale at the end of 1993, the Church Commissioners were legally obliged to waive all monies owing them, as they had agreed to indemnify Cedarvale against any loss of investments made on its behalf. This had been done at the insistence of their partners, and recommended by Hutchings and Shelley, to ensure the financial credibility of Cedarvale within the Ashford Great Park Partnership. By the end of 1993, the money loaned to the Partnership through Cedarvale totalled £45.9m, including rolled-up interest (i.e. interest accumulating year on year) of £15.43m.

Shelley and Hutchings had also persuaded the Church Commissioners to act as guarantors for the repayment of bank loans obtained by Ashford Great Park (Phase 1) Ltd to fund further development costs. At the end of the day, those loans, which were transferred into the Ashford Great Park Partnership, totalled £41.2m, which included a substantial amount of rolled-up interest loaned back to the partnership. The grand total of the loans, all unsecured, was £87.1m – for agricultural land which came to be worth just £3m.

And because of the Commissioners' strategy of concealing true costs – and, therefore, eventual losses – in their annual accounts, the true figure may never be known. For example, based on information available at Companies House, the Commissioners had invested £37m by the end of 1991, which, in their annual report, was put at between £10m and £20m. The following year their investment had escalated to £42m, yet their annual report put the figure between £3m and £5m. The reports deliberately concealed the massive sums of money the Commissioners were pumping into the Ashford Great Park Partnership and gave no clue to the massive losses that would eventually be incurred.

The indemnity provision of a further £41m, made available by the Commissioners through Cedarvale, to cover partnership losses, took the total to near the £88m loss publicly acknowledged. But that provision may have been exceeded, and, unless the full figures are published, the Church of England may never know the full extent of the Commissioners' financial disaster.

However, the known figure of nearly £88m, and the interest costs, surprised neither Myers nor Landau. Said Myers: 'We are businessmen, and we know what the cost of money is. I am not surprised because I had to monitor it. It was being monitored the whole time. We knew exactly what the roll-up of interest was.'

Landau, emphasizing the cost of the planning process, blamed much of it on the fees which Myers claimed he was keen to see radically reduced: 'Have you any idea of the planning that goes in to try and make certain you create the best development ... the optimum development opportunity ... it doesn't just happen. You have to employ an architect, you have to employ a quantity surveyor, you have to employ a planning consultant. You'll have road traffic consultants, environmental consultants. I would like to ascertain a breakdown and find out how much has been paid to all those specialist people.'

He would not be surprised, he added, to discover that there had been 'various' firms continuously working on the Ashford Great Park project 'for several years. You could ask Mr Wells. I bet you there would be people from his organization, Chesterton, who received huge amounts of monies, who were on that job for many, many years.'

A further considerable cost, according to Myers, was caused by the need to sack a number of consultants who weren't up to the mark. 'We on the management committee were monitoring the success or otherwise of various consultants and on several occasions we had to dismiss them and get someone else because they were not up to standard.

'This was a hotbed of activity. You couldn't work at the slowest pace, because you had to get all your expertise in their specialist subjects all going at the same speed, because if one person is lagging behind everyone else has to stop ... We used to have meetings with 20 or 30 people round a table, which used to last from eight in the morning to eight in the evening.'

But Eric Parkinson claimed very little was actually achieved. 'At the outset,' he said, 'it was a small group trying to move it forward. Then, in leaps and bounds, it ended up involving a cast of thousands. I mean, we used to go to these meetings and they were a farce. There wasn't effective management. There were working groups for this and working groups for that ... when Martin Landau came in, there was one board, and a board underneath that, a management board, and, really, the project needed three of our people just to live with [who was doing what] day in, day out.'

Michael Hutchings when asked where the money went, replied, 'I certainly should do,' but then claimed he really had no idea at all. 'When I was there, finance was very strictly controlled. When the thing was first started, the other two partners had incurred expenditure, and as the Church were paymasters, that had to be set straight; there were then the options that had to be exercised, there were some professional fees and rolled-up interest. But when I was there I think the figures, from memory, were nearer to £30 million. But when the story broke it was about £80 million, and I really have no idea how they managed to get to that.' It was a curious defence of his participation, as much of the expenditure was incurred prior to his resignation from Cedarvale in April 1991 and he would have authorized it. 'I cannot conceive, even with interest rates, of that sort of level … I know Cookson took very large fees out of that, but he had an agreement with Ashford Great Park (Phase 1) Ltd. Yes, there were some fat fees being taken up but nothing that would get you near to £87 million.'

Shelley was politely vague about the entire matter. 'I really can't remember much about it.' He admitted having more of a 'hands-on involvement' with the successful Gateshead MetroCentre than at Ashford Great Park. Was Michael Hutchings more in the driving seat with Ashford Great Park? 'Mr Hutchings was the property expert. You must remember that the Secretary of the Commissioners can't have a hands-on involvement in everything.' He declined to comment on the financial calibre of the Commissioners' partners. 'It is a long time ago since I was involved in that, and I think it is best left like that.'

James Shirley, who was appointed with Hutchings and Shelley to Paysystem – later Cedarvale – in December 1988, resigned in August 1990. Shirley was replaced by Shaun Farrell, who worked in the Commissioners' property department and would later replace Hutchings as Commercial Property Manager. He, too, declined to comment on the fate of the Commissioners' £87m. He curtly referred all questions to the Commissioners' Press Office. Andrew Brown, employed by the Commissioners as an ecclesiastical administrator, was also a director of Cedarvale, and he was equally opposed to making any public comment.

Company secretary to Cedarvale, Paul Bussy, was similarly unwilling to comment on the Commissioners losses, adding: 'Before you go any further, I work for a firm of accountants called Coopers & Lybrand. Anything to do with the Church Commissioners has a confidential nature attached to it, and I am afraid I am not prepared to discuss anything without the Church Commissioners' say-so.' He, too, referred inquiries to the Commissioners' Press Office.

Someone who, according to Hutchings, really knew the financial complexities and problems of Ashford Great Park was Peter Sutcliffe, a colleague of Wells' and a partner in Chesterton International, who acted as chairman of the Ashford Great Park Partnership. 'He was the one who really headed up Ashford. He is the one who really knows what happened,' claimed Hutchings. But, predictably, Sutcliffe, out of deference to the Commissioners, declined to comment on his role, or, in particular, on their losses.

Following the retirement of Jim Shelley in June 1992, one of the early moves of his successor, Patrick Locke, who had been eagerly waiting in the wings for some months to assume the Secretary's crown, was to personally engage the services of Richard Lay, the chairman of international property consultants, DTZ Debenham Thorpe, to report on the management of Ashford Great Park. Locke was known to be concerned by the dual role of Chesterton, who were acting as adviser to both the Commissioners and the Ashford Great Park Partnership. In a confidential report of 20 October 1994, commenting on Chesterton's initial report which recommended the Commissioners' involvement in the project, DTZ was critical of Chesterton's role, claiming they had 'failed to deal adequately with the important issues ... Furthermore, we disagree with much of the comment they make and their overall advice.'

On 25 February 1993, in an exercise to clean up the books, the Church Commissioners, through CC Projects, another of their wholly-owned subsidiaries, purchased the interest of Ashford Great Park (Phase 1) Ltd for £1, thereby wiping out the loans. By then, Ashford Great Park (Phase 1) Ltd had a deficit of £4.3m with negligible assets of just £13,361. The value of Ashford Great Park (Phase 1) Ltd's investment in the Ashford Great Park Partnership, which in 1991 stood at £23.1m, was written down to £100. Land once valued in the Partnership the previous year at £79.4m was now worth, as agricultural land, just £2.7m.

The Commissioners also agreed to waive a £15.7m loan which had been made to Ashford Great Park (Phase 1) Ltd between 1989 and 1992. They did so in the forlorn hope of retrieving an unexplained loan of £4m made by Ashford Great Park (Phase 1) Ltd to its shareholders – Imry and Nedaclaret – out of the Church Commissioners' initial advances.

Questions asked of Myers about the loan and its purpose were swept dismissively aside by Landau, who suggested it was in accordance with the Commissioners' traditional practice of providing loans to partners with the interest being claimed by the Commissioners to provide income and, as a charity, protect their non-trading status. It was, he added, part of normal development costs. 'You think it was a bung to George Graham? Who was it supposed to have gone to? Why don't you ask the Church Commissioners?'

In return for the Commissioners agreeing to forego the remainder of the loan – £11.7m – the board agreed to assign ownership of the £4m loan to the Church Commissioners, which gave them the legal right to collect the money directly from the shareholders, Imry and Nedaclaret – which, not surprising, they have been unable to do. It was a desperate effort on the part of the Commissioners to at least try and claw back a fraction of their long-lost millions.

But the Commissioners could, in fact, do no other than waive the loans due to an extraordinary decision which freed their partners, Imry and Nedaclaret, from any obligation to repay them. The decision, which was the cause of a substantial part of the ultimate losses incurred by the Commissioners, was taken by Hutchings after it had been originally agreed that each company would be responsible for its own share of development costs. Wells claims that despite his written and verbal warnings, the Commissioners agreed to granting non-recourse unsecured loans to their partners, which meant the money could not be recovered in the event of default. Said Wells:

> The original intention of the agreement was that each partner would be responsible for their contribution to the costs of the partnership. The Commissioners would then use their best endeavours to procure the loan on behalf of all three parties as they felt that they were able to get better terms. However, in the event, during negotiations, this was changed by the Commissioners despite our written advice to the contrary, as we were very concerned about the exposure of the Commissioners to this significantly increased liability. Our advice was not taken. Somehow or other, although it was spelt out very clearly, both orally and in writing, the message didn't get home that you were considerably increasing your risk by lending the money to

your partners. I mean, the risk was lousy. We said that we strongly advised against it. All you can do is go down in writing to your client and say this really is something you must not do. But, ultimately of course, it is not a property decision, and, ultimately, we are merely their property advisers.

Hutchings claims the original agreement was restructured because at that time neither Imry nor Nedaclaret could raise their share of development costs until the project had received planning permission. He therefore agreed, on behalf of the Church Commissioners, that they wouldn't need to do so until planning permission had been granted.

'Okay, you could say it was imprudent with hindsight, but ... they couldn't actually raise the money until planning permission had been agreed. So the idea was, as soon as planning permission was received, they would actually divvy up their proportion, so it was a third, third, third.' Assuming, of course, that everything went well. If it didn't, as events indeed proved, the Commissioners would carry all the losses.

'Everyone was saying we'd get planning permission. That, I was assured, wouldn't be a problem. Even so, we weren't going to be in that position for ever. There was a cut-off date. By late '91, irrespective of whether planning permission had been granted, they each had to stump up their third. Of course, they went broke, but that is so easy to say with hindsight. I don't know about Cookson, but certainly not with Imry. Nobody believed there was anything wrong with them.' Hutchings may not have thought so, but, even then, Imry was widely known to be in some difficulty, and, just eight months after the Commissioners signed the partnership deal, the company was taken over by Marketchief. From that point, the Commissioners had even less chance of seeing the return of their money.

As for Nedaclaret, a cursory check at Companies House would have revealed that Cookson's company was of negative financial worth and one around which, in more cautious days, the Commissioners would have steered a wide berth. Northern England Development Associates Ltd was a company with a share capital of

£25,000, with Cookson owning 24,849 shares. Its company accounts in 1986 showed an accumulated deficit of £118,092. In that year, Cookson had paid fees totalling £119,896 and expenses totalling £45,529 to J. Cookson & Partners, his management services practice. As he did later on a much larger scale, on the dividends paid by Nedaclaret to European Land, he both owned the company and would take massive fees from it.

Hutchings admits that he was always aware of Cookson's financial worth.

> I always knew he was a one-man band, but, nevertheless, if someone has put the finances together, which we had been assured he had ... we knew he wasn't a PLC but at that stage, before planning permission was refused, we were told that he had sufficient resources to meet his obligations. We knew he wasn't in the Land Securities mould, but we thought he was good for a bob or two. I suppose ultimately, because I was in charge, it must be my responsibility. But, on the other hand, if you employ agents ... perhaps it was naive ... [but] they said these are perfectly sound people, so I didn't feel it was necessary to do another investigation.

Shelley said he could remember little of the Commissioners' dealings with Cookson. 'I can't remember what steps we went through to ascertain whether he was a suitable partner. Mr Hutchings was the property expert. It has been a long time since I was involved in something like that ... I am not willing to talk.'

Confirming that his company had carefully vetted the financial worth of their prospective partners, Wells said: 'Full checks had been made and [the Commissioners] knew perfectly well these companies were companies of no substance, which made it even worse lending them money. Imry was in a much stronger position.'

Sir Douglas claimed, however, that neither he nor his Assets Committee colleagues received information to indicate that any of their proposed partners were less than financially sound. He recalled that, to the contrary, the Assets Committee were informed at the early stages of negotiations by Wells and Hutchings – 'who inquired more deeply into it' – that they 'were fully satisfied'. He added: 'We were told they were reputable people. They came armed with references, not least from their bankers, particularly in the case of Cookson, and Landau and Myers ... exactly who Myers was, I don't know. Anyway, Myers was one of them. They came armed with excellent references. They came with good references, bankers' references. I remember going round the table at the time, at an Assets Committee meeting, and saying, "I've never heard of them. What is known of them?" Most people looked blank. Others said, yes, they'd heard of Mr Cookson and Landau, and knew nothing to their detriment.'

Sir Douglas admitted that neither he nor his committee colleagues saw for themselves bankers' letters of reference. 'But the Assets Committee was certainly told about it ... which of them was it? ... behind Cookson? Memory fades. One of the big clearers was, in fact, backing Cookson quite substantially. I am quite sure that when the proposal to go in with Mr Cookson on Ashford ... we were told that Mr Cookson had bankers' letters of comfort.

'I remember pretty clearly that we were told that Cookson was supported by one of the banks. I think it was the NatWest.' Of the public criticism of the Commissioners' partners, and Jim Cookson in particular, Sir Douglas commented: 'People have said things like, "Y'know, everyone knew this chap was dodgy." I simply said, "Well, it would have been rather nice if you had told us at the time." But nobody did.'

Jim Shelley was unable to recall what inquiries were made to establish Cookson's financial credibility, or who might have carried them out. 'It was some time ago, but one was looking at this sort of thing the whole time.'

Myers and Landau denied Hutchings' claim that the Commissioners agreed to the loans on condition they would be repaid once planning permission had been granted. Said Myers, 'I don't think Michael would say something that's untrue – I think he's just muddled.' Landau commented: 'Why would we go to [the Commissioners] if it were not for them to put up the money for the development?' Ashford Great Park was, they said, like any other co-development venture they had undertaken with the Commissioners, whereby the Commissioners provided the development capital. 'This was not money loaned to Imry,' said Myers. 'It was a loan to a special-purpose vehicle [Ashford Great Park (Phase 1) Ltd], which was completely different.' It was, he insisted, the way the Commissioners wanted the partnership structured to protect, as a charity, its tax-free status. 'If Imry had owed the money, the Church would have sued us, wouldn't they?'

The degree of the Church Commissioners' lack of clout was underscored by their efforts to get Barclays, the new owners of the Imry Group, to repay Imry's share of the loans. According to Hutchings, Patrick Locke, the new Secretary to the Commissioners, was confident that Barclays would play the game and return every penny. Hutchings says when he asked Locke, over lunch, whether the Commissioners would get their money back, he replied: 'I don't see any problem with that. Barclays are there.'

In the event, of course, the Commissioners didn't get their money back. William Wells confirmed that the Commissioners asked Imry to repay the loans. 'They thought Imry would do the gentlemanly thing, but, of course, it doesn't always work that way in business.'

Such dismissive treatment of the Commissioners, claimed Hutchings imperiously, certainly wouldn't have happened in the Commissioners' halcyon days, when they held the respect of those with whom they did business, and especially during the reign of Lord Silsoe. 'He would have been straight round to the chairman of Barclays to talk about it ... He was a significant player. I don't think the Commissioners were taken terribly seriously.'

Not only did the Commissioners' request fall on deaf ears, but they went on to pay Imry £1m for their shares in Ashford Great Park (Phase 1) Ltd, which, by then, was a totally worthless company. Said Hutchings, 'I don't see how their shares could be worth anything. Why do you pay to get them out? I don't know.'

Myers, confirming the purchase of Imry's shares, said it was 'a settlement figure' agreed between the Commissioners and the new Imry regime under Stefan Wingate's Marketchief in September 1989. 'When the company was taken over, there was a new relationship with the Church Commissioners and our partnerships were dissolved. On each one of them there was a negotiation for the Church to acquire our shares because they wanted 100 per cent ownership. As the financing partner, if they were going to take these things on long-term, they figured our 50 per cent wasn't worth a lot, so why not buy us out.'

According to a Millbank source, who was closely involved in the Ashford Great Park disaster and who insisted on remaining anonymous, the Church Commissioners also paid Imry 'hundreds of thousands of pounds' following a threat of legal action by way of compensation 'for future loss of profits ... If it had gone to court it would have been very messy and very expensive. The Commissioners didn't want that. Imry were hardly in a position to complain, as they had taken the project to the Commissioners, but that's the way the Commissioners were. I told them that they should tell Imry to get stuffed.'

At one stage, the Commissioners themselves had seriously considered taking legal action for compensation against one or more of their former partners. They sought the advice of solicitors Lovell White Durrant, of Holborn Viaduct, London, who claimed that, while, in their view, there were three specific areas where a negligence action might be successful, the level of damages would be unlikely to cover legal costs. Apart from confirming that they use the firm of Lovell White Durrant, the Commissioners declined to comment.

Jim Cookson was unable to respond to his many critics. He died of cancer at the age of 56 on 22 July 1993. His widow, Mrs Susan True Cookson, a director of the parent company, European Land, vigorously defended her husband's role in Ashford Great Park.

'The things that have been said about my husband have been totally untrue,' she said. 'He had the leading people in the country working on that project for him. Everything my husband did went through the best accountants, the best lawyers. My husband did nothing crooked. He couldn't have done. They wouldn't have gone along with it, and nor would the Church Commissioners have dealt with him under those circumstances.'

European Land went into receivership, said Mrs Cookson, because the National Westminster withdrew from an agreement to loan 'an amazing amount of money', which she declined to specify. 'But the sort of projects my husband was doing were that sort of thing ... we would go for years without any money coming in at all because projects took so long, and when they did it was brilliant. They were long-term investments and very much larger than most people did. He had a vision which I don't think many other people in the country had, and I think that when people got involved they knew exactly what the situation was.'

Her son, Charles Calvert, who was employed by his step-father's company as new projects manager, said the NatWest loan was planned to finance a multi-million pound 50-acre residential and light industry development in Darlington. NatWest's refusal effectively scuppered European Land's involvement. Cookson had already acquired land options and had applied for planning permission in November 1990, which was subsequently granted, but by then European Land had disappeared from the scene.

In June of that year, Cookson had also submitted a planning application to Newcastle-upon-Tyne City Council for a £750m Great Park project similar to the one in deep trouble at Ashford. This mini-town was no less ambitious. Set in 2,000 acres of woods and farmland near Newcastle Airport, it would include 5,000 houses, a business and industry zone, a hotel, a conference centre, a championship golf course and, he added, create 15,000 jobs.

Cookson also promised to create a one-acre country park, plant more than a million broad-leaf trees and develop 'ecology trails' to wild flower meadows, wetlands, pools and a riverside walk. With the development planned on Green Belt land, Cookson knew it would meet fierce opposition, but, at a press conference to announce the scheme, his comments did little to assuage environmentalists' concerns. He is quoted as saying: 'The Green Belt is fine for rabbits, but you must have living space for people. You cannot keep the lid on it indefinitely.'[1] The company set up to handle the development was NEDACIN – an acronym for Northern England Development Associates and Coal Industries Nominees, British Coal's pension fund – which was putting up the development costs.

But with mounting financial pressures, Cookson was unable to continue, and when European Land went into receivership, Coal Industries Nominees took over NEDACIN and continued negotiations with the city council. A council executive described Cookson as 'very impressive. He certainly sounded as if he knew what he was talking about. He definitely looked the part. But we always took what he said with a pinch of salt. We always thought his plans for Newcastle were too grand. We are now working with NEDACIN on a much more modest scheme, which we think is supportable.'

On 27 October 1992, the result of the public inquiry held on 3 December 1991 into Ashford Borough Council's Local Plan, was issued. Ironically, it came down on the side of Ashford Great Park (Phase 1) Ltd, which, in its objection to the council's development proposals, had argued that theirs was superior. The Department of

Environment inspector recommended that the company's proposals be included in the Local Plan rather than Ashford Borough Council's. He believed Ashford Great Park's proposals had 'greater implementability' – it was more feasible – than the council's; it had better 'landscape coherence' – more fitting with the prevailing landscape; and the 'critical massing' was more attractive – a more viable self-supporting community structure.

As a result, the council amended its draft Local Plan to include Ashford Great Park (Phase 1) Ltd's proposals; this was agreed in June 1993, with planning permission for limited development being granted on 21 September 1994 – almost seven years after the first application was submitted by Cookson's Bigscan company on 25 November 1987, and five years and eight months after the Church Commissioners entered into a partnership agreement with Imry and Nedaclaret in January 1989.

Later that year, on 8 December, the House of Commons Social Security Committee, chaired by Frank Field, the combative Labour MP for Birkenhead, began their inquiry into the business dealings of the Church Commissioners who, as trustees of a pension fund, were answerable to Parliament. It was attended by Sir Michael Colman, who had recently been appointed to succeed Sir Douglas Lovelock as First Church Estates Commissioner, Patrick Locke, Secretary to the Commissioners, and Mrs Margaret Laird, Third Church Estates Commissioner.

During a two-hour hearing, Colman, in reply to a question from Labour MP Jeremy Corbyn, agreed that it had been 'crazy' to invest millions of pounds in the proposed development of land without planning permission. Asked why he believed it had taken place, he said: 'At the time they thought that the value represented by the complete buildings in the drafts put before them were sufficiently attractive to justify purchasing the land and entering into a scheme with a partner, to prepare for planning permission to build and develop several properties on that site. The reality has been very different.'

In a briefing note dated 21 September 1994 to the Social Security Committee, the Commissioners acknowledged that reality, adding that they did not intend to 'undertake any speculative development at Ashford. Although Ashford Borough Council's decision will help market the land, demand for development land at Ashford is still depressed.' The development of Ashford Great Park would take 'many years to implement, unless there is a dramatic change in demand in the area'. The planning permission agreed by Ashford Borough Council for limited development of the site did nothing to reduce the Commissioners' losses. Its development potential, Colman later confirmed, was not 'commensurate with the money spent'.[2]

Such was the concern of the Social Security Committee at the losses incurred by the Commissioners over Ashford Great Park that it recommended in its report of March 1995 on their investment activities that the Archbishop of Canterbury 'should appoint a totally independent investigator into all aspects of this scheme'.[3] The report was highly critical of the Commissioners for failing to have a clear policy or 'due procedures to assess the partners' ability ... to raise the necessary capital to fund their share of the investment'.

The Social Security Committee's recommendation led to the Archbishop of Canterbury authorizing an investigation, which was put into action by Alan McLintock, Chairman of the newly-created Audit Committee, in May 1995. McLintock appointed Sven Tester, a retired partner in chartered accountants KPMG, of Blackfriars, London, to carry it out. He was given access to all papers and people involved in the project. One of McLintock's colleagues on the Audit Committee, Viscountess Brentford, a Church Commissioner, a Lay Chairwoman of Diocesan Synod, and a much-respected chartered accountant herself, said at the time that Tester's findings were likely to be made public, 'although the report is at the request of the Archbishop of Canterbury and for his eyes. What he chooses to do with it will be up to him.'

Less than twelve months after the Social Security Committee's recommendation, McLintock had received Tester's report. By May 1996 it had gone through its final draft before arriving on the desk of the Archbishop of Canterbury at Lambeth Palace. And when Sir Michael Colman and Patrick Locke appeared together for the third time before the committee on April 1, Frank Field and his colleagues were keen to learn of its whereabouts.

After twice referring questions about the report to McLintock's office, Colman insisted that its publication was not his responsibility – 'the report is in the hands of the Chairman of the Audit Committee and is being made for the benefit of the Archbishop of Canterbury and, although it is true to say that I and the Commissioners will get a copy, it is not actually being done for us.'[4] Field, claiming that he and his colleagues had 'supported' the Commissioners against allegations by 'outside organizations' that the investigation was 'a fix' to avoid unnecessary expenditure, said that the request was a *quid pro quo* in return for that support. They wanted the report to be made available to ensure that there had been a proper inquiry,

> because one of the things we will obviously want to see is whether Mr Tester recommends that you should refer some aspects of the development to the police for criminal investigation. I think it is very important that if he made those sorts of recommendations it was clear and open that the Commissioners were not seen to be trying to protect previous and past office holders.

Colman said the report's publication could be complicated by possible legal difficulties. 'That is why I think you should discuss it with Mr McLintock because he may need some help in that direction.' Field said that as the report was being prepared for the Archbishop, 'I do not think our powers such that we can compel another parliamentarian to produce papers anyway, so we will depend on a graceful response from His Grace on that issue.'

But, almost two years after the Social Security Committee's recommendation, the report was no nearer to being made public. The Archbishop of Canterbury, Dr George Carey, said: 'The investigation into Ashford Great Park will be reported to the Board of Governors as well as me personally. There are strong arguments for making the gist of such a report public in due course, but this has to be subject of various legal and other considerations which are still under discussion.'5

A significant contributor to Tester's investigation was Martin Myers, who had been excluded from the Lambeth Group inquiry after Lovelock and Patrick Locke had told Coopers & Lybrand investigator Peter King that it would be 'inappropriate' to include the property development company in his inquiries (see Chapter 11). Tester, said Myers, asked 'very searching questions', to which he responded in writing. Myers professed to welcome Tester's visit.

Following critical comment on Imry in the Lambeth Group report and, in particular, in the Social Security Committee report of March 1995, which accused the company of being unable to meet its financial commitments, Myers was prepared to tell anybody who would listen how unfairly his company had been treated, and he seized the opportunity of Tester's visit to maintain, although not with total accuracy, that throughout his dealings with the Commissioners his company had been financially sound.

'He thanked me most profusely for putting him in the picture, and giving him the correct information,' said Myers. He claimed Imry had been badly treated by the Social Security Committee report 'because everybody who was called to give evidence blamed Imry'. For the record, not one witness did so, but, in explaining their 'motives', Myers claimed they wanted to 'throw off any blame' from themselves. 'To lay the blame at our door was quite a disgrace.' He believed that Tester's report would not be made public. 'It will be swept under the carpet ... but what can you do? I think we have been very badly treated.'

The man whose ill-founded enthusiasm was a principal factor in the Ashford Great Park fiasco remained to the end supremely sanguine about it all. In a radio interview, Sir Douglas Lovelock declared that the loss of nearly £88m was 'very unfortunate ... you win some, you lose some. That's inevitable.'[6] And, as he later told members of the Social Security Committee when he and Shelley were questioned about the Commissioners' reckless investments, 'winning some and losing some' was simply 'the name of the game'.[7]

Meanwhile, back in Edinburgh, Harte and Ellison, the two men behind the concept of Ashford Great Park, were not a penny richer. More than a decade later, they were still waiting for the multi-million pound pay-off their daring vision had once promised. Instead, they were locked in a lengthy legal battle for money they claim the Commissioners are obligated to pay them, through Cedarvale, under the terms of their deal with James Cookson. Said Harte: 'We are not very happy at the way things have worked out. Frankly, I have never found any of the major players in property investment and development to be the most honourable of people. Everybody has made money out of this except us. And, of course, the Church Commissioners.'

1. *Daily Mail*, 1 June 1990.
2. Social Security Committee, Second Report, *The Church Commissioners and Church of England Pensions*, 29 March 1995, Q. 38.
3. Social Security Committee, Second Report, *The Church Commissioners and Church of England Pensions*, 29 March 1995, p. xvi.
4. Social Security Committee, Fifth Report, *Church of England Pensions*, 26 June 1996, Q. 39.

5. *Hansard*, reply to written questions, 15 October 1996.
6. *File on Four*, Radio 4, 5 October 1993.
7. Social Security Committee, Second Report, *The Church Commissioners and Church of England Pensions*, 29 March 1995, Q. 331.

CHAPTER EIGHT

Ethical Investments?

While Sir Douglas Lovelock and his Assets Committee colleagues were sinking deeper into difficulties in the face of depressed income, mounting borrowings and increasing expenditure, they were also under siege over another controversial issue which for over 15 years had caused deep and acrimonious divisions within the Church of England. Such was the bitter chasm between the two sides that the dispute ended up in the High Court, which, claimed a bishop, Lovelock tried to thwart by a 'dirty tricks' campaign.

The pressures caused by this legal battle were so intense that they began to undermine the Assets Committee's work, according to David Hopkinson, who was chief executive of M & G Investment Group, and a key adviser on the Commissioners' Stock Exchange investments. 'All the time this property thing was going sour, the Assets Committee was spending ... at least half of their time with the law case [in the High Court] ... And all my experience in the investment world is that when you start publicly going for an investment manager, and that is what we were, he gets defensive and his eye gets taken off the ball. Jim Shelley did practically nothing but deal with this case for months on end.'

Rather than property, the issue was the ethical investment of the Commissioners' sizeable shares portfolio. The dispute had its origins in the decision by the Church Commissioners in the early fifties to ditch safe but low-yield gilt-edged shares and fixed interest securities for more profitable but riskier ordinary shares. The essential question was whether the Commissioners were investing in companies whose activities might be considered unethical or harmful to God's created universe and people. Such reassurances as were given by the Commissioners about the ethical purity of their equity investments achieved little in quelling growing concerns, which were aroused all the more in the early years by the Commissioners' refusal to reveal the details of the portfolio on the grounds that confidentiality was a necessary strategy in their dealings with companies.

As the pressure upon them increased, the First Church Estates Commissioner at the time, Sir Ronald Harris, always sensitive to the mood of the Synod, attempted to cool passions by issuing a list of commercial and industrial markets in which, he said, the Commissioners would not invest. Part of a policy statement published in the Commissioners' annual report and accounts in 1972, the list proscribed investments 'directly in companies operating wholly or mainly in certain trades – armaments, gambling, breweries and distilleries, tobacco, newspapers, publishing and broadcasting, and theatre and films – or in Southern Africa'.

The reference to South Africa had a particular significance. It was designed to ease the concerns of those who were becoming increasingly alarmed by a growing international human rights problem – the South African white minority government's policy of apartheid which for many years had permitted social and economic discrimination against and exploitation of millions of black workers.

But the statement simply raised more questions, which, to the intense frustration of the Commissioners, refused to go away. It marked the beginning of a campaign by a few of the Church's more socially concerned spirits, who, unlike the majority of Synod members at that time, were campaigning for political and economic action to end apartheid. The declaration of the Commissioners' banned list in 1972 coincided with the founding of Christian Concern for South Africa by a group of churchmen in London, and a more radical group called End Loans to South Africa, founded by a Methodist churchman, which in the mid-eighties staged a 12-hour prayer vigil outside No. 1 Millbank, claiming that the Commissioners' refusal to sell their shares in South African-related companies was 'almost a blasphemy' and a 'sin against the Holy Spirit'.[1]

Throughout the seventies and eighties, the issue caused increasing division within the Church of England and was a constant feature of Synod business. In May 1979 the British Council of Churches issued a report, *Political Change in South Africa: Britain's Responsibility*, which claimed that 'decades of close economic relationships and the intensified pressure exerted upon British firms in the last five years' had failed to bring about the desired political changes. The report called for a dramatic alternative: investment sanctions against South Africa through a policy of 'disengagement'. The BCC insisted that such disengagement remained the only effective way of opposing apartheid, 'until such time as it is clear that all the people of South Africa are to be permanently entitled to share equally in the exercise of political power'.

That November, the General Synod, following a debate of the BCC report, went some way to supporting its recommendation. It encouraged 'widespread consideration ... for economic disengagement in support of efforts to secure a more just society in South Africa'. It also drew the attention of companies with interests in South Africa to a seven-clause Code of Conduct agreed two years earlier by the European Community aimed at promoting better working conditions for black workers in South Africa. The resolution illustrated the extent of the U-turn that had taken place within the Church of England. Eight years earlier the General Synod had actually criticized the World Council of Churches for awarding grants to finance the work of anti-apartheid supporters.

Disquiet within the Church of England over the ethical calibre of the Commissioners' investments led to the publication in July 1980 of a Working Paper by the Industrial Committee of the General Synod's Board of Social Responsibility. Called *The Ethical Use of Investment Funds*, it said the Commissioners could not use their funds 'purely to promote socially desirable ends if this conflicts with their prime duty', but it also believed that a list of banned investment categories had 'a limited usefulness'. With the growth in multi-national companies, it was 'increasingly difficult' to keep track of their interests. 'Indeed, it is virtually impossible for investors to keep out of every questionable company and to keep their portfolios "clean".'

Nevertheless, for investors not to ask questions about the morality of their investments was to be 'careless, even irresponsible, stewards'. Although there were many constraints on business already, there were also moral constraints. 'Wealth and jobs are good, but not at any price.' It argued for 'a minimum concern to avoid social injury and for a policy of constructive engagements on the basis of it ... [which] may imply that institutions should disengage, step by step, from those companies whose activities do not seem to match up to what they regard as right'.

A policy of 'constructive engagement', said its supporters, gave investors access to the offices of key decision-makers, to whom they could express their concerns on employees' working conditions or on other ethical issues. It was this rationale which the Commissioners steadfastly owned in defence of their investments.

Shortly after the publication of the paper, and perhaps in response to it, Millbank opened its doors to *The Times*, and that in particular of its investment manager, Mr Alistair McDonald. The result was a bland article published on 12 August 1980 (entitled 'How the Church keeps its portfolio clean') clearly designed to promote the ethical purity of the Commissioners' shareholding policy. In a series of extraordinary claims, McDonald said that the Commissioners were so meticulous in their investments selection that the 'investments team' not only took 'note' of who the directors were but also their business connections. Once a company looked 'fairly acceptable' on 'management, financial and ethical' grounds, a 'modest' amount of money would be invested. The research team would then try to 'get closer to management and how they operate'.

Much was done at a personal level, said the article, with pressure quietly exerted on company chairmen and managing directors to 'fit in' with the Commissioners' code of business ethics. If a company refused to come to heel, 'we can always get the Archbishop to write'. McDonald was also quoted as saying that most British businessmen 'still obey the express wishes of the Church', a remarkable vote of confidence in the Christian faith of corporate man. There was also the Church's political clout. 'We can exert pressure on government ... the Church of England is the state church. The Church Commissioners are represented in government, and, of course, the Prime Minister is a Church Commissioner. The Home Secretary, the Chancellor of the Exchequer, the Lord Chancellor, the Attorney General, the Solicitor-General, are all *ex officio* Church Commissioners. It is sometimes very useful to have a Chancellor of the Exchequer as a Church Commissioner; we have been able to influence things in a minor way.'

They were grandiose claims. Only the most gullible could believe that the Church of England could even hope to 'exert pressure' on leading ministers of state to induce a company to comply with the Commissioners' code of ethics.

By 1982, the General Synod's attitude towards South Africa had hardened further still. At its session in July, a motion calling for the 'progressive disengagement' of all investments in South Africa was supported as the 'only appropriate basic policy to adopt'. It asked the Board of Social Responsibility to enter into discussions with the government and 'other appropriate bodies' as to how the policy might best be implemented. One of the 'appropriate bodies' was the Church Commissioners themselves, who, as independent guardians of the Church's historical assets, were not obliged to follow the Synod's injunctions.

The force of feeling in Synod was such that Sir Ronald Harris began to talk privately of countering criticism of the Commissioners by lifting the veil on their property and Stock Exchange portfolios.[2] Discussions within Millbank agreed that a period of greater openness might serve the Commissioners better. It would not mean a change in policy, but a concerted campaign to explain the merits of their investments. Certainly the Commissioners' refusal to disclose the contents of their portfolios had won them few supporters and had aided the credibility of their opponents' campaign; a time of *glasnost*, in taking the initiative to the parishes, could serve them no worse.

So, in their annual report and accounts of 1983 (p. 8), the Commissioners revealed for the first time their very considerable Stock Exchange and property holdings. Described 'as a further move in the direction of openness', total assets valued at £1.63 billion were made public, of which £604m was invested in the Stock Exchange and £904m in commercial and residential property, and agricultural land. Total net income was £71m. The shares portfolio showed investments of £22.28m in Shell Transport and Trading, £16.67m in Unilever, £14.29m in Marks & Spencer, £12.46m in GEC, and £11.44m in Beecham. The Commissioners had equity holdings of more than £1 million in each of 158 companies, of which 98 were British, with the remainder in America, Europe, Australia and the Far East. The biggest overseas holding was £10m in Royal Dutch Petroleum.

At the same time the Commissioners published in the report the result of a 'full review' by the Board of Governors of the Commissioners' ethical investment guidelines. Not unexpectedly, it endorsed the policy of 'constructive engagement'. The Commissioners also claimed to have a policy of 'disengagement' – 'insofar as they do not invest in South African companies or companies having a significant stake in that country'.[3] It was an enterprising interpretation somewhat removed from that on which the Synod had based its call for 'progressive disengagement', and this 'blend' of strategies singularly failed to appease the anti-apartheid faction.

As part of the Commissioners' 'open door' strategy, four brochures on their work were published and a touring exhibition undertaken to 12 dioceses. But it was a public relations exercise which failed to mute strident voices within the Synod and elsewhere who remained adamant that investments, no matter how 'minimal', in any companies with interests in South Africa should be withdrawn. They were reinforced by a call from the South African Council of Churches who, claiming that overseas investments were propping up apartheid, urged British firms to disinvest completely from the South African economy.

Although Sir Ronald Harris had initiated the move to open the Commissioners' books, he had retired by the time it became a reality. In his place was Sir Douglas Lovelock, who was far less interested in Synod business or its concerns, and it was to Lovelock that the Bishop of Birmingham, the Rt Revd Hugh Montefiore, as chairman of the Board of Social Responsibility, and the Bishop of Guildford, the Rt Revd John Gladwin, the Board's secretary, had the hapless task of calling, on the instructions of the Synod, to seek the Commissioners' support for 'progressive disengagement' from the South African economy.

Montefiore found it a depressing and fruitless business. 'Lovelock just didn't listen. He always came out with the same story, that he couldn't accept the Synod's ruling ... because it would have meant divesting from multi-nationals which, he said, had very small interests in South Africa. I saw him year after year to present the Synod's case ... but it was to no avail.'

With the growth of multi-national corporations, the Commissioners began to claim two further reasons to justify their 'minimal' investments in companies with South African interests: to withdraw from all companies with South African interests – in the UK alone their investments were spread over 65 major companies – would restrict investments to a degree that would significantly affect income, and possibly put the Commissioners in breach of their legal duty to maximize income; it would also, they argued, threaten the employment of black workers. It was for the latter reason that at one time Montefiore himself had not approved of total disinvestment – although he 'very honourably' put Synod's argument to Lovelock – until he heard Archbishop Desmond Tutu, then a bishop, give it his support.

Whatever diligence the Commissioners claimed to deploy in monitoring their investments, doubts persisted among some in the Synod who had developed an inherent mistrust of all the Commissioners said or did. One of the Commissioners' more persistent and vociferous critics was Frank Field, an Anglo-Catholic churchman and a co-opted member of Synod in 1985. As Labour MP for Birkenhead, Field, of course, would be enjoying a few years later the chairmanship of the House of Commons' Social Security Committee appointed to quiz Lovelock and others on the Commissioners' investment policies. Lovelock's imperious and disdainful manner intensely infuriated Field, who would gladly seize every opportunity to challenge the First Church Estates Commissioner's high office.

Two years after the Commissioners' decision to make public their portfolios, Field decided to put to the test the Commissioners' statement on ethical investment guidelines. He examined a report by the Department of Trade, who were monitoring companies with interests in South Africa, and discovered that 44 companies, who had substantial interests in South Africa and in whom the Commissioners had shares totalling more than £50m, had failed in part or whole to respond to the EEC Code of Conduct. Two companies, Trusthouse Forte and Sun Alliance, had 'consistently refused' to do so, while 18, including General Accident, Shell and Midland Bank, had failed to give direct answers to part or all of the code's question on collective bargaining and the freedom to join a trade union; 17 companies, including Tarmac, Scapa, and Norcros, had failed to pay black South African employees above the minimum recommended level; three companies had failed to commit themselves in principle to equal pay and job opportunities; 20 companies failed to provide details to show that training schemes encouraged the advancement of black employees; and three firms had failed to publish company policy on recruitment of white employees from outside South Africa.

The findings, based on a survey carried out by Field himself of returns from the companies over a two-year period, from 1983 to 1985, also revealed that the number of black employees paid below the minimum recommended wage level had actually increased at one company from four to 32. There was 'little evidence', claimed Field, 'of any pressure by the Commissioners to improve performance or the quality of information'. His findings certainly seemed to ridicule the Commissioners' defence of their investments, that their involvement in such companies ensured they adopted 'enlightened employment policies'. They also seriously undermined the Commissioners' claim that they did not invest in companies which had a 'significant stake' in South Africa.

Field referred the results of his survey in a letter to the Archbishop of Canterbury, Dr Robert Runcie, urging him to ask the Commissioners to approach the 'offending' companies and use their influence to persuade them to co-operate more fully in supplying relevant information to the EEC. 'The defence for investing in companies operating in South Africa is that these companies should make the running in a policy which disengages from apartheid. Crucial to such a move is the implementation of the EEC Code.'⁴

Unsurprisingly to Field, nothing came of his letter to Runcie. He believed that both the political structure of the Church of England and the authority of the Assets Committee which was a central part of its fabric, would ensure his protests came to naught. 'It was the old boys' network,' said Field. 'They kept their snouts out of each other's troughs.' The Commissioners not only continued to invest in the companies cited by Field, but the following year, in 1986, actually increased their shareholding in Shell from £17.73m to £24.71m.

Lovelock and his colleagues on the Assets Committee dismissed such efforts by the likes of Field as tiresome headline-grabbing tactics. One of the more outspoken members, David Hopkinson, believed they were seen as fair game for people who resented their independence. 'The Commissioners did a lot of good things. They were in the ethics of investments ... long before anybody else, and whether they did it right or wrong, they did try.'

Their critics had no understanding of the complexities of huge investments, whether in property or shares. 'You must not emblazon abroad what you are doing, because the market moves against you when you are the size of the Church Commissioners. The Church simply doesn't understand that. They find it difficult to run the accounts of a church and understand them ... let alone £2.5 billion of assets. You must not underestimate the effect of the fact that everybody bitches about the Church Commissioners incessantly. No matter what they do, it is always wrong.'

Certainly Lovelock remained outwardly unmoved by his adversaries. He saw the Commissioners' income from their shares portfolio rising year on year – by 1986, it had increased to almost £45m, an increase of more than 17 per cent over the previous year; and their total income was up by £6.5m to £100m. He was well pleased that the profit line showed that he and his colleagues were fulfilling what they saw as their role of investing assets to maximize profits in the interests of clergy stipends and pensions. 'These people were no doubt sincere in what they saw as their duty as members of the Church,' said Lovelock, 'but we were equally sure of our duty, which was to do all in our power to get the best possible returns from our assets in the interests of the clergy, past and present.'

The division with Synod, and the wider Church, over the issue of South Africa reached a more ominous depth when two senior churchmen, exasperated by Lovelock's constant reference to the Commissioners' duty in law whenever the matter was raised at the Synod, decided to seek legal opinion. They were the Very Revd Alan Webster, the Dean of St Paul's, and the Revd William Whiffen, a member of the General Synod and a parish priest in Milton Keynes, Buckinghamshire, who had worked with the Missionary Society in London, and for seven years as treasurer to the United Church of Southern India in North Kerala. Webster was also a member of the Board of Governors and a Commissioner and had used the influence of his position, informally but unsuccessfully, to bring about a change of heart within the Commissioners' ranks.

They went to law in December 1986. The seed of that decision came out of a resolution at the July session of the Synod following a major debate of a motion by the Bishop of Coventry, the Rt Revd Simon Barrington-Ward, which requested 'banking and financial institutions, trans-national corporations, and all bodies with significant links in South Africa, to take whatever steps are in their power – including acts of disengagement – to increase the pressure on that economy, and [urges] the Church's financial bodies to give a clear lead in this direction.' The 'financial bodies' referred to the Central Board of Finance, of which the First Church Estates Commissioner was also chairman, as well as the Church Commissioners.

Whiffen, Webster and their allies thought the resolution, which had the support of the Commissioners, was fine, as far as it went. But they believed it offered the Commissioners a get-out clause: they would continue to argue that it was not in their power to end their investments in such companies because it would be contrary to their legal duty to maximize profits. Whiffen responded by tabling a private member's motion for the November session of Synod. It urged the Synod to call on the Church Commissioners and the CBF to cease immediately all investments in companies with 'significant or substantial' interests in South Africa. The motion was also critical of the Commissioners' 'progressive disengagement' policy for not allegedly being in line with that envisaged by the Synod resolution of 1982. In introducing his motion Whiffen claimed that the combination with 'constructive engagement' was 'neither hot nor cold and deserved to be spat out of the mouth, like the church in Laodicea'. They had also failed to give a 'clear lead' in disengaging from the South African economy, in accordance with the Synod resolution that July.

But, doubtful that the Synod would support such a tough line, Webster tabled an amendment which requested the Commissioners to disinvest from all companies with interests in South Africa who employed more than 5,000 people, a restriction that would, it was calculated, disbar the multi-nationals with interests in South Africa.

The case of Whiffen and the anti-apartheid faction turned on whether the Commissioners were a charity, which the Commissioners in their annual reports acknowledged they were, or a pension fund. It was considered crucial in deciding where the Commissioners' primary duty lay. The Commissioners had stated in their 1985 annual report (p. 8) that, according to a recent legal ruling on those responsible for the management of charitable funds, financial considerations must be the major factor in all investment matters.

But Whiffen argued that that ruling was based on a pension fund case – Cowan vs Scargill[5] – when the former NUM leader unsuccessfully claimed that the trustees of the miners' pension fund were wrong to invest in the development of gas-fired power stations rather than coal-fired stations, even though, in the opinion of the trustees, it maximized pension fund profits. That ruling, said Whiffen, made it clear that in a non-charitable trust, such as a pension fund, the primary concern was for the beneficiaries. But in a charitable trust, such as that managed by the Commissioners, the primary purpose was quite different.

'In a charitable trust, it is for charitable purposes,' he told the Synod. 'What the Commissioners seem to forget are the terms of their foundation statute of 1840. Their purposes are not only to provide finance for the cure of souls "but to do it in such a manner as shall be deemed most conducive to the efficiency of the established church".' Even if this was interpreted, as it was by the Commissioners, 'to secure better provision for the maintenance of the parochial ministry' – as the Ecclesiastical Commissioners Act of 1840 also stipulated – the point was the same, claimed Whiffen.

'The clergy as such are not the beneficiaries of the Commissioners.

The work of the Gospel, the cure of souls, the efficiency of the Church are the charitable purposes of all that the Commissioners do. That means that social and ethical considerations, which I might call Gospel considerations, must come first.'

Lovelock responded by claiming that since the July resolution the Commissioners had pulled out of another large company – the third that year – because its profits from South Africa were considered to be too large. He emphasized that one 200th part of the Commissioners' income came indirectly from South Africa – 'It has fallen further, and I am in no doubt that it will continue to fall' – but added that Whiffen's motion would mean selling immediately half of their equities. As with Webster's amendment – to disengage from all companies with South African interests employing more than 5,000 people, which would mean withdrawing from nine companies – the result would 'seriously unbalance' the Commissioners' portfolio

> and harm our beneficiaries ... and make us more vulnerable to swings in the economy. I do not need to apologize for our concerns about this. Our money helps the Church's work and witness. More and more we are like a pension fund. Pensions are a first charge on our income, and the Church's pensioners are just as entitled to capital protection as other pensioners from other schemes.

He challenged a legal opinion which believed that the charitable objectives of the Commissioners were for 'the advancement of Christianity by and through the Church of England'. Everything flowed from that. 'But this is wrong,' insisted Lovelock

> Our statute requires us to augment the remuneration of the parochial clergy. Of course we want to advance Christianity, and I hope and believe that we do; but that is not the actual role laid upon us by our statute. If anyone doubts me – and I have the opinions of many legal advisers, stretching over years and including those we have today – let him ask himself this question: if our function is to advance Christianity through the Church of England, if we are free to do anything that comes under that heading, why in an hour's time am I going to commend to the

Synod a new Measure enabling us to do what we cannot do now, namely, to contribute to the Church Urban Fund?

He said the law was there to safeguard the funds of parochial church councils who had entrusted them to the Central Board of Finance, 'so that churches may be kept in good repair for years to come'; it was to 'protect pensioners who may live for 30 years, widows not yet widowed, and dependants not yet orphaned. It is not just a question of income. It is safeguarding the capital base on which these pensions and other payments will be based. Even if there were no law on the subject at all, we would still have to do the best we could for our beneficiaries.'

Lovelock made it clear that even if the Synod supported Whiffen's motion and Webster's amendment, the Commissioners would not fall in line. 'I must say plainly that neither the law, nor the responsibilities which we believe ourselves to have, allow us to act in accordance with them. The July motion was accepted in good faith and it will be pursued. It would, in my view, be much better to allow this ringing endorsement of the Church's consensus view to remain on the record and not be overtaken by something else which could not unite us as the July motion did.'

The debate was adjourned until the Synod session the following February, when both the motion and amendment fell. In anticipation of their fate, and to save face, a much-diluted motion was agreed by Whiffen, and carried by 219 votes to 14. It welcomed 'such disinvestment as has been undertaken by the Church Commissioners and the Central Board of Finance; and urges both sides to pursue vigorously the policies – including progressive acts of disengagement to increase pressure on the South African economy – advocated in the resolution passed overwhelmingly by the Synod in July 1986.'

Whiffen and Webster were now determined to challenge Lovelock in law. It was legal opinion that Whiffen had quoted in presenting his private member's motion, and to which Lovelock had responded. A month later, Webster was responsible for a major discussion of the Commissioners' ethical investment policies by the Board of Governors, of which august body the Archbishop of Canterbury was chairman and Lovelock a member. It was a valiant but forlorn political exercise, which galvanized little support.

Two months later, Whiffen, Webster, who retired that year as Dean of St Paul's, and Elliot Kendal, a retired Methodist minister who was secretary of the Christian Concern for South Africa movement, went to Millbank for a meeting with Lovelock, Viscount Churchill, the Central Board of Finance's investments manager, and Patrick Locke, then deputy secretary to the Commissioners. The meeting had been requested by Whiffen and Webster, with one question on the agenda: would Lovelock agree to going 'hand in hand' to court to seek a judicial review of the Commissioners' legal obligations?

It was, once more, a forlorn exercise. Following his triumph at the Synod, which, in effect, supported the Commissioners' investment strategies, what had he to gain by going to court? Lovelock curtly declined. According to Whiffen, Lovelock said that if the issue went to court and the review, as he anticipated, went in their favour, it might actually compel the Commissioners, in accordance with their fiduciary duties, to invest in companies which hitherto they had voluntarily proscribed. It was seen by Whiffen and his colleagues as a veiled threat; this was their first and last meeting.

Although Whiffen and Webster were looking for the most harmonious *rapprochement*, there was another, more pragmatic, reason behind their approach to Lovelock. Lovelock's acquiescence to a joint application for a judicial review would have achieved their objective at a fraction of the costs. At that time they were being advised by Andrew Phillips, a senior partner in a City-based firm of Bates, Wells and Braithwaite, who was personally sympathetic to the anti-apartheid movement and ethical investment in general. He donated his services free of charge. But it had become a matter which required the services of legal heavyweights, which led to the engagement of Mr Timothy Lloyd QC, an expert in charity law, and barrister Christopher Heath, who specialized in ecclesiastical law. Although their costs were funded by a group linked to the South African liberation struggle, there was little money to spare.

It was the agreed opinion of Lloyd and Heath that the Commissioners' legal duties in supporting the clergy were only a means to the end of promoting Christianity throughout the Anglican Church, and that the maximizing of profit for the clergy was not the principal consideration of the Commissioners' responsibilities. Lloyd believed the trustees owed 'a duty of undivided loyalty to the charitable purposes which their trust are there to promote or achieve'. If the Commissioners were a charitable body, then he believed the case was clear that the overriding duty was 'to act in a way that is consistent with the charitable purpose; and to that end it may be necessary on occasions to accept less than the maximum financial return'.

The Commissioners' legal standard was carried by Owen Swingland QC, himself a Church Commissioner. It was his opinion that the Church Commissioners were bound by law to pursue an investments policy where financial considerations were paramount. He maintained that the Commissioners could take ethical considerations into account only inasmuch that they did not cause the Commissioners to sacrifice 'their general duty to make the best investments'. For the next two years, legal opinions were exchanged without relief to either argument.

At Phillips' suggestion, Whiffen and Webster decided in 1988 to form a body called the Christian Ethical Investment Group (CEIG) in order to give greater credibility to their campaign, which was attracting an increasing number of supporters, including some senior churchmen. Its official platform was the promotion of a stronger ethical investment policy in the Church of England, and one of its early members was the Rt Revd Richard Harries, who had been appointed Bishop of Oxford the previous year. Until then, as Dean of King's College, London, he had had a relatively low profile, known more as a theologically liberal thinker and a writer; but he was a passionate supporter of the anti-apartheid cause and a former president of the End Loans to South Africa movement.

He and Whiffen had met at a public meeting organized by Christian Concern for South Africa in 1986. On joining the CEIG, Harries soon became involved in the legal preamble with the Commissioners. By November 1988, he had become the group's public figurehead. Following yet another legal letter to Millbank, Lovelock's reply of that month went to Harries. It said that Owen Swingland 'does not think Mr Lloyd carries the matter any further and continues to think that our stated policy is right. The Board of Governors agreed.'

Harries and Whiffen claimed they did all they could during these days to reach 'an accommodation' with Lovelock and his colleagues over a judicial review, but to no avail. Their pursuit of actions less litigious were greatly frustrated, said Harries, by Lovelock's tactic of moving the goalposts whenever it suited his reply.

Sir Douglas Lovelock claimed on every issue of significance that the responsibility [of setting investments policy] belonged to the Assets Committee. But, in rugby terms, if you went for the ball with Lovelock, he would put it that

way to the Assets Committee, or that way to the Board of
Governors, depending on whatever served his argument.
So you could not in the end pin anybody down to anything, because at the centre was a single figure moving
things around as he wanted. That revealed a fundamental
lack of accountability that has been recognized by all these
reports [the Lambeth Report] ... that was why so many
of us were frustrated by the Church Commissioners: you
couldn't pin anybody down to anything.

The problem lay, he believed, with the Assets Committee's far-reaching autonomy enshrined in the Commissioners' constitution. They
were ultimately responsible to Parliament, 'but what does that mean?
It doesn't actually, in fact, mean very much. Then you've got the
Church Commissioners who are ... all the diocesan bishops, plus
some of the great and the good, like the Attorney General and so on
but they only meet once a year [for a] ... report and a lunch.'

Few of Harries' episcopal peers wished to be associated with the
new bishop's high-profile campaign, at least, not publicly, although
nine quietly supported the aims of the Christian Ethical Investment
Group. Equally, few were prepared to be so cynically dismissive as
the Bishop of Peterborough, the Rt Rev Bill Westwood, a rumbus-
tiously mordant character, who in 1985 was appointed to the Assets
Committee – he also that year became a member of the Board of
Governors – to advise on ethical matters.

He said: 'By and large, I had no sympathy for them. Well, I
thought that ... there's a great deal of fashion in social and moral
thinking   y'know, just like trousers   and really this was a bit of
the flavour of the month. I took the view, which a number in South
Africa held, that it really was better for us to invest in South Africa
and exercise an influence ... so that you were well involved [and]
you were therefore forced to train your staff, and you would have
brought a lot of improvement in the administrative business skills of
black Africans by being there.'

Yet, said Whiffen, this was not his privately held view. 'He was
quite sympathetic to what we were doing, and told us we were right.
I was quite surprised when I once saw him being interviewed on television and he was quite critical of what we were doing. In the end, it
seems he preferred the status quo.'

In March 1990, Harries called a press conference to announce legal action against the Church Commissioners. He was seeking, he said, a High Court ruling to ensure that the Church's equities portfolio – then worth £778m – was governed by Christian, not purely financial, considerations. Harries and his colleagues believed they had done all in their power to bring Lovelock to a different understanding, but, they insisted, he continued to choose to ignore the express wishes of the General Synod that the Commissioners should effectively disengage from South Africa. 'The Church Commissioners, in the form of Sir Douglas Lovelock, had made it quite clear that they weren't prepared to budge any further on that. In the end, we felt forced to take this action, because Douglas Lovelock during the whole time appealed to the law to justify his actions. We felt we had to test out the law.' It had been suggested that the matter be settled by arbitration, added Harries, 'but ... it was a matter of how the law was to be interpreted. We were interpreting the law differently and that had to be resolved in the courts.'

To Lovelock and the Assets Committee, of course, the law was clear, and had to be obeyed. 'It is the law,' he said. 'Are Christians allowed to say, "Yes, I'll obey this law because I agree with it, but not that one because I don't." To me, that's immoral. At the end of the day you can argue the ethical issues either way, but you come right up against charity law, and what I've found irritating, and I'm not easily irritated, actually, is that it is only the Church of England that is expected to [consider ethical investments].'

Harries stated at the press conference that, although South Africa was the spark, it was no longer the central issue. The collapse of apartheid had been, with the repeal of discriminatory laws, a process of disintegration throughout the eighties until, by now, it had largely ceased to exist. He was now looking for a radical 'review of the whole investment issue',[6] such as low-cost housing, and substantial investment in deprived inner-cities designated by the Church as Urban Priority Areas. But, privately, Harries admitted that if the Commissioners had backed down over South Africa, the court action wouldn't have taken place.

It may be that other issues may have emerged ... about how much should go into low-cost housing, how far environmental considerations should be taken into account, and so on. But certainly, on [South Africa], if they had been prepared to respond more wholeheartedly to what the Synod had called for, we would have been satisfied.

Harries took the opportunity at the press conference to launch a fighting fund to raise £25,000 for estimated legal costs, adding at the same time: 'This is a friendly, rather than hostile, action. We are seeking to co-operate with the Church Commissioners as much as possible. There is a genuine dilemma here and it's in the interests of the Church Commissioners that it is resolved.'[7] Lovelock could not be blamed for remaining unconvinced. 'I don't think you can have a friendly court action. It is a contradiction in terms,' he said.[8] He confirmed the Commissioners' robust resistance to the principle of the action. 'Our job is to protect and defend the parochial clergy. It is sad that we have to use the money which should be going to them to do so. But we cannot allow their interests to go by default.'

Until that time, Harries was considered by some as an evens-favourite candidate to succeed Dr Robert Runcie as Archbishop of Canterbury, who was due to retire the following January. Harries claimed to have no such ambitions, as the political consequences of his legal action probably confirmed. 'It was slightly amusing that when people were putting me on the list, this [legal] action was being taken,' he said. 'The fact of the matter is that I didn't want to be Archbishop of Canterbury – I think I am well suited to my present job and George Carey to his – but ... if I had wanted to be Archbishop of Canterbury, it would certainly have scuppered my chances.'

1. *The Times*, 29 July 1986.
2. *The Times*, 19 July 1982.
3. Church Commissioners, Annual Report and Accounts, 1983, p. 8.
4. *The Times*, 10 September 1985.
5. CH. 270, 1985. Judgement was given by Vice-Chairman Sir Robert Megarry.
6. *The Times*, 27 March 1990.
7. Ibid.
8. Ibid.

CHAPTER NINE

Questions in the House

Two months after the press conference, on 21 May, questions about the legal action were asked in the House of Commons of Michael Alison, Tory MP for Selby, North Yorks, and Second Church Estates Commissioner, the Commissioners' representative in Parliament, by Ian Gow, Tory MP for Eastbourne, who was killed several weeks later by an IRA car bomb, and Simon Hughes, Liberal Democrat MP for Southwark and Bermondsey, and a committed Christian.[1]

Having received from Alison a full explanation of the Commissioners' investment policy towards South Africa, Gow asked:

> Is it really the case that the Bishop of Oxford has it in mind to bring legal proceedings involving the Church Commissioners concerning the investment policy of the Church of England? Instead of indulging in absurd litigation of this kind, should not the bishop and the Church be engaged in the business saving the souls of the people, clothing the naked, feeding the hungry and healing the sick? Can my Right Hon. Friend assure the House that this mischievous bishop will not be considered for appointment to Canterbury?

Alison replied: 'It is not, alas, in my gift – even on this important occasion – to give a definitive answer to my Hon. Friend's final question.' But he could confirm that the Bishop of Oxford seemed intent on taking legal action against the Church of England which could only bring the Church into disrepute. 'The action is bound to be adversarial and will be perceived publicly as hostile. I hope that the Bishop of Oxford and his associates will decide to withdraw it.'

Hughes now stood to say that, while he could understand the motives of the Bishop of Oxford, he wished to be associated with the comments of Gow and Alison:

> The Bishop of Oxford's action seems to be a distraction from more important priorities. Will the Right Hon. Member for Selby urge the Church Commissioners to sustain their present policy of not investing in South Africa until and unless they are advised by the Christian churches in South Africa to change that policy? [The South African Council of Churches had, in fact, made this request some nine years earlier.] Will they above all not be over-hasty in a decision to change their policy under pressure from the Government or anyone else, but rather lead and advise the Government as to what their policy should be in the interests of the souls as well as the bodies of people in South Africa?

Alison replied: 'I repeat that the Church Commissioners do not invest directly in South Africa. The complexity of disentangling even that residual investment, which is associated with some of the largest household names in British industry, would be considerably detrimental for the clergy and pensioners whom we have to support. We could not wait an imprimatur of approval from the churches in South Africa to consider changes in that large overall investment.'

Meanwhile, Harries believed he was the victim of a 'dirty tricks' campaign at Millbank. He alleged that Lovelock made a public issue over the costs of the legal action. 'I think Douglas Lovelock wanted to distract the Church's attention from the poor performance of the Church Commissioners by focusing on the issue of costs. They employed the most expensive lawyers to defend their case instead of going to their normal lawyers, and he wanted to turn public opinion against me by the idea that I was really wasting the Church's money on something which could have been resolved in another way.'

There was another 'dirty trick' which Harries claimed. He also received a letter from Dr Robert Runcie asking him to call off his legal action. The then Archbishop of Canterbury, he said, was in 'a difficult position as Chairman of the Church Commissioners ... and pressure was put on him to write to me an official letter asking me to withdraw, which, of course, he had to do in his official capacity as chairman.' But Runcie, 'a good friend then and now ... rang me up to say that it was coming.' He claimed: 'The pressure to write the letter was put on Runcie by Sir Douglas Lovelock,' adding that it was leaked to the media before he had received it. It was all part of 'a very carefully orchestrated campaign to prejudice church opinion against me and the action'.[2]

Lovelock at first denied playing any part in the letter or having any prior knowledge of its existence, but, in a subsequent interview, said: 'I didn't make any actual request for [the Archbishop of Canterbury] to [write the letter]. He and I had occasional meetings ... That subject came up and I probably said something like, "This is taking up an inordinate amount of my time and it will damage the Church whoever wins the case, and I really think it is a great pity." I don't remember ... whether I said to him, "Perhaps if you asked him not to proceed", or whether he said, "Would it be a good idea if I asked him not to proceed" ... Nor do I have the slightest sense of guilt about it. It was the right thing to do. That the Bishop of Oxford didn't see it that way is a matter for him.'

Harries declined Runcie's suggestion that, in the greater interests of the Church of England, the action should be withdrawn. During a BBC radio interview two days after the story appeared in the national media, Harries said: 'I am going to tell him I think the Church ought to give a much clearer lead in this area. Ethical investment ... is an idea whose time has come. Investment can be, and should be, an instrument of the Gospel.'[3] While lawyers for the two sides were preparing for the High Court, Harries was successfully urging members of the Oxford Diocesan Synod to support a motion calling for the withdrawal of its funds of £2m from the Central Board of Finance, in protest at its investment links with South Africa. The diocese's ethical criteria opposed investments in companies which employed more than 1,000 workers in South Africa or had an annual turnover in South Africa of more than £100m, or derived more than £10m in annual profits, or more than 3 per cent of their world-wide profits from South African interests. It was agreed that the money would be transferred to the Amity Fund managed by the Ecclesiastical Insurance Group. Despite a strict ethical investments code, it had reportedly outperformed the CBF by a considerable margin.

The Amity Fund's performance at that time, following its launch in March 1988, strengthened the argument of Harries and the CEIG that ethical investments did not mean lower profits – investment returns in just over two years had gone up by 31 per cent, compared to a 27 per cent rise in the All Share Index.[4] They might also have been bolstered by ethical investment research data at that time which showed that, in the UK, £69bn of pension fund money had been invested avoiding companies with South African interests; in America, the figure was $300bn in public and private funds.[5]

At about this time, Lovelock and the Assets Committee were also facing a heavy broadside from another quarter, which came in a critical report, *Faith in the Countryside*, published in mid-1990 by the Archbishop's Commission on Rural Areas (ACORA). It was a report gestated with some difficulty, not least through suspicions that its draft had been leaked to the media through Millbank to scupper a principal recommendation that the Commissioners be abolished and their duties devolved to the dioceses. It caused great anger within the commission, which was chaired by Lord Prior, the then chairman of GEC, formerly Jim Prior and, successively, secretary of state for unemployment and Northern Ireland under Margaret Thatcher.

ACORA had been set up two years earlier with a brief to examine 'the effects of economic, environmental and social change on the rural community', the changing role of the Church in the countryside, and 'the theological factors which bear upon the mission and ministry of the Church in rural areas'. It aimed to complement the Archbishop's commission on urban priority areas, whose report, *Faith in the City*, attracted considerable media attention when published in December 1985.

Among its principal recommendations was that bishops on the Board of Governors and the Church Commissioners should form a small group to examine the moral and ethical implications of investments and, following a debate in Synod, make recommendations to the Board. It also proposed that the Commissioners should include in their annual report an account of how their activities reflected the recommendations. Apart from its own ethical investment guidelines, added the report, the Assets Committee had no framework to relate their investment decisions to the mission of the Church.

The report was critical of the Commissioners' attitude towards more environmentally favourable farming practices, land sale and development, and rural welfare policies because of their adverse effect on income.[6] Their policy of selling development land at maximum profits irrespective of local feelings, it stated, often portrayed the Church of England as 'rich, grasping and unheeding of local views'. It was also critical of the 'very great gap' which existed between the parishes and the central administration, which had worsened over the previous 20 years. 'The Commission feels that the serious division between the administrative centres of the Church and its local operating arms, the parishes, is sufficiently serious for it to be adversely affecting morale and leading to confusion of objectives. We regard the building of morale as crucial.'[7]

The solution was a recommendation that, if morale was to be rebuilt and the challenge of the Church's mission met, it was 'very important' that as many decisions as possible were taken at diocesan or parish level, 'and we also believe that there are a number of aspects of the Church Commissioners' work which might be devolved to the dioceses'.[8] It further recommended that the Archbishop of Canterbury set up an inquiry not later than 1992 to establish to what extent this could be done. Like the Commission's recommendation that a group be formed to examine the moral and ethical implications of investments, Runcie, shortly to make way for Dr George Carey, declined to pursue it.

But the recommendation that some of the Commissioners' work should be taken over by the dioceses concealed the real wishes of the commission members. The draft recommendation had been, in effect, that the Commissioners should be abolished altogether, and their £2.4bn-worth of assets equitably shared amongst the 43 dioceses, each responsible for the management of stipends, pensions and housing. 'The recommendation was a recognition that at parish level people ... are capable of managing their affairs,' said the Revd Jeremy Martineau, joint secretary to ACORA, and who, on its recommendation, was later appointed the Church's National Rural Officer. 'We believed it was the feeling of the age ... and we wanted to push the responsibility down to where it was really understood.'

A confidential copy of the first draft was sent to Lovelock at Millbank in early May 1990 for the Commissioners' factual comment. On 13 May, under the headline, 'Church faces big shake-up', a story based on the draft appeared in the *Sunday Times*. It quoted a comment from Humphrey Norrington, a director of Barclays Bank, and a member of ACORA: 'We want to apply good business management principles to the church ... the aims of the Church Commissioners are in conflict with local aims. The Commissioners are run very coldly and distantly.' The leak incensed Lord Prior, who, with joint secretary Ewan Harper, the author of the report, considered an investigation to discover who had been responsible. Said Harper: 'We decided in the end that setting up our own investigation wouldn't necessarily create any benefits and would destroy the very good morale within the commission.'

But the leak led to the commission being 'forced to tone down and re-write that section of the draft,' said Martineau. 'I don't know where the pressure came from ... But I know why – it was because whoever leaked it did not like some of the recommendations we were devising and wanted to scupper them, which he succeeded in doing.'

There was some suspicion that a member of the commission itself was responsible for the leak. Lovelock strenuously denied that Millbank was involved. 'That's rubbish! ... My experience of many leaks in Whitehall and elsewhere is that you seldom know who was responsible ... with great courtesy and quite correctly, the ACORA secretariat gave us the opportunity to make a factual comment on a kind of summary of all their recommendations. Someone at that stage thought it sensible to leak it. It certainly wasn't me. I haven't the faintest idea who it was.'

Harries began his legal challenge before Vice-Chancellor Sir Donald Nicholls in the Chancery Division of the High Court on 7 October 1991. He was formally accompanied as co-plaintiffs by the Revd William Whiffen, now an honorary Canon – 'in case the bishop dropped dead or was appointed Archbishop of Canterbury', said Whiffen – and by the Archdeacon of Bedford, the Ven. Michael Bourke, who had become the chairman of the Christian Ethical Investment Group the previous year.

During the hearing, Mr Timothy Lloyd QC, presenting the well-aired argument of the Bishop and his co-plaintiffs, said they disagreed with the Commissioners' belief that they had a duty to get the best possible financial return from their investments in order to support the Church's work. 'There are circumstances in which that duty has to give way to considerations derived from Christian morality. To invest funds in a particular type of business or to manage their assets in a particular way would be incompatible with the purpose of promoting the Christian faith through the Church of England.'

While, he agreed, the Commissioners already took ethical considerations into account to a certain extent, their policy meant that they would avoid shares seen as morally unsatisfactory only if they could find other, equally rewarding, shares to buy as an alternative. It did not reflect wider moral concerns. The Commissioners' interpretation of the law meant that the only company in which they could not legally invest would be one committed to destroying the Church of England or one that promoted atheism. Lloyd said the court was not being asked to rule whether the Commissioners' investment policy was incompatible with promoting the Christian religion, but whether they were mistaken in their belief that the law prevented them giving weight to ethical concerns.[9]

For the Commissioners, Mr Robert Walker QC, argued that the Commissioners would be acting 'fecklessly' if they followed Christ's cautionary words in the Sermon on the Mount about not storing up treasures on earth. 'It might be a sign of outstanding sanctity in an individual but it would be neither permissible nor admirable in people in the position of stewards responsible for the stipends, pensions and housing of present and future generations of Church of England clergy.' As a further example of 'Christian fecklessness', he read the words of Jesus from St Matthew's Gospel:

Consider how the lilies grow in the fields; they do not work, they do not spin; and yet, I tell you, even Solomon in all his splendour was not attired like one of these. Set your mind on God's kingdom and his justice before everything else, and all the rest will come to you as well. So do not be anxious about tomorrow; tomorrow will look after itself.

Such advice, he said, was of no value to the Church Commissioners, who were trying to manage investments to support the Church into the 21st century and beyond. He also quoted the biblical warning: 'You cannot serve God and Mammon', comparing the Commissioners with the Army Catering Corps which like the fighting regiments, had the duty of vanquishing the Queen's enemies, but did so by supporting the rest of the army. He concluded: 'It may be said that the Commissioners' investment policies already go too far in ethical discrimination.'[10]

On 25 October 1991, Sir Donald Nicholls issued a written judgement in favour of the Church Commissioners. He could not, he said, give the declarations the plaintiffs were looking for: that the Commissioners 'are obliged to have regard to the object of promoting the Christian faith through the established Church of England' and that, secondly, 'in the exercise of those functions, the ... Assets Committee may not act in a manner which would be incompatible with that object'. The fundamental difficulty he had in making these declarations was their ambiguity:

> ... the object which the financial payments made by the Commissioners seek to achieve is the promotion of the Christian faith through the established Church of England ... And it is clear that in managing their investments, the Commissioners do have regard to that object. That is shown by their ethical investments policy. Thus, there is no need for the court to make the first declaration. But the matter goes further. The first declaration is not merely unnecessary. 'Have regard to the object' is a loose phrase, and there is a real danger it will mean all things to all men. Such a declaration should not be made.

Neither, he said, would he make the second declaration:

> The phrase I have used when considering the position of charity trustees is 'conflict with' ... even if this change were made to the wording of the second declaration, I do not think such a declaration would be of assistance to the Commissioners. In particular, it would not deal with how the Commissioners should proceed when confronted with

differing views on whether, on moral grounds, a proper investment is in conflict with the objects the Commissioners are seeking to promote.

Earlier in his judgement, Nicholls had said that when property was held by charity trustees to generate money, the purpose of the trust was best served by the trustees seeking to obtain the maximum return consistent with commercial prudence. In most cases, investments should be made solely on the basis of well-established investment criteria, and for the single purpose of generating money.

Trustees couldn't properly use assets held for investment for non-investment purposes, although they were not prevented from acting as responsible landlords or responsible shareholders; but they must not use their assets to make moral statements at the expense of the charity's income. Trustees 'should not make investment decisions on the basis of preferring one view of whether on moral grounds an investment conflicts with objects of the charity over another' unless there was no risk of significant financial detriment.

The Commissioners' objects as trustees were incorporated in the legal statutes of their predecessors, Queen Anne's Bounty and the Ecclesiastical Commissioners. The revenues of the Bounty were to be used 'for the augmentation of the maintenance of ... parsons, vicars, curates and ministers ...' while the revenues of the Ecclesiastical Commissioners were 'for the cure of souls in parishes where such assistance is most required, in such manner as shall ... be deemed most conducive to the efficiency of the established church', which, in context, 'must mean making financial provision for those who have the cure of souls'.

The heart of the plaintiffs' case was a contention that the Commissioners' policy was erroneous in law in that they were only prepared to take non-financial considerations into account as long as they did not significantly jeopardize accepted investment principles. It was implicit in the Commissioners' evidence that they did regard themselves as constrained in this way, and such constraint had led to no error of law on their part.

He referred to the Diocese of Oxford's investment policy, which, although far more restrictive than the Commissioners' ethical investment guidelines, did not seek to exclude every company which had a South African business connection. Between two such alternatives there could be no right or wrong answer. It was 'a question of degree'.

Another moral question was raised by the sale of land at below open-market value for low-cost housing, and the suggestion that to invest instead in an expensive housing development with a higher rate of return would undermine the credibility of the Christian message by the affront it would cause to needs of local people unable to afford such housing. Said Nicholls, 'The Commissioners are not a housing charity.' They were right to contend that 'local housing needs are, or should be, reflected in local planning policies. When planning permission is available for a particular type of development, it is not a proper function for the Commissioners to sell their land at an under-value in order to further a social objective on which the local planning authority has taken a different view.'

Nicholls ruled that each side would pay their own costs, which totalled £200,000. It meant, said Lovelock in passing the blame to the Commissioners' opponents, that their bill of £100,000 would come out of money allocated for clergy stipends, which would mean about £9 less for every serving clergyman in the country. Mr Andrew Phillips, the solicitor for Harries, Bourke and Whiffen, said his firm and the barristers it briefed would not take fees beyond the £30,000 raised by the bishop's supporters.

In a statement issued after the hearing, Lovelock said that the Vice-Chancellor's decision had 'totally upheld the policy we have followed for so long. Of course, we accept that the bishop acted from the very highest of motives.' Nicholls' decision left Harries 'very disappointed'. He said: 'We wouldn't have gone to law unless we thought we had a very good chance of winning. We didn't do it as a theatrical gesture.'

Lovelock received Nicholls' judgement with great relief. He believed that once and for all the matter of the Commissioners' ethical investments policy had been settled and this henbane that had taken such firm root in the business of Millbank and the Synod was no more.

In his words, it had been almost a decade of 'deep frustration, because the same issue would come back and come back and come back … One had to say the same thing again and again and again. There was no mechanism for final settlement, so things simply went on.' The South Africa apartheid issue was, he said, 'the most time-consuming single thing I ever did. It was totally unwanted, totally unnecessary, utterly futile and very expensive.'

Three months after the High Court hearing, the Ethical Investment Research Service, a London-based organization founded in 1983 by the British Council of Churches and Christian Concern for South Africa and which monitors the Stock Exchange to provide information on ethical investments, published a report on the Commissioners' shares portfolio.[11] Based on accounts to December 1990, it revealed that in addition to maintaining throughout the eighties considerable shareholdings in British companies with major investments in South Africa – British Petroleum (£20.2m); Shell (£21m); and Unilever (£16m) – they also had £6m in ICI subsidiary, Nobel Explosives, which made warheads; £3.25m in Tomkins, which owned gunmakers Smith and Wesson; and £8m in Hanson, which owned cigarette makers Imperial Tobacco.

The report also stated that nearly two-thirds of the Commissioners' investments were in companies with subsidiaries in one or more of 35 countries listed by Amnesty International as having oppressive regimes; more than a third of the firms had been prosecuted for water pollution, 41 per cent for using tropical hardwoods, and 44 per cent for selling products damaging to the ozone layer.

While Sir Donald Nicholls' judgement brought an end to legal hostilities, Lovelock was mistaken if he thought he would hear no more of Harries and company. Soon after Nicholls' judgement was made public, Harries announced that he intended to put another ethical investments motion before the General Synod.[12] He and his Christian Ethical Investment Group colleagues insisted that the judgement did not go far enough in defining the ethical responsibilities of charity trustees. As a result, a private members' motion was tabled, not by Harries but co-plaintiff Michael Bourke, which called for 'a stronger and clearer ethical investment policy', as had been proposed in *Faith in the Countryside*. It also requested the Board of Governors and the Central Board of Finance to draw up 'practical guidelines ... [and] identify any legislative changes which may be needed'.

However, in 1993, Bourke was appointed Bishop of Wolverhampton, severing all ties with the CEIG and its aims, and the motion fell. In his place emerged the Revd Canon Hugh Wilcox, a vicar from Ware, Hertfordshire, a recent recruit to the group and a former assistant general secretary of the British Council of Churches, who, in the same year, was appointed a Church Commissioner, and, in 1994, clerical alternate to the Assets Committee.

Wilcox's motion was carried overwhelmingly at the General Synod in July 1995, although it was effectively pre-empted eight months earlier when the setting up of an ethical investment working group chaired by Lovelock's successor, Sir Michael Colman, was announced by the Commissioners 'in response to the growing interest in, and complexity of, ethical issues' to provide 'an important resource to the central Church investing bodies in order that they can, with integrity, continue to produce good financial returns for the benefit of the Church'.[13] But the timing of the news allowed Harries and his colleagues to add what they saw as a most important amendment to the motion, effectively one of the recommendations of *Faith in the Countryside*. It was that the working group should submit annually a detailing report on its activities to the Synod.

It was seen as a major step in ensuring a strong synodical grip on the Assets Committee's property and Stock Exchange portfolios. 'It is the first time that the ethics of the Commissioners have got to be reported to the Synod in detail,' said Whiffen. 'They could see [the private members' motion] was coming to the top of the list and I think one can be fairly certain in saying that the Ethical Investment Working Group came about as a result of the pressure of the motion.' Wilcox, now vice-Chairman of the CEIG, was appointed to the working group in 1995.

The CEIG claimed another considerable advance for the biblical basis of their work when the General Synod the following February overwhelmingly supported a private members' motion endorsing the aims of Jubilee 2000, a new charity campaigning to lift the massive economic burden of unpayable debt from the world's poorest countries. It also urged the Archbishop's Advisory Committee on the Millennium to include their aims in its proposals, and the Board for Social Responsibility and diocesan development representatives to 'develop appropriate responses'. The motion came from CEIG member David Webster, a retired financial journalist who was appointed a Church Commissioner and a member of the Board of Governors in January 1996. 'This motion was all about, in effect, ethical banking, and wouldn't have seen the light of day at one time,' said Whiffen.

And in June 1996, Harries became poacher-turned-gamekeeper when he was appointed Chairman of the Synod's Board for Social Responsibility, which oversees social, industrial and economic affairs; international and development affairs; home affairs; and race and community relations. The appointment was seen as part of a 'bridge-repairing' exercise with the ethical investment faction which was begun shortly after Colman's appointment. Behind the initiative was Colman himself, who travelled to Oxford for 'a warm and productive' meeting with the bishop. Said one of the bishop's associates: 'At one time, the bishop certainly wouldn't have been invited. He was considered too far from the establishment.'

Such developments confirmed that a sea-change had taken place in the attitude of the Church at large towards the issue of ethical investments, and, most tellingly, within Millbank itself; for all that, Whiffen believed there was little sign that the Commissioners accepted that a major overhaul of investment policy was needed. 'The tenet that the Commissioners intend to serve both God and Mammon, which was stated during the High Court action, is still their basic policy. We have to realize that for a Christian, and indeed for the Church, responsible shareholding, which includes both ethical investment and shareholder action where necessary, is an essential part of the mission of the Church. There is no other way for the power and grace of Christ to influence the whole Western capitalist market economy.'

1. *Hansard*, Oral Answers, 21 May 1990, p. 14.
2. Recorded author interview with Rt Rev Richard Harries, Bishop of Oxford, 17 March 1994.
3. *The Guardian*, 18 June 1990.
4. 'Money Mail', *Daily Mail*, 20 June 1990.
5. Ethical Investment Research Service, *The Ethical Investor*, November 1993.
6. Archbishop's Commission on Rural Areas, *Faith in the City*, 1990, 12.43.
7. Ibid., 12.51.
8. Ibid., 12.53–4.
9. *Daily Telegraph*, 8 October 1991.
10. *Daily Telegraph*, 10 October 1991.
11. *Sunday Express*, 5 January 1992.
12. *Daily Telegraph*, 26 October 1991.
13. Ethical Investment Working Group, First report to General Synod, GS Misc 483.

CHAPTER TEN

Downfall

By 1990, the borrowings incurred by the once prudent Commissioners were almost £520m. The Commissioners had begun very modest borrowing, in a way which placed no strain on their income, as early as 1980, but a massive increase in borrowing was seen by the Assets Committee and Jim Shelley as the Commissioners' only recourse following a protracted dispute with the National Audit Office (NAO), their auditors since 1948, over their accounting practices.

In order to achieve their property investment ambitions, the Assets Committee had needed to overcome two obstacles. First, they had to ensure that their tax-free status as a charitable body, which prohibited them from becoming directly involved in property activities, was protected; second, they needed a way of investing millions of pounds in property developments while receiving an income during construction and letting to cover the costs of clergy stipends, pensions and other obligations.

Both obstacles had been overcome through the device of creating wholly-owned subsidiaries to whom they loaned the necessary funding to meet their share of costs. The interest on such loans was then treated as income to use for distribution. At the same time, the development company would capitalize the interest as any other cost which would be recovered when the development project was eventually sold.

The strategy of wholly-owned subsidiary companies had principally been used in office development and the US market. By 1990, the Commissioners had no less than 17 subsidiary companies, with three holding companies in America, who, in turn, had 17 subsidiary companies. Through these subsidiaries, the Commissioners became funder, developer, and, later, speculator, while remaining within charity laws. But capitalizing interest and treating it as income was a misleading practice which artificially inflated the Commissioners' income at the expense of their capital base.

More seriously, the Commissioners, faced with the need to increase income further still to meet rising expenditure, had introduced a variation to the ruse by paying subsidiary companies for project management services which they hadn't performed. Indeed, the subsidiary companies were merely shell companies and lacked both the staff and resources to carry out such services; these would be carried out by the Commissioners' own staff. Nevertheless, the subsidiary company would pay a 'dividend' to the Commissioners equal to the bogus fees, and this was then recorded in their books as gross rental income. The Commissioners thus had another way of increasing their 'income' by millions of pounds.

To calculate even approximately how much the Commissioners generated in this way is not possible – Millbank declined to reveal the figure – but it was widespread between 1984 and 1986 and fees paid to one of the Commissioners' subsidiary companies during the course of a year, and subsequently returned to the Commissioners as a 'dividend', totalled £3.2m. The company in question was CC Projects Ltd whose dealings with the Commissioners were a matter of concern in May 1987 to the National Audit Office. In a letter dated 13 May to E. S. Young, Director of the Home Affairs Division of the NAO, Shelley described the transaction as 'a simple commercial one'; this, in a reply dated 14 May, Young rebuffed as an over-simplification in 'both the nature and intention'. The essential reason for the transaction, said Young, appeared to be to provide a device to translate a proportion of the Commissioners' capital funds into revenue 'to meet current needs'.

He added that as the Commissioners' auditor, the NAO was primarily concerned with the extent to which such transactions could be properly regarded as falling within the provisions and intention of the 1947 Church Commissioners Measure. They were clearly material in amount, particularly since the £3.2m turned a possible deficit in 1986 into a declared surplus on the General Fund account. Young was also concerned that the bogus fees had not been recorded by the Assets Committee. While he understood the Committee had given its approval, there was no documentation or minutes recording their assent; this cast into doubt the extent to which the Commissioners had approved the decision.

The directors of CC Projects Ltd, and other similar companies, were none other than Michael Hutchings and Jim Shelley. 'Jim and I got paid the most amazing fees,' said Hutchings, 'which we then covenanted back to the Church. All we were trying to do was to ensure that there was some income received during the development stage.' Like the practice of capitalizing the interest on loans to their subsidiary companies, it was done to achieve a smooth income flow. 'I'd always had it hammered in to me that development is difficult for the Church because you can't have these spells where you have two years, let's say, when nothing is generated, and then you have an absolute bonanza in year three.'

The scheme had been devised, said Hutchings, in response to the NAO's objections to the Commissioners' counting interest on loans to subsidiary companies as income. Both schemes embarked upon by the Commissioners were undertaken with the approval of Coopers & Lybrand, who had, said Hutchings, been involved in 'every single scheme that was ever devised'.

Sir Michael Colman, then Chairman of Reckitt & Colman plc, the £2bn-a-year manufacturers of pharmaceutical, household and toiletry products, who succeeded Lovelock as First Church Estates Commissioner, claimed: 'By not consolidating the accounts, [the Commissioners] created this misleading impression about the amount of income available. In the world I come from that is illegal. I naturally found it very strange to see a situation in which this obligation did not pertain.'[1]

Coopers & Lybrand's report revealed that the Commissioners' practice in investment and trading activities had been to look upon all property transactions as capital, with both gains and losses being treated as movements on reserves. This occurred whether a gain or loss had actually been realized through a sale, or merely through revaluation. The effect of the practice, in property developments, promoted capital growth and prevented over-distribution of profits as income. On the other hand, when market values fell, it protected the income account by diverting what were effectively trading losses to the reserves. Coopers & Lybrand were critical of the practice, stating that it did not mirror normal company accounting practices and eroded the capital base.

While the Commissioners were doing nothing illegal, as they were not subject to the constraints of the Companies Act, the NAO considered such creative accounting strategies were not best practice. But for their exemption under the Companies Act, they would have been compelled to consolidate the accounts of their subsidiary companies into the Commissioners' accounts, which, under normal accounting rules, would mean that loans within the group would cancel each other out, with no external borrowings on which interest was being paid. The project management charges, a means by which the Commissioners were capitalizing a proportion of their own overheads, would be similarly cancelled out.[2]

In 1987, the NAO insisted that the Commissioners consolidate the subsidiary companies' accounts (although this was not done until 1992). The NAO's injunction caused some division within the Assets Committee. According to Hutchings, David Hopkinson and Joel Burnett-Stuart believed that their strategies were permissible company practice, as did Coopers & Lybrand. But Lovelock insisted they should comply with the NAO. 'Being a civil servant, he thought it was inappropriate, but the rest of them were all in favour [of contesting the NAO's ruling].' There was some frustration that the Commissioners hadn't used the services of Coopers & Lybrand to audit their accounts. Said Hutchings: 'The NAO were used because they were so much cheaper. In the end, they worked out a darn sight more expensive.'

The Assets Committee decided that, in the light of the NAO's attitude, there was only one route open to them. They would need to borrow the money necessary to fund the major retail projects they hoped would provide the level of rental income – and increase the value of their capital assets – required to help meet their burgeoning level of expenditure. Certainly, in this way, it was possible to account interest on loans to subsidiaries as income without falling foul of auditing guidelines. It was also seen as an opportunity for the Commissioners to make a half per cent profit on the additional borrowings they would take on to fund the equity shares of their joint venture partners. In fact, it was the final act on the road to financial disaster.

Approval for their borrowing requirements was virtually a matter of rubber-stamping in days of record-breaking consumer spending, when some banks were recklessly obliging in their eagerness to loan money. In December 1987, an unsecured floating rate facility of £140m was agreed with the National Westminster, which actually was approved by the Assets Committee two months later. By June 1988 it had been increased to £250m. During 1989, the loan facility was increased to £300m, with a $20m revolving facility for the benefit of Deansbank Investments Inc, the Commissioners' US company, which later that year was increased by $30m.

In 1991, the Commissioners' borrowings were increased by a further £100m to complete their development programme. Separate loan facilities were arranged during 1988 and 1989 with the Sumitomo Bank (for £74m) and Royal Scot Leasing to fund respectively the disastrous development at Ashford Great Park and the Gateshead MetroCentre.[3]

The rise in the Commissioners' borrowings – from £4.7m in 1987 to £518m in 1990 – was as foolish as it was dramatic. Apart from two projects – The Marlowes and the Gateshead MetroCentre – they were short-term borrowings at floating rates. While some were secured on property, most were unsecured, and the Commissioners guaranteed the loans taken out by their subsidiaries. Their terms were arranged and agreed by Shelley, who subsequently reported the increasing levels of borrowings to the Assets Committee for their approval; this was duly forthcoming. The £100m loan arranged in 1991 was reported no more than orally to the committee,[4] such was the astonishing neglect of its responsibilities.

Another equally irregular practice revealed by the Coopers & Lybrand report, which Hutchings described as 'an internal accounting exercise' and took place, he claimed, with the knowledge of the committee, was for project appraisals to be based on figures, usually at about 8 per cent, that did not reflect the true rate of interest at which funding would be borrowed. In reality, short-term borrowings were at almost twice that figure. It prevented the appraisals from demonstrating that some projects would result in a significantly lower capital profit, and possibly a capital loss.[5]

Hutchings said he based his reports on interest rates of about 8 per cent 'to show [the Assets Committee] what they would be funding a development at if they were A. N. Other pension fund. If they chose not to use their own resources, and borrow the money because it was actuarially more attractive solution to them, that was up to them. But that's what they did and they did it with their eyes open.' The committee, he added, was given a separate statement reflecting the true rate of interest. He was 'irritated' by the Coopers report because it implied he had deliberately concealed the true costs. '[The report] was saying, "Michael told me we were only borrowing at 8 per cent." There were bankers on that committee. They knew full well we weren't borrowing at 8 per cent. They knew the differential was going to enhance income to meet expenditure.'

It was all done, he claimed, to respond to calls for more money from the Commissioners' General Purposes Committee, responsible for the distribution of income, and of which Lovelock was chairman. 'When there was this desperate cry from the General Purposes Committee to find more income ... you had it then £300m in short-term loans earning 15 per cent. Wonderful! That's your short-term income produced just like that.' William Wells, whose company would produce feasibility studies based on interest figures supplied by Hutchings, subsequently discovered what Hutchings was doing, 'but it was absolutely irrelevant to us.'

To the sublime Shelley, as he asserted in the Church Commissioners' Annual Report and Accounts 1990 (p. 27), the Commissioners' borrowings were 'in accordance with normal commercial practice'. It was the kind of bizarre and misleading statement that greatly disturbed those within the Church of England who believed that much was wrong at Millbank. The Commissioners were not a 'normal commercial' institution, but a closed fund with no new money coming in, whose exposure to high-risk property speculation meant they were already extremely vulnerable to market conditions.

Even the likes of the ICI and Unilever contributory pension funds, with a positive cashflow, had their fingers badly burnt when they were tempted to invest in property development in the 1970s. Both finances and performances were badly damaged.[6] In the same year's accounts, Shelley was also surprisingly upbeat about the Commissioners' worst property investment performance for years. Although property values had dropped by 16 per cent, he declared triumphantly that it compared favourably with an average institutional decline of 20 per cent.

According to Hutchings, Shelley was a most enthusiastic advocate of borrowing. 'Suddenly, there was this feeling ... just go for it. Before that, [if] I wanted to spend £30m on this development somewhere, we'd have to think, "Now where is that £30m coming from? Are we going to have to sell some equities there, or are we going to have to sell some retail there" ... But once borrowing started, it was almost as if there was a constant source of cash.' A borrowings limit agreed at £350m was soon increased to £500m – with the blessings of Coopers & Lybrand, said Hutchings. 'As far as they were concerned, Jim wanted to give away more and more money and this was the perfect way of doing it.

'The net effect of all this borrowing was that there was an enormous amount of unused cash in the Church to fund the development programme, which was put in the short-term loan portfolio.' The capitalized interest on the short-term loans in earlier days provided 'a phenomenal income' which was distributed as perpetuity income. 'They distributed some huge sums, and that's where it all went wrong. Jim's attitude was not to worry, we'd find the money [to meet their financial commitments].'

William Wells, like Hutchings and one or two others close to Millbank, believed Shelley's innate optimism was becoming 'dangerous'. He said: 'One of the real problems why they were so driven at this time was because they were over-distributing significantly to their beneficiaries. They were endeavouring to achieve returns on capital employed which were wholly unrealistic ... That drove them to more and more of this [borrowing], and if you've got someone who is a born optimist ... largely uncontrolled by his board [the Assets Committee], the inevitable will happen.' Shelley, he claimed, was oblivious to the risks to which the Commissioners were exposing themselves. 'He didn't think he was sticking his neck out. I just think he saw that everything was going fine. Whenever you told him that you didn't think things [were going fine] ... [he'd reply] "Nonsense. You're far too pessimistic." '

But, by 1991, even Shelley must have become acutely aware that the Commissioners were in deep trouble. Pressures on them had been compounded by rapid increases in interest rates. In 1987, when the major borrowings began, the rate had increased from about 8 per cent, to almost double by 1990. In fact, in 1991, the rolled-up interest payment was a crippling £52m, almost as much as their pensions bill of £58m.[7] In addition to pensions, they had to find a further £95m to cover stipends – £62.5m – and other costs which, in happier days, they had agreed to fund. With the rolled-up interest charge, their total expenditure was

£205.6m. Their income: £181.6m.[8]

Their calamitous state would have been evident as early as 1988 when, for the first time, expenditure exceeded income. With rolled-up interest of £13.4m,[9] and other expenditure totalling £125.4m, their income was £129.9m.[10] The Commissioners had borrowed beyond their capacity and were unable to service even the interest.

Even Shelley was forced to face the foolishness of their borrowings, and the terms which he agreed, when he appeared, with Lovelock, before a House of Commons Social Security Committee hearing on 14 December 1994. He first defended the principle of borrowing if the terms were right, but then added: 'I readily admit in the euphoria of the 1980s, we got the terms wrong. For example, we were borrowing with a flexible interest rate. We could so easily have borrowed a tranche at a fixed rate for, say, ten years and that would have greatly ameliorated the problem. We were also borrowing too much on speculative schemes. I think we should have been keener to get tenants before we launched into borrowing and the scheme.'[11]

Lovelock, while agreeing that the Commissioners' borrowings had been as high as 25 per cent of their assets, tried to argue that it was common for the borrowings of a property company or a pension fund to reach 50 to 60 per cent. He confirmed, however, that the Commissioners were neither a pension fund nor a property company. He claimed later in a personal interview that, when news of the level of borrowing broke, he felt disappointed and let down: 'I wasn't very pleased. But I still repeat: these were people of complete integrity. They thought they were carrying out the Asset Committee's wishes.

'They hoped, and believed, that in spite of the increase in the borrowing requirement, the projects would still be successful … They thought the recession would not come, or, if it did, that it would be a shallow one. They were wrong in all these things.' He had not asked questions because he was not a property man. 'On the Assets Committee, there were people who did, and who started to ask some questions later on … when people started to get alarmed by the danger signals they were seeing.'

A member of the Assets Committee, claimed Hutchings, who was unhappy with the way in which the Commissioners were moving so heavily into borrowing was David Male. 'He specifically raised the matter of borrowings and he was told to shut up.' He also objected, added Hutchings, to property investments in America and the borrowings that followed. 'He actually believed in saying whatever he thought about any particular venture, instead of agreeing the party line over lunch, so he was not very popular. But I think he was reined in, if that's the right word.'

In desperation, two courses of action were pursued in an attempt to ease the Commissioners' worsening predicament. The first was a legal exercise authorized by Hutchings, which brought Coopers & Lybrand back into the arena. In late 1990, Hutchings instructed their accountants to look at ways of removing the straitjacket the NAO's ruling on consolidation had placed them in, which made it impossible for them to continue to use interest on loans to subsidiary companies as income.

At considerable cost, Coopers & Lybrand sought the opinion of Queen's Counsel, which, in a report from Coopers & Lybrand dated 25 January 1991, supported the Commissioners' accounting practices. Hutchings, even at that late stage, wanted the Commissioners to fight their case in court if necessary. Coopers' report went on to suggest that the cost of the Commissioners' property department could also be charged to property developments, which would increase the Commissioners' income by the same amount. The case was argued by comparing the Commissioners' position to some investment trusts who had begun charging a portion of their overheads to their investment accounts.

The report compared the Commissioners to a commercial organization and drew an analogy between clergy stipends and dividends. But, according to a chartered accountant and a senior company executive who had taken a close interest in the Commissioners' investment activities, the report was in this respect flawed. 'Trustees' responsibilities are unlike those of a company director. A trustee has a duty of care and so must choose less risky investments ... than a commercial company. Many of the Commissioners' problems arose precisely because they were in high-risk investments inappropriate for trustees.' But whatever the report's recommendations, they were academic. Said Hutchings: 'It was simply too late. Everyone knew the writing was on the wall.'

The other initiative was, in the circumstances, more practical, and controversial. The Assets Committee agreed to raise urgently needed income by 'gilt-stripping', or asset-stripping, which had the effect of undermining the value of their capital assets. It is a way of creating short-term income at the expense of long-term interests. But for a closed fund, it is generally considered an imprudent policy. In particular, it is contrary to the constraints of the Church Commissioners Measure 1947, which allows income to be raised exclusively through investments, thereby protecting assets for future stipends and pensions.

'Gilt-stripping' means buying gilt-edged government securities just before interest payments are due (which is usually every six months), and then, once the interest has been received, selling the securities at a capital loss. It is normal commercial procedure to allocate a portion of the yield on the sale to restore capital, and to take only the profit on the sale as income, but instead the Commissioners accounted all the interest as income following the sale of the securities. To cover shortfalls in income at short notice, they began to indulge in gilt-stripping in 1987 to raise £2.4m. However, it was not until 1991 that Shelley referred in the Commissioners' annual report to what he euphemistically described as 'special temporary measures'.

Gilt-stripping in that year raised £4.9m[12] and was used, said Shelley in his report, to help pay £8.5m in clergy community charges, which the Commissioners had agreed to do following a General Synod debate. An unusually contrite Lovelock explained to the Social Security Committee that the Commissioners gilt-stripped because 'we thought we could safely change the basis of our capital in order that more income could be obtained. As things turned out, we went too far in that direction, but every single thing was done to meet a request from the Church and to help the Church. There was no wrongdoing. There was no sleaze.'

Later, though, in a personal interview, Lovelock was considerably more bullish. He said he had had no compunction in resorting to gilt-stripping, despite the consequences to the capital base. 'At the time there was no doubt in my mind that it was necessary to do it. We had a great need for additional income ... We were being pressed ... to relieve the clergy of the community charge ... to improve clergy pensions, and ... to spend a good deal of money on parsonages to renovate them ... The only way we could see to do that was by asset-stripping. It sounds vaguely improper, but it isn't. It is done by every investor ... when they need extra income.'

He was highly critical of people, particularly those within the

Church, who later attacked the Assets Committee's decision, 'jumping up and down and saying, of course, they never wanted the extra income, that it was entirely the Assets Committee that decided in its wisdom that it would be nice to have a bit extra. I regard people like that with unadulterated contempt … Far from saying they didn't want it, you would find that they were among those who were saying, "Are you sure that is all you can manage? We'd like a bit more." I've nothing but contempt for that argument.'

Sir Michael Colman told the Social Security Committee that he was 'very uncomfortable' with the practice when all the yield was distributed as income. He reassured the committee that the practice, which Lovelock said had been introduced as a short-term solution, would cease. But pressure was put on Colman from the House of Bishops, with the support of the Archbishop of Canterbury, to continue with gilt-stripping, to take 'the easier option' so the Commissioners could maintain sufficient income for 'the pastoral care of clergy and churches'.[13] By 1994, the Commissioners had produced £56.7m in this way,[14] which was criticized in the second report produced by the Social Security Committee as 'legalized sleight-of-hand'. Between 1990 and 1996, there was an average annual income shortfall of about £14m which was largely met through gilt-stripping and dipping into the Commissioners' reserves for about £33m, a resort which undermined the ability of the fund to meet its longer-term commitments.[15]

The alternative to the 'easier option' had been for the Commissioners to cut back on their allocations and leave the parishes to pick up the balance. But people in the pews were still incensed by the magnitude of the Commissioners' foolishness and the turmoil it had wrought on the Church and, horrified by media stories of pensions in peril, threats of church closures, parish mergers and fewer clergy, they were in no mood to dig deeper into their pockets to ease the Commissioners' lot.

Even so, the Commissioners were so strapped that, in order to meet pension costs, it was necessary additionally to cut back on stipends allocations by £4m in 1991–92, increasing to £5.5m through to 1995, which reduced their share from £65m to about £48m. Further cuts were forecast for 1996 and beyond to bring expenditure in line with income. But Shelley, in his 1991 report, just months away from the scandal that would envelop Millbank, remained indomitably optimistic. 'We now have clear but realistic targets for income and expenditure for the period ahead,' he announced. 'We are confident that, given reasonable economic recovery and modest inflation, we will meet and, if possible, improve on these targets.' Even he, by then, must have known the game was up.

Certainly those members of the General Synod who could read a set of accounts, had for some time been asking awkward questions about the true state of the Commissioners' property portfolio. Among them was Mike Tyrrell, group development manager of an international building materials manufacturer with a turnover of more than £1bn, and Chairman of the Christian Ethical Investment Group.

At the General Synod in York in July 1992, Tyrrell queried something he had spotted in the notes in the 1991 accounts. They revealed a property write-down of £186m, which gave the first firm indication of the depth of the Commissioners' troubles. He told Synod that he thought something was 'seriously wrong', but even he didn't realize how close to the truth he was. Lovelock curtly dismissed Tyrrell's comments, bluntly stating that Tyrrell did not know what he was talking about.

But Lovelock's opinion was not shared by one of his committee colleagues, Philip Lovegrove, a merchant banker, who earlier that year had been appointed by the General Synod as an associate member to the Assets Committee. His specially-created non-voting appointment was connected with gathering disquiet within Synod, and among some members of the Board of Governors, about the Commissioners' property investments performance. It was thought in the best interests of the Church to have someone on the 'inside' who could get the information necessary for a more informed understanding of what was happening. Lovegrove, a member of Synod since 1977 and Chairman of the St Albans Diocese's Central Board of Finance, privately told Tyrrell that he had every reason to be concerned.

Sir Douglas Lovelock's curt and superior attitude in responding to questions, regardless of the subject or the occasion, did little to ease the love–hate relationship between the Commissioners and Synod. The Commissioners' synodical critics believed Millbank to be too secretive and powerful, while Lovelock and his colleagues saw Synod as a grasping, ungrateful lot, who, in the words of David Hopkinson, 'can't wait to get their hands on us.'

Resistance within Millbank to incisive questioning exacerbated considerably the relationship between the two sides. Even formal requests from Church Commissioners, in whose name the Assets Committee made their decisions, were thwarted. Viscountess Lady Brentford, a much-respected chartered accountant, who was elected to Synod in 1990 and appointed a Church Commissioner in 1991, was 'horrified' by the level of borrowings and the size of the property portfolio when she read the Commissioners' annual report and accounts for 1991. She began asking questions in Millbank about risk evaluation procedure and the Asset Committee's long-term plans, 'but I was shunted to one side as if the questions had never been asked.

'You had to be enormously self-confident to get past an extremely patronizing attitude … you were left wondering what was going on. To find things out, you would either have to be very aggressive or have powerful friends, and at that time I didn't know anybody. I think it was one of the problems all the Commissioners faced. You were treated like … a minor irritant.' She felt that unless she had the information she wanted, she was powerless to do anything. She whiled away her time on the Housing Committee but, in her exasperation, intended to resign unless she was able to get access to the information she wanted. Then, in 1992, she was elected to the Board of Governors, which brought about an overnight change of attitude in Millbank to her presence and questions. By then Shelley had departed and Lovelock was getting ready to clear his desk.

The Commissioners' 1991 annual report also caused considerable anxiety to one member of the Board of Governors. He was John Smallwood, a former deputy chief accountant of the Bank of England, and a vastly experienced Church Commissioner of 24 years' standing. Such was the dismay of Smallwood, at that time also Chairman of the Southwark Board of Finance, and who was a former deputy Vice-Chairman of the Central Board of Finance, that he sent a six-page letter to Lovelock based on his analysis of previous years' reports and accounts, pointedly querying the balance of property portfolio to equities, equities against gilts, and the size of borrowings.

Lovelock's reply, in predictable style, was to state that the Assets Committee was aware of the points he was making 'and do know what they are doing … this is the responsibility of the Assets Committee'. Before writing the letter, Smallwood had also expressed his worries to other members of the Board of Governors to whom the Assets Committee, under its exclusive powers, was responsible but not accountable. It was, said Smallwood, 'very difficult, without being extremely nasty, to go beyond polite questions.' The Governors did not want to 'snarl things up'. He reported to the Governors Lovelock's response to his letter, but by then the Governors had already approved the Commissioners' all-revealing accounts and decided to pursue the matter no further.

As Lovelock was an *ex officio* member of the Board of Governors, frank discussion of the Assets Committee's shortcomings, at least formally, raised its own problems. The comments of the Rt Revd John Waine, Bishop of Chelmsford and an influential member of the Board of Governors, typified the Board's attitude: 'When there were questions about how we were financing our operations, and to some extent the level of borrowings, the assurance were given that all was well and that there was no cause for anxiety ... one worked on the assurances that others who were perhaps better qualified were able to give on these matters.'

The 'closed shop' politics of Millbank were no recent obstacle. During the previous decade many had been the call for greater accessibility to the Commissioners' inner sanctum. One of the most vitriolic came from the Ven. Archdeacon J. D. R. Hayward, who, as General Secretary of the Diocese of London, published in March 1984 his own widely-distributed report on the shortcomings of the Commissioners as the central financial authority for the Church of England.

On behalf of his diocese, in a paper entitled *The Diocese of London's Reply*, he claimed that competent managers existed at diocesan level and 'the time had come for less centralization'. Quoting the Commissioners' annual report, which showed that 43 dioceses together disposed of £136m of capital compared with the Commissioners' assets in 1982 of £1368m, he questioned 'whether it is in the best interests of the Church of England that the centre should hold so much of the Church's disposable wealth. The holding of such a vast investment pool raises grave questions of ethics, efficient management, control and accountability.'

The Church 'had seen no evidence' to substantiate a claim that the Commissioners had brought expertise to the management of assets entrusted to them. In calling for an 'authoritative inquiry into all aspects of the Commissioners' work and functions', Hayward said that he and his colleagues were not saying that the Commissioners' management had been poor, 'only that we have nothing but their word for it that it has been good, and this is not a healthy state of affairs'.

Five months later, he spoke at General Synod against a proposal to integrate the Pensions Board and Church Commissioners as such a move would abolish a body answerable to the General Synod and hand over its functions to one that was not 'a body which comes here, and whose three Estates Commissioners are members of this Synod, but which is answerable, not to this body, but to Parliament'.

With remarkable prescience, he went on: 'I believe that, over the next ten years at least, the nature of these two bodies will change. The Commissioners, who have now been in existence for 150 years and who have, over the last 30, accumulated to themselves powers which they never had in the beginning, are really ready and ripe for reform. Unless they are reformed and made more accountable to the will of the Church, as expressed through this Synod, we shall not have a happy and unified Church.'

Hayward was seen as the ideal person to monitor the activities of the Commissioners, or, more accurately the Assets Committee, when Mrs Betsy Haworth retired as Third Church Estates Commissioner in 1989. His name was put 'very strongly' to Dr Robert Runcie, said a retired senior bishop. But Runcie believed the appointment of such an outspoken personality would cause a major row. Instead, he confirmed the appointment of Mrs Margaret Laird, former head of religious studies at a private school in Bedford, whose views on the competence of the Assets Committee fitted less threateningly into the political culture of Millbank.

The efforts by Tyrrell and others to alert the episcopal hierarchy to the financial mire in which the Assets Committee was sinking, and the Church with it, may have seemed at the time to have been to no avail. Tyrrell was surprised that the media covering the General Synod failed to pick up his observations on the beginnings of the property write-downs. But, given the power of the Assets Committee and Lovelock's insistence that all was well, and an evident reluctance by the Board of Governors, of which the Archbishop of Canterbury was chairman, or indeed the General Synod to pursue the matter more diligently, what more could be done to bring matters to a head?

A well-placed tip-off to the media was seen as the solution to attract the attention of Carey and company. Smallwood was suspected by another governor as being the source, as was Lovegrove, who, according to a member of Synod, 'was instrumental in blowing the whistle'. In fact, neither played any part in breaking the story to the *Financial Times*.

Certainly John Plender, the journalist responsible for exposing the Church's financial plight, received some help from within the Church of England, albeit from an unlikely source. It came from Oliver Marriott, a church warden of Garton-in-Holderness parish church, near Hull, a former financial editor on *The Times*, and a keen reader of the small print in the Church Commissioners' annual reports and accounts. Marriott, author of *The Property Boom*, which recorded the Commissioners' first move into property development in the mid-fifties and which Plender plugged in his article for its background information, was openly contemptuous of the Church of England's structural bureaucracy and what he saw as the Church Commissioners' crass negligence of their fiduciary duties. He co-operated with the *Financial Times* because he believes that Plender, 'more or less, is the best financial journalist around.'

The publication of the story in the *Financial Times* on 11 July 1992 was timed to coincide with the annual General Synod in York to cause maximum embarrassment to the Church. Appropriately, it was Lovelock's last Synod. With considerable chutzpah, given his leading role in the great financial disaster that had just broken, he rose to move a resolution that, 'in the light of the current and project financial situation facing the Church of England', the Synod urge all Church members to give not less than 5 per cent of income.

He went on to say: 'I suppose that this will be my last speech on finance – my favourite subject, if not Synod's. As the sound of sobbing dies away, I must say how grateful I am for their past indulgence.' Referring to the buoyant years of the eighties, he said the growth of income had allowed the Commissioners to pay for the Community Charge, parsonage renewal, the car loans scheme, and others.

> Not unnaturally, expectations rose that this would go on and on. Then came the recession ... the Commissioners have no magic button to press which is not available to

other people. We provide the money that we do by means of dividends and rents, and both are down ... In the recent newspaper publicity, much has been made of the reduction in the value of our property portfolio, but ... everybody's property values are down ... What matters most is that our Church Commissioners' income remains flat. I would not want to deny that we have made mistakes. But I think it is fair to point out some of the rather spectacular mistakes that we did not make.

Lovelock, with some audacity, then spent one or two minutes pointing out recognized investment calamities that the Assets Committee had been smart enough to avoid. He went on to say that the average contribution by Church members at that time of £3 a week needed to be increased to about £5. 'Some Church members have been made redundant. All have been hit by the recession. Some may feel that that is simply beyond them. If they can conscientiously say that, so be it, but there are many who could give much more.' The Church was not, he insisted,

> ... in a crisis. It is a manageable problem, but it is a serious one and we should not underestimate it, or we shall blunt our message on giving ... I must deal, as the Synod would expect me to do, with the recent newspaper publicity. The first thing that needs to be said is that we have not lost £500m ... Some years [our assets] go up and some years they go down. There is not an institution or company in this country of any size, I expect, whose capital value has not gone down in the last year or two ... Our borrowing was high. But we could not have had the MetroCentre without heavy borrowing, because we have no stock of capital; we have no new funds.

He added, on both counts inaccurately, that the Gateshead MetroCentre had 'traded very well' in spite of the recession, and that returns on the Commissioners' investments had during his tenure been consistently higher than the rate of inflation. Times, he stressed, were difficult 'and we, the Commissioners must be, and we are, ready to learn from the experience of recent months and years.' In urging support for his motion, he said the successful attainment of the Church Urban Fund's target of £18m – the Commissioners' plight, incidentally, forced them to end their £1m-a-year contribution – 'demonstrates the Church's ability to respond to a clearly articulated need and challenge. A sound infrastructure, with much help, it must be said, from the Commissioners, imaginative leadership in the centre, in dioceses and in parishes in partnership; I believe that if we can get this message across to the Church about the financial challenge they will respond in the same way and as they have done before.'

He concluded: 'I am sorry to have talked all the time about money, but we have a Gospel to proclaim and it takes money to proclaim it. I will report everything that is said in this debate to the Assets Committee and they will reflect upon it carefully.' It was a remarkable speech, both for the lack of contrition and for the impudence of his solution to a problem for which he was ultimately answerable. He remained unrepentant to the last.

The Archbishop of Canterbury thanked Lovelock for his 'thoughtful' speech, adding: 'He may not have heard much sobbing, but we were grateful for all that he has given.' He said serious points had been made about the management of funds and about judgements on investments: 'I want to assure Synod that these will be examined closely by the Church Commissioners and others concerned.' But none of the criticisms should detract from the underlying and long-term challenges that faced the Church: the need for a shared vision, 'of which sacrificial giving is a natural and joyful part.'

> We should be grateful for our past but not enslaved by it. Grateful too for all the material resources which our Church has inherited from the past and for the care and skill of the Commissioners and many others. We as a Church have lived on the capital of that past, but we cannot do that much longer. The time has come to work energetically and confidently for a future which, under God, we can control and direct through sacrificial and faithful giving.

Whatever the criticism made of him, Lovelock insisted, ever the quintessential civil servant, that he took none of it personally. He was simply doing his job, he said at his £300,000 home in its own spacious grounds in Old Coulsdon, Surrey. 'I don't see the criticisms that have been made in the later years, or the praise that was heaped on us in the early years ... being of me personally. Perhaps I am too much the civil servant. I have certainly not lost any sleep over it.

'Of course, where I was complacent or not assiduous enough at looking into something, I regret that ... but over a period you do some things better than others. Some things I think I did pretty well. It was I, more than anybody else, who got the very large sums out of the Department of Environment to compensate for the Community Charge [and] saved the Church many millions of pounds on the introduction of the council tax by the concessions I got.

'Those were things I felt my experience qualified me to do, because I knew my way round Whitehall and I knew most of the ministers concerned. The property world is not my world. But over the years I have been influenced by neither bouquets or brickbats. That is not the way I am made. No civil servant is, who is worth anything. You must retain a certain detachment.

'... This is going to sound horribly arrogant, but then I am arrogant sometimes ... in my career in the Civil Service, I have been involved in issues *vastly* greater than any of these, and with people whose standing in our national life is on a different plane. And at the risk of sounding arrogant, I have to say they didn't upset me too much, and nor has this.' His errors had been ones of omission rather than commission, he said. 'I have enough strength of personality, I think, to say to those who came [to the Assets Committee], "Look, I don't give a damn that a year ago you asked us to do so and so and it worked, I am not happy about this one." There were one or two occasions when I should have [objected], so should other members of the Assets Committee, and they know it.'

While he was very much at home with the structure of Millbank, with its ranks and scales of pay organized on similar lines to Whitehall, his central difficulty was the

> ... extraordinary nature of the Church of England, of which, by the way, I am a loyal and keen member, at the central level, where there is this very uneasy tension between the commercial imperative and the logical imperative. I had to live with that and I found it very

odd indeed. There is no doubt that, although it may be inevitable, it does make more difficult the kind of calm, dispassionate judgement we exercised at Whitehall.

The great problem of the central Church of England is that no one, repeat no one, is in charge. There are a number of power centres – Lambeth, with the Archbishop; the Synod, the dioceses, the bishops in their splendour, the Church Commissioners, and all those other bodies, some of which I was on. But there is no single person who can do as we were accustomed to at Whitehall, who can say, 'Okay, I've listened to everything you've said. I've weighed up the objections and *this* is what we're going to do.' No one at all. Just a series of power centres, all floating around. I found that very, very odd, indeed. I found that terribly frustrating.

What had he learnt from his time as First Church Estates Commissioner? 'The only thing that men learn from history is that men learn nothing from history … I've learnt that you shouldn't put too much weight on the experts, even if they have delivered the goods before. I ought really to have known that.'

On 30 June 1992, eleven days before the *Financial Times* story was published, Jim Shelley, the man who couldn't say no, retired after 37 years' service to the Church Commissioners, nearly seven of them as Secretary, to his home in Basingstoke, Hants. His departure was observed in the Commissioners' annual report and accounts, with the comment that 'he gave himself unstintingly to our work. His tact and understanding smoothed relationships and fostered many achievements, of which the MetroCentre may be singled out. His many qualities were strengthened and supported by a deep commitment to the work of the Church of England and our contribution to it.'

Shelley declined to make any comment on his part in the Commissioners' downfall, other than to agree that he had found it difficult to argue against the financial requests to utilize the Commissioners' income. 'There is probably some truth in it. Obviously one was there to help. One wanted to get as much benefit to the clergy as one could.'

He had, he said, been out of touch with the Commissioners, 'and I don't think what I've got to say would be of any great value.'

For the record, the Assets Committee's property specialists – Brian Howard, the deputy chairman, and David Male, who was made a CBE in the Queen's birthday honours list in 1991, also declined to be interviewed. Male, President of the Institution of Chartered Surveyors from 1989–90, who was appointed a member of the Assets Committee in 1989, retired in 1993. He said: 'I regard the matters discussed during my four year term of office as a Church Commissioner as confidential, and therefore regret that I am not able to provide you with the information which you have requested.' Male's predecessor, Chris Briant, who spent eight years on the Assets Committee and who was centrally involved in its earlier property decisions, died in July 1993.

Howard also retired in 1993, after 16 years as a Commissioner, both on the Board of Governors and the Assets Committee. Controversially, he was appointed by the Archbishop of Canterbury to sit on the Lambeth Group, whose priority was to investigate the activities of the Assets Committee. Howard declined to be interviewed on the grounds that members of the group had agreed to make no individual comment. He also declined to comment as a member of the Assets Committee. He would only do so with the permission of the Bishop of Chelmsford, as Chairman of the Lambeth Group, or Patrick Locke. Permission was not forthcoming.

Joel Burnett-Stuart retired on 8 March 1994 after nine years on the Assets Committee. He, too, declined to comment. Sir John Starkey resigned suddenly as a Commissioner in 1992 following a heated argument at a meeting of the Assets Committee. Starkey refused to confirm the details, but it was over his belief that the committee had failed to exercise control over the executive officers, such as Shelley and Hutchings. 'I felt market forces had contributed to the result, but it was more mismanagement than market forces. Because I too had been responsible for the decisions the Assets Committee made, I felt I had no alternative but to resign.'

David Hopkinson – 'they'll be glad to see the back of me' – retired on 30 July 1994. He was one of the more widely-experienced churchmen, elected to the General Synod in 1979 and appointed a Commissioner in 1982, who had sat on the Board of Governors. His parting comment was: 'The things that were done in the eighties and the nineties ... could have been jolly right. If we hadn't had three years of 15 per cent money rates ... and they slightly overdid the borrowings ... because the only way to have this closed-in fund bigger is actually to have successful property development, [but] all these people who go round wringing their bloody hands about this ... They've been jolly pleased to have it in the past.'

The Bishop of Peterborough, the Rt Revd Bill Westwood, retired in 1992 after six years on the Assets Committee and Board of Governors. 'I thought I was flavour of the month while I was on the committee but really it was a waste of space. What you needed was someone who knew more than I did about the things they were dealing with.'

One of the first of the Executive to go was Michael Hutchings. It was agreed with Patrick Locke, Shelley's successor, that his resignation 'would suit all sides'. With the dramatic cutting back planned for the Commissioners' property portfolio, he was told there would be little scope for his 'entrepreneurial flair. [Locke] thought I would be terribly unhappy,' said Hutchings.

'He said that we had to conform, that we had to be like everybody else. It was no good us being so heavily into property. I asked him if he thought we could really work at the property portfolio, and he said he thought we were beyond that. He said there was such a momentum of disbelievers who just wanted bread today and forget tomorrow. We talked about it ... over four or five months, and it became clearer and clearer to me that I didn't have an ally in the place.'

Friendless or not, Hutchings was comforted on his departure with a pay-off of a year's salary of £51,000, plus a further year's salary for consultancy work on four projects, although he did little work on any of them. 'I think they acted absolutely properly,' he said. 'That is probably why I don't feel any bitterness towards them.'

Much criticism was heaped on Hutchings, by implication, as in the Lambeth Group report, or more directly in the general media, either for his maladministration of administrative duties and unorthodox standards or extravagant personal lifestyle and apparent lack of remorse. Others, perhaps more accurately, saw him as the Commissioners' scapegoat.

He had all the classic qualities necessary to make him vulnerable: highly individualistic, he was not inculcated, despite his years at Millbank, with the sterility of the civil servant persona; he was not by temperament inclined to the discipline of office organization and structural efficiency; hence he was not a team player, one who would instinctively seek the wisdom of a collective decision. All this was known of Hutchings, and when things go wrong such people are stereotypically suitable for any opprobrium that might follow.

But Hutchings was promoted to the highly responsible position of commercial property manager for none of these qualities; they came with the famed 'golden nose' able to sniff out what at the time were seen as excellent property investments. He was shrewd, intuitive and quick to take an opportunity. He was also eager to please, and he used these qualities in energetic and obedient pursuit of the Assets Committee's property investment strategy. That he was allowed so much freedom of licence to express his aberrant style in crucial areas was a major error that cannot be laid at his door.

Hutchings, though, was merely one of the factors that came together in the Commissioners' defeat. They all needed to be in place – from the appointments of Hutchings, Shelley and Lovelock and the insularity of Millbank to the apathetic miserliness of a long-cossetted Church and a deep economic recession – for all that befell the Commissioners to come about. If any had been absent at the critical time, the history of the Church of England would, to this point, have remained unchanged.

1. Social Security Committee, Second Report, *The Church Commissioners and Church of England Pensions*, 29 March 1995, Q. 89.
2. Lambeth Group Report, July 1993, Para. 505.
3. Ibid., Paras. 508–515.
4. Ibid., Para. 511.
5. Ibid., Para. 910.
6. *Financial Times*, 11 July 1992.
7. Social Security Committee, Second Report, *The Church Commissioners and Church of England Pensions*, 29 March 1995, Para. 64.
8. Church Commissioners' Annual Report and Accounts 1995, Ten Year Financial Record.
9. Social Security Committee, Second Report, *The Church Commissioners and Church of England Pensions*, 29 March 1995, Para. 64.
10. Church Commissioners' Annual Report and Accounts 1995, Ten Year Financial Record.
11. Social Security Committee, Second Report, *The Church Commissioners and Church of England Pensions*, 29 March 1995, Q. 259.

12.   Ibid., Appendix 12.
13.   Ibid., Q. 178.
14.   Ibid., Appendix 12.
15.   Lambeth Group Report, July 1993, Para. 618.

CHAPTER ELEVEN

The Lambeth Inquiry

Within 48 hours of the publication of the *Financial Times* story, the Archbishop of Canterbury, Dr George Carey, moved to announce at the General Synod in York that an inquiry would be held into its allegations. Three months later, an assembly of distinguished senior churchmen and businessmen, which came to be known as the Lambeth Group, met under the chairmanship of the Bishop of Chelmsford, the Rt Revd John Waine, to begin that inquiry. It was not an appointment that the 63-year-old senior bishop particularly welcomed. As deputy Chairman of the Board of Governors, he suspected that others might think that the Lambeth Group's efforts might be less than assiduous in getting to the truth.

'I understood those who said that it sometimes helps to have a patently independent chairman,' he said. 'I certainly asked the question whether the opinion was firm that I should take this on. I was told it was. I was aware that there were those who were very critical of the fact that I was chairing it. Friends of mine were saying, "You shouldn't have to do that, and we feel for you." But my own view is that if the Church asks you to do something, and it is believed that you are the person to do it, then you have to have a very good reason for saying no.' He believed he was appointed because he was a senior bishop 'with years of experience' of the Commissioners.

His colleagues on the Lambeth Group were Peter Baring, Chairman of Barings plc until the Nick Leeson securities scandal forced his early retirement in April 1995; Derek Fellows FIA, formerly Executive Director of the Securities and Investments Board

171

and former Chief Actuary of the Prudential Assurance Company; Sir John Herbecq, a Church Commissioner, Chairman of the Chichester Board of Finance, and a former Second Permanent Secretary to the Civil Service; Assets Committee member Brian Howard, deputy Chairman of Northern Foods, formerly deputy Chairman of Marks & Spencer; Alan McLintock CA, Chairman of the Woolwich Building Society, and Chairman of the Church of England's Central Board of Finance; Canon John Stanley, a Church Commissioner, Vicar of Huyton, Prolocutor in Convocation for the Province of York; Maurice Stonefrost CBE, Chairman of the Municipal Mutual Insurance, formerly Chief Executive of British Rail's Pension Fund, and former Director General of the Greater London Council; and James Tuckey FRICS, managing director of MEPC.

If Waine's chairmanship was considered by some to be unwise, two other appointments caused eyebrows to be raised considerably higher. These were Brian Howard, deputy chairman of the Assets Committee, and accountants Coopers & Lybrand, who were engaged to investigate the Commissioners' investment activities. For Howard had been a central architect of the committee's grand retail schemes and had been party, by design or neglect, to the crippling borrowings that financed them, and Coopers & Lybrand had been responsible for much of the Commissioners' creative accounting policies. Both were being invited to play key parts in judging the consequences of their own actions.

In the face of public criticism, Waine defended Howard's appointment on the grounds that he was 'able to explain and to speak, and to answer questions in the group as to how the Assets Committee operated, the kind of decisions that they were called upon to make.' But with suspicion of the Commissioners at its strongest within the Church, the appointments to the Group of Howard and of Coopers & Lybrand were seen as a serious gaffe. Frank Field, Chairman of the House of Commons Social Security Committee, compared Coopers' appointment to 'inviting Mrs Thatcher to run the Scott Inquiry'.[1]

Coopers & Lybrand were not unknown to the Social Security Committee, the company having been brought before its members during a parliamentary inquiry into the Maxwell pension funds scandal. Field took full advantage of their appointment to undermine the credibility of the Lambeth Group inquiry. When the Archbishop of Canterbury and the Bishop of Chelmsford appeared before the Committee on 26 April 1994, Field commented, 'Some of us felt that Coopers & Lybrand ought to be investigated, not just the Commissioners.'[2]

Carey, when asked by Field who had been responsible for their appointment, said he had taken 'soundings from a wide circle of friends, colleagues and professional people in the City and elsewhere. I did not find at any point any questioning of the abilities of Coopers & Lybrand.'

Field wanted to know why Coopers & Lybrand, as their auditors, hadn't alerted the Commissioners. 'One of the groups which could and should be "whistle-blowers" are the auditors. For each of the joint companies set up by the Commissioners, Coopers & Lybrand were the auditors at the time the funds were lost. Therefore, it seems to some of us that their role needed to be investigated. Why did they not whistle-blow? Why was it that His Grace had to learn the extent of the financial crisis from the *Financial Times*?'

It had not been learnt, he added, from the professional people employed to audit the accounts and presumably raise the alarm if things were wrong. 'They were wrong, were they not, to a massive extent.' Waine agreed. Mistakes had been made and compounded. 'There is no question about that,' he said. One of the problems had been of accountability and exchange of information, which, he added, had been 'fortunately highlighted in the Lambeth Group report'.

The Social Security Committee, in its report, remained derisive of Coopers & Lybrand's appointment, claiming that the Lambeth Group report would have

> gained more immediate and widespread support if a firm of accountants or consultants with no connections with the Commissioners had been given the investigating task ... While we have our doubts about the wisdom of the choice of auditors for the task, we do not dissent in any major respect from their analysis, as far as it went. It did not cover fraud, although the Church Commissioners proved such an easy target to developers to whom they entrusted vast sums of capital that fraud was probably superfluous.[3]

Frank Field later described the appointment of Coopers & Lybrand as 'a blinkered decision' which 'typified what was wrong with the

Church Commissioners. It was the old gang network operating, which always had, from Sir Robert Peel onward. Little groups always coalesced round them.'

Whatever parliamentary questions or criticisms might lie ahead for Bishop Waine, the inquiry had barely got off the ground before he encountered a more parochial problem in the form of a highly indignant Sir Douglas Lovelock, who insisted that neither Shelley nor Hutchings, key figures in the inquiry and who by then had left Millbank, should be interviewed. Lovelock, reported Hutchings, was 'damn angry', insisting that it was 'inappropriate' to put two 'ex-civil servants' in such a situation. Waine was aware of Sir Douglas's objections, 'but we were certainly sure in our mind that we wished to speak to them, because we were concerned that there should be no "no-go" areas.' Lovelock thought otherwise. A short but plain exchange followed before Lovelock was compelled to back down.

Among the questions asked of Hutchings, some concerned allegations of property deal 'sweeteners' of holidays abroad. He denied emphatically ever being offered bribes, or having knowledge of them. William Wells was asked similar questions by the Coopers & Lybrand team, which was led by Peter King, a partner in the company. 'I was questioned very closely and I said that, as far as I knew, nothing like that happened, but then we wouldn't necessarily know. I will say this on the record: there has been a bit of a history with the Church Commissioners that they have had a number of people over the years who have thoroughly enjoyed being entertained, with very good dinners and who enjoy drinking wine and the like. If the Commissioners did not want that to happen, they should have done something about it. They knew perfectly well it was going on.'

Allegations of corrupt practice weren't unknown within No. 1 Millbank prior to the innuendoes of media reports. David Hopkinson, the committee's equity investments expert, admitted he had been told about 'things that one wouldn't be very excited about. Weekends here and there, and that sort of thing.' Hopkinson – 'that sort of thing is anathema to me' – said the person claimed they had taken place about five years earlier. I said, "Well, why the bloody hell didn't you tell me five years ago?" This was somebody who said to me, "Didn't you know about … that sort of thing going on?" … and one didn't.' Hopkinson didn't pursue the matter, or discuss his conversation with others in Millbank. It was the likes of Hopkinson on the Assets Committee, incidentally, who gave Lovelock succour. 'One of my great comforts as Chairman of the Assets Committee and being myself a generalist was the knowledge that there were people in the room who probably would be able to steer us clear of the more unsavoury beasts that roam that [commercial] jungle.'[4]

The Group came up against other 'no-go areas' in their attempts to conduct a purposeful inquiry. Unknown to Waine, Lovelock and Patrick Locke, who, as the newly-appointed Secretary to the Church Commissioners attended the Lambeth Group meetings, told King that it would be 'inappropriate' to interview the management of the Imry Group, the property development company which over the years had undertaken about 15 co-ventures with the Commissioners involving tens of millions of pounds, including the Ashford Great Park project.

Asked why he had not spoken to Imry, King said: 'It was the view of the Commissioners at the time that it was not appropriate for me to … or necessary for me to see Imry.'[5] Who were the Commissioners? 'That was Douglas Lovelock at the time and Patrick Locke, who was the Secretary.' It seemed it was considered to be outside the terms of his brief, which was 'to examine and report upon the Commissioners' borrowings and the information flow for the management of their assets'.[6]

It was Carey's wish that there should be 'no recriminations' and, for this reason, the brief may have been purposefully narrow. Yet failing to interview property developers who were closely involved with the Commissioners, if only to expunge any rumours or suspicions and to gain a clearer understanding of their relationships, did little to sustain Carey's claim to the Social Security Committee that the Lambeth Group inquiry was not 'a whitewash'.[7]

However, King did have a meeting with Martin Myers, managing director of the Imry Group, following publication of the Lambeth Group report. Myers had taken exception to a section in the report which, in analysing estimated and actual costs of partnership developments between 1985 and 1989, claimed the Commissioners' share had increased overall by more than £400m due, among other reasons, to the 'failure' of partners (whose interests the Commissioners were forced to buy). Myers believed that his company, widely known in the property world as a major partner of the Commissioners, had been identified by implication and unfairly impugned.

Myers said he had consulted peers in the property world who believed that 'failure' in that context implied that Imry had failed to fulfil their financial obligations. 'Perhaps it is natural for ... either advisers to the Church or within the Church [to] look to some sort of scapegoat, but I think it is incredibly unfair to look to Imry for that scapegoat, because all these transactions the Church undertook with us [they did] on advice from their advisers. There is no question of the Church ever seeking recourse against Imry. They don't have any grounds for that ... if we had been called [to give evidence], we could have proved that the debacle was nothing to do with Imry. I think we have proved that beyond all reasonable doubt. If we had failed, as they said in the report ... why on earth didn't they sue us?'

To little surprise, the Lambeth Group report made no mention of the extensive role that Coopers & Lybrand had played in the Commissioners' accounting strategies, which, at best, exceeded the constraints of the Church Commissioners Act 1948 by which the Commissioners were bound to protect their capital assets. At the same time, it was due to Peter King's initiative that the report was substantially more wide-ranging than his brief had allowed. In the opinion of John Plender, the *Financial Times* journalist whose story broke the news of the Commissioners' massive losses, King was right to 'ignore their extraordinary restrictive terms of reference which, if followed, would have resulted in a report of little value and much needless expense'.[8]

Published on 22 July 1993, and based on what the Archbishop of Canterbury described as a 'very rigorous analysis of the problems',[9] it confirmed what was widely known, that the Assets Committee had taken on commitments well in excess of income. The Group's principal conclusions were that:

- The Commissioners' Assets Committee increased an already large exposure to property; the problem was compounded by borrowing to finance speculative property development. This has resulted in the overall performance of the portfolio of assets under the direction of the Assets Committee being below average, particularly in the last five years, partly because of the underperformance of the property sector in general and partly because of the underperformance of the Commissioners' property portfolio relative to the sector.

- The Assets Committee failed to ensure that they had regular and accurate reports from the executive management to enable them to control the commercial property developments adequately.
- The Commissioners have taken on commitments to finance clergy benefits which are in excess of the Commissioners' financial capacity. Inadequate attention has been given to ensuring that the Commissioners' commitments are kept in line with their resources. The performance of their equity investments was considered 'satisfactory' and the sales of certain residential property and agricultural land 'well-judged'.

The report recommended that since the contribution by the Commissioners to the cost of pensions, stipends and housing could not be maintained at its present level their future contribution must be reviewed, with regard to the need to preserve their capital. The creation of a separately constituted pension fund was recommended, and regular contributions should be made to it to ensure future liabilities were covered. The level of pensions should be more flexible, and related to, for example, price increases rather than stipends.

The responsibilities of the Assets Committee should be reviewed and they should make a formal report quarterly to the Board of Governors on their investments and other activities. An Audit Committee should be appointed by the Board, and a commercial accountancy firm with wide audit experience should be appointed to audit the Commissioners' accounts. The Commissioners should aim to avoid speculative property development and continue to have regard to their special character as a major investor for the Church of England; should normally avoid borrowing and cease to generate 'temporary income' through 'coupon trading' (gilt-stripping).

Finally, it dealt with the Church's management structure:

> The nature, the constitution and the management of Church affairs are very different from and more complex than most other organizations, within which large-scale assets and liabilities are managed and financial returns deployed. It would be appropriate for the Church to review its overall organizational structure in the light of its present-day activities and requirements.

Commenting on the bureaucratic complexity of the Commissioners' operational mechanism, the Lambeth Group said it believed the Church would benefit from a simpler organizational structure:

> If this already existed we believe that the questions which now need urgent answers would have been dealt with earlier and that, in consequence, the Church would not now be faced with the need to make major decisions under pressure of time.

But the issue that most concentrated the attention of retired clergy and widows, reading the report in the parishes, was that of pensions. Media speculation and comment, some ill-informed and some disturbingly accurate, about the Commissioners' resources to meet their commitments had heightened widespread concerns. The Lambeth Report offered little comfort, merely confirming suspicions that the Commissioners, in permitting expenditure to exceed income, had been no more competent in ensuring their capacity to meet their commitment to clergy benefits than they had been in the management of their property portfolio.

The burden of pensions that had come to bear so heavily on the Commissioners' income had its origins in the Clergy Pensions Measure of 1926 introduced by the Church Assembly, the forerunner of the General Synod, and launched with a capital sum from the coffers of the Ecclesiastical Commissioners, topped up annually by contributions from the Church Commissioners, the Church Assembly, and the clergy themselves. The payments were little enough, but they allowed, at last, men of the cloth, who had devoted their lives to the Church, the luxury of retirement.

Over the next 28 years, payments were improved to meet changing economic conditions, but the fund's growth became increasingly complex. The managing of its assets proved too burdensome for a Pensions Board which had been established by the Measure for its control and administration. In 1954, full responsibility for the fund and the investment of its assets, by which time totalled £8m, was transferred to the Church Commissioners' Estates and Finance Committee (later known as the Assets Committee), with the Pensions Board continuing its administration. At the same time, contributions by members and the Church Assembly came to an end.

Further improvements were introduced and charged to the Commissioners' income, such as non-contributory pensions for widows and the pension payments of bishops. They were followed in 1967 by a lump sum retirement payment and the lowering of retirement age from 70 to 68 in 1969, and to 65 in 1971. At this time, the pensions bill of £5m represented only 15 per cent of the Commissioners' income of £33.1m, placing no great strain on their resources; and temporal life was proving a little more agreeable for retired clergy.

Even so, the annual pension of the clergy in 1980 was just £2,000. With no other means of support, it compared miserably with the pension provisions of the secular world. Recognition of retired clergy's financial plight had led to. the setting up two years earlier of a working party committee comprising three members of the Assets Committee and three members of the Pensions Board, which was co-chaired by the then First Church Estates Commissioner, Sir Ronald Harris, and the Chairman of the Church of England Pensions Board, Mr Howard Gracey. Its purpose was to formulate a strategy for making clergy pensions more realistic to the economic demands of the modern world.

Out of a series of meetings emerged what came to be known as 'the three aspirations'. The 'aspirations' were: a full service pension of two-thirds the previous year's national minimum stipend; a widow's pension at two-thirds the clergy pension; and a retirement lump sum based on three times the clergy pension. They were so named by Sir Ronald, who, wily in the ways of the General Synod, did not want to be held a hostage to fortune.

It would be unwise, he advised his committee colleagues, to put them forward as proposals. He did not want the Assets Committee to be compelled by any connotation of commitment or timescale.

When the three 'aspirations' were put before Synod in 1980, they were enthusiastically received, and it was overwhelmingly agreed that they should be pursued. By now, pensions represented 24 per cent – £14.4m – of the Commissioners' total income of £59.3m, but the 'aspirations' were still considered to be easily affordable and realized by 1990 under Sir Douglas Lovelock. A two-thirds pension was achieved by April 1, 1985; the widow's pension based on two-thirds of clergy pension in 1988; and a retirement lump sum three times the clergy pension in 1990.

Said a Governor: 'If we had been asked to put a timetable to the achievement of those aspirations, it would have been 20 to 25 years, whereas, because the income was buoyant … we achieved those aspirations within 10 years.' And in doing so put unsustainable pressure on the Commissioners' income. The implementation of Harris's 'three aspirations', with clergy retiring at a younger age on a fatter pension linked to stipends, guaranteed a rapidly increasing pensions bill for a growing number of retired clergy, which by 1991, stood at 10,500 clergy and widows, and which would soon exceed active clergy of about 11,400. By 1991, the cost of pensions – £58m, accounting for 35 per cent of the Commissioners' investment income of £166.5m – had almost trebled, an increase of almost twice the rate of inflation: an astonishing 325 per cent compared to an RPI growth rate of 173 per cent. Overall, the Commissioners' total expenditure had risen by 260 per cent.[10]

During that decade the Commissioners had also agreed to fund a number of generous benefits and obligations, from the equity-sharing loans scheme and interest-free car loans totalling £17.4m to 6,700 clergy to the renewal and renovation costs of clergy housing through the Parsonage Renewal Fund and one-off payments such as individual community tax bills totalling over £8.5m and selective grants to cathedrals. The projected costs of some of these schemes were seriously under-estimated and added millions to the Commissioners' bill, which, until the Coopers & Lybrand investigation, had been concealed in annual reports.

But, in one of the most damning indictments of the Commissioners' stewardship, it was revealed that costs had got out of control largely because the Commissioners had failed to introduce a safeguard fundamental to pension funds: an actuarial assessment to ensure there would be sufficient income to meet the future costs of pensions and other benefits. There was, in particular, inadequate information on clergy retirement ages.

A short-term assessment undertaken within Millbank in 1986 proved dangerously inaccurate. Pension costs projected for the period to 1995 underestimated the actual cost for 1992 by 15 per cent, and for 1995 by 22 per cent. The assessment used assumptions which were unrealistic, said the report. They forecast annual increases of 5 per cent in the national minimum stipend – to which pensions were two-thirds linked – when, in fact, the increases over the following five years were between 6.3 per cent and 15.4 per cent, an average rate of 8.8 per cent.

Based on core assumptions, and the Commissioners' current asset distribution at that time, actuarial consultants Bacon & Woodrow, engaged by the Lambeth Group to report on the Commissioners' pension liabilities, forecast that by the year 2010, pension costs would absorb 90 per cent of their total income. The report also revealed that the Commissioners' liabilities exceeded the total value of their assets – £2.1bn against £2bn.

The blame for the lack of a reliable actuarial assessment was passed between Sir Douglas Lovelock and Mr Howard Gracey, the long-standing Chairman of the Pensions Board, like a hot potato.

When Gracey appeared before a Social Security Committee hearing on 26 April 1994, with the Archbishop of Canterbury and the Bishop of Chelmsford, he admitted that no actuarial assessment had taken place as if the Commissioners had been a pension fund. 'There was no valuation of liabilities on a traditional actuarial assessment, beyond back-of-envelope calculations which I have done myself to make sure there was not a silly situation,'[11] he said – an extraordinary comment for someone of his professional standing and experience, closely involved with the management of what in effect was one of the biggest pension funds in the country.

But his office had supplied some actuarial information to the Assets Committee, he said during a personal interview shortly after the Social Security Committee hearing. With Roger Radford, Secretary to the Pensions Board, by his side, he said it had been based on 'the numbers of likely pensioners, and certain assumptions

[on] the cost of paying pensions to those people.' The numbers proved to be 'very close, in fact'. The final costs, said Radford, turned out to be greater because of an inflationary surge in the late eighties. Radford maintained that their role had been simply to supply the projected clergy figures.

The Pensions Board had offered to provide a detailed projection of both pension costs and income following a decision in 1987 by the Assets Committee that, having achieved the second of the three 'aspirations', a monitoring of costs should be made. But the offer was declined. The Assets Committee responded by stating that as it had other liabilities, 'it was not the responsibility of the Pensions Board to project the income or the Commissioners' other liabilities'.[12] The subsequently incomplete assessment that was supplied by the Pensions Board was based on stipendiary rates of increase which the Assets Committee had specified – assumptions which, the Coopers & Lybrand report had revealed, were 'unrealistic', leading to pension costs considerably higher than forecast.

Confidential minutes of the General Purposes Committee also revealed that as late as 1991, the Assets Committee, at a meeting with the General Purposes Committee, 'discouraged' a recommendation that a full actuarial assessment should be carried out. The General Purposes Committee, which was responsible for the allocation of the Commissioners' income, and of which Lovelock was chairman and Gracey a member, was criticized by the Social Security Committee for failing to spot at the time either the inadequacies of the figures supplied by the Pensions Board, or the over-optimistic income growth rate of 5–8 per cent forecast by the Assets Committee in 1988.[13]

When, nine months later, on 14 December, Lovelock, accompanied by Jim Shelley, appeared before the Social Security Committee, he did nothing to counter any presupposition that the fault lay squarely with Gracey and the Pensions Board, making no reference to the offer by the Pensions Board to provide a full actuarial report of the Commissioners' income and outgoings.

In response to Frank Field's point about the financial pressures placed on the Commissioners by the three 'aspirations', and the lack of actuarial data, Lovelock said it was clear that 'we ought to have had, several years ago, the analysis which ... goes into enormous depth as to the extent of the obligation which these aspirations have led the Church and the Commissioners into.' Everyone needed to take the blame. Shelley thought there had been an 'age profile, but I do not think it was looked at very carefully, and I do not think a full actuarial examination was put in hand. You correctly addressed that to the Chairman of the Pensions Board.'

Seizing, it would seem, every opportunity to absolve the Assets Committee from blame, Lovelock, when asked by Field if he thought it unreasonable to think that the chairman of the Pensions Board should have been advising him on the dangers and pitfalls, replied: 'Yes, I think that is a fair point, chairman.' He further agreed with a suggestion that the 'primary responsibility' for an actuarial assessment had lain with the Pensions Board, adding, 'I am not here to cast waves elsewhere.'

Lovelock, no more to his credit, believed the problem had been caused by the rejection of a proposal he had put before the General Synod in 1984 to merge the Pensions Board and Church Commissioners – 'this kind of thing will always happen if you have two bodies charged with the administration of what is in fact the same thing ... I am absolutely convinced that if one body, instead of two, had been operating in this area it would not have happened.'[14]

Lovelock, of course, knew exactly what the Pensions Board had been doing. It was a smokescreen quickly blown away by Field when the following month Gracey again appeared before the Social Security Committee. Now aware of the offer from the Pensions Board, following a lengthy explanatory memorandum from Gracey, and the contents of the General Purpose Committee's minutes, Field remarked that it appeared 'Sir Douglas's memory [had] played tricks with him'.

He said Sir Douglas believed the problem had occurred 'because it was a cock-up of the type which occurs naturally ... everybody thought everybody else was making these calculations, when in fact they were not.' Speaking directly to Gracey, he went on: 'In fact, the cock-up theory may be there, but it is a slightly different cock-up theory in that the Pensions Board was prepared to undertake the more detailed work and the Commissioners, in the form of the First Estates Church Commissioner, thanked you for your kind offer but declined it.' Field added: 'I merely mention it, Howard, because it quite significantly changes your position in the story.' To which Gracey, duly vindicated, replied, 'Yes.'[15] Although the record had now been set straight, the Social Security Committee, in its first report on the Commissioners, nevertheless recorded its disappointment that Gracey, as 'the Chairman of the Church of England Pensions Board, had not been more effective in pursuing the need for a review of income and expenditure'.[16]

Frank Field, incidentally, would have had good cause to remember Lovelock's proposal in 1985 to the General Synod that the Church Commissioners and the Pensions Board should merge. At the time he was a co-opted member of Synod and, with many others, strongly opposed the idea. It was Field's first debate – and signalled a brief career in the Synod. 'It made sure that I wasn't co-opted again,' he said.

'I objected on the basis that I had helped to establish a group of ex-clergy wives and the only body that had behaved with any sense of Christian charity towards them was the Pensions Board. The thought that they should be gobbled up by the Commissioners seemed to be bad policy.' He believed it was a move by Lovelock to enlarge his power base.

The political manoeuvring was 'a terrible business'. Field believed that it contributed to the breakdown of Shelley's predecessor, Kenneth Lamb, who, after five years in office, retired in July 1985 due to ill-health, and died in June 1995. 'This must have contributed to his breakdown, the way they were behaving,' said Field.

Lovelock believed his proposal was opposed on 'largely sentimental' grounds. Stipends and pensions were 'a seamless robe', he claimed; either the Commissioners and Pensions Board should have merged, or been taken over by another body. He believed the Commissioners could have run the administration of pensions more efficiently.

Said Field: 'We now know that that is the last thing that would have happened.'[17]

By the time the Lambeth Group report was published, Sir Douglas Lovelock had retired, still heroically insisting that the Church hadn't done too badly by him, and that all would come well in the end. The office of First Church Estates Commissioner was taken this time not by a civil servant but a businessman of proven record.

He was Sir Michael Colman, Eton-educated and a member of Boodles and the Cavalry Club, whose family founded the Colmans Mustard of Norwich business in 1814, and which merged with Reckitt, manufacturers of household products, in 1938 to become Reckitt & Colman, whose turnover in 1995 was £2.35bn. Colman was appointed company chairman in May 1986 and retired in August 1995. Having run his company's pension fund and also been director of finance, he was vastly more experienced than his predecessors in understanding the commercial world.

Support for his appointment came from much the same faction which, seeking an end to the civil service hegemony in Millbank for a commercially more astute and informed leadership, had opposed Lovelock's appointment. This time, it was claimed, pressure was put on the Prime Minister, responsible for the appointment, to back Colman. 'If we had our way in opposing Lovelock's appointment, we may well have avoided all the disasters that followed,' said a senior churchman.

Colman, of trim and unpretentious dress and manner, a firm believer in delegation, loyalty and commitment, also believed in leading by example. Anticipating the belt-tightening times that lay ahead and the financial sacrifices that the parishes would be called upon to make, one of his first moves was to decline his salary of about £65,000 a year. His style of communication was also forthright. When a member of the Social Security Committee, before whom Colman would appear a few months after his appointment, remarked, in referring to the practices of the Assets Committee and lack of resignations, that 'the whole thing stinks ... I feel very unhappy about the whole set-up,' the new First Church Estates Commissioner replied: 'So you should be.'[19]

Recommendations of the report relating to the Commissioners' financial and project monitoring structures were rapidly implemented. Alan McLintock, Chairman of the Church's Central Board of Finance, which managed the purse-strings of the General Synod, Derek Fellows, a former Chief Actuary of the Prudential – both had sat on the Lambeth Group – and Viscountess Brentford were appointed to an Audit Committee to keep a close watch on the Asset Committee's financial management; a Deputy Secretary for Finance and Investment, whose responsibilities included evaluating and forecasting 'the financial consequences of the Commissioners' liabilities and proposed policy commitments', was appointed; a professionally qualified chartered surveyor was appointed to manage the property portfolio; DTZ were appointed as independent valuers of the portfolio; new guidelines were agreed with the Board of Governors on how it was to function; two sub-groups of the Assets Committee were established to scrutinize property and equity investments; and commercial accountants were appointed to audit the Commissioners' accounts.

The Assets Committee itself underwent substantial changes. Only Philip Lovegrove, appointed by Synod as an associate member, survived. He was joined, as the committee's deputy chairman, by Sir Richard Baker Wilbraham, a former director of investment bankers Schroders, and chairman of the Bibby Line Group; Jeremy Newsum, Chief Executive of Grosvenor Estate Holdings; Godfrey Richardson, senior investment partner in Knight Frank Rutley until early 1993; R. Martin Shaw, managing director of Baring Asset Management Ltd, responsible for worldwide institutional business; the Bishop of Blackburn, the Rt Revd Alan Chester, a member of the Board of Governors and appointed by them to monitor the implementation of the Lambeth Group report; and, to reinforce a policy of greater accountability to Synod, the Revd Canon Hugh Wilcox, Prolocutor of the House of Clergy of the Convocation of Canterbury. Richardson and Newsum were joined by Sir Christopher Wates, Chairman of the Wates Building Group, to form the sub-property group.

Changes in the mechanical structure of the Commissioners took place without resistance. They were seen as necessary and long overdue. Persuading others to accept what he saw as the necessary immediate measures to tackle the tough times that lay ahead was, for Colman, another matter. Alarmed at the high level of over-distribution of income – at that time £151m based on assets of £2.4bn – and its erosive effect on the capital base, Colman wanted to introduce without delay a massive reduction in the Commissioners' annual contribution to clergy stipends, possibly as high as £30m, with the parishes taking up the shortfall. The proposal was received with dismay. Many within the Church, who believed that Colman had arrived from Reckitt & Colman with a magic wand, thought it would cause real hardship and damage in the parishes.

He said he 'confronted [the Board of Governors] with the full picture' so they could see why the Commissioners had to modify their practices 'in order to live with the obligations we have as

Commissioners'. He believed that some of his colleagues saw him as being 'very awkward and very prickly', but they understood what they were being asked to do. All the same, Colman was urged to consider a more graduated change. The House of Bishops, with the support of the Archbishop of Canterbury, also applied pressure for a less painful option, so that the Commissioners could maintain sufficient income for 'the pastoral care of clergy and churches'.[19] Colman reluctantly agreed to continue to 'gilt-strip', a practice which he had admitted to the Social Security Committee left him 'very uncomfortable'. During his first year at Millbank, it generated income of £13.6m, and £12.9m the following year.[20]

The Commissioners, already criticized in Parliament for pursuing a policy that exceeded their statutory powers, said in a news release issued in March 1994 that 'gilt-stripping' was being carried out in the context of phasing cuts while maintaining, 'as far as possible, the integrity' of their investment portfolio. It added that they had sought Counsel's opinion, which stated the practice did not constitute a breach of trust if it was carried out 'with a view to balancing the investment strategy as a whole and compensating for a low yield on other investments with a greater potential for capital growth'. Nevertheless, 'gilt-stripping' would be phased out as soon as possible. Yet it was still being used to raise income in 1997.

However, while Colman was compelled to back down over the speed at which reduced levels of income should be introduced, little conflict was provoked at Millbank. Colman was confident of the Board of Governors' support – and, equally so, that the Church's members would respond to a call to raise more money to meet a greater share of the stipends bill totalling £157m, of which, on Colman's arrival, the Commis-sioners were producing £58m. 'What they object to,' he said, 'is pouring money down a big hole in the centre [Millbank] which they mistrust. If it is organized in such a way that people see the money going to things that they mind about – their own church, their own incumbent – they feel very sorry if they are not supported. What they don't like is all sorts of churchy appointments which they don't think are necessary.' With about £370m coming from the parishes, it meant that the parishes would need to find less than 10 per cent to close the gap between the

Commissioners' income and expenditure; not, he predicted, 'an unmanageable task'.

Out of the Lambeth Group report came an announcement by the Church Commissioners that a firm of actuaries would be appointed, on the back of Bacon & Woodrow's findings, to provide independent advice about their liabilities and investments strategy. The final choice was marked: both because it went against the views of Colman, and it gave further proof, if any were necessary, that the Church was either arrogantly indifferent to public opinion or genuinely but incredibly naive.

After public criticism for the composition of the Lambeth Group and the appointment of Coopers & Lybrand, the company chosen to provide the 'independent' advice was R. Watson & Sons, who had not only been auditors to the Robert Maxwell pension fund, but whose chairman was Howard Gracey, the Chairman of the Commissioners' Pensions Board. Frank Field was not alone in publicly describing the appointment as 'mind-boggling'.[21]

Bacon & Woodrow had been seen initially as the obvious choice. They were well appraised of the problems and consequences of the Commissioners' ineptitude, and were unsullied by involvement with Millbank's coterie of favoured specialists and advisers. The Social Security Committee were quick to pick up on the matter when, for the second time, Colman appeared with Patrick Locke and Howard Gracey before them on 12 January 1995.[22]

Questioned about the 'apparent conflict of interest' caused by Watson's appointment, Colman said that the Commissioners had been 'pressed' by the Board of Governors to consider Watsons. The Board, he added, was 'insistent' that discussions take place with both companies. There were Board members who felt Watsons were 'in some respects superior' to Bacon & Woodrow. Given the overwhelming presence of bishops and senior churchmen, and a handful of distinguished lay representatives with little, if any, actuarial experience, it is difficult to imagine who on the Board of Governors might have been qualified to underwrite that superiority.

The company the Commissioners subsequently recommended was, of course, Watsons, and Colman was 'instructed to go away' and announce the appointment. Gracey, himself a member of the Board of Governors, excluded himself from all discussions, Colman reassured the committee, adding that, in subsequent dealings with Watsons, the pensions board chairman had allowed him to deal independently with the company and had not sought to interfere. 'In fact, I would be very quick to let him know if he did seek to interfere in any way.'

Earlier, Sir Michael said that discussions had taken place about the position Watsons might find themselves in if they wanted to make comments which might have adversely reflected upon their chairman. 'I made it very plain to them that one of the conditions of their appointment was that they had to treat us as clients and the interests of clients had to predominate over any other considerations they might feel inclined to take into account. If I felt at any time they were not observing that integrity, they would be out of the door.' He agreed that their appointment could be seen as 'an additional, perhaps unnecessary, complication', and it was his inclination to avoid that.

Commenting on the appointment of R. Watson & Son, the Social Security Committee's report concurred with Sir Michael's 'inclination' to avoid an unnecessary complication by appointing Watsons, and regretted 'that the Commissioners did not select a firm wholly uninvolved with their past activities'.

1. Social Security Committee, Second Report, *The Church Commissioners and Church of England Pensions*, 29 March 1995, Q. 24.
2. Ibid., Q. 116.
3. Ibid., Para. 30.
4. Ibid., Q. 272.
5. Personal telephone interview, 13 February 1995.
6. Lambeth Group Report, July 1993, p. 3.
7. Social Security Committee, Second Report, *The Church Commissioners and Church of England Pensions*, 29 March 1995, Q. 116.
8. Ibid., Appendix 12, Para. 2.
9. Ibid., Q. 167.
10. Lambeth Group Report, July 1993, Appendix 3.
11. Ibid., Q. 129.
12. Ibid., Memorandum submitted by Mr Howard Gracey, p. 50.
13. Ibid., p. xxvi, Para. 78.
14. Ibid., Q. 206–212.
15. Ibid., Q. 397–398.
16. Ibid., p. xxvi, Para. 78.
17. Telephone interview, 5 July 1994.

18.   Social Security Committee, Second Report, *The Church Commissioners and Church of England Pensions*, 29 March 1995, Q. 41.

19.   Social Security Committee, Second Report, *The Church Commissioners and Church of England Pensions*, 29 March 1995, Q. 178.

20.   Ibid., Appendix 8.

21.   Telephone interview, 5 July 1994.

22.   Social Security Committee, Second Report, *The Church Commissioners and Church of England Pensions*, 29 March 1995, Q. 379.

CHAPTER TWELVE

Paying for the Future

A 57-page report by Watsons on the Commissioners' management of pensions and assets allocation strategy, based on a 20-year projection, was published in July 1994. This revealed, in their words, that the Commissioners had been sitting on a 'time-bomb' whose fuse had merely been shortened by the disastrous performance of the property portfolio.

Confirming much of the findings of the Bacon & Woodrow report, Watsons concluded that for some time the Commissioners had been over-committing their resources and over-distributing their income without any clear understanding of the accumulating financial burden and their sensitivity to inflation. It was not simply an issue of 'short-term imbalance of expenditure and income'. It could not be resolved without action by the Commissioners to reduce a long-term over-commitment of resources.

Action, in particular, was required to close the gap between the level of expenditure and the income available. Any solution which involved simply increasing income would further jeopardize the ability of the Commissioners to meet future obligations. The over-distribution of income had led to a decline in the real value of the asset base and if the Commissioners' current asset allocation policy continued the amount available for stipends would diminish rapidly.

> The primary cause of the problem is not the way in
> which the Commissioners' assets have been managed,

although poor performance on the commercial property portfolio exacerbated the situation and accelerated its impact. The accumulating unrecognized liabilities can be likened to a time-bomb waiting to go off: poor performance within the assets portfolio merely shortened the fuse.

It confirmed Bacon & Woodrow's opinion that pensions would soon demand all the Commissioners' income. An early casualty would be discretionary support for needy dioceses, which would come to an end by 2010. Financial support of all non-pension obligations, from stipends to cathedral grants, would soon follow, and even after all other expenditure had been eliminated, there would still be insufficient income to meet the full cost of pensions.

Pension costs were projected to increase over the following 20 years at an average of about 1 per cent above the Retail Price Index, with the cost of the Commissioners' other commitments expected to increase by about 1.5 per cent above RPI. However, Watsons' long-term assumption of a total investment return of 9 per cent, based on a substantial portfolio shift from property to equities and on a core assumption that total investment returns would exceed the retail price index by 5 per cent, predicted a growth in investment income of 1 per cent *below* RPI.

In the long term, even a major restructuring of the Commissioners' assets, from property to less spectacular equities, would do nothing to resolve the deficit between assets and liabilities. The Commissioners were set on a course which, said Watsons, they could not afford to continue. 'Under optimistic scenarios for investment performances, inflation or increases to stipends and pensions, the immediate problems might appear to diminish. It would, however, be foolhardy to plan on the basis of optimistic assumptions.'

Watsons' report confirmed that the only solution lay in establishing a separate pension fund, with contributions from the dioceses – already mooted in the Lambeth Group report to wide agreement – although there was one major obstacle. Unlike the trustees of a conventional pension fund, who could use capital, if necessary, to help meet pension liabilities, the Commissioners' obligations allowed no such flexibility. As a permanently endowed charity, the payment of pensions could only be met through investment-generated income, thereby ensuring that their capital remained intact in perpetuity. The report called for this obstacle to be removed through legislative action.

Watsons maintained that this restraint was 'inappropriate in relation to the Commissioners' real liabilities, and unnecessarily constraining to their ability to adopt the most suitable investment policies ... the Commissioners' objectives should instead recognize the need to protect the real value of the assets and hence the real level of income available for distribution.'

The report by Watsons caused a fresh series of consultations, nationally and regionally. Sir Michael Colman, Howard Gracey, Chairman of the Pensions Board, and Alan McLintock, Chairman of the Central Board of Finance, discussed the report's recommendations with the House of Bishops and with chairmen and secretaries of diocesan boards of finance. They also met diocesan boards of finance representatives at a private conference and a consultative group of diocesan board of finance chairmen and secretaries.

But several diocesan representatives were uneasy about the timetable proposed by the Commissioners, fearing that changes might be rushed through the General Synod in the belief that they had the widespread agreement of the dioceses. It was argued that time was needed to consult with parishioners, who would be picking up the bill. Further concern was expressed about the fact that, while clergy pensions would depend on the uncertain generosity of parishioners, the pay of bishops would remain within the guarantee of the Commissioners' budget. There was also a strong challenge to the Commissioners retaining £11m a year to cover their costs while other church bodies had to obtain agreement for their budgets from those who paid the bills.

Some saw the circumstances as providing a unique opportunity to do better by less wealthy parishes. One diocese in enthusiastic support of a more egalitarian approach was that of the Archbishop of Canterbury. Mr David Kemp, diocesan secretary, claimed that the proposals tackled the problems in 'piecemeal fashion'. There should, he claimed, be a new mechanism for the support of poorer parishes, not merely a readjusted continuation of the present system. 'There must be a radical financial review,' he said.[1]

Disillusioned and angry dioceses were adamant that the Church Commissioners, in whom their confidence had all but disappeared, should play no part in managing a separately funded pension fund. The Chairman of York Diocesan Board of Finance, Bryan Sandford, who, as chairman of a consultative committee of diocesan boards of finance, had spent 18 months talking to dioceses nationwide, reported back to Sir Michael and his colleagues that the dioceses had made it 'very, very clear that [they] ... wanted nothing whatsoever to do with the idea of paying money to the Church Commissioners'. In addition to their lack of confidence in the Commissioners, they also believed that pensions should be under the control of the Church.[2]

Watsons' actuarial projections and recommendations led to a joint report by Colman, Gracey and McLintock, first discussed at a conference of chairmen and secretaries of the Church of England's 43 diocesan boards of finance in May 1995, who agreed with its 'general thrust'. It favoured a pensions structure with costs shared through contributions based on 18.5 per cent of stipends – subsequently revised to 19.3 per cent – which, based on the average stipend at the time, would mean that parishes would have to raise each year about a further £2,500 per clergyman. It was considered 'the best way to finance pensions in the future by widening the financial base of ministry, which the Commissioners' over-commitment has shown to be too narrow and still too reliant upon historic resources'.

Another option, with the Commissioners' funds exclusively committed to pensions, and which had the backing of those who believed that historic resources should fund pensions while church members' giving should bankroll current ministry, was considered not to be in the interests of the wider Church. Such a pension fund, it was claimed, would hurt needier dioceses by replacing endowment funding with discretionary funding. They would become dependent exclusively on the willingness of less needy dioceses for support. It would simply recycle funds originally held in trust to support needier dioceses and 'would be a breach of faith for those from whom much of the Commissioners' funds derive'.

It was also feared that the Church would no longer be a central authority able to 'target funds strategically in line with its national priorities'. If the 'spirit of partnership' was to be honoured, both historic and current resources should fund the total costs of ministry. 'In most walks of life, accruing pension liabilities are recognized as funded as current employment cost. As a practical way of proceeding, it seems appropriate that today's Church should fund today's ministry as the cost (including the accruing pension liability) arises rather than landing the problem on the shoulders of future generations.'

In sharing the cost of pensions with dioceses, the joint report proposed that the Commissioners would finance past and current pensions while the parishes met the costs of the pension contributions of future clergy, which would go into a separate pension fund. The move would reflect 'the important principle that pensions are deferred pay, and that the pension liability being accrued by the clergy serving in our parishes today should be recognized and financed by the whole Church as part of the overall cost of ministry. It provides a disciplined and transparent mechanism for raising additional support for ministry, and it provides a more visible security for clergy which will accord more closely with wider pension practice.'

It would mean the transfer of £1.34bn of the Commissioners' assets – £580m of which was calculated for discretionary increments – to a separate pension fund for retired clergy, a liability that would exist until about 2050, by which time the last of the beneficiaries would have died. But in order to meet their pension liabilities, the Commissioners would need to use capital. Without it, income from assets would fall far short of projected pensions expenditure. In accord with Watsons' recommendation, the joint report called for legislation which would empower the Commissioners to do so.

The alternative would require maximizing income by concentrating their assets in high income-yielding investments such as gilts – at the expense of future capital and income growth, which had proved so costly in the eighties – or cutting back further on non-pension expenditure. But that would, in addition to pension contributions, place an impossible financial burden on dioceses. The use of capital, 'subject to appropriate safeguards', would give flexibility to the management of pension liabilities 'in a way which does not impose unmanageable pressures either on their investment policy' or other expenditure.

A transitional support fund was also proposed to help ease the impact on parishes while adjusting to the cost of meeting pension contributions. Assets of £68m were later earmarked for distribution on a sliding scale of three to ten years – later limited to seven years – depending on the wealth of the dioceses. The size of the task dioceses and parishes faced in funding pension contributions was not under-estimated, said the joint report. By the year 2000, they would total about £36m – the Commissioners planned cuts between 1995 and 1997 to about the same order to bring income and expenditure into line. But it was, acknowledged the joint report, a tall order, 'especially following several years of substantial cuts'.

Parishes and dioceses were urged to absorb the cost of pension contributions as quickly as possible. The cost of the transitional support would affect the Commissioners' capacity to help poorer dioceses in the longer term. 'If the endowed capacity to help the poorer dioceses is too weak, this will affect those dioceses long after the issue of transitional allocations has been forgotten.' The Commissioners also later earmarked £1.1bn in the discharge of their commitment to support poorer parishes, including the costs of bishops' salaries, cathedral grants and retirement housing, and £67m to cover staff pensions.

The discussions with the diocesan boards of finance led to agreement on five key principles:

- Recognition that the current arrangements for meeting the overall costs of ministry are not sustainable and that the base of financial support for the Church's ministry must be widened and enlarged through increased giving and other means.
- Confirmation by the Commissioners of their continuing ability to meet their existing liability for past service, including pension increments, the precise method of doing so to be determined.
- Pension contributions for future service to be raised from dioceses (through funds raised from parishes) and provided by Diocesan Boards of Finance as a recognized component of the current cost of ministry (to be included in a Fund separate from the Commissioners' funds).
- Transitional provisions to phase in the impact of pension contributions on dioceses and parishes.
- The introduction of legislation to empower the Commissioners to use capital for pension purposes.

The principles, stated the paper, were 'intended to provide the foundations for arrangements which will provide continued security for clergy and greater financial stability for the Church as a whole.'

The five principles, the 'foundation stones' of the most radical and far-reaching change to take place in the Church of England since the creation of the Church Commissioners in 1947, received the overwhelming endorsement of the General Synod in July 1995, and that November it approved a draft pensions Measure which proposed two separate schemes – one for past service, a closed and ultimately self-liquidating scheme funded by the Church Commissioners, and the contributory scheme for future clergy funded by the parishes.

The Measure introducing the legislation for the two pension schemes was scheduled to receive final approval from the General Synod in July 1997. The date set for its implementation: January 1998.

But, even before the 'principles' contained in the report by Colman, Gracey and McLintock were put before the General Synod, where agreement was far from sure, there was uncertainty even within Millbank over the way in which the Commissioners' liabilities for retired clergy should best be funded.

As actuarial assessments are essentially sophisticated guesswork, there was no way of knowing whether a single transfer of assets of £1.34bn to the Pensions Board, projected over a span of 50 years, would prove too little or too much. If it were too much and a surplus emerged, who would enjoy its benefit? Would it be distributed as a pension bonus, or would it be returned to the Commissioners to help meet its non-pension beneficiaries, such as those in the poorer parishes? On the other hand, if it proved inadequate, would there be calls on the Commissioners to make up the shortfall, to the detriment of their other beneficiaries?

On one side there were those who considered the Commissioners' pensions liability to be paramount and wanted the capital to be handed over from day one to ensure that the money was in the pension fund to meet the Commissioners' liabilities, while others, anxious that non-pension beneficiaries should not lose out by any overfunding, were fearful that transferring the capital in one lump sum might result in precisely that. In the middle, the majority were trying to make up their minds which of the options was right. By 1 April 1996, when Sir Michael and Patrick Locke had been summoned yet again to appear before the Social Security Committee before it presented its final report, the division was no nearer to repair.

Sir Michael personally supported what he described as 'a more prudent' strategy. He thought it would be financially imprudent to transfer such a large sum of money without first seeing contributions from the parishes and dioceses establishing the level required. He believed it would be wiser for the Commissioners to transfer capital to the fund on a pay-as-you-go basis, and, once a record of contribution flow had been established and a capital fund built up, to negotiate their remaining liabilities with the fund trustees in return for further capital. That way, he argued, the pension fund would be able to adjust for any under- or over-funding.

But Howard Gracey preferred a strategy that was somewhere in between Sir Michael's preference and a once-for-all payment – a phased transfer of assets, which, spread over a period of time, would minimize the risk of over- or under-funding as future transfers could be adjusted to eliminate any surplus or deficit. It would require, however, close tracking of assets performance and liability costs.

Such was his apparent frustration that Sir Michael appealed to Field and his committee for an opinion to help resolve the matter. He told the Social Security Committee that he believed his approach 'would be the prudent way to go about it'. But that would not satisfy the 'somewhat excited political interests either on one side or the other, and therefore the Commissioners have a real difficulty in resolving that issue in a way which I would regard as being common-sense and in the interests of good husbandry.'

'I would find it very helpful, chairman, if your committee was to express an opinion which would help us to form a view, particularly on the political dimension, because, if it is going to be decided on this basis, it would be very difficult for us to handle, particularly if it was not in keeping with what I personally regard as being a financially prudent way of dealing with it.'[3] The statement indicated a conflict of some seriousness within Millbank, an issue that some believed perhaps even challenged Colman's position as First Church Estates Commissioner.

The political dilemma for Colman was in fixing priorities: if pensions had absolute priority, then payment of capital would need to be made, but if they were on an equal footing with the Commissioners' non-pension obligations, such as supporting the poorer parishes, a legal obligation decreed by Measure, then a more flexible, pay-as-you-go approach appeared to be the safest. The issue created, he told the Social Security Committee, 'a real political aspect ... which the Commissioners are not competent of themselves to determine.'[4]

Field warmly welcomed Colman's request for his committee's opinion, which amounted to Field's opinion. That it should be so openly sought by a senior servant of a Church whose workings he had little time for was flattering. He responded that Colman's personal choice was 'eminently sensible'. He also thought it was important that the Commissioners' priorities should be stated in a Bill or Measure, with first priority inflation-proofed pensions, followed by the protection of poorer parishes. 'That would then give the pensioners some security that their pensions were going to be met and that it would not depend on the whims of Commissioners who may decide to pay them in future from the flow of income.'

It would also, he added, leave the Commissioners with maximum flexibility over the size of their portfolio and distribution.[5] In return for possibly supporting his preference for maximum flexibility, he asked Colman whether it would not be reasonable to expect any Bill or Measure coming before Parliament to list those priorities 'very clearly in rank order'. It would, replied Colman, 'be helpful'.[6]

Colman had no problem with Field's proposed reciprocal arrangement. He wanted the committee's support for the pensions Measure that would be ultimately going before Parliament and saw no reason why the wishes of the Social Security Committee should not be incorporated in the legislation package. He thought it shrewder to enlist the goodwill of Field and his committee at that stage, rather than probably encounter opposition at a later, more crucial, stage of the legislative process.

But Patrick Locke, sitting by Colman's side, was less keen on any political interference by Field and the Social Security Committee in the drafting of the Measure. Since 1919, under the Church of England Assembly (Powers) Act, also known as the Enabling Act, the Church of England had been empowered to draw up its own framework of legislation, which Parliament might either accept or reject, but not amend. Once passed, a Measure had all the statutory power of an Act of Parliament. During the previous 77 years, the Church of England had come to keenly guard its unique legislative powers.

Behind the closed doors of Millbank, the degree to which the Commissioners were prepared to comply with the Social Security Committee's wishes proved to be markedly less than Colman's response had suggested. In a letter to Field dated 30 April 1996,[7] Colman, after confirming that pensions were a legal liability on the Commissioners that 'no one would wish to change', added that, while no rigid order of priority was laid down, an order was effectively produced in the way their balance of income was allocated. 'To establish an order in statutory terms would be difficult if all the discretions are to be kept and, if they are kept, there has to be a degree of flexibility.'

He said the Commissioners were 'urgently examining' the possibility of including in the Measure – 'if its scope allows' – a statement that their traditional function of using surplus income to support poorer parishes remained their primary purpose. He concluded his letter by adding that the statement could be combined with an undertaking that the Commissioners would do their best to maintain pension increments in line with the retail price index. 'Whatever the outcome of that examination, you may accept my assurance that to give priority to that purpose will be the Commissioners' aim.'

In fact, Field found Colman's assurance far from reassuring, although not altogether unexpected. He understood the style of Millbank well enough to know that, even with the arrival of Colman, ranks would close to protect its political powers, but he remained much concerned. He believed the need for the Commissioners' spending priorities to be protected by legislation had become all the more necessary following the publication of a singularly significant report on the Church of England's structure which had been produced by a commission set up by the Archbishop of Canterbury under the chairmanship of the Bishop of Durham, the Rt Revd Michael Turnbull.

Among other fundamental changes the Turnbull Report proposed an Archbishops' Council in which sweeping powers of executive responsibility would be invested. (See Chapter 13.) Much of the authority of the Commissioners would be transferred to the Council, and their influence greatly diminished. Colman's letter did nothing to ease the fears of Field and his colleagues, that, unless priorities were inscribed in legislation, the historical legal and moral obligations, no longer protected by the Commissioners' independence, might become vulnerable to the vagaries of the Church's political forces, with the support of poorer parishes at particular risk.

Two months after the letter, the Social Security Committee's second and final report on the operation of the Church of England's pension funds was published. It called for a full parliamentary debate to establish the Church's calls on income from the Commissioners' assets, but went a stage further and listed what the committee saw as the order of priorities: past pension obligations, payments and allocations for stipends for poorer parishes; redundant churches and other historic buildings; payments to cathedrals; episcopal administration; episcopal and cathedral housing; financial provisions for resigning clergy; central Church functions and Commissioners' administration; and administration costs and other bodies. They should, said the report, be clearly stated in legislation.

The committee's report continued that there was an air of unreality about Parliament being expected to approve a Pensions Measure laying duties and obligations upon an institution that was facing 'virtual elimination. Even if the argument were accepted that legislation by separate Measure was the correct way to proceed, it would be essential in our view for Parliament to settle first the post-Turnbull institutional structure before re-defining roles and duties with respect to pension arrangements.'

The Social Security Committee was equally concerned about the style of pension that the Church Commissioners, the Pensions Board and the Central Board of Finance had endorsed to manage future pensions, and which the General Synod appeared to favour. It was highly critical of a pension plan similar to the traditional company occupational scheme with defined benefits. There were several models which could be implemented, but

> it does not appear that the process of consultation considered in any real depth which model would be appropriate to deal with a contributory scheme for the clergy.
>
> While such a fund clearly offers a greater degree of security than the unsustainable pay-as-you-go scheme, which has been operating in the Church of England since the 1950s, it would be quite understandable if members of the clergy who have experienced anxiety

over their financial protection for old age remained somewhat skeptical of the ability of the Church authorities to deliver on their promises.

The alternative of personal pension schemes deserved the fullest consideration before legislation was put before Parliament. The property rights of a personal pension plan were less risky than the voluntary nature of contributions through the parishes than those from a viable trading company.

The Social Security Committee then delivered a scathing attack on the Archbishops' Council, the Pensions Board and trustees recommended by the Turnbull Report to manage and administer the proposed pension plan.

We would not be at all surprised if substantial numbers of clergy preferred to opt out and retain individual property rights over their accumulating invested contributions rather than to rely on promises and performances of central institutions barely distinguished from those who have let them down in the past.

It went on to cast doubts on the legality of the new pension fund under the new Pensions Act 1995, believing that further consideration needed to be given to whether a company pension model was appropriate for the Church of England. While clergy were regarded as 'employed earners' for national insurance and tax purposes, it was doubtful whether there was an identifiable 'employer' to guarantee any defined benefit promise in accordance with the act. 'So there must be some concern that ... there may be some sort of expectation that ultimately the Church Commissioners' assets might be raided in future if the optimistic projections about the willingness of the laity to increase their voluntary donations were not borne out in reality.'

The Social Security Committee, suspecting that the Church might attempt to exempt itself from the legal requirements of the 1995 Pensions Act through the introduction of a Measure, warned that such a move 'would surely be unacceptable to Parliament unless the most persuasive arguments were advanced, and enforceable guarantees were in place, to demonstrate that the position of the clergy would be in no way jeopardized by the removal of statutory protection ... the Church Commissioners and Synod must ensure that the powers they are seeking in the draft Pensions Measure will provide for the full application of the legislation Parliament has passed to regulate and control pension schemes'.

It also responded cautiously to the Commissioners' proposal to use capital if they were to meet their pensions expenditure, which included funding the cost of transitional support to the dioceses. Field and his colleagues were opposed to any open-ended licence, recommending that the Commissioners should be allowed to dip into capital for no longer than five years – 'and that the Church Commissioners should undertake to inform Parliament of the exact size and nature of any funds transferred from capital to income and the Church Commissioners should give an undertaking that "coupon trading" will cease.'[8]

The alarm caused at Millbank by such a time limit was subsequently expressed by Michael Alison MP, the Second Church Estates Commissioner, during a Commons debate on the Social Security Committee's report on 17 July 1996. He said the five-year timeframe left uncertain whether the Commissioners could continue to manage their commitments. 'I know that many in the Church of England would prefer the Commissioners to acquire a permanent power to spend capital on an unlimited scale, including the power to transfer capital to a new pension fund.' Referring to the uncertainty the Commissioners would face, he added: 'It is in this context that some in the Church of England find a major attraction in being allowed to have a fixed and final capital transfusion ... to wipe out future liability in one fell swoop.' He said the Church would press for a seven-year limit to capital, which would harmonize with the period proposed for 'transitional' payments to dioceses to help ease the impact of pension contribution costs. At the end of that period, with parishes having proved their willingness and ability to meet the costs, it would be simply a matter of legislation finishing 'what had already been well begun'.[9]

In reply, Frank Field said it was the form of the new pensions fund proposed in the draft Measure – modelled on a company pension scheme – which 'most concerned' the committee. It would mean, he said, that dioceses and parishes would be asked to accept unqualified, open-ended financial liabilities. He believed that the

Synod, the diocese board of finances and parishes, would find the proposed scheme unsatisfactory for three reasons.

As charitable bodies under the Charities Act 1992, it was clear that they should not commit themselves to debts amounting to more than their assets, yet that is what they would be asked to do. While the Commissioners would have the resources to meet their past service liabilities, the dioceses and parishes 'cannot know that they will have the resources to meet [their] responsibility ... That is not to say that they should not meet them, but that they should design a pension arrangement so that they can meet them.'[10] They would be taking on liabilities, said Bernard Jenkin, Conservative MP for Colchester North, a member of the Social Security Committee, an adviser to the Legal and General Group, that they couldn't control because the pension scheme benefits would be decided by the trustees.

The committee's second concern, said Field, and one already expressed at diocesan level, was the way in which the security of clergy pensions would depend on the generosity of parishioners while those of bishops, deans 'and what are extraordinarily called the higher clergy' would be met out of the Commissioners' historic resources. 'That is not acceptable,' he warned. 'It will cause problems in this House and even greater problems with the laity in our parishes.

'They will fear that is not fair treatment of those who bear the burden of the day, especially those who have the toughest parishes, whose children are often beaten up at school because they speak with slightly different accents and whose houses are regularly ransacked by yobboes ... We should treat that group as the most privileged, and not subject it to risks to which we are not willing to put bishops, deans and other clergy.'

Thirdly, it claimed it was 'a fantasy' even if the House agreed to vote over half of the Commissioners' assets to a new pension fund that it would end the Commissioners' responsibilities. They would not be able to defend the rest of their assets from a company pensions scheme that, he claimed, wouldn't be able to maintain its income flow. There would be enormous moral pressure on them to hand over yet more assets to meet any deficits that the dioceses and parishes were unable to meet.

Underlining his committee's preference for a personal pension plan for the clergy, he said it would be sustainable in the long term and would safeguard the Commissioners' remaining assets once they had discharged their current past service liabilities. It would be a simple form of pension plan that would be easily understood. 'The assets that would be built up would be in the name of the priests. The assets would not be collectively owned, lost or damaged if anything untoward happened to the scheme.' A unit trust-backed, 'individually-owned' personal pension scheme would also 'allow parish churches and diocesan boards of finance to enter into legal agreement honestly, knowing that their commitments can be fulfilled. The Church, by seeking such a Measure, would unlock the debate that we need about how to universalize second-funded pension provision.'

While Frank Field had doubts that people in the pews would be prepared to take on the burden of finding the money necessary to meet the additional cost of pensions, the Archbishop of Canterbury was sufficiently confident to declare that he believed parishes would increase their contributions by as much as 30 per cent if necessary. He told the Social Security Committee, when he and the Rt Revd John Waine appeared before Field and colleagues on 26 April 1994, that the Church had gone through 'a major evolution' in the last 25 years.

'We are giving more from the parishes for the maintenance of the clergy. It is now increased to three-quarters of the giving; £450m out of £600m comes from ordinary Christians and this statistic indicates it is ... £2.70 a week or so ... if you look at it in that way it is not a large amount we are talking about ... I am quite confident that the Church can find that money, and where we put before people an imaginative claim on their time and their ideals ... I have proved again and again that people will respond positively.'

His confidence was shared by Waine. 'The Church Commissioners are not the Church of England,' he said. 'The Church Commissioners have been major contributors to the ministry of the Church of England, but increasingly over the past years, quite apart from recent losses, the contribution of the Commissioners proportionately has got less and the contribution of parishioners has got more.

'When the matter of our investment policy hit the headlines, there were certainly shock waves that went through the Church. But my own perception is that people have now generally in the Church, certainly in the House of Bishops and the parishes as well, come to recognize that we are in a more difficult financial situation but that if they believe in the mission and the work of the Church, then it is actually within our competence to be able to manage this and to pay for it. After all, other denominations have always had to and we have been somewhat cosseted.'[11]

Dr Carey said earlier that the plight the Church found itself in was perhaps a matter of collective responsibility. 'I think the lesson that we have learnt from operating as a big business – because the Church Commissioners is a big business in the amount of money it spends – is that we as a Church must be more responsible for all we do. That it is why it is uncomfortable for any of us who are bishops to apportion blame, because we are Commissioners, and all of us must perhaps criticize ourselves that we were not more careful at the AGM of asking the kind of question of how money was being spent and the build-up to a very big problem which was going to confront the Church.'

He hoped the Church of England was an open Church that would become more transparent. 'We have learnt some bitter lessons. I certainly, as Archbishop of Canterbury, would not want to be put in this position ever again, not for my own sake but for the sake of the Church.'[12]

Field, offering his sympathy to the Archbishop who, he said, had been under media fire for some considerable time, ended the hearing with the advice: 'Don't let the buggers get you down.' To which Dr Carey replied: 'Thank you very much indeed, I shall bear that in mind.'[13]

1.   *Church Times*, 16 December 1994.
2.   Social Security Committee, Fifth Report, *The Church Commissioners and Church of England Pensions*, 26 June 1996, Q. 131.
3.   Ibid., Q. 84.
4.   Ibid., Q. 86.
5.   Ibid., Q. 85.
6.   Ibid., Q. 87.
7.   Ibid., Appendix 7.
8.   Ibid., p. xvi (ii).
9.   Clergy Pensions, *Hansard*, col. 1088, 17 July 1996.
10. *Hansard*, p. 1092, 17 July 1996.
11. Social Security Committee, Second Report, *The Church Commissioners and Church of England Pensions*, 29 March 1995, Q. 173.
12. Ibid., Q. 138.
13. Ibid., Q. 184.

CHAPTER THIRTEEN

An Extensive Overhaul

The conclusion of the Lambeth Group report that 'it would be appropriate for the Church to review its overall organizational structure' created the opportunity for a radical restructuring of the Church of England's cumbersome, costly and inefficient bureaucracy.

The recommendation that the Church should undergo a structural 'review' was by no means discouraged by Dr Carey or his advisers. It is thought indeed that the initiative for the recommendation came from within Lambeth Palace. The Archbishop had long felt a sense of frustration at the number of executive authorities where personal power bases protected sectional interests detrimental to the effectiveness of the wider Church. He believed they promoted division rather than cohesion, confusion rather than clarity, and thwarted the leadership that he, as Primate of All England, was expected to give.

He had a zealous ally in Dr David Hope, shortly to be appointed Archbishop of York, who felt that much of the work of the General Synod's boards and committees was 'a colossal waste of time'.[1] While Bishop of London, he had decentralized his diocese's top-heavy administration with an energy that alarmed Church traditionalists. He closed down London's centralized Industrial Mission to encourage industrial chaplains to work within the parish; the 30-strong Higher Education chaplaincy was slimmed down, with pastoral care for students being mostly provided by the college's parish; and a chaplaincy at Heathrow Airport was axed – he insisted it should be undertaken by local churches. His appointment to York, it was thought, was advanced by the enthusiasm he shared with Dr Carey for a comprehensive overhaul of the Church.

So, following the publication of the Lambeth Group report, Dr Carey began a consultative process to establish one of the most important commissions ever undertaken within the Church of England. Its work demanded a membership of wide-ranging experience and skills, both sacred and secular, including an understanding of the Church of England's political and sectional factions.

Two of the appointees were considered inevitable – Sir Michael Colman, the First Church Estates Commissioner, and Alan McLintock, the Chairman of the Central Board of Finance, the General Synod's financial executive. As the Church Commissioners were in line for virtual emasculation, it made political sense to have Colman in the operating theatre. Like McLintock, and Howard Gracey, Chairman of the Pensions Board, who was also appointed to the Commission, Colman was at the heart of the turbulence. And, like McLintock, veteran of many a closed-doors synodical skirmish, his corporate shrewdness and acumen would not be out of place.

Their colleagues were a combination of corporate heavyweights, ecclesiastic worthies, and grassroots diocesanism. The top appointments included Lord Bridge of Harwich, a former appeal law lord, former Chairman of Parliament's Ecclesiastical Committee, and Chairman of the Review of Synodical Government; Sir Brian Cubbon, former Permanent Under Secretary of State for Northern Ireland and Home Office; and Prof. David McLean, QC, Chairman of the General Synod's House of Laity, Pro-Vice Chancellor and professor of law at Sheffield University.

In addition to Colman and McLintock, the corporate caucus was completed by John Jordan, a KPMG consultant, and former head of the company's operations and financial management, and Humphrey Norrington, former vice-Chairman of Barclays Bank. The Very Revd Dr David Edwards, Provost Emeritus of Southwark, the Ven. Stephen Lowe, Archdeacon of Sheffield, Bryan Sandford, Chairman of the York Diocesan Board of Finance, and Sylvia Green, Secretary of the Hereford Diocese, completed the team. Predictably, there were public criticisms that the Commission's membership failed to include the 'ordinary' churchgoer, an admonishment Lambeth was prepared to endure rather than risk the Commission being undermined by people whose well-meaning but unprofessional opinions would contribute little to its objectives.

The position of chairman, whose views needed to chime with Dr Carey's ambitions for the Church, offered a wide array of sympathetic bishops, few of whom would be grieved by the thought of the General Synod and its endless committees being cut down to size. But the pedigree of Michael Turnbull, the Bishop of Rochester, Kent, for the previous seven years, met the requirements to a degree: he had a credible middle-of-the road political profile, at the age of 58 had the energy to take on the chairmanship, enjoyed a supportive relationship with Dr Carey, and was a fellow evangelical from a not dissimilar background. A former grammar schoolboy and the son of an insurance manager, who read geography at Keble College, Oxford, he moved out of mainstream ministry in 1976 to become Chief Secretary to the Church Army because he felt attracted to its world-wide frontline work with the poor.

The invitation from the Archbishop to chair his Commission came out of the blue. He was equally surprised by another invitation from Dr Carey which followed a couple of months later – to become the next Bishop of Durham, the fifth-ranking English See, to replace the controversial liberal theologian, Dr David Jenkins, who was retiring. By the time Turnbull and his wife, Brenda, moved to the bleak, historical grandeur of Durham in the autumn of 1994, he was deeply involved in the work of the Commission, a commitment that at one stage had caused him to wonder whether he was able to take on the Durham Bishopric.

News of the Commission and its purpose – to 'review the machinery for central policy and resource management machinery in the Church of England, and to make recommendations for improving its effectiveness in supporting the ministry and mission of the Church to the nation as a whole' – was announced in a news release on 16 February 1994. The Archbishop, keen to maintain the initiative for action that he had imposed since the news of the Commissioners' mismanagement of assets had broken 18 months earlier, wanted the Commission's report by the following summer, a deadline which later provoked criticism that the work of Bishop Turnbull and his colleagues had been rushed.

During the next 17 months, the Commission met almost monthly at Lambeth Palace, and at three weekend sessions at residential centres in Kent and Sheffield, to examine the infrastructures of the Church's five executive authorities – the General Synod, including its numerous boards and councils; the Church Commissioners; the House of Bishops; the staff structure of the Archbishops of Canterbury and York; and the Pensions Board. They received more than 470 written submissions of evidence.

The Archbishop had invited Turnbull to be radical in the Commission's recommendations. He did not disappoint. The 152-page report, which cost £100,000 to produce and was made public on 20 September 1995, proposed the biggest structural upheaval since 1534, when, in the wake of the Reformation, Parliament passed the Act of Supremacy to make the monarch the head of the church in England.

The Commission's most radical recommendation was the creation of a 17-member National Council – or Archbishops' Council, as it would be later renamed – in which would be invested sweeping powers and authority through which all executive bodies would operate. It would be responsible for all policy and resource issues and propose strategies to deal with them. The Council would be chaired by the Archbishop of Canterbury, with the Archbishop of York as vice-Chairman. 'The buck would stop with the Council and it would be answerable for its work,' said the report.

The Council should take responsibility for assessing the overall financial and 'human resource' needs of the Church, 'including not only their effective stewardship but taking active steps to enhance them'; determining the distribution of income from the Church Commissioners' assets; redistributing resources to help redress financial inequalities of dioceses; fixing the budget for ministry training and national Church responsibilities; and overseeing the work of its own committees and boards. It would also draw up the Synodical legislation necessary for the introduction of the proposed changes. The Council, in short, would have supreme powers and authority.

The Commission's judgement on the Commissioners, the General Synod's influential 26-member Standing Committee – described as the 'Church's Cabinet' – and Policy Committee, its Central Board of Finance, the Advisory Board of Ministry and the

Pensions Board, was severe. It recommended that their functions should be taken over by the Council, with the Commissioners reduced to managers and trustees of assets. The 30-strong Board of Governors and the office of the Third Church Estates Commissioner should be axed.

The multifarious boards and committees would be replaced, it was proposed, by four policy and resources departments, each headed by executive chairmen appointed by the Archbishops and approved by the General Synod, which would 'work closely with the Archbishops in the development of the Church's overall strategy'. The policy and resources areas were designated as: resources for ministry (human resources); mission resources; heritage and legal services; and financial resources. The Council would also have independent external auditors and an Audit Committee 'to strengthen the process of accountability'.

Prompting media comparisons to a business corporation – with the Archbishop of Canterbury as Chairman of the Church of England plc – the analogy was reinforced by the Commission recommending the creation of a new role of Secretary General, who would act as the chief executive officer of the Church at national level. He would be in charge of a senior staff team which would help 'provide the dynamic, strategic initiative the Council would need to fulfil its role'.

But the parallel with the board of a business corporation was false, said Dr Carey. 'The Archbishops' Council will only be able to operate through consultation and consent of the General Synod, the bishops and the dioceses,' he said. 'It should certainly help to overcome the fragmentation and inertia of the current set up but the autonomy of the dioceses and parishes will continue as before.'[2]

Central to the corporate framework recommended by the Commission would be a Business Committee, which would work alongside the four departments and the Secretary General, and would be responsible for communications between the Archbishops' Council, the House of Bishops and Synod. Its chairman would be a member of the Council, appointed – as the best man for the job, it emphasized – by the Synod from among members of the Houses of Clergy and Laity.

The General Synod would be represented on the Council through the appointment of six 'non-executives': the Synod's clergy and lay leaders – the Prolocutors of the Convocations of Canterbury and York and the chairman and vice-chairman of the House of Laity – and two bishops representing the House of Bishops. The Archbishops would also have powers to appoint a further three members, which would be approved by Synod, with skills and expertise not otherwise available to the Council 'and essential to the fulfilment of its task at any particular time'. It added that this power should be 'permissive and limited' so that there were not more than three such people on the Council at any one time.

Membership of the council would be between three and five years, renewable for one further period. Those who were not members of the Synod would become *ex officio* members which would enable them to represent the Council's business to the Synod and be answerable to it. The Archbishop of Canterbury would be President of the Council, with the Archbishop of York as vice-President. This was later amended to a joint presidency to enable the Archbishop of York to help ease the pressures on Dr Carey.

To increase administrative efficiency and reduce costs, the staff of the Church Commissioners, the Pensions Board, the Central Board of Finance and the Archbishops' staff – apart from the Archbishop of Canterbury's personal staff – would be combined to produce a central secretariat, probably based at Church House, where it would service the four new departments, the House of Bishops, and the Council. The Commission wanted to see the staff develop 'a coherence and singleness of purpose which the present structures do not permit.'

The practical advantages of a Archbishops' Council, argued the Commission, were clear: 'for the first time, all the responsibilities at national level for ministry would be brought together in one place so that a coherent strategy for ministry and training for ministry could be developed. For the first time, a single body at national level would be responsible for overseeing the financial flows within the Church, and for helping the dioceses and parishes in managing them. For the first time, a single body would be responsible for developing with the dioceses a comprehensive pensions policy and arrangements for financing that policy.'

The Commission, which discovered that Church House was serving more than 100 committees, said it was essential to move away from the committee culture, and resist re-inventing 'the plethora of committees which abounds at present'. It believed the way in which separate bodies at national level worked was detrimental to the Church.

> Problems can arise from excessive loyalty to one body. Communication between the various national organizations is limited. There is a risk of people not knowing what is happening or of duplicating each other's work. In general, the Church makes great use of committees and standing bodies, often carefully balanced in terms of churchmanship, geographical representation, clergy and lay membership and so on, instead of assembling for a limited time teams with the skills needed to do a specific job. An issue which can be quite straightforward can be looked at repeatedly by different bodies with little value added. Little distinction is made between matters which need to be handled thoughtfully, carefully and with wide consultation, and matters which can properly be dealt with more swiftly and decisively. There is also an emphasis on producing reports rather than securing practical outcomes.

The chaotic committee-bound culture, with no single focus of decision-making and strategic planning, had led to widespread dissatisfaction, causing people to lack confidence in the national performance of the Church, especially, in recent years, the Church Commissioners. It had also resulted in people in authority having no shared sense of collective responsibility for furthering the mission of the Church, and for finding ways of addressing the problems. 'While many people participating in the Church's governance can stop things happening, few (if any) can make things happen … The system places a great burden upon (and potentially gives too much influence to) the few who try to co-ordinate its working and master its complexities.'

The existing system prevented the Archbishop of Canterbury from fulfilling his role – 'the Church of England looks to the Archbishop of Canterbury as its national leader and he is often seen as the only person able to speak for the Church as a whole. This is a heavy responsibility but one for which he is given little executive power … because of the fragmented and incoherent character of the Church of England's own national machinery.'

The Commission, concerned that their proposals might be seen to give too much power and control to the Archbishops and their board of 'directors', said that the Archbishops' Council should take care to respect the roles of the parishes and the dioceses. It reassured them that the Archbishops' Council would carry out much of its work in direct contact with the dioceses, and, aware of the damage caused by the Commissioners, added that they 'should seek to restore the confidence of the dioceses and parishes in the work of the Church at the national level, much of which is performed in support of them.' The Archbishops' Council should not undertake any function that could be more effectively or appropriately performed at diocesan level.

The Commission believed the Church of England underestimated its strength and potential. 'Indeed, because so much of the important work of the Church takes place in the parishes, deaneries and dioceses, it would be wrong to exaggerate the importance of the impact of changes at the national level. Within these limits, however, there is now a significant opportunity to improve the way in which the Church can work as one body. Our report seeks to build on the existing strong foundations of the Church, so that its strong potential can be fully realized.'

The most radical restructuring, as widely expected, was reserved for the Church Commissioners, whose management of the Church's assets was politely described as 'flawed'. In proposing that the Archbishops' Council take over all their functions, the Commission recommended that the number of Commissioners, with far fewer functions to perform, should be reduced from 95 to 15.

Its membership would consist of the two Archbishops, the First and Second Church Estates Commissioners, three Crown appointments, two bishops elected by the House of Bishops, a dean or provost, and two clergy and three lay members elected by the Houses of Clergy and Laity. This composition, claimed the Commission, broadly reflected the balance between Church and State.

Essentially, the Commissioners – 'as an independent trust as guardians and stewards of the centrally held historic assets of the Church' – would carry out the functions of the Assets Committee, whose membership, the Commission recommended, would be replaced, a matter which had been enacted by the time the Commission's report was published. The committee would concern itself solely with the day-to-day management of assets, under a new regime of scrupulous monitoring which had also been put in place following the recommendations of the Lambeth Group.

Said the Commission: 'What is important is to protect the body managing the assets from undue pressure to over-distribute.' The Assets Committee would report directly to the Commissioners whose external auditors would liaise annually with the Audit Committee recommended by the Lambeth Group to scrutinize all aspects of the work of the Assets Committee and the Commissioners themselves. The assets would remain ring-fenced, 'so that neither the Commissioners nor any other body within the Church could spend the capital from them unless authorized by legislation to do so'.

The Archbishops' Council would also take over the Commissioners' role as the Central Stipends Authority, to which it was appointed in 1972 by the General Synod to set the stipends of bishops, deans, provosts and residentiary canons. But the Commissioners would no longer continue to pay their own administration costs – £6.5m a year – nor contribute to the administration costs of other central bodies. They would be mostly borne by the dioceses to make more money available for selective distribution, 'and to introduce greater transparency' in central costs.

The legal obligations, duties and responsibilities of the Commissioners would be no less safe in the hands of the Archbishops' Council. 'Unless and until the obligations were changed by law, the Council would discharge them. If it failed to do so, it would be breaking the law ... The key difference would be that the Council, as a policy body, would be in a position to look at the existing pattern of demands on the Commissioners' funds and to consider if they represented the best way of meeting the current requirements of the Church.'

If they did not, the Archbishops' Council would either make necessary adjustments in accordance with its administrative discretion or power or seek necessary legislative changes through Synod. And if legislation removed a function funded by the Commissioners' income, the 'freed' money would be made available for distribution to needy parishes in accordance with the Commissioners' historic purpose. The Commissioners would also have to be satisfied that any proposed new expenditure, unless otherwise authorized by legislation, was similarly allocated.

To ensure that the Archbishops' Council had distributed income in accordance with its functions, it would issue the Commissioners with a certificate, with any balance of funds made available to needy parishes. It would be 'a check to ensure compliance, not as a detailed audit'. But it would be reinforced by a Measure which also would require the Archbishop's Council to give the Commissioners information on request about the purpose to which income had been put.

Summing up, the Commission said their recommendations involved 'massive changes', with the Commissioners losing the majority of their functions. The composition would be totally changed and their staff merged into the central secretariat. 'Nevertheless,' it added, 'we believe that a radical refocussing on the Church Commissioners' core function would restore them to their appropriate place in the central structures of the Church. We note that this approach is in line with the recommendations of the House of Commons Social Security Select Committee.'

But the Commissioners would continue to manage the investment of assets, which had precipitated the Church of England's financial crisis, while transferring other responsibilities, which they had carried out satisfactorily. This was noted for its irony, and it caused those responsible for their administration to feel they were paying the price for the incompetence of others.

Said Colman: 'A lot of people, who have been involved with the Church Commissioners over many years, feel very deeply that they have been caught up in [the mismanagement of assets] ... and that has been used as an excuse in a sense to deprive them of work that they have carried out for many generations and [of which] they feel quite proud ... in the sense that their achievements have been quite significant.'[3]

Before loading them onto the tumbrel, Bishop Turnbull and his colleagues graciously attempted to defend the Commissioners, implying more than once that they had done their best in the face of unreasonable demands by the General Synod.

> The present pattern of the Church Commissioners' functions reflects their desires and their efforts over the years to meet the requests of the Church for help and

support. The General Synod has made decisions about policy, and while the Commissioners have sought to provide the resources needed, it should have been clear to all that the resources available were not sufficient to sustain all the commitments entered into.

… The support which the Church Commissioners have in the past been able to provide may have served to obscure the fact that the fundamental responsibility for the maintenance of the ministry rests with the bishop and his diocese. Some parts of the Church may have expected too much from the central endowments.

Undoubtedly so, but the fact that the Commissioners buckled under such pressures and remained quiet for so long served to compound their mistakes.

The Commission had considered recommending the abolition of the Commissioners, or, at least, the transfer of their asset management function to another central body, but decided it would be wrong for the capital of the historic assets to be eroded or dispersed. It also decided against recommending that the Archbishops' Council take on the responsibility, believing it was more 'prudent' for the bodies responsible for decisions about asset management and decisions about expenditure from their income to remain separate.

The Commission also respected the conditions on which the assets were originally accumulated.

The State has an interest in the origins of the assets, played a part in arranging for their surrender, and was the source of some of them. It is therefore appropriate that the assets should be managed by a body in which the historic partnership between the Church and the State continues to be embodied. We hope the State as well as the Church will find these reasons persuasive.

Fully aware of the political sensitivity of the management of the Church's historic assets, particularly in the thinking of the Social Security Committee, the Commission's reassuring comments were interpreted by some as an attempt to pre-empt Parliamentary criticism that the relationship between the Church and the State had already been undermined by the restructuring of the Church Commissioners, who, through *ex officio* appointments of government ministers, historically formed the bridgehead with Parliament.

A further blow to the standing of the Church Commissioners was threatened by the proposed sale of their prestigious premises at No. 1 Millbank. The Commission, in recommending a cost-cutting central staff pool to serve the various bodies taken over by the Archbishops' Council, believed that it would be better accommodated at Church House in Great Smith Street. The additional costs, it was suggested, would be met by the investment income of capital raised by the sale of the Millbank property, currently valued at £25–50m.

Church House, owned by the Corporation of the Church House, an independent body founded by Royal Charter, would become the Church of England's national office, with the Charter being amended to give the Archbishops' Council control of the building. As the employer of the staff of the national office, the Commission believed it was right that the Archbishops' Council should have effective control of the building to allow the proper discharge of its responsibilities, including working conditions and control of costs. In the longer term, it suggested the Archbishops' Council consider relocating administrative staff out of London.

The Turnbull Commission was keen to see the House of Bishops play 'a more sharply focused and purposeful role' in the institutions of the Church. Subject to the 'strategic approval' of the General Synod, it should give guidance in helping the Church to develop its broad direction. The Archbishops' Council should regularly seek the views of the bishops on what they saw as the Church's priorities. The bishops, in turn, would be invited to ask the Archbishops' Council to pursue particular issues.

With the Archbishops, the bishops would regularly develop 'an articulated vision', which would be debated by the General Synod. 'The Church could thus forge the shared sense of direction and broad unity of purpose which some now feel it lacks,' said the Commission.

A more clearly focused and 'regular collective approach' by the bishops would not 'suppress openness of debate or difference of view within the Church ... The reflections of the bishops on the issues of policy and resources being handled by the Council would enrich the theological and intellectual quality of the debate on them in the Church as a whole.' It was appropriate for the House of Bishops, as a college of 'chief pastors' with a responsibility for oversight, to offer vision and guidance. They were best placed to propose broad directions because 'they have the most general knowledge of their dioceses and thus, collegially, of the whole Church'.

The General Synod did not emerge unscathed from the Commission. It was acknowledged that the Synod had many critics, as confirmed by the letters columns of religious newspapers. But it had no doubt about the validity of the principles which led to its establishment. The Church

> must have a national body with power to deal with the legal rules which are to govern, and facilitate its work. If it is to be true to itself, an Anglican church must incorporate within such a body the episcopal leadership of the Church, and representatives of the clergy and the laity. Those elements must be present if decisions on matter of controversy, which may need to be settled by a legislative process, are to be acceptable as reflecting the mind of the Church.

The Commission defended the Synod against criticism that as a national forum it was no more than a 'talking shop'. Its deliberative role was considered to be no less important than its legislative role. The Commission believed the Church needed a forum at which leaders and representative members could reflect together and make known the views of the Church.

They were also for 'seeking together to know the mind of Christ. If a synod is one means by which the Church grows in understanding ... it is to be expected that its conclusions on difficult issues will sometimes have a tentative quality.' The Commission believed, however, that the Synod would lead to a more coherent and responsive central structure which would ensure that the General

Synod's debates and decisions were informed 'by clear and up-to-date policy analysis and information about resources'.

It rejected arguments in favour of the General Synod being the 'principal decision-making body on policy and resources'. The Commission questioned whether the Synod could be a 'governing body' making executive decisions as well as a legislative and deliberative assembly. It would, it claimed, be logistically impossible.

> Quite clearly, an assembly of some 566 members, drawn from all over the country and meeting twice, or occasionally three times, a year, cannot be an executive body.
>
> As a representative assembly, it must be able to question, to seek and obtain information, and to express opinions which will influence, often decisively, the formation of policies. But it cannot itself be the forum in which those policies are formulated. The General Synod has its own role in governance: its legislation binds the church, its resolutions influence Church opinion. It will often be invited to approve policy proposals. In terms of the central structure, however, its role is primarily reactive.

In proposing the abolition of the Synod's Standing Committee, and its Policy Committee, the Commission believed they had been rendered largely ineffective by the fragmentation of the central structure. The Archbishops' Council would provide for the first time a forum 'properly equipped' to carry out the executive role.

The Business Committee proposed by the Commission would be responsible for the organization and management of General Synod business and meetings. A principal function would be to ensure that proper consideration was given by the Synod to business brought to it by the Archbishops' Council. The Synod would elect its chairman and the majority of seven members, with the Archbishops, the Prolocutors and the chairman and vice-chairman of the House of Laity as *ex officio* members. The Secretary-General would also be a member. The overlap in membership between this 'important' committee and the Archbishops' Council 'would ensure that the respective functions of each are well co-ordinated'.

The General Synod would retain its distinctive role as a national legislative body, and an important element of its powers:

control over expenditure, although it emphasized that the budget as a whole, including clergy stipends and pensions, would be prepared and presented to the Synod by the Archbishops' Council. However, the Synod's scrutiny of costs would take on increased importance through the Council taking responsibility for a larger area of central expenditure.

Sensitive to the political nuances of the General Synod, and concerns that the Council might be too autonomous, the Commission attempted to underline the importance of the assembly on five counts: Council members would be either directly elected or approved by the Synod; all members would be members of the Synod; the Synod would play a role in providing many of those involved in the work of the Council; the Synod would have total legislative control where the Council's proposals required legislation; and, 'perhaps most significant of all in practice', there would be 'an important measure of public accountability of the Council to the Synod'.

It stressed that the relationship between the General Synod and the Council would be an 'important part' of ensuring effective communications between the dioceses and the central structure. 'The principles of synodical government would be fully protected, and indeed more coherently expressed. In its practical working, the Synod would be better informed, and be provided with a wider overview of the life of the Church and its financial and manpower needs.'

In reviewing the Church's financial structure, the Commission proposed significant changes to shift much of the burden of administrative costs from the centre to dioceses. Over the years, the Commissioners had either taken on, or contributed to, the administrative costs of a number of Church bodies whose activities were not directly related to asset management functions. As a result, the Commissioners incurred expenditure totalling £15.7m in 1994, of which £7.6m went to pay over half the administrative costs of the Church's national activities – which account for 3 per cent of the Church of England's annual running costs of £615m – while the dioceses paid the remainder.

'Every pound used to finance central costs results in one pound less being available for selective allocation to the needier dioceses,' said the Commission. In the changing financial climate, such administrative costs should come out of the budget for national

Church responsibilities, with as much as possible being funded by the dioceses, which would allow the Church as a whole to 'decide, in the context of its overall priorities, what elements of central expenditure should be met from the income from the historic assets (which would otherwise be available for allocation to the dioceses) and what should be met from apportionment on the dioceses nationally.' Administrative and support costs provided by the Commissioners should be confined to matters associated with their management of assets, and to their historic obligations to diocesan bishops' costs and cathedrals, although their level of expenditure would be determined by the Archbishops' Council.

The central administration of clergy stipends should be billed to dioceses, and the management costs of any assets transferred for pensions would be met by diocesan contributions to the pension fund. 'It is our view that all other administrative costs and grants should be met by the dioceses through the budget for national church responsibilities.' To ensure easier monitoring of expenses, the Commission proposed that bishops 'and others' charged their Council business expenses to the Council's budget or relevant committee, rather than their own general expenses account. 'In this way, it would be possible to see the true cost of each activity.'

Under the Commission's proposals, the dioceses would need to find a further £9.5m a year. It proposed that the costs met by the Church Commissioners of Pension Board administration, support for 'other bodies', and national church functions, which totalled £6.4m, should be shared by the dioceses, who would also be directly charged with suffragan bishops' costs of £2.8m and clergy stipends administration costs of £300,000.

While the figure apportioned to the dioceses would currently increase from £13.2m to £19.6m, it would result in two important consequences: the substantial reduction in central costs would mean that more money would be available for the needier dioceses, and, as the proportion of central costs included in the national budget for Synod approval would be much higher, it would mean greater synodical accountability. The transfer of funding responsibility was an important way of ensuring that the Church could respond more flexibly to those in greatest need by releasing more of the Commissioners' funds for discretionary allocation. How the precise mechanics of their proposal would work in practice would need to be discussed by dioceses and the national Church bodies.

While significant savings should be seen to be within the grasp of the Church, the primary objective of the Commissioners' proposed restructuring was to increase the effectiveness of the Church's national organizations. 'It would be contrary to our underlying objectives if the new staffing structure were to be based merely on bringing the existing organizations together and looking for efficiency savings.' Until the Council had worked out its plans in detail, it was impossible to be precise about its running costs. For the first two or three years, it would be unwise to expect any worthwhile savings. Indeed, the process of transition was likely to have an adverse financial impact for which provision had been made through the Central Board of Finance's budget.

But looking beyond the initial stages, the Commission had made broad calculations, based on reasonable assumptions, which forecast savings of between £750,000 and £1m per year. The Council, which would be expected to review the support given to Church bodies such as the Church Urban Fund, 'alongside other national Church responsibilities', should set these figures as its target.

In acknowledging the efforts in recent years to reduce the Church's administrative costs, such as the Church Commissioners' reduction of their staff from 400 to 270 since 1980, it encouraged the drive for continued realistic economies. It had not found 'immediate scope for further drastic reductions' in central costs.

> Instead, we have sought to identify the most appropriate level within the Church's organization for aspects of the Church's mission and ministry, and then to ensure that all those functions which belong at the national level are carried out not only efficiently and effectively, but also economically ... We have also set out more clearly than hitherto has been done what should (and consequently what should not) be financed from the Church Commissioners' income.

Aware of the damage done to confidence in the Church's handling of finances, the Commission put forward a three-point 'charter' to ensure greater accountability. Parishes should be provided by dioceses with a statement of the cost of ministry in their parish, with a breakdown of contribution to activities funded at a diocesan and national level; parochial, diocesan and national activities should be seen as supportive of each other, while policy-makers should communicate more effectively how money is spent to those who are providing it; and an acceptance of giving to, and being supported by, others:

> ... trusting others to make decisions is inherent in the image of the Church as the body of Christ but that trust should be reciprocated by open, fair and understandable means of discerning need and of reallocating resources ... We believe that money flows within the Church must be rationalized and better explained.

Legislation should be introduced to allow accounts and trust funds, which by law must be held at national level, to be managed by dioceses, which would eliminate the flow of money between dioceses and the centre and the 'many transactions' it entailed. It supported the view of the Church Commissioners that diocesan pastoral accounts and diocesan stipends fund capital accounts should come under diocesan management. All relevant trust monies, it maintained, should be held by the dioceses. Once legislation had been passed, dioceses should have the choice either to invest locally or in national investment funds.

But the Commission rejected calls to allow parishes to fix clergy stipends. It would be neither in the interests of pay equality or cost-efficiency. 'Each parish is part of a national Church which has a responsibility to ensure that all its stipendiary clergy are paid at a fair level.' The Central Stipends Authority, responsible for setting that level, existed to encourage equality of stipends, both in the interest of equity and to encourage clergy mobility. It would not be efficient or 'appropriate' for parochial church councils to run their own payroll system. Fewer than 20 staff handled the central payroll, including tax and 'many other matters' related to the payment of 17,600 serving and retired clergy. However, while a central payroll meant economies of scale, the Commission suggested that dioceses might want to consider taking on the function. 'It is a sound principle that monies for stipends and, especially, for pensions should be pooled and held at one remove from the parish.'

Commenting on the Church's increasing dependence on giving and less on income from the Church Commissioners' inherited assets, the Commission believed that parishes and dioceses could increase income by widening their fundraising efforts beyond the traditional appeal for church building repairs. The Church Urban Fund had demonstrated that there was a considerable willingness by individuals, trusts and companies to support 'clearly focused good causes' which contribute to areas of need. 'We believe that individuals and organizations, both within and outside the Church, would be ready to fund certain "mission" projects in which people are actively involved in Christian programmes,' said the Commission.

It recognized that, with parishes and dioceses having to bear the burden of increased giving,

> ... a hard challenge and painful decisions lie ahead for all of us. Nevertheless, we do welcome the increased reliance on voluntary and sacrificial giving. A living Church should depend primarily on its living members for its survival and growth. Those who are giving should be able to see how their money is being spent and have the opportunity, directly and indirectly, to influence those decisions.
>
> This expectation plays a healthy part in ensuring that scarce resources are used efficiently and effectively. Our proposals seek to enhance the accountability of those taking policy and resource decisions, whilst stressing that those directly charged with responsibility for taking decisions should have the trust of the Church as a whole.

In summarizing, the Commission underlined the importance of its recommendations being implemented in their entirety – or not at all. It urged that

> major recommendations be taken as a package of inter-related reforms. We do not believe the necessary changes would be achieved if only some of our recommendations were implemented.

... We are unanimous in making these proposals for reform. We are confident that they would enable the central institutions of the Church to be more effective and efficient in making policy and in directing resources. We hope they will be implemented swiftly so that the Church can more effectively work as one body in the service of God and his world.

1.   *Daily Telegraph*, 16 February 1994.
2.   Response to written questions, 15 October 1996.
3.   Social Security Committee, Fifth Report, *The Church Commissioners and Church of England Pensions*, 26 June 1996, Q. 45.

CHAPTER FOURTEEN

Ominous Warnings

Grassroots response to the Turnbull Report proved difficult to measure. An invitation to the Church at large to respond to the Turnbull Commission resulted in no more than 33 parishes out of 13,025 bothering to do so. Only five of 900 deaneries expressed a point of view, while 25 dioceses – more than half – made their comments known. The official 'spin' on what others perceived as disappointing indifference in the pews was that the Church was having difficulty in keeping pace with progress.

Of almost 200 Church bodies and individuals who responded to the report, less than 20 rejected its main recommendations, or criticized it with a severity unlikely to be mollified by amendments, according to a White Paper[1] produced by an Archbishops' Advisory Group, and published four months after the Turnbull Report to consider the general response to the report and to help form a legislative framework.

The most persistent criticism, doubtless from those who saw the authority of the General Synod being usurped, was of the Archbishops' Council's accountability to Synod, which, it was thought, should be more clearly defined and reinforced by legislation. There was also criticism of a Council whose membership would be substantially appointed by the Archbishops. The proportion of elected members should be higher, it was claimed.

High on the list of concerns was that the Turnbull Report threatened to put too much power into the hands of the Council. It was likened to the Curia, the papal court and government of the

Roman Catholic Church. Critics felt that 'appointments should reflect the comprehensive character of the Church of England and ensure effective consultation. Many people are concerned that the Archbishop of Canterbury should not be placed in a managerial mould nor lose his status as an arbiter of last resort, and that the distinctiveness of his office and that of the Archbishop of York should be preserved.'

Regret had also been expressed 'in some quarters' that the Church Commissioners had not been replaced by a new body of trustees, although 'in the main' the reasons for retaining the Commissioners in an asset managing role had been accepted. Others thought it 'incongruous' to transfer away from the Commissioners functions which they had 'performed best', notably the Pastoral Measure and the support of bishops and cathedral clergy.

In reply to a popular claim that the Archbishops' Council would be too powerful with little accountability, the Council would not, said the Paper, take decisions wholly in isolation, but would be 'locked into a network of relationships, in particular with the House of Bishops and the General Synod'.

The Paper rejected also a suggestion that a revised Standing Committee of the General Synod could fulfil the role of the Archbishops' Council. It did so on three counts: the necessary coherence among the Boards of the General Synod and other national bodies required 'a new mechanism' which could effectively bring policy and finance together; the executive and legislative functions are distinct, nor could it be assumed that the wider Church would think it right for every function to come under the Synod's control; and there could be no guarantee that Parliament would agree to a revised Standing Committee taking on the functions of other bodies.

Criticism that the composition of the Council should reflect a stronger elected element could not be supported, said the Paper. 'Election is not the only means by which the accountability of the Council is to be assured. Other means include the General Synod's power to approve appointments to the Council; to set the budget and approve or not approve legislation; and to question and hold Council members to account.' There was also 'a balance to be struck between representativeness and competence to undertake the duties laid upon it'.

But it agreed with concerns that the link between the Council and the Church Commissioners was not strong enough. It should be strengthened to ensure that the Commissioners were kept fully aware of the Council's policies. To provide that link, the Paper said it would 'seem sensible' to appoint the First Church Estates Commissioner to the Council. This would also go some way to meeting a similar criticism, that there needed to be 'a clearer line of answerability' between the Commissioners, the Council and Parliament so that the Commissioners could be kept fully informed on the way in which the Council was discharging its historic trust responsibilities, and thereby able to answer questions in Parliament.

But it defended the Turnbull proposal which would give the Archbishops the power to nominate to the Council up to three people with special expertise. It was feared that it would lead to the Archbishop of Canterbury, also with authority to nominate the four executive chairmen, packing the Council with his supporters. In rejecting the criticism, the Paper said the object of the proposal was to ensure that the Council had available the appropriate specialisms to assist in its core task of furthering the mission of the Church.

Underlining the Council's accountability to Synod, the Paper said that it would not be able to impose its will on the Synod or the Church. If it was to be effective, it would have to convince others – Synod, House of Bishops, dioceses, parishes – of the wisdom of its proposals. Its authority would be a product of its perceived competence. 'The General Synod's role will be far from that of a rubber stamp. It will be involved in a complex inter-action with the Council, whose views and actions it will be able to influence and help shape.'

The view of the Turnbull Report that the House of Bishops should 'play a more sharply focused and purposeful role among the national institutions of the Church' was generally welcomed, although the suggestion that it should develop, at regular intervals, an 'articulated vision for the direction of the Church' was seen by some as a visionary role that was potentially threatening, either to the different views within the Church or to the scope for clerical and lay leadership. 'It does not however follow,' said the Paper, 'that an attempt by the House to articulate such a vision would carry either risk.'

The Paper attempted to allay fears expressed by dioceses that the Turnbull proposals would lead to a coherent national organization at the expense of dioceses and parishes. In fact, it said, in many ways their position would be enhanced.

A substantial part of the White Paper responded to comments and criticisms of the restructuring of the Church Commissioners and their functions. While some believed the Commissioners should be wound up and others queried the logic of leaving with them the management of assets, while transferring those functions they had managed well to the Archbishops' Council, the majority accepted the case for retaining the Commissioners with the asset managing function, 'partly as an aspect of Church/State arrangements and partly as a way of ensuring that ... those managing the assets in future are protected from too much pressure to spend.'

It was generally accepted that the responsibility for deciding on the allocation of discretionary funds should be transferred to the Council, along with the role of setting clergy stipends, as was the proposal that the support of bishops should be the subject of discussion in a joint bishoprics committee comprised of Council members and the Church Commissioners. There was also general support for the reduction in the number of Commissioners, although there would be need for consultation with the Government and others.

Opinion was divided over the Council taking over the Commissioners' trust and administrative functions. Some thought it would bring greater coherence, while others questioned the level of responsibilities the Council would be taking on. The Paper, in distinguishing what the legal liabilities undertaken and funded by the Commissioners were, said they could be summarized as support of bishops and cathedrals, and their responsibilities under the Pastoral Measure.

It was thought 'sensible' to phase the transfer of the Commissioners' responsibilities to the Council, partly to allow for full discussions to take place with various bodies, but also to ensure 'an orderly move to new organizational arrangements, including the possibility of lightening the burden on the dioceses in the initial stages of implementation'. For these reasons, the Paper proposed including in the draft legislation an order-making power to allow for a phased transfer.

Some commentators believed that the Commissioners, freed of their expenditure responsibilities, would no longer have the incentive to achieve income levels 'most helpful' to the Church's financial obligations. They might be more inclined to investment strategies calculated to build up their assets. The Commissioners, however, would be kept informed of the Council's assessment of needs, said the Paper, and with the First Church Estates

Commissioner a member of the Council, would be made fully aware of those needs.

They could also be made by statutory duty to take account of the Council's needs when formulating their asset investment strategies, along with their obligation to preserve the capital value of the assets. The Councils' joint presidents, the Archbishops of Canterbury and York, would, as Commissioners, be able to maintain effective liaison between the two bodies. 'In the end, arrangements will need to be made which enhance trust between the Council and the Commissioners,' said the Paper. It believed that criticisms made of the Turnbull Report should be seen

> ... against the background of a general acceptance that reform is needed and that this should be broadly along the lines set out in the report. Several of those who have responded have made it very clear that the expression of concerns should not detract from a strong, overall support for the proposals ... A number of people have said that the Report should be accepted in its entirety as quickly as possible to avoid a long period of introspection and continued uncertainty for staff of the bodies affected as well as in the wider Church.

The Turnbull Commission's proposal to greatly reduce the authority of the Church Commissioners in number, power and responsibilities caused alarm amongst some senior churchmen. They believed it posed a serious threat to the link between the Church and Parliament historically represented by the Commissioners. It could be misconstrued, they feared, as a move towards disestablishment, with the Church running off with the Commissioners' assets, a third of which, in the form of Queen Anne's Bounty, Parliament claimed for the nation.

Among them was the Second Church Estates Commissioner, Michael Alison, who, during a 'take-note' debate on the White Paper at the General Synod in February 1996, said the proposed 'massive attenuation' of the Commissioners' powers and resources would remove them from the heart of the Church of England family to a place at the margin – 'to become, in effect, the family stockbroker'. It was on this 'marginalized role and function', with the number of Commissioners reduced from 95 to 15, that the Commissioners would continue to embody the important and historic partnership between Church and State.

He was concerned that a draconian overhaul of the Church Commissioners could precipitate a harsh response from Parliament, which might even challenge the Church's right to retain the assets of the Queen Anne's Bounty. He could not imagine a Turnbull Measure being debated in this Parliament or the next 'without this sensitive issue being raised'.

Carey agreed under pressure to a considerable U-turn to placate certain politicians and senior churchmen. A Steering Group set up by the Archbishops' Advisory Group, of which Carey was Chairman, recommended that the number of Commissioners, which the Turnbull Report proposed should be reduced to 15, should now be almost doubled to 29. This disappointed Turnbull, who believed that 20 was the maximum number that could effectively be responsible for policy and the Commissioners' day-to-day affairs.

It meant reinstating nine of the *ex officio* government appointees, who, Turnbull believed, were of no practical relevance or political significance to the Commissioners' functions. They were the Prime Minister, the Home Secretary, the Lord President of the Council, the Lord Chancellor, the House of Commons Speaker and the Attorney General. The remaining three would represent the city of London, the city of York and Oxford and Cambridge Universities.

The Steering Group's revision of the Church Commissioners' number was later discussed with the Government 'and other interested parties'. Both the Steering Group's report and the White Paper emphasized 'the Church's recognition of the need to preserve existing levels of accountability to Parliament and the Government in respect of the uses to which the income from historic assets vested in the Commissioners is put'.

Seven months after the publication of the Turnbull Report, Frank Field and his colleagues on the Social Security Committee were ready to put Millbank back on the rack. Their interest focused in particular on the Commissioners' historic assets, and specifically on the Queen Anne's Bounty, which, as government stock, was transferred with Parliamentary approval to the Church Commissioners in 1948, when the Ecclesiastical Commissioners and Queen Anne's Bounty merged to form the Church Commissioners.

Frank Field interpreted the move to give control of the Commissioners' assets to the Archbishops' Council as a devious attempt to effectively 'appropriate' the income from Queen Anne's Bounty. If any such change was planned by the Church, it should only be done through a Parliamentary Bill, argued Field, and not by Synod Measure.

The point had been forcefully made in the Social Security Committee's first report issued 14 months earlier, when, in antici-pating legislative changes to the Commissioners' role, the commit-tee said it believed that Parliamentary legislation was the 'right course' for three reasons. First, as the Church of England's historic resources were contributed to directly by the Monarch – through the Queen Anne's Bounty – and the taxpayer, they belonged to the nation as a whole. Only Parliament could speak for this group, claimed the committee.

Second, as a result, a Measure would severely curtail debate on the Commissioners and smack of the 'excessive secrecy' which, claimed the committee, had been a major factor in the per-manent reduction of the Commissioners' income. Third, the Commissioners' powers and structure not only required 'careful definition', but there was an equally important task in deciding to whom the Commissioners should be responsible. 'The complexities of the existing interlocking relationships would appear to point to an Act of Parliament as the least contentious way forward.'[2]

When Colman and Patrick Locke appeared before the Social Security Committee on 1 April 1996, Field was quick to bring this contentious issue into his sights. He suggested that the proposal of taking the Commissioners' income while leaving them with the assets could be cynically seen as 'a neat way' of circumventing par-liamentary legislation. Said Colman: 'I would not like to comment on that. It had not occurred to me. You are better able to discern what is going on than I am.'[3]

Field, who outside the House of Commons had made no secret of his mistrust of the Church's motives, continued to pursue his concerns three weeks later when Philip Mawer, Secretary-General of the General Synod, Brian Hanson, its Legal Adviser, Bryan Sandford, chairman of the consultative committee of the diocesan boards of finance, Howard Gracey, Chairman of the Pensions

Board, and Martin Slack, the Pensions Board actuary, took their turn with the Social Security Committee.

It was Mawer, who was guiding the drafting of the Measures, whom Field most keenly wanted to question. The tone and nature of questions left no doubt that he wanted the Church of England to clearly understand which legislative assembly would be supreme in enshrining in statute the course it wished to take. Moreover, the mischievous speculation on which questions were based suggested that Field was intent on spreading as much alarm as possible within Millbank and the Church.

Clifford Forsythe, Ulster Unionist MP for Antrim South, raised the curtain, as briefed, with a question on the scope for Parliament or the Social Security Committee to 'intervene' in the drafting of the Pensions Measure. Mawer emphasized that the Church wanted to preserve the 'essence' of the 1919 Enabling Act which empowered the then Church Assembly, the forerunner to the General Synod, to legislate on Church affairs. He said that meetings had taken place with parliamentary authorities to discuss a compromise proposal, which would allow views to be made known at an informal meeting under the auspices of the Commons' Ecclesiastical Committee. They would be conveyed to the General Synod's draft revision committee and Synod itself. It would allow, said Mawer, 'for parliamentary views to be expressed at a crucial formative stage of the legislation.'

It would also mean, he added, that when the Measure came before the Ecclesiastical Committee and the two Houses, it could be clearly seen to what extent parliamentarian views had been taken into account. They were 'exceptional arrangements' which would be limited to two Measures – relating to pensions and any further changes to the Church Commissioners' powers and control of assets – which sprang 'from the fact that together they go to a fundamental aspect of relations between Church and State as … currently embodied in institutional forms.'[4]

The Church hoped that its proposal would show the adaptability of the 1919 Act while not upsetting 'the basic understanding' with Parliament.[5] Under the Enabling Act, 'very important' matters had been before Synod and, subsequently, Parliament. He cited as examples the Worship and Doctrine Measure and the Ordination of Women to the Priesthood Measure.

But to Field, those were internal matters which could not be compared to the proposed Measures. These were 'matters which affect historic resources which may not be, some could argue, within the total charge of the Church, but these are assets held in stewardship. Does Synod concede that in this territory it is in a unique situation in its relationship with Parliament in that it is seeking to legislate on historic assets of the Church of England which it holds in trust and some would argue does not have in ownership, and that the interest in those assets is far wider than what Synod could possibly entertain?'[6]

Mawer conceded that the two Measures were particular forms of legislation which warranted exceptional treatment. It was for this reason, he said, that the Church was keen to make arrangements for dialogue in line with the proposal he had put before the committee. But he continued to maintain that the legislation should come within the envelope of the 1919 Act.

Neither side was prepared to give way. Field continued to insist that the fate of the historic assets and their ownership were issues too important to be left to Measures, while Mawer remained equally insistent, claiming that the Pensions Measure, which would stipulate the level of assets income committed to pensions, would prevent what the Social Security Committee feared: the total absorption of assets income due to the demands of their funding and its consequence to the Commissioners' obligations, above all the giving of financial assistance to needy parishes.

Field also believed that the parliamentary process would be more efficient if legislation was by Bill. Mawer thought otherwise. It was because of the time it took Parliament to deal with Church legislation that the General Synod had been empowered under the 1919 Enabling Act. Only a few people in Parliament were 'properly and rightly' interested in Church matters.

Not so, claimed Field, citing the women's ordination Measure and changes in the election of Bishops as positive examples of parliamentary interest. Parliament would not want to get involved in proposals that dealt with the internal affairs of the Church, but it spoke for 'a wider constituency' which had helped to build up the historic assets, and it was here that Parliament might want to exercise its rights.[7]

Bernard Jenkin, Tory MP for Colchester North, turned up the heat by claiming that the Social Security Committee was seeing a 'huge transformation' in the relationship between the Church and 'the centre, the State ... What we are effectively seeing is a privatization of the Church of England where the payers, the providers, the rich congregations, the contributors, are going to be gaining far more influence over the ownership and control of the Church of England as an institution at the expense of the Church Commissioners, who have historically been answerable to Parliament, which has made the Church the national Church.

'The Church is transferring from being a national organization, which belongs to everybody, churchgoer and non-churchgoer alike, to the nation, to becoming a more congregationally-based organization, less like an established Church. That is what you seem to be saying, more in the control of the Archbishop and the Archbishops' Council.'[8]

Mawer, who had said nothing of the kind, explained that while there was a shift of responsibility, accountability and power within the Church, it did not follow that the Church of England was being privatized or in the thrall of richer parishes. 'The Archbishop and House of Bishops, and everybody else in the Church of England in senior positions I am aware of, is committed to the concept of the Church of England as a national Church. I would dispute the notion that the status of the Church of England as a national Church is focused on, as it were, and solely embodied in the Church Commissioners and its relationship with Parliament. That is clearly an element in the national nature of the Church and in its established nature. In the Turnbull Report there is no proposal to change that relationship.'

Field, apparently still convinced that the plan to transfer the Commissioners' powers to an Archbishops' Council was a devious route to avoid Parliamentary legislation, attempted to ensnare Mawer, as he had Colman, by suggesting that if the Turnbull Commission had proposed winding up the Commissioners, as indeed had been considered, it would have required a Bill.

Mawer's reply, that in his opinion it could have been dealt with by a Measure, failed to deter Field from imposing the central and cynical point of his questions: 'Is it not possible therefore that some clever person thought the way round this would be: "We will make them hand over the money but leave them with the assets and therefore we will not need a Bill but we have got really what we want?" '

With a hint of contempt, Mawer dismissed the charge. 'It requires a degree of Machiavellian intent which I can honestly say was not present at any session that I attended of the Turnbull Commission,' he said. 'We have not dissembled over what we are about, and what we are about … is not appropriating assets or seeking to appropriate assets to the Church from the Commissioners, because it is a Church–State body and we share with the State and interest in those assets.'[9]

Field, assisted by Clifford Forsythe, then played his ace card: the future of Queen Anne's Bounty. It was one that Field frequently enjoyed playing to tease and taunt Millbank, even suggesting two months later in a public comment that, as they belonged to the whole country, the Bounty's assets – valued then at about £900,000 – should be distributed between all religions.[10]

But he now wished to know of Mawer how the Church had reacted to the General Synod comment of Michael Alison, who, he said, believed the Commissioners might lose the Bounty if they pressed ahead with proposed Measures. As Field had deliberately or otherwise misquoted Alison, Mawer, after correcting Field's account, sidestepped the question. However, Forsythe asked what Mawer's reaction would be to Parliament setting up a Special Joint Committee to consider hauling back the assets of the Queen Anne's Bounty.

Mawer's response was not as outraged as Forsythe might have hoped. It was, he said, a matter for Parliament to decide. 'We would be anxious to co-operate with it if it was set up and we would hope that it would be willing, and no doubt it would, take Church evidence and views. The ambit of the Joint Committee's report or review would be very important.'

Field pursued another scare-mongering tack. He invited Sandford to agree – which he was disinclined to do – that a growing force of evangelicals within the Church, aware of how much money the laity would be required to find, would seize the opportunity to launch a doctrinal *coup d'etat*. The evangelical lobby, he added dramatically,

> might feel this offers it the God-given opportunity for a final push back to the roots prior to the Tractarian movement, in other words it will be an evangelical–protestant Church … It would not be impossible for [the evangelicals] to put you in their sights, that your view is far too civilized, far too rounded, far too tolerant

of opinions you might not share, and they might not share, and that you are clearly a person who should be removed if what they feel is the right policy to be pursued is to be pursued. Do you see that as a possible worry, that as the laity become more educated in the power they do have now, not the elite laity but the rank and file laity, there could be a movement to have a Church in their image, rather than accept that the truth is often many sided?

To a seeker of truth, whose career in the Commons had doubtless brought him into touch with the truth of many things and from every side, Sandford's reply must have been a disappointment. He was, he said, professionally involved in health and safety management. Risk management, therefore, was part of his tool kit. He thought what the chairman had said was possible, but not probable.[11]

Field, now in political overdrive, saw further subterfuge in the power the proposed Measures would have in allowing the Archbishops' Council to merge poorer parishes. It would not be able to protect them in the way in which the Commissioners had. There could be differences of opinion over what constituted a poor parish and whether they had tried hard enough to raise money, said Field. The Archbishops' Council could 'cleverly use language' that they were supporting the poorer parishes while actually merging them with others.

'We are moving from a system of checks of balances in the Church of England, which is like the British constitution, to one where there will not be those checks and balances, and one will be depending on people's decency to ensure the least powerful do not get squeezed out.'

The call was taken up by Jeremy Corbyn, the left-wing Labour MP for Islington North, who asked how the Church would feel if Parliament, in fulfilling that duty, wanted to examine the Church's books to make sure that such parishes were not being neglected and consequently closed down, whereas the wealthier parishes could carry on much as before.[12]

In reply, Mawer said support for the ministry in poorer areas was contained in three elements: the first objective was to try and increase the total amount of money available for distribution.

The 'sealing off' of the pensions liability and the new pension arrangements were designed to try to stop the 'sapping' of the Commissioners' resources and create a base 'from which we can try to increase the total amount which is available for the support of ministry in poorer parishes and the other responsibilities of the Church Commissioners.'

The second element was to ensure that the total money available went to areas in greatest need, and, to that end, the Commissioners had been discussing with dioceses ways of ensuring that allocation. The third was the 'mutual support' fund for dioceses to support one another 'and so, leaving the Commissioners and the historic resources out of the picture, that money will actually flow between the dioceses from richer to poorer.'

Field insisted that the historic role of Queen Anne's Bounty had been distorted by the demands on the Commissioners' income to pay pensions. The Queen Anne's Bounty had been set up to augment money to poorer parishes, but in taking on the pension commitments that primary aim had become a secondary consideration. It was for this reason that the Social Security Committee had attached so much importance to the expenditure of the Commissioners' income by the Archbishops' Council being prioritized in legislation, those priorities being pensions liabilities, poorer parishes and historic Church buildings.

But there was, said Mawer, a two-fold problem in trying to put priorities into legislation: 'One, the priorities you have mentioned are not the only obligations of the Commissioners. They also have obligations to bishops and cathedrals, for example, from where they got a lot of their assets originally. While many may not argue in favour of these beneficiaries, they certainly have a moral claim to some aspects of the funding that is available. The other problem is, of course, that at the end of the day there is only one pot of money. You are always having to judge conflicting claims within that pot. This is where the whole question of laying down priorities becomes a difficult and moving issue.'

Corbyn continued to insist that nevertheless there lay a duty on Parliament to ensure that the poorer parishes argument was to the fore.

> I think the worry that many people have, and it has
> been expressed to me, is that because of the loss of

money through investments and so on, and the quite understandable and quite legitimate demands of the pension fund, that the Church will simply cease to exist in the poorest inner urban areas of the country in ten or 20 years' time, because there will be so many parish mergers, there will be so little money going into them and such difficulties for those congregations to raise that money that they will simply cease to exist. That is the area where Parliament has a responsibility as a national institution to ensure that poorer parishes exist.

On 26 June 1996, the House of Commons Social Security Committee issued its final report on the operation of the Church of England's pension funds. Its recommendations caused widespread concern by proposing, as anticipated, to take legislative power away from the General Synod for the first time since the introduction of the 1919 Enabling Act. It threatened, some believed, open conflict between the Church and State, with the establishment of the Church itself at peril.

Parliament's approval would be required, it warned, if the General Synod wanted to change the status of the Church Commissioners and their power of control over the nation's historic assets. The General Synod, it recommended,

> should report to Parliament on the extent to which it can implement the Turnbull proposals without the need to seek Parliament's approval; and any further changes to the power of the Church Commissioners either to sell assets to meet current liabilities, or to transfer any assets to a new pension fund covering past commitments, or to change the existing powers of the Church Commissioners over the control of their assets should be presented to Parliament in the form of a Bill where it can be debated carefully and fully.

The report called the Turnbull Commission's proposal to give the Archbishops' Council full control over income from the assets an attempt to bring about a 'most fundamental change in the effective ownership of the historic assets' in a manner that was less than proper. 'Sensing that their appropriation would require an Act of Parliament, the Commission evidently hit upon the idea of leaving the assets with the Church Commissioners but adding a most fundamental proviso' – allocating income on the Commissioners' behalf in return for an annual certificate that the Council had discharged the Commissioners' trusts obligations.

In proposing a new Church of England Bill, the report called for 'full parliamentary scrutiny' of the proposals for altering the Church's historic endowment, with, in particular, a full debate on the priorities for calls on Commissioners' assets. It added that Parliament had not been faced before with the kind of Measures flowing from the Turnbull Report. Parliament did not believe that the ordination of women, for example, changed in any fundamental respect the threefold ministries of bishops, priests and deacons. The Alternative Service Book was also presented to Parliament as precisely that; it was merely an alternative to the Book of Common Prayer and not as its replacement.

> Similarly, on past form, it is unlikely that Parliament will see the establishment of the Archbishops' Council as an area in which it should have a decisive say. The moving of ecclesiastical furniture – for that is what most of the Turnbull proposals involve – is well within the letter of the 1919 Enabling Act. But where Parliament is likely to wish to have a decisive say is over the question of the Church's historic resources.

In reviewing Parliament's responsibilities, the report said that one of the most important aspects of the debate over the Church Commissioners' assets was the fulfilment of the Commissioners' historic role of providing support for poorer parishes. 'One reason for bringing to an end unsustainable rises in the Commissioners' pension commitments is the need to preserve the parish system which is the hallmark of our national church. Inner cities and rural areas alike face increasing difficulties in maintaining the existing structure of parochial clergy, which contributes greatly to the life of the community.' The question of priorities for calls on the Church Commissioners' assets was 'crucial, and it is particularly on this point that the will of

Parliament should be expressed'.

The report, contesting claims for the Church's right to legislation exclusive of Parliamentary involvement, said that when the 1919 Enabling Act was introduced some MPs found such 'a large change' difficult to accept but were placated by the fact that Parliament still had the right to generate legislation on Church matters and still had the ultimate power to reject Measures put before it by the National Assembly. Implicit in the 1919 'settlement' was the assurance that Measures would have to be fully considered before being presented to Parliament, but the Social Security Committee was 'seriously concerned that in the aftermath of the exposure of the Church Commissioners' shortcomings major new proposals are being rushed along without sufficient detailed examination of their constitutional and financial implications'.

The report was dismissed by Mawer as 'ill-advised and ill-founded' and 'a curious hotpotch'.[13] He added that interference by Parliament in Church legislation could 'rekindle the debate about disestablishment'. It could, he warned, lead to MPs imposing solutions on the Church. 'It would set a potentially dangerous precedent in respect of legislation on other Church matters. It is, quite simply, unacceptable.'

Although John Major's government made it clear in May 1995, during a House of Commons debate on the Social Security Committee's earlier report, that no grounds could be foreseen that were likely to impel the Government to object to legislation by Church of England Measure, a similar prospect under a Labour Government seemed less likely. On 10 June 1996, shortly before the Social Security Committee's report was published, Frank Field wrote to shadow Home Secretary Jack Straw, MP for Blackburn, for a meeting to discuss an informal timetable for the introduction of a Bill. Straw's only reservation was on keeping the contents of a Bill to a timetable – 'but I very much agree with you that there must be a full Bill as far as any changes to the Church Commissioners' control over the historic assets of the Church of England are concerned.'

Some would see the composition of the Social Security Committee to be in keeping with the almost surreal strain that tainted the inquiries held into the Church Commissioners' financial downfall. The appointment of the Social Security Committee's chief inquisitor, Frank Field, to orchestrate Parliament's investigation was, for different reasons, no less curious. A high-profile figure, described as a policy adviser to Labour leader Tony Blair, and well known for his bitter contempt for the Church of England establishment, he had seized every opportunity from the day the *Financial Times* published its story to publicly ridicule and disparage both the Church Commissioners and the Church of England to a degree that should have disbarred him from any part of the Social Security Committee hearings.

Field, who describes himself as a low church Catholic, was aware of criticisms of prejudice towards the Church of England, but brushed them aside. 'I think they are endlessly scratching around trying to deflect attention [from themselves],' he said. 'I can understand when they say "You've got a chairman who is motivated against us' ... [but] it doesn't sound very savoury. On the one hand, I am accused of not being a good politician because I am not partisan, and then all of a sudden the Church is saying ... this guy [is] running this campaign against us.'[14]

Nevertheless, the spectre of the Church's disestablishment was brought to life more than once by Field and his colleagues during questions on the most acceptable means of legislation – by Bill or Measure – following the Turnbull Report proposals. It may have been mere political mischievousness in search of media coverage, but, more alarmingly, it perhaps also suggests that a Labour Government would be ready and willing to intervene in Church affairs and thereby precipitate a crisis to bring an end to more than 1,000 years of Church–State links. It could yet prove to be the Church Commissioners' final legacy.

1. *Working as One Body: a framework for legislation*, GS 1188.
2. Social Security Committee, Second Report, *The Church Commissioners and Church of England Pensions*, 29 March 1995, p. xxxiv.
3. Social Security Committee, Fifth Report, *The Church Commissioners and Church of England Pensions*, 26 June 1996, Q. 54.
4. Ibid., Q. 106.
5. Ibid., Q. 108.
6. Ibid., Q. 114.
7. Ibid., Q. 126.
8. Ibid., Q. 129.
9. Ibid., Q. 164.
10. *Daily Telegraph*, 21 June 1996.
11. Ibid., Q. 147–149.
12. Ibid., Q. 209.
13. *Church Times*, 12 July 1996.
14. Recorded interview, 5 July 1994.

Postscript

By the end of 1995, the Commissioners' investments strategy had undergone significant repositioning to improve long-term income. Its main plank was a radical slimming down of the property portfolio to less than 30 per cent of assets, with UK and overseas equities being increased to more than 50 per cent. Through the sale of much of its retail sector, notably the Gateshead MetroCentre, which totalled £400m, property was cut back from 58 per cent to 39 per cent – £554m – of total assets, while equities were increased from 36 per cent to 49 per cent. Property sales were also a major factor in the total return of the property portfolio – 17.8 per cent compared to the market return of 4.1 per cent based on the Investment Property Databank Index.

The buoyant performance of equities, substantially increased from £1.1bn to £1.4bn, and funded by the sale of property and some fixed interest investments, was largely responsible, in addition to an improvement in agricultural property values, for a £300m increase in the Commissioners' total assets, taking them to £2.7bn, almost level with the 1989 record figure of £2.931bn.[1] Their value was confidently predicted to reach £3bn in 1996. There was also good news on the Commissioners' level of borrowings, which had been reduced from £518m in 1990 to £23m. Said a member of the Board of Governors: 'A tremendous job is being done in turning round the Commissioners' fortunes in a relatively short period of time. The books at last are being competently balanced.'

In balancing the books, greater responsibility inevitably fell on the parishes to increase their financial support. In 1995, for example, giving was increased by 7 per cent to raise £81.7m towards a clergy pay bill of £155.4m, of which £41.7m – down by 8 per cent – came from the Commissioners' net income of £137m. The parishes were also expected to find a further £10m in 1996, as the Assets Committee continued to reduce expenditure to bring it closer to a sustainable level. Church members by now had stoically accepted the consequences upon their pockets of the Commissioners' past foolhardiness. Indeed, the need for them to take greater financial responsibility for the Church and its ministry was considered by many to be no less than right and proper and, moreover, long overdue.

It was argued that the Church Commissioners' historical assets had featherbedded the Church of England for too long. The overwhelming majority of its members had become dependent on the Commissioners' allocations to pensions and stipends to a point that encouraged little regard for the biblical teaching of tithing, and nor, as long as the money was coming in, was greater ownership of the Church's ministry in this way deemed necessary. However, once the trauma of the Commissioners' misdeeds had been worked through the Church's collective consciousness and the shock of the headlines had given way to phlegmatic if not disgruntled acceptance, all that had befallen the Commissioners was seen by some within the Church in a new and illuminating light.

The force of circumstances, they realized, would compel parishioners to become more financially accountable and responsible for what they claimed was so vital and central to their existence. It would give them a new and decisive role, however reluctantly welcomed by the more moribund communicant, that would markedly advance an important decentralization, shifting financial autonomy from Millbank to where, it had long been claimed, it should be – in the parishes and dioceses. In this way, it was wryly observed, much good had come of the Commissioners' financial follies.

Among senior churchmen who welcomed the apparent irony of the Commissioners' calamities was the Bishop of Coventry, the Rt Revd Simon Barrington-Ward. He believed it had caused 'the people in the parishes to come alive to the Gospel and see the need to give for the cause which really should be at the heart of their lives.' It had been a principal spiritual lesson to emerge from all that had happened.

'There is no doubt in my mind that great good has come out of it. I think it has been a very beneficial thing. I think people have begun to see what sacrificial giving is about and what it means. A different scale of giving is now required across the whole church, and what is exciting is the extent to which that has been happening. Although we still have to get the message across to the whole Church, that if they want to support the mission they have got to give more, there has been a magnificent response, which is empowering people to take greater ownership of the Church and its mission,' he said.

At diocesan level, a greater awareness had also developed of the Church's responsibilities, with goals being seen as objectives to which everyone should contribute.

> In all areas of the Church's work, I think we have got to see a new collaborative pattern of ministry which draws more imaginatively and dynamically on the skills and expertise of people at every level. Although it is still early days, I am beginning to see evidence of this happening, even in small village church congregations, where in gatherings for prayer or Bible study I have met with a transformation of individuals or groups which is bringing out a real sense of greater aliveness to the Gospel. The events of the past have also, I believe, brought about a greater understanding of the simple fact that people in the pews must own the Church and its purpose in this world as children of God in the Church of God.[2]

Canon Dr Christina Baxter, Dean of St John's College, Nottingham, and Chairman of the General Synod's House of Laity, believed that the financial downfall of the Commissioners 'served as God's catalyst to the national Church', which, she agreed, had caused the present generation of churchgoers to take responsibility for the central structures of the Church. 'We had grown up in a furnished house, never really thinking about the age, condition or arrangement of the furniture.' A consequence of the circumstances that revealed the Commissioners' difficulties was similar to someone 'throwing open the blinds so that we could see what the actual inefficient situation was. Refurbishment is not given to each generation; one does it in the light of the experience of proceeding generations with as clear a vision as possible of the demands which the next will be facing.'

It had come, she believed, at a providential time; in an age of ecumenical collaboration, with churches willing to work together, and when the need had now been recognized 'to be engaged in a massive turning round of the Church of England from maintenance to mission, from pastoral ministry to proclamation of the Kingdom of God. The structures which we need to support these new ministerial opportunities are not the same as the ones which have served our old priorities well.'

Whatever spiritual lessons it might have learnt, Dr Baxter hoped that the Church had come to know more of the quality of humility

> ... in the way we think of ourselves and how we relate to other faith groups in the nation. Apparently, financial security lured us into forgetting what it means to live by faith, and prevented us from asking searching questions about the appropriate use of money. That can no longer be the case, so we have also had to learn a new mutuality, in which we share the resources at our disposal and take counsel for the good of all. We have also had to relearn the importance of trusteeship, so that we realize that we are only stewards of these goods which Christians of past generations have so generously bestowed upon us, and which we must hand on to future generations.
>
> I think it has forced us to face in a new and more radical way the Christian virtue of 'give as you go', so that we take seriously that most spiritual activity of giving generously, proportionately and regularly from the wealth or poverty which God bestows upon us. I think that that in time will produce two more important fruits: namely, responsibility for how we choose to spend these gifts, and prayerful accompaniment of their spending. Neither of these are yet universally evidenced in the Church of England.[3]

Nevertheless, the Archbishop of Canterbury, Dr George Carey, is of the opinion, and perhaps predictably so, that the Church, as it approaches the challenges of the new millennium, has every reason for doing so with confidence.

> I believe that we are emerging from financial and organizational challenges in a healthier and stronger condition.

We shall be less reliant on the bounty of previous generations and more confident in our faith and vision. I
believe that the Church is now more systematically
committed to outward-looking mission and service and
that its special position in our national life is still widely
valued by many different people, including many of
those who do not themselves go regularly to Church.
Despite media stereotypes, the Church of England is in
good heart and as eager as ever to preach and live out
the Gospel of Christ.[4]

None would deny that in the last decade the Church of England
has survived one of the most turbulent and revolutionary periods of
its history as its finances, structure and reputation were undermined
by a convergence of circumstances, aided and abetted by the
Commissioners' key decisions. Certainly, through central restructuring, not least the Archbishops' Council, the Church of England will
become a more efficient and streamlined administrative machine.
The many-splendour'd bureaucratic leviathan that had run the
Church of England for so long will soon be no more, and the more
professional, open and accountable system that will emerge from its
demise will unquestionably prove more effective in supporting the
Church's ministry. But its work will only prove truly effective in
doing so if it is accompanied by another no less radical and revolutionary change – in the hearts of Christians.

At a General Synod debate in February, 1996, five months after
the publication of the Turnbull Commission report, *Working as One
Body*, the Archbishop of York, Dr David Hope, referred to a comment in the White Paper on the report, which stated that the
Commission's main purpose had been 'to enable the Church's
national structure to serve more effectively the Church's mission to
the nation'.[5] Said Hope:

We need to keep this central and overriding objective
very clearly before us throughout the process on which
we are now embarked.

There can be no other purpose, in my view, because
unless it is that with which we have been entrusted as a
Church – the Missio Dei – in worship, witness and service,

which is and remains the clear focus of all our business, we can do as much restructuring as we like and it will make little or no difference. What we are engaged in is not just the conversion of structures but the conversion of hearts and minds and lives, attending to those spiritual needs which are so vitally necessary for the renewal of our Church and of its engagement with the world. So I hope that we shall not pursue a merely managerial and organizational exercise simply as an end in itself.

It is on the central truth of this statement that the future growth and development of the Church of England hangs. Indeed, all the structural changes and hierarchical repositioning and shrewd business acumen in the world will not make a jot of difference to the effectiveness of the Church of England unless there is a heartfelt willingness at parish level to take the love of Christ into the streets and gutters. The Church, primarily, is not in need of money. That will follow once its members are prepared to follow the gospel of Jesus and develop a far greater sense of mission.

It has been rightly said that Jesus was not crucified between two ornate brass candlesticks in the pomp and circumstance of a cathedral, but between two thieves in the rubbish tip of a city so cosmopolitan that his name was spelt in three languages. It was amongst the lower levels of society, the Bible tells us, that he spent his ministry; not with the wealthy, the powerful and influential, who, then as now, doubtless preferred their possessions to his promises. As Jesus was wholly obedient to his Father's will, he was exclusively where his Father wanted him to be. It must surely follow, therefore, that if Christians are to model their lives on Jesus, they too must embrace society's broken, despised and helpless rejects.

There was a man called Peter, perhaps in his late sixties, a bent, shuffling figure of no prepossessing feature, who was a prison visitor at Strangeways Prison in Manchester. I saw him weekly, as we passed each other with a nod of acknowledgement. I knew nothing of him, other than that imparted by another prison visitor. It was this: in addition to Strangeways, Peter called weekly at a local hostel for down-and-outs, many of them alcoholics who had no home but the streets. The purpose of his visit was to wash and shave those who were willing to let him do so. He would also polish their shoes. When the prison visitor who told me about Peter asked why he did these things, his reply was: 'To give them dignity.'

In Derby, there is a young couple, with four children, who several years ago decided to dedicate their lives to working amongst young children. In faith, they gave up their work to become involved full-time in child evangelism through local schools and youth work. Their Friday night group, Explorers, attracts no fewer than 90 young people, many of whom have been brought to Christ, and through them, their parents. In May 1997 they opened a church, financed by their own fund-raising efforts, which grew out of their child evangelism.

An alcoholic of many years, whose wife was on the verge of leaving with their three children until he went into a rehabilitation hospital where he committed his life to Christ, has for the last 10 years been working as an inner-city mission church pastor on one of the worst crime-ridden council estates in Europe.

A young woman gave up a lucrative career in television and an enjoyable lifestyle in London to work, with her Brazilian husband, among the street children in Belo Horizonte in Brazil; they have now established two night hostels there and bought a farm in the neighbouring countryside where children are clothed, fed, educated and taught about Jesus.

A former prostitute and drug addict, who was sexually abused as a child and raped in prison, came to Christ in extraordinary circumstances. She is now married to a minister in Horley, Surrey, and is currently planning a walk from John O'Groats to Land's End urging women to pray for famines and the healing of broken marriages.

Through these people, whom I have known personally, one sees the work of Jesus Christ. They are the living evidence of the power of God at work, and any one story is more persuasive of the awesome reality of his love than the highest theology or any number of eloquent sermons. These people are aware of how much their sins have been forgiven. And because they have been forgiven much, they are able, through the grace of Christ, to love much.

Conversely, there are those who consider themselves to be 'good' Christians, law-abiding citizens who pay their taxes and keep their gardens tidy, but their spiritual lives are kept in a straitjacket by ritual legalism. Their spiritual growth may even be neutralized by the materialism of a destructive Western culture in which they place their trust, rather than in God, because of the threat it poses to the reassuring security of their material comforts. If God is to be glorified by deed and service – and, as James makes clear, faith without action is meaningless – Christians must allow the Holy Spirit to break them free of the ghetto mentality that separates the church from the world and which gives Christ such a bad press.

In trying to be obedient to God's will, the wonderfully comforting fact is that it doesn't matter if the Christian succeeds or fails. God isn't impressed by target figures or bottom-line 'profits'. His heart is filled with no less joy at the seemingly hopeless efforts of the Christian handing out gospel tracts on a street corner in Grimsby than at the hundreds who may make a commitment to Christ at a Billy Graham crusade.

The Decade of Evangelism launched by the Archbishop of Canterbury in 1991 was a brave and proper initiative based on the Church's central role as commanded by Jesus Christ in his great commission 'to go and make disciples of all nations, baptizing them in the name of the Father and of the Son and of the Holy Ghost' (Matthew 28:19). But it cannot succeed unless more Christians are willing to live in the strength of Christ's teaching.

The church that is alive and thriving is the one where Bible study home groups are encouraged, where the skills and expertise of its members are used to network with the local community, including, essentially, schools, youth organizations, political parties and the local media; where, crucially, young people are engaged in active street mission, particularly amongst those whom society despises; where a letter-writing 'unit' responds to media issues, local and nationally, in defence of God's word and his standards; where regular contact is maintained through home visits or telephone with Christian brothers and sisters in distress, who, by default, are so often hurtfully ignored; and where a prayer group meets weekly to intercede on behalf of the church, for the marriages and wellbeing of its members, for growth both in spiritual maturity and number of membership, and for all the church's outreach activities. Such a church is truly alive in Christ.

The Church of England may well need more money, but, much more urgently, it requires a spiritual sea-change towards the mission fields. And that will happen only when men and women in the pews – and no doubt some bishops – have regained their faith in God. This, through his Grace, he will restore in abundance, but first there must be the simple but sometimes difficult act of heart-deep repentance: to seek his forgiveness for a pride and arrogance that has disgraced his name and Church; for a wilful disobedience of his Word; and for a hardness of heart and indifference of attitude towards Christ's 'widows and orphans' – the vulnerable, the defenceless and deprived.

All that has happened to the Church of England in the last decade has not happened by mere chance or misfortune. If God is in control of all things, especially the future of his Church, his purpose has been at the centre of it all. As the Archbishops of Canterbury and York have said in different ways: the administrative machinery is now in place to make the Church of England financially and organizationally more efficient. The question remains to be answered: is the will in place to make the Church of England more spiritually dynamic in bringing an unbelieving world to the saving grace of Jesus Christ?

The Church Commissioners' Assets Committee and those involved in its work latterly pursued profits with a recklessness that took them closer to Mammon than God. The time is approaching when the Church of England will stand or fall on its willingness to be no less reckless – in abandoning itself to trusting in the power of God and the leading of the Holy Spirit.

> The King will reply, 'I tell you the truth, whatever you did for the least of one of these brothers of mine, you did for me.'
>
> Matthew 25:40

> The Church as it now stands, no known human power can save.
>
> Thomas Arnold (1795–1842)

> And I tell you that you are Peter, and on this rock I will build my church, and the gates of Hades will not overcome it.
>
> Matthew 16:18

1. The Church Commissioners Annual Report and Accounts 1995.
2. Personal interview, 20 February 1997.
3. Written response, 27 February 1997.
4. Written response, 3 October 1996.
5. *Working as One Body: A Framework for Legislation*, GS1188.

Appendix

ASHFORD GREAT PARK PARTNERSHIP STRUCTURES

Ellison Harte Developments Ltd
Purchased options on 2,000-acre site at £7,000 per acre = £14m
Agreement to sell options for £655,000 plus £3.5m to:

Northern England Development Associates Ltd (NEDA)
Managing Director: Jim Cookson

Claret Developments Ltd
Managing Director: David Ackroyd
Puts up £655,000

European Land
(Parent company to NEDA
and Nedaclaret: owned by
Jim and Susan Cookson)

Equity Partnership

Nedaclaret Ltd
(Holding company for project)

**Imry Merchant
Developers Ltd**
Put up £5m to buy options

Bigscan Ltd
(Formed by Nedaclaret and Imry to buy and sell land)

Ashford Great Park (Phase 1) Ltd
(Acquired all shares in Bigscan Ltd)

Paysystems Ltd
(Church Commissioners)

Cedarvale
(Shareholding: 10%)

Imry
(Shareholding: 45%)

Nedaclaret Ltd
(Shareholding: 45%)

Ashford Great Park Partnership
(Set up to protect tax exemption status of Commissioners
who could not be seen to be operating as a trading company)

Cedarvale Ltd
(Shareholding increased to
33 1/3 % in October 1989 –
just six weeks prior to the
result of the final planning
appeal being announced)

Imry
(Shareholding: 33 1/3 %)

Nedaclaret Ltd
(Shareholding: 33 1/3 %)

Ashford Great Park Partnership

Index

Rachman, Peter 27
Radford, Roger 181–2
Ramsey, Dr Michael, Archbishop of Canterbury 19
Rayne, Lord Max 13–17, 23, 26, 48
Rennison, Jennifer 92–3
Richardson, Godfrey 186
Ritblat, John 79, 80
Robert Fleming Holdings 76
Rosehaugh plc 30, 31
Royal Scot Leasing 51–2, 151
Runcie, Dr Robert, Archbishop of Canterbury 32, 34–5, 86, 124, 136, 138, 161
St Enoch's Centre, Glasgow development 52, 55–6, 73
Samuel, Basil 23
Samuel, Howard 23
Sandford, Bryan 194, 208, 233, 237–8
Sankey, Martin 38
Shaw, R. Martin 186
Shelley, Jim:
    on American investments 74
  and Andrew Oakes 64–5
  appointment 45–6, 169
  and Ashford Great Park project 83, 84, 88–9, 101, 103–4, 108, 115
  and Hutchings 68, 69
  and income generation 147–9, 151, 152–4, 157–8
  and Lambeth Group inquiry 74
  and pensions 182–3
  and property investments 62
  remit 45, 49–50, 56
  retiral 59, 159, 166–7

and South African investments 117
Shirley, Jim 84, 103
Silsoe, Lord see Trustram Eve, Sir Malcolm, Lord Silsoe
Singh Sabha Gurdwara sect 36
Slack, Martin 234
Smallwood, John 159–60, 162
South Africa, investments in 118–44
South African Council of Churches 122
Stanley, Canon John 172
Starkey, Sir John 49, 167
Stockwood, Dr Mervyn, Bishop of Southwark 40–1
Stolzenberg, Wolfgang 96–7
Stonefrost, Maurice 172
Stopford, Dr Robert, Bishop of London 41
Stratton, Peter 37
Straw, Jack, MP 242
Sumitomo Bank 84, 151
Sussex Gardens development 17
Sutcliffe, Peter 85, 104
Swingland, Owen 130

Tester, Sven 113–15
Tower Ramparts, Ipswich development 45
Trillo, Rt Revd John, Bishop of Chelmsford 39
Trinity Quay development 72
Trustram Eve, Sir Malcolm, Lord Silsoe 38
  appointment as First Church Estates Commissioner 12–13, 14, 15
  on Estates and Finance Committee 18–19, 21, 22